BY EMILY GIFFIN

Meant to Be

Meant to Be

A NOVEL

EMILY GIFFIN

DOUBLEDAY CANADA

Doubleday Canada and colophon are registered trademarks of
Penguin Random House Canada Limited

Library and Archives Canada Cataloguing in Publication

Title: Meant to be / Emily Giffin.
Names: Giffin, Emily, author.
Identifiers: Canadiana (print) 20210366494 | Canadiana (ebook) 20210366508 |
ISBN 9780385689762 (hardcover) | ISBN 9780385689779 (EPUB)
Classification: LCC PS3607.I28 M43 2022 | DDC 813/.6—dc23

Meant to Be is a work of fiction. Names, characters, places, and incidents are the
products of the author's imagination or are used fictitiously. Any resemblance
to actual events, locales, or persons, living or dead, is entirely coincidental.

Jacket design: Elena Giavaldi
Jacket illustration: Serena Marangon
Book design: Victoria Wong
Title-page image: © Pacha M Vector / iStock / Getty Images Plus

Printed in the United States of America

Published in Canada by Doubleday Canada,
a division of Penguin Random House Canada Limited

www.penguinrandomhouse.ca

10 9 8 7 6 5 4 3 2 1

Penguin
Random House
DOUBLEDAY CANADA

For Jennifer New,
whose generous heart
makes everything more special

Meant to Be

Joe

I don't remember my father. At least that's what I tell people when they ask if I do. I was barely three years old when he died. I once read that it's impossible to have memories much before the age language fully develops. Apparently, we need words to translate our experiences, and if memories aren't encoded linguistically, they become irretrievable. Lost in our minds. So I've accepted that my vague recollections of the day he was put to rest at Arlington National Cemetery are fabricated—an amalgam of photographs, news footage, and accounts from my mother that were somehow planted in my brain.

But there is one memory that can't be explained away so easily. In it, I am wearing red footie pajamas, padding down the wide-plank wood floors of our home in Southampton. It is nighttime, and I am following the white glow of Christmas lights, along with the hum of my parents' voices. I reach the end of the hallway and peer around the corner, hiding so I don't get in trouble. My mother spots me and orders me back to bed, but my father overrules her, laughing. I am overcome with joy as I run to him, climbing onto his lap and inhaling the cherry-vanilla scent of his pipe. He wraps his arms around me, and I put my head on his chest, listening to the sound of his heart beating in my ear. My eyelids are heavy, but I fight sleep, focusing on one gold ball on our tree, wanting to stay with him as long as I can.

I guess it's possible that this memory, too, is illusory, a scene I imagined or dreamed. But it almost doesn't matter. It *feels* so real. So I've decided that it *is,* clinging to it as the one thing of my father's that belongs only to me.

I know what people would say to this. They'd say, No, Joe, you have so much more than that. You have his wristwatch and his rocking chair. You have his eyes and his smile. You have his *name.*

It always comes back to that name—Joseph S. Kingsley— which we also share with *his* father, my grandfather. The *S* is for Schuyler, the name of the family who landed in New Amsterdam via the Dutch Republic in the seventeenth century. Somehow, we spun off from those folks—as did the Oyster Bay Roosevelts— privilege and wealth begetting more privilege and wealth as a handful of families intermarried, curried favor, and became increasingly prominent in business, the military, politics, and society. My great-grandfather Samuel S. Kingsley, a financier and philanthropist, had been close friends with Teddy Roosevelt, the two boys growing up a few blocks apart in Manhattan, then attending Harvard together. When Samuel died in a freak hunting accident, Teddy became a mentor to my grandfather, recruiting him for his Great White Fleet and eventually introducing him to my grandmother, Sylvia, a fiery young suffragist from yet another prominent New York family.

Joseph and Sylvia married in 1917, right before my grandfather shipped out for the First World War. While Joseph commanded a Sampson-class destroyer and earned the Navy Cross, my grandmother continued to battle for women's right to vote, helping to organize the "Winning Plan," a blitz campaign that lobbied southern states to ratify the Nineteenth Amendment. Her fight would last longer than the war, but on August 18, 1920, the suffragists finally got the thirty-sixth state they needed when a young man in the Tennessee statehouse changed his vote at the eleventh hour, crediting an impassioned note he'd received from his mother.

My grandmother would tell this story often, citing it as an auspicious sign for her own son—my father—born that very same summer day. Two more boys and three girls would follow, making six kids in total, and although each had unique gifts and abilities, my grandmother turned out to be right. My father *was* special, her eldest son emerging as the standout of the Kingsley clan.

My father excelled in everything as a boy, then graduated at the top of his class at Harvard before matriculating at Yale Law. When World War II broke out during his second year at Yale, he entered the NROTC, then joined my grandfather in the Pacific. Whole books have been written about their time in combat, but the most significant moment came in late 1944, when the two Joseph Kingsleys found themselves side by side in the Battle for Leyte Gulf, the rear admiral and lieutenant junior grade narrowly surviving a series of kamikaze attacks, along with a typhoon, before securing the beachhead for the Sixth U.S. Army. Upon their return home, a photo was snapped of my grandmother embracing her husband and son on the tarmac. The image would appear on the cover of *Life* magazine, along with a one-word headline HE-ROES.

After the war, my grandfather served in Truman's State Department, while my father pursued his love of naval aviation. He completed advanced flight training, then went on to test pilot school, kicking ass and taking names. Nobody worked harder, earned higher marks, or had more raw ambition than my father, but he also knew how to have a good time and could drink anyone under the table. He was a man of contradictions or, as one

biographer described: "Rugged yet debonair, brash yet intro-
verted, Joe, Jr., was a disciplined dreamer and a risk-taking per-
fectionist."

It's a description I've often returned to in my mind, though I
find myself wondering whether it was true, or if people just see
what they want to see.

One thing I know for sure, though, is that my father had no
enemies. It's a claim heard in eulogies or biographies, especially
about men who die young, but in my father's case, it was the
truth. Everyone loved him. Of course, that included women, and
to his mother's frustration, he loved an awful lot of them as a
young man—and had trouble choosing just one.

That all changed in April 1952, when my father attended a
state dinner at the White House and met my mother, Dorothy
"Dottie" Sedgwick. The daughter of a diplomat, Dottie was a gorgeous, young socialite, fresh out of Sarah Lawrence, who had just
been named to *Look* magazine's best-dressed list. What intrigued
my father the most, though, wasn't her beauty or style but her
poise and worldliness. She seemed so much older than her nineteen years, and after overhearing snippets of a conversation she
was having with Queen Juliana of the Netherlands, he was smit-
ten.

Later that evening, he asked her to dance, and the two hit it
off, talking and laughing as he twirled her all over the White
House ballroom. The following morning, *The Washington Post*
ran their photo in the lifestyle section, along with a description of
my father's finely tailored ivory dinner jacket and my mother's
powder-blue chiffon gown. The society pages followed every
move of their ensuing courtship, and by the time they were engaged a year later, Joe and Dottie were household names. America's sweethearts.

A lavish wedding was planned in the Hamptons, but the Korean War put things on hold, as my father returned to combat. From the cockpit of his F-86 Sabre, Captain Kingsley would down six enemy aircraft, becoming one of only two navy aviators to achieve ace status, before returning home to marry Dottie in the summer of 1954. Their wedding was *the* social event of the year, solidifying my mother as a fashion icon. Women everywhere, including Audrey Hepburn, emulated her tea-length wedding dress, paired with elbow-length gloves.

Shortly thereafter, my father announced his bid for New York's junior Senate seat. He ran as a Democrat but garnered vast bipartisan support and won the election handily, becoming a rising political star. My grandmother was thrilled and my mother relieved, believing that politics would keep her husband out of harm's way. For several golden years, they were happy, splitting their time between Georgetown, New York City, and Southampton.

But in the fall of 1957, just as my parents were planning to start a family, *Sputnik 1* ushered in the Space Race, and my father grew restless, dreaming of flight. My mother begged him to stay the safer course, but my father had an iron will, and eventually he left the Senate for NASA, the agency he had helped create. Anyone alive at that time knows that astronauts were larger-than-life figures, revered as America's greatest heroes in a global conflict between democracy and communism. The ultimate goal, as President Kennedy proclaimed before a joint session of Congress, was "landing a man on the moon and returning him safely to the Earth." It seemed an impossible dream to most, but not to my father and his cohorts in the early days at Cape Canaveral.

My mother put on a brave public face, as all astronauts' wives were required to do, but she lived in constant fear of what might happen at the end of the next thirty-second countdown. To make matters worse, she suffered a series of three miscarriages. Her doctor couldn't find a medical explanation, but my mother believed it was stress over my father's occupation. Her heartbreak was compounded by resentment.

Then, miraculously, in December of 1963, she had a healthy baby boy—*me*—and things were good again, especially after my father promised her that he would leave the space program by my third birthday. It was an arbitrary deadline, and he ended up asking for a slight extension so that he could accept one last mission—a low Earth orbital test of the Apollo command and service module scheduled for February 1967.

Of course, that mission never flew. Instead, on January 27, 1967, a flash fire broke out in the cabin of the module during a simulated rehearsal, asphyxiating the four men inside: Gus Grissom, Ed White, Roger Chaffee, and my father, Joseph Kingsley, Jr.

The rest is history, as they say. The shock of the nation. The endless *if only*s and *what should have been*s. Much was made of the idea that my father likely would have returned to public service after his final mission, with aspirations beyond the Senate. Most pundits believe he would have secured the Democratic nomination over Humphrey in 1968 and beaten Nixon in the general election to become the thirty-seventh president of the United States.

Instead, a nation mourned its fallen hero and pinned its hopes and dreams on a little boy.

For much of my childhood, I didn't see it this way. All I knew was that people revered my father, which made me proud and happy. I liked it when strangers stopped me on the street to talk about him. Mostly they offered condolences or shared an anecdote about what he'd meant to them. Sometimes they talked about the day he died, everyone seeming to remember exactly where they were when they heard the news. Regardless of what they shared, my mind would inevitably return to that moment on his lap in front of our Christmas tree.

As I got older, there was a shift. I still viewed my father as a hero, but I began to feel the heavy weight of so many expectations. People often used outlandish descriptions like *heir apparent* and *America's prince,* prodding me to honor my father's "legacy." Meanwhile, my mother constantly brought him up, comparing and measuring me, especially when I got in any kind of trouble in school. Didn't I want to be a great man like my father? I learned to stare back at her and nod as solemnly as I could. I certainly wasn't going to tell her the truth. That I really just wanted to be a *good* man. My *own* man.

My mother would have fainted if she heard me say that. One of her favorite passages in the Bible was "For unto whomsoever much is given, of him much shall be required." I knew where she was coming from. Being a Kingsley meant access to the best private schools, private clubs, private bankers, private planes. I was grateful for the blessings in my life. But damn. My father was killed in a fiery explosion when I was three—which, from my vantage point, felt a hell of a lot more like "From whom much is taken, much is expected."

Bottom line, I would have traded all the pride and privilege of being a Kingsley for a regular name like Smith or Jones and a dad who wasn't dead. Hell, I would have traded it for far less. Maybe just a few more years with him and more than one memory that might not even be real.

CHAPTER 2

Cate

My father died in a car accident in Nevada when I was three. I was too young to understand, grasping only what my mother told me: that my dad wasn't coming home and that we were going to live with my grandmother in a place called Hackensack. I remember packing up our apartment in Las Vegas and loading our belongings into the back of my mom's blue Pinto. I cried saying goodbye to Pepper, my black kitten, who we left with a neighbor because my grandmother was allergic. It later struck me as odd that I felt sadder about Pepper than about my father.

When I got to kindergarten, I noticed that my classmates put dads in their drawings, along with brothers and sisters and dogs. I had a grandmother, but she was mean to my mom, so I left her out of my pictures. Once I drew my father standing on the other side of me, and my grandmother got mad, calling him a loser, making my mom cry.

A short time after that, my mom and I moved into our own apartment. We didn't see much of my grandmother anymore, which was fine by me. Even better, my mom let me get a new cat, which I named Pepper, Jr. Around that time, she also gave me a photograph of my dad—the only one I'd ever seen. It was black and white, but I could somehow tell that he had blond hair and blue eyes like me. In it, he is leaning on a doorframe, wearing a plaid shirt and cowboy boots. He has long sideburns, and his expression is plain—not happy or sad. It's not a lot to go on, but from there I filled in the gaps, imagining that he had been the strong, silent type, rugged and intrepid and a bit mysterious. Like the Marlboro Man. My mom didn't corroborate my vision, but she didn't contradict it, either. In fact, she didn't talk about him much at all, and I learned not to ask questions. It made her too sad.

Eventually, my mom began looking for a new husband. She was beautiful—taller and thinner than other mothers, with long blond hair that she set in rollers at night. Wherever she went, men stopped to talk to her. She also met a lot of them at the Manna Diner, where she worked as a waitress. They'd ask for her phone number, and she would pretty much always give it to them, even to the bald, ugly guys, because she said you never could tell if a fellow had money. My mom talked incessantly of money and men, making both seem like prerequisites to happiness.

In my mind, it didn't add up. I was poor. I was fatherless. But I was still happy. I loved our cozy, cluttered third-floor apartment at Queen's Court with its shag green carpet and concrete balcony with a bird's-eye view of the parking lot. I would sit out there for hours, playing with my Barbies while I waited for my mom to get home from work. There was always something exciting happening down below—from a kickball game to a screaming match to a make-out session—and it was almost always more entertaining than whatever Gloria, the old lady who babysat me, was watching on our color television, its small screen distorted with zigzag lines and sometimes a white-out blizzard of fuzz. As far as I was concerned, our television was the only thing that needed an upgrade. Otherwise, I thought our life was just fine.

Until my mom got a new boyfriend, that is. Whenever she did, things got messed up. Either I would get kicked out of the bed my mom and I shared and be forced to sleep on the hard, scratchy sofa, or she would disappear for days at a time, leaving me with Gloria. The worst part, though, was what happened when those men inevitably vanished, and my mom would sleep, drink, and cry all hours of the day. Eventually, she would get over it, but only when another man came along. She didn't know how to be happy without one and constantly dreamed of our being rescued and taken to a nice house in Montclair. I'd never been, but she said it was a suburb in New Jersey where rich people lived.

In theory, I understood the fairy tale she was after, and I was hopeful she would find it, for her sake and mine. I dreamed of a kind stepfather, imagining Mike Brady: a handsome architect who kissed my mom in the kitchen and helped me with my homework. Even better if he came with three sons, a dog, and an Astroturf backyard complete with a swing set and teeter-totter. In reality, I knew that wasn't going to happen. I also intuitively understood that *no* man was better than the *wrong* man. If only my mom had agreed.

When I was ten years old, she met Chip, a cop who came into the diner and charmed her over his sliders and coconut cream pie before leaving a tip bigger than the check. His phone number was written on the back.

"He's *perfect*," my mom said as she got ready for bed that night, slathering Oil of Olay on her face and neck.

"And he wasn't wearing a wedding ring?" I asked—because that had happened a few times.

"I'm *positive*," she said. "I checked his hand the second he sat down."

"And he had good manners?" I asked.

This was her favorite screening device, though she went out with the rude ones, too.

"Yes," she said. "Not a crumb left on the table, and he even stacked his dishes and folded his napkin on his plate."

This seemed a little extreme to me, like a red flag of a different kind. My mom and I were messy and liked it that way, calling our bed a "nest"—which we never made.

When I pointed this out, she interrupted me. "I'm telling you, Cate. He's dreamy. And I'm going to marry him."

She sounded so certain that I almost believed her this time, and I was excited when Chip came over a few days later to take my mom out on a date. Without her even asking me, I put on a dress, along with a ribbon in my hair, determined to make a good impression. If things didn't work out between them, I wasn't going to be the reason, as I had been in the past, when other men decided they didn't want the "baggage" of a kid.

When Chip walked into the living room, I stood up from the sofa, where I'd been quietly reading a book, and made eye contact with him. I was shy, so that wasn't the easiest thing to do. It didn't help that he was taller and bigger than her usual boyfriends.

"Hi, Cate!" he said in a booming voice that matched his stature.

"Hello, *Officer Toledano*," I said, as my mom had instructed.

"Call me Chip!"

I glanced at my mom, who nodded her permission.

"Hi, Chip," I said.

Beaming down at me, he handed me a plastic bag and said, "I brought you a little something."

I smiled and thanked him, expecting candy or a drugstore trinket, the two most common gifts given to me by my mom's boyfriends. Instead, I reached into the bag and pulled out a boxed Barbie *with* a Ken doll. The tanned Malibu couple sported matching teal and purple monogrammed swimsuits. I was sold.

I SHOULD HAVE known better, of course. It all turned out to be a ruse—a *really* good act that lasted nearly three months, just long enough for Chip to propose and my mom to say yes. Shortly after that, Chip showed his true colors, and I realized that he was not only a neat freak but also a jerk, putting my mom and me down at every turn. I quickly came to hate and fear him, and did my best to talk my mom out of getting married. But she didn't listen, making endless excuses for him. Her favorite was all the stress he was under as an "officer of the law"—she'd say that there was no more difficult job in the world.

"Things will be better once we're married," she promised me. "Just hang in there and give him a chance."

I tried to believe her. I *wanted* to believe her. But Chip's moods only worsened, along with his verbal assaults and threats. I told myself there was no way he'd physically hurt my mom, no matter how mad he got, because men didn't *hit* women, especially policemen, who were the good guys.

One Saturday night in December, Chip invited my mom to the chief of police's Christmas party. She was excited and spent all afternoon primping in our bathroom as I played the role of her lady-in-waiting, handing her various makeup brushes and bottles of lotion and perfume and advising her on jewelry and shoes. When we were finished, she looked more gorgeous than usual, her blond hair feathered around her face, her fingers and toes lacquered red to match her sparkly sequined dress. When he arrived, I went to the door with her, excited to see Chip's reaction, expecting him to gush over her. Instead, he looked my mom up and down, made a face, and said, "You're going for the hooker look tonight, I see?"

My heart sank, and my mom's face fell.

"Who are you trying to impress anyway?" Chip said, his words slurring like he'd been drinking. "Nick?"

Nick was Chip's partner—who I'd noticed was a dead ringer for the Six Million Dollar Man. Unfortunately, my mom had made the mistake of sharing my observation with Chip a few weeks earlier; he'd promptly lost his mind, accusing her of wanting to fuck Nick. I'd heard the f-word before, but never as a verb and not in any relation to my mom.

"I got dressed up for you," my mom explained, desperation in her eyes. "Not Nick."

"Well, I think it's a mighty big coincidence," Chip said. "You look like shit when it's just the two of us and then you put on that dress when you know Nick's going to be there."

My mom stammered that she would change into something else as he continued to berate her, following her down the hall to our bedroom. I stood frozen in the hallway, wondering if I should go with them or escape to Gloria's apartment. Sensing that my mom might need reinforcements, I decided to stay by her side, and even forced myself to take a deep breath and defend her.

"Chip. Just so you know, she didn't buy that dress for Nick. She bought it for *you*. It cost a lot of money, and she thought you would love it."

I knew it was the wrong thing to say because Chip began shouting at the top of his lungs that I was a rude, spoiled brat. He then turned his wrath back to my mom, questioning the way she had raised me and whether he even wanted to be married to someone with such a disrespectful brat of a kid. By then, my mom's makeup was ruined, mascara streaming down her face as she sobbed that she was sorry. That we were *both* sorry.

"What are you sorry for, Jan?" he yelled.

I could tell it was a trick question, and my mom knew it, too.

"For everything," she whispered, which seemed like a safe response.

"For being a slut?" he said.

My mom opened her mouth to answer, but he cut her off, yelling louder. "For wanting to fuck Nick?"

"I don't—" she whimpered. "I only want you—"

"For all the guys you've fucked in town? Look at you in that slutty dress. The town whore of Hackensack. Jesus, we *have* to move."

As he continued to rant, my mom frantically went through her closet, then pulled out a brown polyester pantsuit. "What about this? Do you like this?"

"Are you serious? Wow," Chip said. He shook his head, then looked at me. "Your mother here has two extremes. She can look like a slut . . . or she can look like a dyke. Whaddya think, Cate? Would I rather be seen with a slut or a dyke?"

I didn't know what a dyke was, but I could tell he didn't consider it a compliment.

"I can't take you anywhere, can I, Jan?" he yelled. "You're an embarrassment. A goddamn embarrassment."

At that point, I felt a surge of hope that he might finally just dump her, like the others had. My mom would be sad for a while, but she would get over it, and we could go on with our lives. Instead, he shoved my mom into the closet door. As she crashed against it, then fell to the floor, he yelled at her to get up and get ready, that they were going to be late. When she didn't move, he kicked her in the stomach. I watched in horror and wondered if I should call the police.

In the next instant, I remembered, with a fresh wave of terror, that he *was* the police, and there wasn't anything anybody could do to stop him.

CHAPTER 3

Joe

Growing up, I didn't have a father or siblings but was very close to my aunts and uncles and cousins, especially on the Kingsley side. Sadly, my father's death wouldn't be the last tragedy in our family, not by a long shot. The year after he passed away, my father's second-oldest sister, Betty, died in a house fire (on Christmas Eve, no less); the following year, my three-year-old cousin Eloise wandered out of their yard in Sag Harbor and drowned in their neighbors' pool; and when I was eight, my oldest cousin, Frederick, died in an avalanche while skiing in the French Alps.

People called it the "Kingsley curse." The phrase infuriated my mother, perhaps because it also terrified her, especially when my cousins and I were having a good time. We loved to take risks on land and water, and I was typically the ringleader—surfing, skiing, hang gliding, rock climbing, you name it. Someone was always being hauled off to the emergency room for one mishap or another, which we cousins wore as badges of honor, keeping a running tally of stitches and broken bones. My mother didn't find any of it even remotely funny and lived in a constant state of dread that I'd be critically injured. I guess I can't blame her for that, given what she and our family had been through, but it still seemed unfair. She wanted me to follow in my father's footsteps, and to me, a sense of adventure came with that territory. I wasn't as smart as my father, but I could be as *brave* as he had been, if only my mother would let me.

Fortunately, my father's mother (whom I called Gary, because I couldn't pronounce Granny when I was little) understood me and gave me the freedom to be exactly who I was. The only thing that she asked of me was that I fulfill my own unique potential. She made me feel special, and when I messed up, she was always the first to forgive me. I adored her, and never turned down the opportunity to spend one-on-one time with her, whether at her home in Southampton or her apartment on the Upper East Side. I especially loved when she would pick me up from school and walk me over to Tavern on the Green for ice cream. We had some of our best conversations over hot-fudge sundaes and root beer floats.

"Tell me what's going on in your world, Joey," she'd always say.

I knew that unlike other grown-ups, who were just going through the motions, my grandmother was seeking an interesting answer.

One afternoon when I was about ten, she asked the question, and I told her about Charlie Vance getting bullied at recess.

"Why was he bullied?" she asked, taking a dainty bite of whipped cream while I took a spoon and dug down deep into mine.

"Because he's a sissy," I said.

"And what makes him a sissy?"

"You know. The usual sissy stuff," I said, explaining that Charlie couldn't throw a ball to save his life and was afraid of spiders and talked with a goofy lisp. And the most egregious example: he was rumored to play with his sister's dolls.

My grandmother nodded and said, "Hmm. And when people tease him, do you stick up for him?"

"Yeah," I said, which was true, but she may have guessed by the look on my face that my efforts to stand up for Charlie were halfhearted at best. Mostly, I just wanted him to fall in line and stop being his own worst enemy.

Gary suddenly put her spoon down and stared into my eyes. "Joey. Are you aware that Charlie might be homosexual?"

I gazed back at her, processing this. It had never occurred to me that Charlie was gay—nor had it crossed my mind that anyone our age could be—but I wanted my grandmother, the wisest person I knew, to think I, too, was wise in the ways of the world. I somberly nodded.

"And if that's the case, Charlie is going to have a very difficult life, Joey," she said. "He can't help who he is, and you need to do everything you can to ease his way."

"I will, Gary," I said, feeling ashamed that I hadn't done more for Charlie to date, and that what I had seen as tomfoolery by my more rambunctious classmates actually had shadings of cruelty.

"You're a natural leader. People listen to you," she continued. "I've watched you in action."

"Where?" I said, picturing my grandmother holding up binoculars to the school yard fence.

"When you're with your cousins," she said. "All the time."

I looked across the table at my grandmother, feeling so proud.

"Did I get that from my father?" I asked. "Was he that way?"

She shook her head, which shocked me. "Don't get me wrong. He was a good-hearted boy like you are," she said. "But he wasn't as outgoing or brave."

I stared at her, finding it hard to believe that I could, at any age, be braver than someone who became an ace fighter pilot and astronaut. I said as much, and my grandmother explained. "He grew into a leader, but he wasn't *born* one. It didn't come naturally to him. Not like it does for you. That's a superpower, Joey. And you need to always use that power for good."

She went on to talk about advocacy and activism, and her work for women's suffrage when she was young, and how much still needed to be done for women and minorities.

"I can see you in that fight for equality," she said. "And maybe it all starts here. Defending Charlie. Will you do that for me? For him?"

I sat up straighter and promised her I would.

In the weeks that followed, I put the kibosh on all bullying of Charlie, and I did it in grand style. Rather than simply defending him on an ad hoc basis, I befriended him, and he was damn near popular by the end of that school year. I know that probably sounds arrogant, but it's the truth. I was pretty pleased with myself.

A COUPLE OF years later, on the first day of the seventh grade, Mr. Wilkes, our headmaster, summoned me to his office and informed me that I was responsible for "shepherding a new student."

I nodded and said, "Yes, sir. What's his name?"

Mr. Wilkes told me that *her* name was Berry Wainwright, and that she had just moved to New York from London. She had attended Thomas's Battersea, he said in a tone that made it clear this was an impressive school.

"Berry as in Barry White?" I interjected. "Or like a strawberry?"

"Like a strawberry, Joseph," Mr. Wilkes said.

"Berry good!" I said, giving him a thumbs-up.

He stared at me a beat, looking weary, then said, "Joseph. I need you to take this responsibility seriously."

"Yes, sir," I said, suddenly feeling a little suspicious of his reason for choosing me for this job—that it had more to do with Berry's parents' social status or net worth. I was only thirteen, but I had seen Mr. Wilkes use me as a pawn like that before, and in that moment, I was annoyed not to be back outside in the courtyard with my friends. I also predicted that I wasn't going to be a fan of this new girl named after a piece of fruit.

But my attitude did a one-eighty the second his office door opened and our guidance counselor brought her in. She was a dead ringer for Tatum O'Neal, and let me just say, there was a reason I'd seen *The Bad News Bears* three times. I got to my feet, as I had been taught to do when a girl enters the room, while Mr. Wilkes rose from his desk and cleared his throat.

"Joseph, this is Berry Wainwright," he said, gesturing toward her. "And Berry, this is Joseph Kingsley the third."

"How do you do?" I said, looking directly into her eyes, another point of etiquette, though also what I *wanted* to do.

"I'm well, thank you. And you?" Berry said.

"I'm good," I said, for some reason relishing my bad grammar, perhaps because I wanted to offset any notion of being the kind of guy who had a Roman numeral after his name.

Mr. Wilkes asked us to take a seat, and for the next few minutes, he droned on about how wonderful our school was and how happy we were to have Berry. He then informed me that her class schedule mirrored mine with the exception of our respective seventh-period math classes.

"Lemme guess," I said with a laugh. "She's in a higher math class than I am?"

"She is, indeed," Mr. Wilkes said, staring me down. "Perhaps if you work harder, you can join her in accelerated math next year."

"Or maybe," I said, keenly aware that self-deprecation was a crowd favorite. "We both work *equally* hard, and she's just smarter than me."

Mr. Wilkes ignored this as he stood and said, "I'll let you two get acquainted before first period. . . . Berry, please know that you're in excellent hands with Joseph."

He gave me a final look that said, *Don't mess this up,* then ushered us out the door of his office.

Now alone in the hall, Berry and I gazed at each other for a few awkward seconds before I cleared my throat and asked the standard back-to-school question. "How was your summer?"

"It was fine," Berry said. "How was yours?"

"It was fun . . . really fun. . . . I did a lot of surfing."

She nodded, looking uninterested but not impolite.

I changed tactics, asking, "Hey, has anyone ever told you that you look like Tatum O'Neal?"

"No," she said.

"Well, you do," I said. "Have you seen *The Bad News Bears*? The movie?"

"No," she said again. "I don't really like sports."

I started to tell her that liking sports wasn't a prerequisite to enjoying the movie but suddenly realized something. "Hey. Where's your British accent? Did you lose it already?"

"No. I never had one. I'm not British," she said, holding my gaze in a way that many girls were incapable of doing—not just with me, but with *any* boy. "My dad worked at the embassy."

I nodded, mentally returning to my theory about her wealthy, connected parents. "What's he do now?" I asked, though I actually didn't care.

She bit her lip. "He doesn't do anything," she said, hesitating. "He died. In March."

Her delivery was so matter-of-fact that, at first, I thought I must have misunderstood her. But then she started blinking, like she might cry.

"Oh. Wow. I'm sorry," I stammered, feeling the rush of empathy that I always had for another kid who had lost a parent. It was a club you didn't want to be in—but a club nonetheless.

"Thank you," she said, a reply that I vastly preferred to some variation of *it's okay*. After all, it *wasn't* okay—those were just words we said to make other people less uncomfortable.

In that moment, I was speechless—rare for me.

I certainly wasn't going to ask any questions about the manner of death. (*Was it sudden?* was the euphemism people used for *Was it an accident?*) Yet it didn't feel right to just move on to a new topic, either. A few more seconds passed before I settled on telling her that my father had died, too. "But I was too young to really remember him," I quickly added. "So your situation is way harder."

"No. They're just hard in different ways," she said, acknowledging something I'd wondered about. Would it have been better if I had known my father? Or would it only have made me more sad? The fact that Berry recognized these nuances impressed me.

"I bet that's why Mr. Wilkes put us together," I said, mostly thinking aloud.

"Maybe so," Berry said. "But please don't feel like you have to babysit me."

"Oh, I didn't mean it like that," I said. "I'm happy to show you around and stuff."

Berry shrugged and said, "Okay. But I really don't need anything. I've changed schools before. It's no big deal."

I nodded, giving her my most earnest look. "I hear you," I said.

"But I'm gonna have to assist you regardless. You wouldn't want to get me in trouble, would you?"

"No," she said, giving me the smallest of smiles. "Of *course* I wouldn't."

BY THE END of the day, the whole school was abuzz with Berry's story. Rumors swirled that she had lost not only her father but also her *mother,* both among the 585 people killed in the infamous runway collision of two fully loaded Boeing 747s on the island of Tenerife. I prayed that it wasn't true—that it was simply some jerk kid embellishing her loss. I mean, surely Berry would have mentioned it if her mother was dead, too.

That evening, my mother, who had apparently talked to Mr. Wilkes about my assignment, confirmed it. She told me that Berry was an only child like me—and was living with her aunt and uncle, both of whom were busy with big jobs. I couldn't believe it. Berry was an *orphan.*

Needless to say, I discharged my duties with the utmost seriousness, which some of my friends mistook as my having a crush on the new girl. I denied it, for although she *was* pretty, my feelings for Berry bore none of the hallmarks of my usual infatuations. I didn't want to kiss her; I just wanted to be friends with her.

At some point, the two of us started spending time together outside of school, hanging out in the park, doing homework at my dining room table, and hitting up record stores all over the city. (Berry had great taste in music—which made up for her being clueless about sports.) She was the best listener, and asked questions about how I felt that would have seemed nosy or judgmental from anyone else. She confided in me, too, telling me heavy stuff about her grief and night terrors. Once, she told me how grateful she was that her parents had been together when they died, even though it meant losing them both. That really bowled me over. I'd never known anyone so selfless or strong.

Over the next few years, Berry and I became closer and closer, and by our junior year of high school, when we both headed off to Andover, she had become an honorary Kingsley, mingling with all the cousins. My mother adored her as much as I did, calling her the daughter she never had. Sometimes, I would come home to find the two of them already chatting away in the kitchen. I found their relationship comforting, like it made all three of us seem more normal. I didn't even mind when they teasingly ganged up on me, though I pretended to be annoyed.

Their specialty was critiquing the girls I liked, or more accurately, Berry would critique them, and my mother would take her word as gospel. While she'd occasionally deem someone worthy of my attention, more often she'd wrinkle her nose in disapproval, dismissing them as being too needy or a social climber, or lacking substance. Over time, all the girls in our social orbit came to see Berry as the Joe Kingsley gatekeeper. Some girls even tried to befriend her to get closer to me. It was a tactic that Berry saw straight through. You couldn't get anything by her.

The only time we ever argued was when I put myself in harm's way with my cousins. Like my mother, Berry had good reason to be afraid—but I never understood why that fear translated to such anger. While others called me reckless, Berry called me selfish and arrogant and stupid.

The summer before our senior year, after one particularly harrowing mishap that involved a capsized kayak and a mild case of hypothermia, Berry wouldn't speak to me for a week.

"What if something happened to you?" she said when we finally had it out. "Your mother would be alone. *Alone*, Joe!"

"She wouldn't be alone. She'd have you."

"It's not the same, Joe, and you know it. We aren't family."

"You might as well be," I said. "And besides, nothing is going to happen to me."

"And why's that?" she asked, her voice rising. "Because you're invincible?"

I sighed, silently acknowledging to myself that I *did* feel a little bulletproof. But I wasn't about to admit this to Berry, so instead I said, "No. Because I'm *resourceful*."

"You took a kayak across the bay in a *thunderstorm*, Joe. That's not resourceful. It's idiotic."

"It wasn't storming when I left."

"And you didn't check the weather? Or think to tell anyone where you were going? That's the *opposite* of resourceful."

"Well, how about the fact that I'm a strong swimmer?"

"Being a strong swimmer doesn't help when you're hypothermic—"

"Hey—I got to the shore, didn't I?"

"Yes, and you also had to break into a stranger's house to take a hot bath!"

"Exactly! Resourceful as *hell*," I said, feeling smug.

Berry gave me a look of contempt, then shook her head. "You're such an idiot."

"But I'm *right*. I'm *here*. Alive and kicking," I said, though I still felt a chill remembering how shockingly cold the water had been, how violently I'd been shivering as I knocked on doors for help.

"*This* time," she said. "Who knows about the next time if you keep this up?"

I hesitated, and then said, "The universe has punished my family enough."

"Oh. I see now," she said. "Silly me. I forgot that the universe is *fair*."

"I'm not saying it's fair," I said, thinking of her parents, as I always did. "But I'm saying—what are the chances?"

"What are the chances that an astronaut is risking his life? Or an idiot who takes a kayak out by himself in a storm?"

I bit my lip and lowered my eyes as Berry kept on going.

"Your dad had a wife and child," she said. "He had *no* business being in the space program. Especially when your mother begged him to quit."

I looked at her, a little stunned by the direction she was now taking. "That was his *dream*," I said.

"So what?" Berry shot back. "How about your *mother's* dream?"

"French literature? Journalism?" I quipped.

The former was her major, the latter her first and only job out of college. Her actual job title had been "inquiring camera girl," for which she wandered the streets of Washington, DC, taking photos of strangers whom she polled about current events and other random topics. Her photos, along with their responses, were in a daily column in the *Washington Times-Herald*. It was a cool gig, but I'd never gotten the feeling that it was her *dream*.

"No, dummy," Berry said. "Her *real* dream. To raise a family with her husband. And watch her child grow up with his father. *That* dream."

"Oh," I said.

"If he had listened to your mother, he'd still be alive. But he was too stubborn . . . too selfish."

"What did my mother tell you?" I said, my stomach twisting in knots.

Berry shrugged and kept on staring me down. "She's told me a lot of things, Joe," she said.

"Like what?"

She took a deep breath, then let out a long sigh. "Well. Did you know they had a deal? That he made her a promise?"

"What promise?" I asked, my face hot.

"He swore to her that he would quit flying when you turned three," Berry said. "Did you know that?"

I shook my head, feeling a wave of intense sadness.

"Well, he did. But he broke that promise. 'Cause he just *had* to do one more mission. His ego was too big—"

I'd overheard these whisperings before from some of my aunts and uncles, along with reading about rumors in the press about my father's infidelity, but nothing had ever been confirmed by my mother. "Berry. Stop it. Right now!" I said as sternly as I'd ever spoken to her—or *any* girl.

But of course, she didn't stop. "It's true," she said. "Your father was selfish, Joe—"

"He was a *hero*," I said, my voice shaking.

"Yes, Joe," she said. "He was a *war* hero. But he didn't *die* a hero."

"Yes, he did!"

"No. He died putting his own lust for adventure and fame and ambition over you and your mother. That's what happened. Face facts."

I couldn't believe her disrespect and felt myself snap. "Shut your damn mouth, Berry!" I shouted.

"No, Joe," she said. "I *won't*. Someone needs to stand up to you—"

"Oh, cut the crap. Lots of people stand up to me," I said, thinking of all the adults in my life who scolded me when I messed up.

"Yes, but you won't *listen* . . . to *anyone*," she said, her eyes suddenly filling with tears.

Now I felt pissed *and* guilty, the worst combination. "Shit, Ber. Don't cry," I said.

"I can't help it," she said, tears now rolling down her cheeks. "The skydiving. Rock climbing without a harness. Riding a motorcycle without a helmet. This idiotic talk about getting a pilot's license. It's all so stupid and pointless. It scares me. It scares your mother."

"I'm sorry, Berry. You're right. I'll be more careful. I promise," I said.

In that moment, I meant it. Not because I believed for one second that anything could happen to me, but because I loved Berry and my mother and didn't want to upset them. So for the rest of that summer, and throughout my senior year, I did my best to keep my promise. Don't get me wrong—I found other ways to upset my mother and Berry; it's just that none of my bad decisions were things that could have gotten me killed. So that was something, at least.

CHAPTER 4

Cate

Despite all my protesting and begging, my mom went ahead with the wedding. She married Chip on Valentine's Day, a permanent stain on the already lame holiday. She kept insisting that he could change. And even if he didn't, nobody was perfect, and the good outweighed the bad, and Chip really did love us, and his temper was a small price to pay for a "better life" in Montclair, where Chip had so generously bought us a house.

If you didn't know what was really going on, my mom and I probably did seem lucky, as there was no arguing that a three-bedroom home in Montclair was an upgrade over our one-bedroom apartment in Hackensack. I'll also admit that I loved having a real, fenced-in, private backyard and my own bedroom, which my mom let me paint a shade called "pink lemonade." Another great part was that my mom no longer had to waitress. In fact, she no longer had to work at *all,* as Chip wanted a "stay-at-home wife" at his beck and call.

But my mom was still wrong. It wasn't a better life—not even close—as none of those improvements were good trade-offs for the sickening sight of Chip coming through the front door with that gun in his holster and a mean glint in his eye. Or the smell of booze on his breath as he called me stupid and lazy—*a loser like your mother*. Or the terrifying noises that came through the walls of my room (and the pillow over my head)—sounds of my mom crying and screaming and begging. For some reason, the begging broke my heart the most. It never worked, and I'm pretty sure it just made things worse.

That fall, I started sixth grade at Mount Hebron Middle School, a cheerful red-brick building on Bellevue Avenue. Like our house, Mount Hebron was an upgrade from my old school with its stench of fish sticks and bleach. I especially loved Miss Wilson, my art teacher, who talked in the most soothing voice and always praised my work. In my case, school *anywhere* was better than home, my safe haven from Chip. But don't get me wrong—my self-esteem was low there, too, and I lived in fear of my classmates discovering the truth about my family.

I frequently reminded myself that nobody knew the names my stepfather called me, and what he was doing to my mom, but I still walked around feeling ashamed. It didn't help that I was the tallest girl in the grade—looming over most of the boys as well. On top of that, I wore all the wrong clothes among so many rich kids. Lee jeans and Braggin' Dragon knockoff Izod shirts from Sears were my staples, as Chip insisted that my mom wasn't going to spoil me with the designer jeans and Lacoste shirts that the other kids were wearing. It was ironic, I often thought. For the first time in our lives, my mom and I were middle-class—yet I'd never felt so poor.

On the weekends, I would stay in my room with Pepper, listening to music (turned down low so I wouldn't disturb Chip), reading Judy Blume novels about other miserable kids, and flipping through my *Bop* and *Tiger Beat* magazines. I didn't like boys in real life, but I had a robust lineup of celebrity crushes that included Shaun Cassidy, Leif Garrett, and Donny Osmond. My hands-down favorite, though, was Joe Kingsley.

Growing up, I'd always known who Joe was. A few years older than I was, he had a famous father who was killed in a failed space mission, and he lived on Fifth Avenue with his glamorous mother. They also had a house in the Hamptons, where they congregated with his aunts, uncles, and cousins, playing touch football, croquet, and other rich-people sports on their sprawling green lawn. I knew these things because my mom could never resist the tabloids with their photos on the covers in the grocery store checkout lines. As a little girl, I didn't fully understand her interest, or why those people were so worthy of her admiration. Though I must admit, I was intrigued by those pictures, too. I especially liked the ones of Joe milling about the city, walking his sheepdog in Central Park or emerging from the subway in his crumpled school uniform and untied shoelaces.

Over the course of that first traumatic year of my mom's marriage to Chip, Joe morphed into a teenage *hunk* (the term the magazines always used), and I became obsessed. Unlike other celebrities, Joe Kingsley never posed for pictures. Instead, he was captured going about his life, often with an endearing, bewildered look on his face. My favorite image, featured as the *Tiger Beat* centerfold one month, was of Joe emerging from the gray surf off Long Island, his tanned chest glistening, his dark hair wet and wavy, a shark's tooth on a leather cord hanging around his neck. I pulled the staples out of his torso, unfolded the poster, and taped it up on my bedroom wall.

On some nights, feeling especially sad and lonely, I would pretend that Joe was my boyfriend. I would make up all sorts of elaborate vignettes, but my favorite was a scene of Joe and me on the beach at dusk. I could practically hear the waves crashing on the shore and smell the salt water and see his dark eyes smoldering as he fastened his shark's tooth necklace around my neck before leaning down to kiss me gently on the lips.

Occasionally, I would feel a little embarrassed for myself, and it would cross my preteen mind that I was doing the same thing my mom had always done: relying on a boy for my happiness. But then I reminded myself that my fantasy of Joe was the opposite. It was my way of avoiding *real* boys who might one day hurt me; it also provided an escape from the man who already *did*.

THE SUMMER BEFORE ninth grade, I underwent my own metamorphosis. Some of it was just the natural progression of puberty and filling out my tall frame with the slightest hips and breasts. But a lot of it came from a dogged determination. I read advice columns in teen magazines about how to "fake it till you make it." I practiced good posture, once even balancing books on my head the way they suggested. I learned how to do my makeup and style my hair. Most important, I bought myself some decent clothes, thanks to a babysitting gig for a rich family who paid me six dollars an hour to watch their kids at the Glen Ridge Country Club. As a bonus, I was getting tanner and blonder, too.

So when I returned to school that September as a freshman at Montclair High, everyone took notice, both the girls *and* the boys doling out the compliments about how pretty I'd "become." By the end of that first week back, Bill Adams, a junior football player, had invited me to a party (I said no), and Wendy Fine, the most popular girl in our grade, asked if I wanted to sit with her at lunch (I said yes).

At first, the attention surprised me. After all, how much could a person change over the course of three months, and why was so much turning on my appearance anyway? It was all further evidence of the "emperor's new clothes" pack mentality. Someone at the top, likely Wendy, had decided that I had some worth, and everyone else was just following suit, giving me a chance.

But I still had to pass the test, and as I sat down at Wendy's lunch table, I reminded myself to smile and pretend to be confident. Meanwhile, Wendy and her cohorts pummeled me with questions. It was clearly an audition of sorts, and I could tell by the looks on some of the girls' faces that they were hoping I'd falter. Kimberly Carrigan, in particular, looked sour, perhaps worried that I might affect her standing as Wendy's best friend.

"So, Cate, do you like anyone?" Wendy asked at one point, her eyes darting over to the football table, where Bill Adams was sitting.

I shook my head no.

"What about Bill?" she said. "I heard he asked you out."

"He didn't ask me out," I said. "He just invited me to a party."

Wendy let out a snort of a laugh and said, "Um . . . that's called asking you out."

For a second, I felt dumb. But I spun it to my advantage, playing cool with the most nonchalant shrug I could muster. "Whatever. I said no."

Several of the girls looked impressed as Wendy continued to grill me. "Why did you say no? 'Cause your dad's a cop? And you'd get in trouble?"

My stomach dropped at the out-of-the-blue mention of Chip. How did Wendy know he was a cop? I started to tell her that he wasn't my dad—that he was only my *step*dad. But then I flashed back to my English teacher talking pityingly about the kids from "broken homes" in *The Outsiders* and bit my tongue.

I shook my head, flipping my hair behind my shoulder like the popular girls always did. "Nah. He's not, like, running around busting parties or anything like that. . . . He's a detective. . . . He works in the city."

Wendy looked impressed, nodding her approval as she told me that her father worked in the city, too. She then returned to the subject of Bill, asking *why* I'd said no. "You don't think he's cute?"

I hesitated, my mind racing. How could I explain that it really had nothing to do with Bill's level of cuteness? I just didn't trust boys. Nothing good ever came from a romantic relationship. I couldn't really say all of that without sounding weird, so thinking of my Joe poster, I blurted out a whopper of a lie. "I'm kind of seeing someone."

"Who?" a few girls said in unison, everyone leaning in, eager.

"His name's Joe."

"Joe Miller?" Kimberly said, guessing another football player.

"No," I said, sipping from my carton of chocolate milk with a straw, buying myself some time. "You don't know him. He doesn't go to our school."

"Where does he go?" Wendy asked.

"Um. He goes to school in Manhattan."

"Oh, *wow*. What year is he?"

"He's a senior," I said.

"How did you meet him?"

"I went to work with my dad one day," I said. "I mean, he worked while I went shopping with my mom. And we met Joe in the park . . . randomly. He was walking his dog."

"Oh, wow. What does he look like?"

"He's *very* cute—with wavy brown hair and brown eyes. . . ."

"Is he tall?"

"Yes," I said, nodding. "I only date tall guys."

"That makes sense. Since you're so tall," Wendy said. "You could be a model."

"Thank you," I said, genuinely taken aback.

Wendy nodded, then said, "Is he romantic?"

"Oh, yeah. He just gave me his shark's tooth necklace on the beach . . . in the Hamptons. It was really sweet. . . ." My voice trailed off, as I knew I was going *way* too far, and suddenly feared that someone would ask why I wasn't wearing the necklace.

That's when I shrugged and said, "He's great, but we actually might break up soon."

"Is he, like, *too* nice?" Wendy asked.

The question confounded me—how could someone be too nice?

"No. He's great," I said. "But, you know, sometimes boys aren't worth the trouble."

FROM THAT DAY on, I was officially popular, scoring invites to the movies and the mall and the skating rink with the rest of the in-crowd. Chip's instinct was always to say no to anything I wanted. But when it came to my social life, the answer became a surprising yes, so long as it didn't inconvenience him. He was more than happy to have me out of "his house" and have my mom all to himself; it was clear he was jealous of anyone or anything that took her time away from him, me at the top of that list.

I began spending as much time as I could at Wendy's house, which was like being at a nice hotel. She had a pool in her back-yard, a console television in her family room, and extensive stereo equipment in her bedroom, along with thousands of eight-tracks and cassettes that her father had gotten for free as a lawyer in the music business. She also had a king-size water bed, and her very own bathroom, attached to her bedroom, complete with a Jacuzzi tub. Wendy was spoiled, but I was more envious of her actual parents than of their money. Other than on television, I'd never witnessed such a harmonious marriage. Mr. Fine acted as if Wendy's mom could do no wrong. He wanted her opinion and cared what she had to say. If anything, Mrs. Fine was the one calling the shots, and it was she, not he, who could be difficult and moody (a trait she passed on to Wendy). I was always nervous when one of them acted bratty, but Mr. Fine never exploded like Chip. In fact, their pouting and complaining only made him bend over backward more.

Meanwhile, I kept Wendy as far away from my house as I could. It wasn't that she was a snob; she never seemed to look down on me or the other girls in our group with less money and smaller houses. But I desperately didn't want her to know the truth about Chip. I knew it wasn't my fault that my mom had married such a monster, and I had a hunch that Wendy would have been really cool and supportive about it. But a greater part of me worried that if she and the other girls found out what was happening at my house, they'd look at me differently. They might even put me in the "white trash" category—a delineation they often used about other stuff that was completely out of a kid's control. At the very least, I worried that Wendy might change her mind about wanting me as her best friend, and I couldn't take that chance. Other than Pepper, our friendship was the only thing that made me feel happy.

As an insurance policy against any form of rejection, I did my best to stay aloof. I pretended that nothing bothered me. I also made it a rule not to like boys. That game was way too risky. Along those lines, I gave up my teen bop magazines and took down my Joe Kingsley shrine, replacing it with a collage of artsy photos cut from the pages of *Vogue*, *Elle*, and *Harper's Bazaar*. There was something about those models, with their passive expressions and irreverent glamour, that I found so intriguing. Inspiring, even. I wanted to be like them—how I imagined they were in real life, anyway—and I came to see clothes and makeup as my own sort of armor. I couldn't change my life in any *real* way, but with fashion, I could construct a different identity—or at least hide my true one. I obviously couldn't afford to shop at The Limited and Benetton and my friends' other mainstays at the mall. Instead, I had to get both creative and resourceful, scouring thrift and consignment shops and stretching my babysitting wages, carefully assembling a wardrobe of secondhand designer goods and various pieces that looked nicer than they were.

It was fun, actually—both the shopping and the styling—and I felt flattered when anyone complimented my outfit or asked if I'd ever thought about being a fashion model. Of course I hadn't— and knew they were trying to be nice. Either that, or they were just confusing style with beauty. It was still nice to hear, though.

Then, one night at the Fines', Wendy and I did our hair and makeup and got all dressed up in our most glamorous outfits. We took turns taking photos of each other with her dad's fancy Nikon. When we got the film developed, I was shocked to discover that the camera seemed to prefer my high cheekbones, wide-set eyes, and fair skin to her golden tan, cutesy smile, and perky ski slope of a nose. Equally surprising, my shots were more interesting. While Wendy stared right into the camera with the most obvious grin, I tried to channel the elusive expressions of my favorite supermodels.

"Wow, Cate! You look amazing," Wendy said, staring down at the pictures. She seemed as surprised as I was, and maybe a little bit annoyed, too. I'd begun to notice that things went more smoothly when Wendy was on top.

"You look even better," I said, then made a joke about how big my nose looked in one of the pictures.

"I *love* your nose," Wendy said. "It reminds me of Christy Turlington's."

"Thanks," I said, thinking that was pretty high praise.

"But if you don't like it . . . you could always get a nose job," Wendy added. "Did I tell you my dad said I could get a boob job for my eighteenth birthday?"

I shook my head and said no, storing this bit of information away in the "Wendy lives on a different planet" file. Man, she really did.

LATER, I SHOWED my photos to my mom, feeling so proud when her face lit up.

"Catherine Cooper! These are gorgeous! We need to get you an agent!"

I laughed.

"I mean it! Or you could enter one of those model search things. . . . I saw one being advertised at the Cherry Hill Mall."

Just then, Chip came around the corner with a can of Coors Light and said, "She's not doing any damn model searches."

"Why not?" I asked, at my own peril.

"They're all run by pimps and child molesters," he said, the authority on everything. "And they're a scam. We aren't throwing money down the drain for some pipe dream."

I exchanged a fleeting glance with my mom, who instantly caved. "You're right, honey," she said to Chip.

"Besides," Chip added, looking at me. "Your nose is too big for you to be a model."

CHAPTER 5

Joe

A few nights before my eighteenth birthday, and just after Berry and I had returned from Andover for winter break, my mother asked if the three of us could have a chat in the living room. The word *chat* was usually a signal that I was about to be lectured, but our grades hadn't yet been announced and I couldn't think of anything else I'd done wrong.

As Berry and I sat side by side on the sofa and my mother took her usual place in the wingback chair next to the fireplace, I watched her pull a cigarette out of the engraved silver box she kept them in. She held it between her fingers without lighting it, a ritual that was part of her latest attempt to quit.

"So," my mother began. "Can you believe it? Only one semester until you're both high-school graduates and off to college."

I nodded as Berry said something about how the year was flying by.

My mother chatted a bit more about Andover generally, asking if we were still happy with our decision to transfer from our old school in the city. We both said we were, and I resisted the urge to make a joke about all the freedom I had now that I was living away from home.

"And you're about to turn *eighteen*," my mother said, giving me a purposeful look that was a clue about the chat to come.

My turning eighteen had always been a thing for my mother, something she had talked about for years. Obviously, I knew it was a benchmark under the law—that on that day, I would become a person who could vote and fight for my country. But it seemed to hold significance beyond that for her, something she saw as representing my official Kingsley manhood.

"Yes," I said, nodding. "I sure am."

She took a deep breath, then said, "Are you excited for your party?"

"Yeah," I said, then corrected myself before she could. "I mean *yes*. Very excited. Thank you."

I still couldn't quite believe that my mother was throwing a big bash for me, at a trendy downtown nightclub, no less. It wasn't like her; she was usually very understated about my birthday, perhaps conscious of not wanting to spoil me or create a sense of entitlement beyond that which automatically came with my name. I like to think she succeeded in that aim, but I was also happy she was making an exception this year.

"And how are your friends feeling?" she asked.

The question was vague—how were they feeling about what, exactly? So I played it safe and said, "Great."

Berry nodded and said, "Everyone is very excited. . . . It'll be so nice to get the old gang back together."

"Yes. It should be wonderful," my mother said as I caught the two exchanging a loaded look.

"Okay. What's going on here?" I said, suddenly suspicious that the two were in cahoots—and my mother had waited for Berry to arrive before having this little conversation.

"Nothing is 'going on,' Joe," my mother said. "I just want to talk to you about some things—"

"Like what?"

"Like certain expectations . . ."

Here we go, I thought, as my mother began droning on about all the adults who would be in attendance, including some notable figures in politics and business, publishing and the law.

I hadn't given much thought to the guest list beyond the names that Berry and I had come up with a few weeks before, and was a little taken aback by the notion that it wasn't just a fun party for my friends and family. There was nothing I hated more than making small talk with adults I barely knew and being grilled about my "future plans"—which, at that point, were nonexistent. I was still waiting to hear back from Harvard, a long shot, along with my backups: Brown, Middlebury, and the University of Virginia.

I did my best to hide my annoyance, as I didn't want to appear ungrateful, and simply said, "Cool. It'll be a blast, I'm sure."

"I hope so. I want you to have fun. But please remember that you're an adult now. And it's time for you to start thinking about cultivating contacts in the working world."

"Doesn't that come *after* college?" I said with a smile.

"No. It starts now," she said. "Your eighteenth birthday is a rite of passage. Things will be different now, moving forward. In the past, you've been absolved of your mistakes—"

"Mistakes?" I said, grinning. "What mistakes?"

"Um. Jumping the subway turnstile. Cheating on that math test. The fake ID," Berry said, then mumbled under her breath, "as if *that* was going to work."

"Thanks, Ber," I said, giving her two thumbs up. "Very helpful examples."

"She's right," my mother said. "Foolish behavior is more easily forgiven when you're a boy. But now the stakes are raised. You'll be under a microscope like never before. I won't be able to protect you, and the press will no longer show you any grace."

"Wait. Is that what they've been showing me to date?" I said, laughing. "Hot damn, I'm in trouble."

Berry elbowed me and said, "Be serious, Joe."

"Yes, Joseph. Please," my mother said. "This is important. What you do from here on out could impact the rest of your life. Do you understand that?"

The statement seemed both melodramatic and obvious, but I played along, just wanting the conversation to be over. "Yes," I said. "I understand."

"Do you also understand that you'll be found guilty by association if your friends—or your girlfriend—misbehave?" she asked, shooting Berry another fleeting, but unmistakably conspiratorial look.

I sighed so loudly that it sounded more like a groan. "*Ohh*. So this is about Nicole," I said.

"It's not about any *one* friend of yours," my mother said. "Although now that you mention her, I do think it's best if you have Nicole come to the party separately—"

"Why?" I said, having already planned to pick her up in a taxi. "That seems pretty rude. Haven't you always taught me to be a gentleman?"

"Normally, yes. It would be rude. But if you arrive with her, the press will know you're dating . . . and they'll start digging into her past."

"Her past, huh?" I said, folding my arms, then giving Berry an accusatory glance.

My mother pressed her lips together a beat, then said, "Did Nicole *shoplift*, Joe?"

"Oh, for the love—" I said, throwing up my hands. "It was a stupid dare . . . years ago. She was only, like, *twelve*—"

"She was actually fourteen," Berry said.

"Right," I said. "A kid."

"But that's your mother's point," Berry said. "She was a kid—and people *still* hold it against her. So now . . . imagine if she was eighteen? She'd be in jail."

"For a two-dollar pair of earrings? I don't think so."

"You're missing the point," Berry said.

"Yes, Joseph," my mother said. "You really are."

"What's the point, then?"

"The dress rehearsal is over now. The public eye will be on you as never before. You're a man—"

"I know," I said, cutting her off. "A Kingsley man."

"Yes. A Kingsley man," my mother said. "And you need to be very careful—and make good decisions. People expect a lot from you. . . . And remember, Joseph, to whom much is given—"

"Much is expected," I finished for her. "I got it."

THAT SATURDAY NIGHT, my mother, Berry, and I arrived at the club early, pulling up in a black limousine. Through the tinted windows, I could see that the press were already in place, waiting to get their shots of us. I scanned the sidewalk, recognizing some of the usual suspects, including Eduardo, the only one I knew by name. Eduardo invaded my privacy as much as the next guy, but he was so damn funny and friendly that I couldn't help liking him.

As the driver helped my mother and Berry out of the car, then escorted them over to the entrance, I stepped onto the curb and grinned at Eduardo.

"Happy birthday, Joey boy!" he called out to me.

"It's Joe!" I shouted back. "I'm a *man* now."

The paparazzi chuckled as they snapped away, staying behind the velvet ropes that were being closely guarded by two thick-necked bouncers mumbling into walkie-talkies.

"Hey! Where's your girlfriend?" Eduardo called out to me.

"Who said I have a girlfriend?" I quipped back.

Eduardo laughed and said, "You *always* have a girlfriend, Joey."

THE PARTY STARTED out following my mother's exact script. My friends and I were all on our best behavior, making polite conversation with my mother and other adults. My friends, especially my female friends, had always been intrigued and impressed by my mother, probably because she was such a legend among *their* mothers, and that night, I watched the subtle jockeying for position and a chance to talk to her. My mother was pleasant to everyone, but she wasn't particularly warm to anybody but Berry, a dynamic that seemed to annoy Nicole. Frankly, everything about Berry seemed to annoy Nicole that night, and at one point she accused me of flirting with Berry.

"Ugh, that's disgusting," I said. "She's like a sister to me."

"But she's *not* your sister."

"She might as well be."

"I still think you like her."

"Of course I *like* her," I said, pretending not to know what she was implying.

"No. I mean I think you have a *thing* for her," Nicole said. "And she's clearly in love with you."

"Stop it. She's my best friend. That's all there is to it," I said, shutting the subject down. Berry was off-limits, and our friendship was not to be questioned.

Of course, my terse reply only amped up Nicole's jealousy and insecurity, and around ten, as my mother and the other grownups were saying their goodbyes, I could feel a wave of girl drama brewing. I chose to ignore it, hoping it would go away, my strategy for any strife. Meanwhile, my friends and I began to drink, the bartenders ignoring the fact that most of us were underage.

Around one in the morning, long after the party was supposed to be over and when things were really turning wild, Berry cut in between Nicole and me while we made out on the dance floor. "Joe, can I talk to you for a second?"

"What the hell is your problem?" Nicole erupted, staring Berry down.

"My *problem* is that Joe is drunk. And it's time for him to go home."

"Stop bossing him," Nicole said. "You're not his mother."

"Well, at least his mother likes me," Berry said under her breath.

It wasn't like her to be so petty, and I couldn't help but smile, which further enraged Nicole. "What's *that* supposed to mean?" she shouted.

"It means: His mother likes me. And trusts me. And you have terrible judgment. So I'm taking Joe home. *Now*." She then turned to me and said, "I'm going to get you a cab. Be outside in five minutes."

Much to Nicole's fury, I did as I was told, gathering my things and saying my goodbyes. Then, just as I was headed out the door, one of my friends yelled that the paparazzi were still camped outside. Our collective judgment impaired, we concocted a convoluted getaway plan that involved a decoy and a protective barrier around me. The idea was to prevent any clear photographs on my path to the taxi, although at that point, it was less about privacy and more just a game. As we all spilled onto the street, one of my friends yelled at Eduardo to "get the fuck out of the way, you fat fuck." Eduardo took it in stride, laughing it off and patting his belly, but another photographer goaded us with insults of his own.

Before I knew what was happening, punches were being thrown, and the city block was illuminated by flashbulbs. Things were a blur after that, but I remember flipping the bird at one of the photographers before Nicole and I got into the backseat of Berry's waiting cab.

"Goddammit, Joe!" Berry shouted, as we pulled away from the curb. "Why would you do that? He has a camera!"

"I know he has a camera! Why do you think I was mad at him in the first place?"

"He wanted to make you mad! He wanted you to react. That's why you don't flip off the paparazzi! You played right into their hands!"

"They deserved it!" Nicole yelled.

"That's not the point, you moron!" Berry yelled back at her.

"Oh my God, Joe!" Nicole whined. "Are you going to let her call me a moron?"

"Berry, please don't call moron a Nicole," I accidentally said, then laughed. "Oops. You know what I mean—"

Nicole glared at me while Berry looked out her window and said in a loud voice, "My God, your mother is right."

"About what?" I couldn't resist asking.

She turned, gave me the most disdainful look, then said, "You're your own worst enemy. Your *only* enemy."

"What's *that* supposed to mean?" Nicole shouted at her.

"It means—he makes shitty choices."

"Like what?" Nicole said.

"Like getting drunk. Like fighting with photographers. Like dating *you*," Berry said. She then turned back to me and said, "This is going to be bad, Joe. This is going to be *really* bad."

In that moment, I sobered up just enough to know she was right.

THE DRUNKEN RUCKUS happened so late—or, as it were, *early*—that the story didn't make it into the morning paper. Instead of viewing the delay as a reprieve, I felt worse with every passing hour, dreading the moment when my mother heard about it.

The moment finally came with the evening edition of the *New York Post*. She walked into my bedroom, where I was still nursing a hangover, and deposited a copy of the paper on my bed. I braced myself for the worst, then looked down. On the front page was a huge picture of me. In it, I was bleary-eyed and disheveled, with my shirttail out and my tie dangling loose. My middle finger was up, a giant *fuck you* to all of New York City, my mother included.

"How could you do this?" she asked in a low, steely voice.

"I'm sorry, Mom," I said, feeling a wave of intense shame.

"I'm sorry, too," she said.

"Why are you sorry?" I asked with a dash of irrational hope that maybe she had seen me as the victim, for once.

Instead, she looked me dead in the eyes and said, "I'm sorry for having so much faith in you. Clearly, I was wrong. You aren't up to the challenge."

I wanted to ask what she meant by "the challenge." The challenge of not getting into trouble? Or the challenge of being my father's son? Somehow, I knew she meant both things—and probably a whole lot more—so I just said again how sorry I was.

She stared at me a long time, looking so sad and disappointed that it broke my heart. "I know you are," she finally said. "But being sorry isn't going to fix this."

I nodded, feeling my throat tighten and a huge pit open in my stomach. "I promise I'll do better," I said. "This will never happen again."

She took a deep breath, like she was going to say something else. But she didn't. She just shook her head and walked out of my room, leaving the newspaper on my bed.

MY MOTHER NEVER explicitly forgave me for what happened on the night of my eighteenth birthday, but she eventually moved on from it, probably because the press did first. They enthusiastically covered my graduation from high school a few months later, followed by my backpacking trip through Europe and my post-Nicole fling with a hot Danish au pair.

By the time I enrolled at Harvard that fall (with Berry still by my side, thank goodness), the nightclub incident seemed all but forgotten. I had a clean slate and was determined to make my mother proud. Following in my father's footsteps, I joined all the right clubs and societies—from the Spee Club to the Hasty Pudding to the *Crimson*. Deep down, though, I felt like a fraud and an impostor, knowing that I had only gained admission to those organizations, along with Harvard itself, because of my name. It was something I brought up to Berry often.

"You need to get over this impostor syndrome nonsense," she said after I bombed a biology exam at the end of our freshman year and confided that it felt like confirmation of my theory. It was a rare sunny day in Cambridge, and we were strolling in Harvard Yard, where kids were lounging and reading and playing Frisbee. "I mean, look around. Half the kids here are blowhards who got in through connections."

"That isn't exactly comforting," I said.

"It's not supposed to be," she said.

"Jeez. I was telling you about my insecurities—and you come back with that?"

"Yes. Because you're doing your best to make those insecurities a self-fulfilling prophecy."

"What are you talking about?"

"I'm talking about your 'aw shucks' self-deprecating schtick."

"It's not a schtick."

"Well, then that's even *worse*. Look, Joe. You know full well you didn't study for this exam."

"Yes, I did!"

"Having sex with Evie doesn't count as studying for biology, Joe," she said, rolling her eyes.

I tried not to smile, thinking of the study session I'd had with my hot TA—and how we'd gotten a little sidetracked. I was also wondering how Berry always managed to keep such close tabs on me. I shared a lot with her, but even the stuff I didn't tell her, she'd always somehow discover.

"Well, it *was* an anatomy exam." I grinned.

Berry made a face and told me not to be a pig. I would have been offended, but I knew she didn't mean it. I was far from perfect, but I treated women with respect. I never cheated, I didn't lead them on (not purposefully, anyway), and I kept my promises. If I said I would call, I would call.

"Just try to do better, Joe," she finally said with a sigh. "You don't have to be your dad. Just be *your* best self."

"And what if this *is* my best self?" I said.

"It's *not*," she said. "And we both know it."

I took Berry's words to heart. For my remaining three years at Harvard, I managed to stay out of trouble and get mostly decent grades. When I did screw up here and there, I took my lumps and apologized with as much sincerity as I could muster. Generally, that was enough, as I discovered that just being a decent, humble guy went a very long way. Unfortunately, humility didn't earn me as many points with my mother, whose bar for me was considerably higher. In fact, I think she sometimes wished I were a little less down-to-earth, seeming to believe that a certain aloofness carried more gravitas. It wasn't so much that she was a snob, or even an elitist, and I never heard her talk down about people, at least not directly. She just wanted me on a certain path—my *father's* path. That was the difference between her and Gary, I think. Gary wanted me to be the best version of *me,* and my mother wanted me to be like *him*. I can't entirely blame her for that—for wanting me to carry his torch and legacy. Perhaps she also felt a responsibility and duty to her dead husband. When I didn't uphold his honor in a certain way, whether it came to my résumé or my relationships, I think she felt that we had both failed him.

The good news was, after going out with a string of girls my mother didn't approve of, I finally found one she really liked. I'd met Margaret Braswell the first week of college; she was one of Berry's three suite mates and by far her favorite. Margaret was intelligent but quiet and unassuming—not hell-bent on proving how smart she was, like a lot of girls at Harvard. She was also very pretty, with big brown eyes and dark hair cut in a short glossy bob. A former ballerina, she was slight—almost wispy— not at all my usual type. The more time I spent with her, though, the more I liked her, and I could tell she liked me, too. It took a while, but we finally got together during the fall of our junior year. My mother was thrilled. Margaret checked all the boxes, including the fact that she came from a "good family"—whatever that meant. In some ways, it seemed as if my relationship with Margaret made up for my lackluster transcript.

"So, Joseph, do you think Margaret is 'the one'?" my mother

asked one cool June evening after finding me on the back porch of our home in the Hamptons.

I'd just gone for a long run on the beach and was enjoying a rush of postexercise endorphins, along with a cold Schaefer, straight out of the can.

The question caught me off guard. Margaret and I had only been dating a year, and I said as much.

"Well, for what it's worth, I think she's perfect for you," my mother said.

I nodded—because in many ways, I did, too. Margaret had such a kind soul, and I loved how nonjudgmental and laid back she was.

"And she'd be a wonderful First Lady," my mother said, staring at me over her glass of chardonnay.

"Jeez, Mom," I said, laughing. "Jumping ahead a little, are we?"

"Perhaps. But I know quality when I see it. She's so smart and elegant and gracious."

"Okay. Yes. She is all of those things," I said. "But you do realize that for her to be a First Lady would require that I not only marry her but, you know, also *win* the presidency?"

My mother waved this off, as if it was just some run-of-the-mill job that anyone could apply for and get. "I realize that, Joseph. That's my point."

I took a sip of my beer and laughed.

"What's so amusing?" she asked.

"I don't know, Mom. That's sort of like saying you want me to be the starting pitcher for the New York Yankees."

She shook her head. "No, it's not. You weren't very good at baseball."

"The hell!" I said. "I made the All-Star team in the fifth grade."

"But that doesn't translate to pitching for the Yankees," she said.

"Well, I wasn't even *in* student government."

"Believe me, I'm aware."

Filled with my usual mixed feelings, I took a sip of my beer. On the one hand, I wanted to make her happy. On the other hand, I wanted to make *myself* happy. It was frustrating that both things didn't seem possible at once, and I went out on a limb and told her as much.

"Of course I want you to be happy, Joseph," she said, as if it were a complete given.

I stared at her, thinking of what had happened my sophomore year when I caught the acting bug and landed the starring role in *The Tempest*. My mother had come to see me on opening night, praising my performance and going on and on about how I'd become a real Renaissance man like my father, rounding out my sportier side. But when I raised the idea of pursuing theater as a major, maybe even a career, she quickly shut it down. In no uncertain terms, she informed me that acting was not a suitable profession for a Kingsley man.

"Well, acting made me happy," I said on the porch that day, unable to resist the comment.

"Joseph, please," she said, taking a sip of her wine. "You aren't considering that again, are you?"

I shook my head—because I wasn't. I also had to admit to myself, with hindsight, that my theater days probably had less to do with a passion for acting and more to do with Olivia Healey, who had played Miranda alongside me.

My mother blinked, then said, "So what *are* you thinking?"

"Well, we know medical school is out," I said.

"Because of your grades?"

"Yes," I said. "And also because I don't want to be a doctor."

"Right," she said. "And you don't care for math. . . ."

"Correct. So no career in finance or engineering for me."

My mother nodded. "So what does that leave?"

I looked at her, thinking that it left a whole lot of shit, but I knew what she was getting at, and what she wanted me to say. I also knew that it lined up with what my grandmother wanted for me, albeit for different reasons, so I played along, humoring her.

"I could always go to law school," I said, running my thumb along the condensation on the side of my beer can.

My mother sat up straighter, her whole face coming to life, as if the thought had never occurred to her—and it wasn't the automatic default of privileged kids across America. "That's a great idea!" she said. "Shall I get you an LSAT tutor?"

"Sure, Mom," I said. "That'd be super."

AND SO I went along on my path of least resistance, studying for the LSAT, then taking the exam, getting a mediocre score to go along with my mediocre grades. I think my mother realized that even with the Kingsley name, I didn't have the credentials for Harvard, Yale, or Columbia, but when I squeaked my way into NYU, she was happy enough. Meanwhile, I was pretty happy, too, if only because I was returning to Manhattan. Four years in Cambridge had been a pleasant diversion, but I missed the action and nightlife of the best city in the world.

After graduation, Margaret and I broke up, both reluctantly and on good terms. The decision had more to do with distance and logistics, as she had joined the Peace Corps and was going to teach English in Malawi. In other words, my mother couldn't blame me for once.

For the next few years, I played the field, much to the delight of the tabloid press. There were a few law school girlfriends along the way, but none of them measured up to Margaret in my mother's eyes—or mine for that matter—so I migrated to the other extreme, hanging out with a bevy of actress and model types, most notably Phoebe Mills. Other than going on a couple of dates with Brooke Shields during college (a buddy of mine at Harvard knew her roommate at Princeton), I'd never been with a woman famous in her own right. My mother preferred the term *infamous* when it came to Phoebe and highly disapproved of her most recent film with Michael Douglas, in which she'd appeared topless.

Phoebe's most controversial moment, however, was her drunken appearance on David Letterman, in which she talked about our relationship in unfiltered terms, suggesting that I was good in bed. It didn't help that she also had a wardrobe malfunction during the segment, which Dave milked for all it was worth. My mother was appalled with the entire spectacle. Berry piled on, calling her trashy and phony and accusing her of using me to amplify her celebrity. I defended her on the margins, pointing out that Berry's pretentious banker boyfriend was a bigger phony than Phoebe. Besides, I said, Phoebe had plenty of her own press and didn't need me for added exposure.

Over time, though, I had to admit that it *was* pretty suspect the way the paparazzi always seemed to know exactly where Phoebe and I would be, at times showing up before we even got there. It was also true that drama followed her everywhere. It became exhausting. To my mother's relief, I finally ended things.

Shortly after that breakup, I graduated from law school (with a 2.9!) and Margaret returned from Africa, taking a teaching job in Brooklyn. That summer, and much to my mother's delight, we began to spend time together again, agreeing to take things slowly as I focused on studying for the bar. That was the plan anyway, but more often, I did other stuff. Like going to Yankees games. And playing poker. And surfing and sailing. And rollerblading in the park. And going to nightclubs where I met *more* models and actresses and enjoyed an occasional one-night stand, all within the rules of our current relationship status.

The predictable result, of course, was that I failed the bar. *Twice.* The tabloid headlines were brutal—the worst they'd ever been. THE HUNK FLUNKS and TWO-TIME LOSER. My mother was mortified, and I was pretty embarrassed, too, though I played it off, cracking jokes about three times being the charm.

Thank goodness it *was*, and in a Hail Mary, I finally passed. From there, I was sworn in to the New York bar and took a job as an assistant district attorney in Manhattan. I was only going to be making forty thousand dollars a year, but my mother and grandmother were pleased, likely because everyone knows that the DA's office is a great path to running for public office. I wasn't sure how I felt about the idea but figured I could cross that bridge later. In the meantime, I basked in their approval, however fleeting it might be.

CHAPTER 6

Cate

When I was little, my mom used to take me down the shore for the day. We rarely spent the night—she couldn't afford the time off work or the price of an Atlantic City hotel room—but every once in a blue moon, we would splurge and stay over. To me, there was nothing more thrilling than the way the boardwalk transformed at nightfall. I loved everything about it. The colorful blinking lights of the rides and arcades, the shiny lure of those souvenir shops, the smell of delicious food cooking in the salty ocean air.

Of course, once Chip came on the scene, my mom and I stopped going, and there was a several-year gap when I never saw the ocean. Fortunately, that changed again when I became friends with Wendy. Her parents had a beachfront condo in Margate, about twenty minutes south of AC, and they would often invite me to stay with them. Wendy and I had a blast there. It was where I learned to drink and smoke and hook up with random guys who I wouldn't have to later face in school. But being on the boardwalk at night always made me a little bit nostalgic, too, thinking about that fleeting, magical part of my childhood when it was just my mom and me.

On one of those trips, Wendy met a boy she really liked. While the two of them were off making out somewhere, I strolled along Steel Pier alone, eating cotton candy and avoiding eye contact. Feeling melancholy and resentful toward Chip, I wasn't in the mood to flirt or talk to anyone at all, so I was extra annoyed when some lady approached me with a bright smile.

"Excuse me," she said in a polished voice. "May I ask your name?"

I hesitated, as it was so instilled in me not to answer these sorts of questions from strangers. But we were in a public place, and this woman didn't look like a kidnapper, so I told her.

She nodded and said, "And how old are you, Cate?"

"Sixteen," I said, warily.

The lady reached into her quilted black Chanel bag, like the one Wendy's mother carried. She pulled her hand back out and gave me a business card.

"My name is Barbara Bell," she said. "I'm a talent scout for a modeling agency."

In a state of disbelief, I looked down at the card and saw the words *Elite Model Management*.

"Is this the same Elite that reps Naomi Campbell and Linda Evangelista?" I asked.

"Yes! One and the same!" she said, looking surprised. "You're familiar with us?"

"Yes," I said, thinking that my fascination with fashion models was paying off.

"And have *you* done any modeling, Cate?"

"No," I said with a nervous laugh. "I haven't."

"Well, Cate, you're a stunning young woman. . . . I'd love to set up a meeting with you and your parents. Do you think that would be possible?"

"Um, maybe . . ." I said. "I'd have to ask them."

My mind was racing. This woman could not be serious. Maybe she was one of the child molesters Chip had warned me about? Then I remembered the photos that Wendy and I had taken in her bedroom—how pretty I'd looked in them—and wondered if maybe she really was a legitimate model scout and saw some potential in me.

"Well, I do hope you give me a call," Barbara said. "Because I really think you have something special."

FOR SOME REASON, I didn't tell Wendy about Barbara for the rest of that week. Maybe I thought she'd be jealous; maybe I worried that she'd be skeptical and dash the hopes I could feel building inside me. In any event, I kept the secret until I got home and told my mom. She seemed to feel that Barbara Bell was for real and was as giddy as a kid on Christmas morning, talking about photo shoots in the Caribbean and catwalks in Europe. For a second, I got caught up in her excitement, but then I reminded myself that my mom didn't always have the best judgment. As much as I hated to agree with anything Chip had to say, he was a little bit right about that. After all, she'd married *him*.

Besides, even if Barbara was legit, she was probably wrong about me. I calculated that for every so-called story of discovery, there had to be a dozen misfires. Girls who seemed pretty or interesting in a certain golden moment—only to get under the bright lights of a studio and falter. I told myself that the whole thing was way too risky. I needed to save myself a lot of trouble and disappointment and just say no.

But every time I thought about throwing away Barbara's business card, a little voice in my head reminded me that this could be my ticket out. My shot to get away from Chip. And maybe not just an out for me, but for my mom, too.

So I went out on a limb and asked for his permission. Miraculously, he gave it to me, likely because he had dollar signs in his eyes. I called Barbara, and the following week, my mom and I boarded the New Jersey Transit train to Manhattan. After arriving in Penn Station, we walked over to Elite's Fifth Avenue offices, then rode the elevator up to the twenty-fourth floor. I was so excited, but it all felt very abstract until we pushed open the glass doors and saw gigantic photos of Linda, Naomi, and Cindy adorning the walls of the reception area.

"Wow," I whispered, getting chills.

"I know," my mom whispered back, shaking her head, staring up at Cindy. "This could be *you* one day."

I took a deep breath as a stylish receptionist looked up and asked if she could help us. I gave her my name and said I had an appointment with Barbara, and she smiled, nodded, and picked up her phone.

A second later, another well-dressed woman arrived. She introduced herself as Tonya, Barbara's assistant, and ushered us down the hall to a conference room with modern furniture and a gorgeous view of the park.

"May I get you something to drink?" Tonya said. "Coffee, tea, soda?"

"Um, do you have Diet Pepsi?" my mom asked in a voice that was a little shaky.

"Yes. We do. And for you, Cate?"

"I'll take one, too, please," I said.

Once alone, my mom and I debated which seats to take, talking in whispers. We decided to sit facing the windows. A moment later, Tonya returned with our sodas poured into tall glasses with cubes of ice and skinny straws and told us Barbara would be right with us.

As we waited, I got more and more nervous, questioning my

outfit, my makeup, and especially my high ponytail, which I worried made me look too young. Then again, maybe that was a *good* thing. I knew plenty of models got their start earlier than sixteen. For the next five long minutes, as I sipped my soda and tried to block out my mom's nervous chatter, I kept thinking that there was no way this could be happening. No way it would work out. At some point, though, I gritted my teeth—literally—and told myself that was no way to approach life. I had to stop panicking. If I didn't calm down and believe in myself, at least a little bit, how could anyone else?

Before I could answer my own question, Barbara walked into the room flanked by two men and made introductions. Everyone shook my hand, then my mom's, before sitting down at the table and making a bunch of small talk about the weather, and our train ride into the city, and my school year so far. At some point, as I started to calm down a little, Barbara segued to the reason we were here, talking about my appearance, praising my features and figure.

"But you're more than a pretty face, Cate," she said. "I watched you on the boardwalk. You have poise and confidence. An *aura*. The trademark of Elite models."

I thanked her, stunned by her compliments. It was the best I'd ever felt about myself.

"We would love for you to join the Elite family," Barbara said, beaming at me.

"Oh, wow . . . thank you," I said, my heart pounding. I was going to be not only a model but part of a family? My mind was blown.

"Is that a yes?"

I nodded, speechless and overwhelmed.

"Wonderful!" Barbara said, quickly turning things over to the men, who began to describe what they called "next steps." They talked about setting up a test shoot to get me headshots and comp cards—basically a portfolio of marketing materials. I would then be assigned a booker at the agency, who would submit my portfolio to various clients and set up castings for me—which were like auditions. From there, I just had to show up to the casting calls and make a good impression. If a client liked what they saw, they would call my booker, send out a contract, and schedule the shoot.

I nodded, but I must have looked uneasy, because Barbara said, "It might sound overwhelming, but that's what we're here for. To help you navigate the process."

One of the men nodded and then chimed in. "Yes. Barbara is right. Elite will be with you *every* step of the way. There is no agency out there who will better protect your interests while also promoting you in this competitive marketplace."

I smiled and said thank you.

"Do you have any questions?" Barbara asked, looking at me first, then my mom.

"No," I said, shaking my head.

"No," my mom echoed.

"Great! Here's your contract. It's standard language that all of our models sign," Barbara said, sliding me a sheet of paper. "Take your time reviewing it. No pressure. If you need to go home first and talk it over with your father—or perhaps a lawyer—that's fine, too."

"No," I said, cutting her off. There was no way I was going to give Chip the chance to change his mind. "I'm ready to sign. Right now."

LATER THAT WEEK, my mom and I returned to the city for my test shoot. When we arrived at the studio, we were met by a small crowd, including a photographer, an art director, a hairstylist, a makeup artist, a fashion designer, and various scurrying assistants. I was told that clothes would be provided for me, and that I should come with no product in my hair and a clean, makeup-free face. I followed instructions, but wasn't happy about the way I looked, and half expected them to cancel the shoot when they saw my flat hair and the huge zit on my chin. But nobody seemed fazed, and the hairstylist and makeup artist quickly got to work.

Over the next two hours, I was transformed multiple times. In the first shot, I wore blue jeans and a white T-shirt with natural makeup and wavy hair; in the second, I had on a black lace cocktail dress with dramatic, smoky eyes and a straighter but still very full hairdo; and in the third, I wore a white string bikini with hair so curly it looked permed and lots of shimmery gold makeup.

Sitting there in the swivel chair and getting my hair and makeup done was the easy part. The hard part was posing under those bright lights with everyone staring at me as the photographer gave me hundreds of instructions to sit, stand, look up, look down, look to the left, look to the right, lower my chin, raise my chin, smile, smile more, smile less, smile with my eyes, don't smile. It was exhausting, and I'd never felt so awkward and self-conscious, like I was playing a game of Twister in high heels and being judged on style points. But as the shoot progressed, things got a little easier, and I learned that the key was to try to relax, ignore all the people in the room, and pretend to be somewhere else, preferably somewhere far away. I was good at that; living with Chip had given me plenty of practice.

At the end of the session, after I was back in my own clothes, the art director gave me a little hug and said, "Great job, Cate. You're a pro."

"Thank you," I said, feeling more relieved than anything else.

Like I'd passed another test and tricked them all into believing I was something I wasn't.

A FEW DAYS later, my mom and I returned to New York for the third time in less than two weeks to meet with my assigned booking agent, a woman named Daisy, who reminded me of Yoko Ono. We chatted for a while, getting to know each other, before Daisy mentioned the test shoot and the great feedback she'd gotten.

"They said you were a very hard worker—and so polite. Which goes a long way in this business."

I nodded, wondering if there was a *but* coming. Perhaps she was about to tell me that the photos hadn't turned out and they needed to redo them. Or maybe the news was even worse. Maybe some higher-up had decided that none of this was going to work out after all.

I held my breath as Daisy splayed about a dozen photos of me on the glass coffee table between us. I looked down as I heard my mom gasp.

"Wow," I said, my eyes darting from picture to picture. I hardly recognized myself. I looked like a movie star.

"Do you like them?" Daisy asked.

It felt like a rhetorical question, but I answered it anyway.

"I mean . . . yes, sure," I said, noticing there was no trace of the zit that had been on my chin the day of the shoot. My skin looked flawless, in fact, and my arms and legs looked more toned and tanned than they were in real life. "I can't believe this is *me*. Did someone doctor these photos or something?"

Daisy laughed, then said that the images had been retouched. It was the first time I'd ever heard that word.

"How do they do that?" I asked her.

Daisy explained that it was a process in the darkroom where they pieced together separate images to create the perfect photo.

"Do they do this with everyone?" I asked. Maybe that's what made supermodels supermodels: they were actually perfect without all the retouching.

Daisy smiled and said yes, everyone. Then she paused and her face got very serious as she said, "Listen, Cate. I want you to remember something as you move forward in your career."

I nodded, listening as intently as I could.

"You're going to be rejected and criticized and picked apart. Endlessly. You'll be told you aren't thin enough or pretty enough or good enough. And ultimately, at the end of it all, you're going to be told you're too old. No matter how successful you become, you will eventually be replaced by someone younger."

The speech was the opposite of what I'd expected, but for some reason it made me like Daisy even more than I already did.

"Do you understand what I'm saying?" she asked, staring into my eyes.

"Yes. I do," I said, wondering what about her statement could possibly confuse anyone.

Daisy pushed her glasses up on her nose and said, "And? Does that scare you?"

This question was more difficult to answer, and I pondered it a few seconds before shaking my head no. What scared me was the thought of Chip putting my mom in the hospital, maybe even killing her. Not the idea of someone telling me I was fat.

"Good," Daisy said. "Because the sooner you realize that there is no such thing as perfection—and this entire business is an illusion—the better off you'll be."

—

OVER THE NEXT month, I returned to the city a half dozen times for casting calls, racking up rejections along with absences from school. Chip seemed to revel in my failure, reminding me that I wasn't model material and gloating that he'd been right—that the whole thing was a scam. He also complained that I should be in school (as if he cared at all about my education) and that my mom should be home, cleaning and cooking and stroking his ego and doing God knows what else she did for him. It made me shudder to think about it.

Then, just as Chip was on the verge of making me quit before I'd even started, I got booked for my first job. Then my second and third and fourth. None of the jobs were with major fashion houses or big brands, and Daisy seemed to think they were small potatoes, but it felt like a lot of money to me. More important, I was gaining valuable experience and building a résumé. Daisy promised that if I kept working hard, it was only a matter of time before I got my big break.

"One minute you're modeling a twenty-dollar skirt for Macy's, and the next you're wearing Versace on a catwalk in Milan," she said.

So I kept working hard and saving what little money Chip didn't take from me. You'd think the funds he siphoned off would have been enough to keep him off my back, but the more I made, the more he seemed to hate me. At first, I thought maybe he was jealous, but that really didn't make sense. How could a middle-aged cop be jealous of a teenaged model? Then I thought it had to do with my mom—that he hated how happy and proud she got when she was looking at pictures of me in catalogs and magazines, because it meant less attention for him. In part, it was probably both of those things.

But I came to realize that it was mostly about power and control. Everything with Chip boiled down to that. It wasn't so much that he hated me, or even my success, but that he resented the confidence and independence that came along with that success. They clearly threatened him. I think he intuitively understood that if I got strong and made enough money, he wouldn't have as much control over my mom. The bottom line was that Chip needed me to "know my place," and if he sensed for one second that I didn't or that, in his words, I was getting "too big for my britches," he went berserk. So I kept a low profile around the house and often reminded my mom, who wasn't as savvy about these dynamics, never to mention my career or casting calls within his earshot.

All the while, I counted down the days until my eighteenth birthday, knowing that I could move out of my house the second it was legally permissible—and that Chip couldn't track me down and drag me back home as some sort of a power play. I felt myself regularly drifting into dream mode, imagining a small apartment in the city—one with two bedrooms so my mom could come with me. We could re-create a version of our old life in Hackensack, only slightly more glamorous, and minus the loser guys.

IN SEPTEMBER OF my senior year, a rep from Calvin Klein contacted Daisy, inviting me to a small, exclusive casting call. The agent said they were looking for a "relative unknown—a fresh face with star power" and that they thought I fit the bill. I couldn't believe it. In my mind, *nobody* was bigger or more iconic than Calvin Klein, except maybe Ralph Lauren, though I preferred Calvin's simple, seductive aesthetic to Ralph's snobbish, preppy one. As excited and hopeful as I was, I was also a little worried. Not about getting rejected, but about getting *picked*. I knew that my landing

Calvin Klein would upset the precarious power dynamic in our household. If Chip could no longer call me "bush league" and "second-rate," it would push him over the edge.

The night before my audition, as I was in bed trying to fall asleep, he went on a rampage. Like clockwork. Through the door of my bedroom, I heard him ranting about me—and of all things, Pepper's litter box. Chip despised Pepper (probably because Pepper didn't give a shit about Chip) and was always threatening to give him away or, when he was *really* pissed, put him down.

I put my pillow over my head, but Chip's voice still got louder. He shouted about what a spoiled, irresponsible diva I was, and how I never "lifted a damn finger around here." When he was right outside my door, I could hear my mom begging him to leave me alone, saying that I needed my sleep for my "big day" tomorrow.

I shook my head, knowing she'd just made things infinitely worse. It was going to be a long night—and we were both screwed. It was inevitable. So before we could go through the whole tired routine of him pounding on the door and threatening to kick it down, I opened it, staring right into his eyes. For one second, he looked surprised—maybe a little disappointed—that I wasn't cowering in the corner.

"I'm really sorry, Chip," I said, facing the music, getting it over with.

"What are you sorry for?" he shouted, his face bright red. He was still in his full uniform, gun in his holster and all, with Pepper's litter box at his feet. "Tell me *exactly* what you're sorry for."

It was the usual song and dance, and one I could never get right. I was either too specific or not specific enough. I was either being flippant or groveling in a way he found disingenuous.

"I'm sorry for not changing the litter box," I said, glancing down at it, keeping my voice low and steady, trying to hit the right note.

"When did you change this fucking thing last?" he yelled at the top of his lungs. "And don't lie to me."

It was a no-win, because I'd changed the litter box two days ago—and the directions on the box said I had three to four days. So I opted to lie, saying, "I'm not sure. It's been a few days. I'm sorry."

"The hell you are. You're a spoiled fucking brat. You think you're too good for this house, don't you?"

"No, I don't, Chip," I said, making fleeting eye contact with my mom, another tactical error. He hated when he felt like she was on my side, especially if that meant we were aligned against him.

"YES, YOU FUCKING DO! AND DON'T LOOK AT YOUR MOTHER!"

I bit my lip, nodded, and mumbled again that I was sorry. But he was already on to his next move, reaching down for the litter box, then raising it over his head with both hands. I stared at him, confused, then realized with horror what he was about to do. Sure enough, he hurled the entire plastic bin at me as hard as he could. I ducked my head as cat litter and pellets of cat poop flew across my room, landing all over my shag carpet, my desk, my bed.

"Clean this fucking mess up. NOW!" he said, looking so satisfied. Downright proud of himself.

I nodded, quickly dropping to my knees and scraping up cat litter with my bare hands. It was a completely futile exercise, especially because the trash can was on the other side of the room.

"I'll get the vacuum cleaner," I heard my mom say.

"No! Don't you dare help her! You do everything for her!" Chip shouted. As he turned and stormed back down the hall, I prayed that he wasn't looking for Pepper. Fortunately, the front door slammed, and his engine turned over in the carport outside my window. Only at that point did I look back up at my mom.

"I'm so sorry, honey," she said, tears in her eyes.

I started to tell her it was okay, like I always did. Instead, something snapped inside me. "Why in the world would you tell him about the casting call?" I demanded to know. "He always tries to ruin everything!"

"I—I—was excited."

"Yeah," I said. "Well, there's nothing to be excited about. I'm not gonna get it."

As I went to get the vacuum cleaner, I realized, once again, that I was screwed and alone. It crossed my mind to call Wendy—and go over to her house for the night—maybe finally confide in her and her parents what was happening in my house. But in the long run that would backfire. Not even Mr. Fine, with all his power, could do anything to stop a police officer. More likely, he'd tell Wendy that it was too dangerous to be my friend. Mr. Fine was a good man, but he would put his child's safety first, the exact opposite of what was happening at my house. Besides, Wendy and I weren't even as close as we had been. I was so busy working that Kimberly had moved back up in the pecking order. Sometimes I felt like Wendy rubbed that in my face, going out of her way to let me know how much fun I was always missing, and how bad she felt for me. To be fair, I think she actually *did* feel sorry for me, as I think Wendy's worst nightmare would have been to miss both homecoming *and* prom, as I had. But her constant sympathy only made me feel more left out, like I was straddling two worlds, truly belonging in neither.

When I returned with the vacuum cleaner, my mom was stripping the sheets and pillowcases from my bed, still talking about Calvin Klein, and how she just knew I would get picked. It was her Stepford Wife robot mode; her eyes were glassy and her voice stilted as she fell into a catatonic denial.

"No, Mom. I'll tell you what's gonna happen," I said, staring at her. "I'm gonna clean this room for the next two hours. And by then, Chip will come home and tell me I didn't do it right and start screaming again and find some kind of an excuse to beat on you. Maybe break your nose . . . And tomorrow I'm gonna show up at that audition looking like a zombie with bloodshot eyes and they're gonna laugh me out of the room. Which is *exactly* what Chip wants."

My mom's chin trembled. "Oh, honey. I'm so sorry," she said. Because she knew it was true.

And, of course, it *was* true. Everything I said turned out to be correct, with only one exception: Chip didn't break my mom's nose; he broke her collarbone.

As CHIP TOOK my mom to the ER, undoubtedly with another lie about her falling down the stairs, I lay awake all night, worrying that Chip's abuse seemed to be escalating. Finally, my alarm went off, and I got up and went to my casting. Afterward, Daisy called and asked me how it went.

"It was a disaster," I said.

"Oh, no. What happened?"

I took a deep breath, fighting back tears. "I don't know . . . I just . . . I didn't get much sleep last night. And I—I just couldn't get it together. They started asking me questions, and I couldn't think . . . I sucked . . . I'm sorry, Daisy."

"Don't apologize to *me*, honey," Daisy said. "This just happens sometimes."

Yes, I thought. *And sometimes your mother ends up in the ER with a broken collarbone. That happens sometimes, too.*

—

A FEW HOURS later, Daisy called me back.

"Cate?" she said. "Are you sitting down?"

"Yes," I said, thinking that she didn't have to coddle me. She had no idea what a thick skin I had. "What did they say? I bombed it, right?"

"No," she said with a giddy laugh. "You got it!"

"What?" I said, confused.

"You got the job. They picked you!" Daisy said.

"There's no way," I said, thinking that it had to be some kind of joke. "I—I practically broke down in tears—"

"I know you did," Daisy said. "They said they could tell you were upset about something, but that they loved your vulnerability. . . . They said you were raw and real and perfect for this campaign."

"They *did*?" I said, in a complete state of disbelief.

"Yes. They did. . . . Congratulations, Catherine Cooper. You're the face of the next Calvin Klein campaign."

CHAPTER 7

Joe

For the most part, I liked being an assistant district attorney. It was hard work, but the hours weren't nearly as bad as what my law school buddies were billing at their big corporate firms—and my cases were a lot more interesting. Instead of arguing over a clause in a contract or reviewing documents for litigation that would never see the light of a courtroom, I was out in the field, talking to cops and witnesses and victims, building a case and preparing for trial. I loved any kind of court appearance. It reminded me of theater in that I had to stand up and put on a really good performance. Sometimes I had a script that I memorized, but I was good at thinking on my feet, too. Basically, I did whatever I needed to do to charm the jury and get a conviction.

In that sense, I had a distinct advantage over my fellow ADAs. Jurors felt as if they already knew me, and for the most part, they liked and trusted me. I could win over most judges, too, many of whom were older and had revered my father. In other words, I definitely benefited from my name. For once, though, I didn't feel guilty about my advantage, since I felt I was using it to help others. I was fighting for justice, just as my grandmother had wanted me to. Every now and then, she would come downtown to see me in action. Afterward, she'd take me to lunch, and we'd talk about the case. Occasionally, she felt sorry for a defendant and expressed mixed emotions about me getting a conviction.

"I have to say, Joey . . . I was really hoping that young man would see an acquittal today," she said one afternoon as we sat in a little bakery.

I chuckled and shook my head. "C'mon, Gary. He was guilty as hell," I said. "They found the crack in his car."

"Allegedly. It could have been planted. At the end of the day, you only had the word of one white police officer. That's not exactly ironclad."

"Okay. But we also got a *confession*," I countered.

She dismissed that, too, and began a whole diatribe about shady police tactics and forced confessions and unethical interrogations.

"And in any event," she said, "does it seem right to put away that kid for *life*?"

"Well, he's eighteen. So technically an adult," I said, feeling instantly sheepish as I thought of my birthday party and how eighteen hadn't seemed so old to me then. "Besides. It was his *third* offense."

"Right. Because he's a teenage *addict*. Addicts typically do things more than once."

I sighed, then said, "Well, I don't make the rules. And neither do cops or judges or juries. That's up to the legislature."

My grandmother conceded this point but insisted that the so-called war on drugs wrongfully targeted minorities and the urban poor. "Joey, have you ever wondered why the sentencing guidelines are harsher for crack cocaine than *regular* cocaine?" she asked.

I shook my head, because I hadn't; I'd just always thought crack seemed worse, somehow more dangerous, more associated with crime.

"Think about it. But for now, let's put that aside," she said. "Let's just talk about pot."

I smiled, surprised to hear my grandmother use the slang term.

"Okay," I said, nodding.

"Which file is more likely to come across your desk—an African American teenager smoking pot in Harlem or a white kid getting high at Columbia?"

"Dang," I said, nodding. "You got a point there."

"You smoked pot in college, didn't you, Joey?"

"Gary! C'mon," I said, smiling.

"Well? Were you ever worried about being imprisoned?"

I shook my head and said, "No. Not really."

"And if the police had raided one of your little parties, and brought you in, what would have happened?"

I bit my lip, imagining how it would have all unfolded, and how far-fetched it was that any scenario would have included a jail cell. "Yeah. I hear you."

"The whole criminal justice system is problematic, Joey."

"Right. Sure. But a lot of the people I prosecute are seriously bad guys, and I feel good about getting them off the street."

"I know, Joey," she said. "And I'm not trying to disparage your entire profession. We need principled prosecutors. . . ."

"But?" I said.

Gary shook her head and said, "There's no but—I just want you to think about the big picture."

"Meaning what? Do you want me to be a public defender instead?"

"I'm not saying that, exactly."

"Okay. What *are* you saying?"

Gary took a deep breath and said, "Well. Didn't you say that it was all about the laws?"

I nodded.

"Well, then . . . maybe the laws—and the sentencing guidelines—need to be reformed."

"Yeah," I said. "Maybe so."

"So . . . we need really good men—and women—as lawmakers, too. . . ."

I smiled. "Gary, you *dog*. I see where you're going here—"

My grandmother raised her eyebrows, smiled, and said, "Just something to think about, Joey."

MEANWHILE, AS I careened into my thirties, my mother returned her focus to my personal life. She would often ask about Margaret, pretending to be casual, making easy-breezy conversation. But the intent was clear: she wanted to know when (not if) I was going to propose. Proposing to Margaret actually felt like something of a given to me, too—we'd even adopted a dog together, a black-and-white Canaan terrier I named Thursday. But it was more of a "far into the future" given than an "any day now" given.

I said as much to my mother one day at brunch, and she looked appalled, insisting that girls like Margaret shouldn't have to wait until their *thirties* to marry.

"Mom, thirty is *not* old. Maybe it used to be, but these days people are waiting to get married."

"Waiting for *what*?"

"Waiting until they're *ready*, Mom."

"Ready for *what*?"

"I don't know, Mom. Financially ready—"

"You're set financially."

I knew it was true, but I still winced inside. "*Emotionally* ready, I meant."

"Please, Joseph. You're *thirty*. And Margaret is even older."

"Only by four months, Mom."

"Still . . . it's not fair to her."

"Margaret is *fine,*" I said, thinking that I couldn't remember a single instance in which she'd pressured me, questioned me, or even so much as dropped a hint. In fact, at the last wedding we went to together, she didn't even get up from the table to participate in the bridal bouquet toss shenanigans—which I thought was pretty darn cool.

"She's *pretending* to be fine, Joseph," my mother said. "And just because she's not giving you an ultimatum doesn't mean there isn't a deadline in her mind."

"Okay, Mom," I said, eager to change the subject.

"I just don't want you to lose her, Joseph."

"I'm not going to lose her, Mom," I said. "Everything is great. We're great. In fact, we're thinking about moving in together."

I braced myself for her reaction.

"Joseph, no. That's a terrible idea."

"Why?"

"It's so disrespectful to her. She deserves better."

"Don't do the why-buy-the-cow thing, Mom. Please."

"Well, it's true."

"It's old-fashioned."

"I *am* old-fashioned. And so is Margaret's mother."

"Well, we're not, Mom. We aren't that way."

"Joseph, trust me, she *is*. She just doesn't want to rock the boat. She wants to make you happy."

"And that's a bad thing?" I said, keeping my voice light. I didn't want to upset her—or myself.

"Look, Joseph," she said with a weary sigh. "Just don't let her get away. I think you'll be really sorry if you do. You need a partner in this life, and I know you think I'm always nagging and pressuring you—"

"Because you are," I said with a laugh.

"I don't want you to have any regrets. I don't want you to ever look back and think, 'Could I have done more? Been more? Done it differently, better?' I'm just trying to help you—"

"I know, Mom," I said, my voice firm. "And I appreciate your concern—I really do. But I got this under control."

JUST A FEW weeks later, Margaret told me that one of her best friends from high school had just gotten engaged, after dating the guy for only six months. She seemed a little upset—maybe even jealous—and I wondered if maybe my mother had been right after all.

"Whoa. Six months? That seems a bit fast," I said, treading carefully.

"I disagree," Margaret said, holding my gaze. "I think . . . when you know, you know."

I knew what she was getting at. More important, I knew that *she* knew that *I* knew what she was getting at. I had to say something. "Yeah. That's true . . . but every relationship is different. Every situation."

"Obviously," Margaret said.

I pretended not to notice her annoyed tone as I added a foot-note. "And who knows, maybe she's pregnant!"

"Oh?" Margaret said, her eyebrows rising. "Because that's why couples get engaged? Because they *have* to?"

"No. I just meant . . . I don't know . . . I just don't want you to feel bad that they got engaged before we did," I said. I'd finally addressed the elephant in the room.

Margaret stared at me for a few seconds before nodding. Then she said, "*Should* I feel bad about that?"

"No," I said.

"Well, then," she said wryly. "I guess I won't."

—

A FEW MONTHS later, as I felt myself getting closer and closer to pulling the trigger on a ring, Margaret had to go out of town for a conference, so I went to the Hamptons for a long weekend and a little final soul-searching.

The morning I arrived, I headed straight out for the beach, taking Thursday for a long walk. About a mile up the shoreline, we came across a photo shoot of some sort. I planned to pass on by, but as we got closer, I spotted a gorgeous blonde who looked vaguely familiar. I lingered in the general vicinity for a moment, tossing the Frisbee I'd brought along for Thursday while trying to get a better look.

It crossed my mind that this wasn't something I should be doing—using my dog as a prop to meet a woman—but I told myself that it was harmless. Besides, just because I was about to get engaged didn't mean I had to stop interacting with half the population of the world. I was capable of meeting someone without it leading to flirtation, let alone sex. Heck, I could even view this as a test. If I couldn't handle a simple interaction with a stranger on the beach, it would be a clear sign that I wasn't ready to get engaged. Better to find that out now rather than later.

Before I could change my mind again, I flung the Frisbee in the general direction of the woman, knowing that Thursday would lead a merry chase. He did, of course, and a few seconds later, I was standing next to her, trying, quite *unsuccessfully,* not to stare. To put it bluntly, she was the most beautiful girl I'd ever seen— which was really saying something, as I'd obviously seen plenty of gorgeous women in my day. Everything about her glowed. Her skin, her pink lips, and her long, shiny hair that looked like sunlight. And that was all before she glanced up to meet my gaze with these *huge,* intense pale blue eyes that melted me. For a few seconds, I couldn't speak. Then I somehow got it together, stumbling over my words as I mumbled a vague apology for my dog. She gave me a remote smile that said she knew what I was up to—like, *Listen, buddy, I'm no dummy; I've seen this dog trick before*— and in that instant, I could tell she had a little edge. Meanwhile, if she knew who I was, she pretended not to.

Over the next several minutes, we introduced ourselves and made small talk. Yet even as she answered all my questions, she retained an air of mystery. Like she didn't *want* to be known. Not by *me*, anyway.

Fortunately, she had a makeup artist with her, and he seemed more than eager for our conversation to last as long as possible. He kept chiming in on Cate's answers with additional color commentary. As we talked, I kept studying her face, and suddenly realized that I *had* seen her before—on a billboard near LaGuardia. I blurted that out, resisting the urge to also tell her that she was even more beautiful in person, somehow knowing that a statement like that, although totally true, would sound like a line.

Meanwhile, I knew I was running out of time—and that she had to get back to work. Any second, I was going to have to say goodbye and might never see her again. It made me panic a little inside. I *had* to see her again.

There was really no way, though, not without breaking my cardinal rule about cheating. Even if I kept it platonic, it would still be cheating given what I was thinking. I had never believed in love at first sight—how could you love someone you didn't know? But this woman gave me that feeling. Like a chemical reaction. A little explosion in my chest.

As I stalled for a few final seconds, I told myself to think of Margaret. That worked for a moment but then backfired, as I had to face the fact that I'd never, not for one second at any point in our relationship, experienced anything approaching this feeling.

The realization made me a little sad, then gave me the justification I was so desperately seeking.

"So I know you have to get back to work, but I'd love to, you know, get together sometime. . . . Do you think I could get your number?"

She stared at me for several seconds, as if genuinely contemplating the pros and the cons. Then, just as I thought she was going to reject me, she nodded. Before she could make a move, the makeup artist was eagerly jotting a number down on the back of a business card.

"Here you go," he said, handing it to me.

I thanked him, then looked back at Cate for permission. "So I can call you?" I said.

She gave me a little smile, then shrugged and said, "Sure . . . why not?"

In that instant, I knew I was screwed.

THE NEXT DAY, after Berry had driven out to the Hamptons last minute to join me, I made the mistake of casually telling her that I'd met someone "interesting" the previous day.

She shook her head, frowned, then said, "Oh, Lord, Joe. I know that look."

"What look?" I said, doing my best to hide my smirk.

"The I-met-a-hot-girl look," she said.

"I didn't even say it was a girl."

"Well? Was it?"

"Yeah," I said, I'm sure looking as sheepish as I felt.

"Okay," Berry said. "And . . . was it a *hot* girl you had no business talking to?"

"That feels like a trick question," I said.

"Ugh, Joe," she groaned.

"What?"

"C'mon, spill it. Who is she?"

"Her name's Cate."

"What's her story?"

"She works in the fashion industry."

Berry raised an eyebrow. "The *fashion* industry? So another model, huh?"

I stared back at her and blinked, feeling a stab of guilt.

She shook her head and said, "Did you get her number?"

When I didn't answer, Berry groaned again. "Shit, Joe. You're going to throw things away with Margaret over a *model*?"

"Whoa, now, Berr," I said. "No one is throwing anything away . . . and there's no need to denigrate the woman's profession."

Berry took a few deep breaths and said, "Fine. You're right. Her job is beside the point. The point is—if you call that girl—*any* girl—things with Margaret will be done. Forever."

"That seems a bit extreme."

"It's true."

We stared at each other in a stalemate that she broke. "Do you love Margaret?" she asked.

"Yes," I said, picturing her sweet brown eyes. "I do."

"Then get your shit together, Joe," my best friend told me. "Once and for all."

CHAPTER 8

Cate

On the morning of my eighteenth birthday, just after Chip had left for work, I woke up my mom and told her I was moving out; my bags had been packed the night before.

"Where are you going?" she asked, sitting up in bed, rubbing her eyes.

"I'm moving in with my model friend Elna," I said. "To her place on the Upper East Side."

It was the first I'd told her of my plan, but she didn't look surprised. "I'm so happy for you, sweetie," she said, blinking back tears. I wasn't sure if they were happy tears or sad. Likely they were both, which was how I was feeling, along with so many other emotions.

"I'm going to come back for you, Mom," I said. "Soon. I promise. I just need to save a little more money—and get my own place. We can be roommates again. Like old times."

"Oh, sweetie—you know I can't do that—"

"Yes, you can, Mom. There are tons of waitress jobs in the city. Really nice restaurants where the tips are just huge. Or you could find something else to do—there are so many jobs to be had—I'd love to have a full-time manager. I could really use the help. What do you think, Mom? You know you aren't happy here. You have to get away from him." By that point, I was rambling—and a little frantic, because I knew it was pretty futile.

"I can't leave," she said, cutting me off, tears streaming down her cheeks.

"Why not?"

"I just can't."

"Yes, you can, Mom!" I said, putting on my best life coach face. "You have to. You know you do."

She took a deep breath and did her best to smile back at me. "Okay, sweetie," she said. "We'll see."

"Yes, Mom," I said, feeling so determined. "We *will*."

A FEW HOURS later, I was unloading my bags into Elna's second bedroom, which had recently been vacated by another friend of ours who had quit modeling to get married. Aside from the guilt over leaving my mom behind, I was excited and hopeful. Elna was the most inspiring person I knew. She had grown up in Johannesburg, South Africa, in the thick of the apartheid era. After her real father was killed in the Soweto Uprising, her mother remarried a bigger monster than my stepfather. He hit her mother but also molested Elna, the abuse starting when she was eleven. Three years and a back-alley abortion later, Elna worked up the nerve to tell her mother what was going on, at which point her stepfather called her a liar; her mother sided with her husband, and they both kicked her out of the house. From there, Elna made her way to Cape Town, living on the streets until she was discovered by a British fashion photographer on the beach at Camps Bay.

Within days of my meeting Elna, she had shared this entire

story with me, sparing no gory details. Beyond the heartbreak of her story, the thing that struck me the most was her complete lack of shame. I had still never told a soul about Chip. Elna would end up being the first.

It was before I moved in with her, but while I was crashing at her place after a late night of work. We were exhausted and punchy, and had another early wake-up, but instead of going to bed, we opened a bottle of red wine, caught a buzz, and curled up in her bed together, talking. At one point, Elna asked why I never dated anyone or mentioned guys. "Are you a lesbian?"

"No," I said. "I just don't have time to date."

"Yeah. But you have time to fuck, don't you?" she said with a little grin. "I mean, everyone has time to fuck."

I laughed, thinking that Elna could be so blunt—so different from Wendy and my old Montclair friends. But given the life she'd led, I guess there wasn't much reason to sugarcoat things.

"Yeah," I said, laughing. "I suppose I *do* have time for that."

"And?"

"And . . . nothing," I said, staring at one of Elna's dangling false lashes. She was so bad about removing them after we worked, sometimes not even bothering to wash her face at night, which was crazy given that she had the most flawless skin I'd ever seen.

"Wait. Are you a virgin?"

"No," I said, then told her about Jared, the Burberry model I'd met on a shoot last summer, my only real boyfriend to date.

"How long did you go out?"

"Only about three months," I said. "And the whole thing was long distance. He works in LA."

"Were you in love?"

I made a face and said no, not even close.

"Have you ever been?"

I shook my head, thinking that there was no way I would bring anyone home to Chip and my mom, which made it sort of hard to have a boyfriend. I went out on a limb and told her as much, alluding to my "difficult home life."

"Difficult how?"

"My stepfather's a dick."

Elna's light green eyes narrowed. "Is he abusive?"

"He hits my mom. He's just a run-of-the-mill asshole to me." I gave her a few examples, including the litter box story, then said, "It's not nearly as bad as what you went through—"

Elna cut me off and said, "Abuse is abuse. And your mother is allowing it, just like mine did."

"Yeah. But there's really nothing she can do."

"Bullshit!" Elna said, sitting up, now animated. "She could protect you. And she's not. You need to leave, Cate."

"I will. As soon as I graduate high school," I said, though I was on the verge of flunking most of my classes due to unexcused absences and missed assignments and abysmal test scores.

"You can get your GED," she said. "It's what everyone does."

"Yeah. It's not just that, though. I can't leave my mom," I told her, explaining how, in recent months, I'd been able to quell some of Chip's attacks simply by giving him cash. And when that didn't work, I'd get in his way—physically.

"Oh. So you pay the bills—and now you're her bodyguard?"

I stiffened, feeling both resentful and defensive at once. "There's really nothing she could do. I think he'd try to kill her if she stood up to him—"

"Well," Elna said with a surprisingly callous shrug. "That's the price of poker."

"Elna!" I said. "You can't blame the victim!"

"*You're* a victim, too," she said. "And she's your *mother*. And

I'm sorry she's suffering, but if she won't protect you, you have to protect yourself. Get the fuck out of there. Every woman for herself."

FROM THAT POINT on, Elna and I were a team, fiercely protecting each other. She became my best friend. In some ways, she felt like the only real friend I'd ever had.

I stayed in touch with Wendy, even after she went off to Cornell, pledging a sorority and falling in love with the man she'd eventually marry. She annoyed Elna to no end, who criticized the way Wendy only surfaced for the big, glamorous moments—like Fashion Week or other high-end parties. "I feel like she uses you," Elna said once.

"I wouldn't go that far," I said.

"Well, at the very least, she's a fair-weather friend."

Maybe that was true, but I explained that it really wasn't Wendy's fault. She was just sheltered, having never worked a day in her life, save for a short stint at the Gap that she quit because she "hated folding." Wendy had absolutely no clue how grueling being a model really was. The obscene hours. The shoots that would last all night. The endless flights and jet lag and waking up in hotels and forgetting where we were. The starvation diets that gave new meaning to running on empty, as we were told that there was no such thing as too thin and some of our friends who had to be hospitalized for anorexia were *praised* for looking like skeletons. Hell, there was really no such thing as a model without an eating disorder; it was more a question of degree and method. Elna chose to binge and purge, but I couldn't stand the feeling of throwing up, so I went the extreme exercise route. Sometimes I'd go to the gym and ride the bike for three hours at a time, paying the price for a few chips and guacamole. Nicotine helped, too, a pack a day being standard fare for most models, Elna and me included.

We did have a no-hard-drugs pact, though—Elna had been down that road and was determined never to relapse. My reason had more to do with wanting to stay in control of my body and mind and emotions. Along those lines, I continued to hold guys at arm's length, noticing that the nice ones generally didn't pursue me anyway, perhaps too intimidated by the toughness I did my best to project. The ones who seemed confident in the beginning turned out to be the most insecure. They talked a big game at first, bragging to their friends that they were dating a model, but most of them could only take so much before a steamy photo shoot or long trip would push them over the edge. Sometimes I would break up with them from sheer annoyance; in other cases, they would preemptively dump me, quickly transitioning to a safer girlfriend with a less threatening lifestyle. Meanwhile, I reminded myself to stick to casual dating with men who couldn't disappoint me.

In the spring of 1995, I was in the Hamptons on yet another Obsession shoot. It was miserable. To be honest, beach shoots were *always* miserable, the sand blowing in your eyes and chafing your skin, to say nothing of the freezing water. That day was actually sunny and sixty, but the wind still made it feel like winter. While the art directors, fashion designers, and photographers wore puffy down coats and boots, I faux frolicked in the ice-cold surf wearing nothing but a bikini and a sheer white linen blouse.

Between takes, the team did their best to warm me up, though that had more to do with not wanting my skin to look blue in the photos than with my actual comfort. During one of those breaks, as I sat under a heat lamp, sipping green tea from a thermos, I spotted him walking toward us with his dog. The one and only Joe Kingsley.

Curtis, my favorite makeup artist and close friend, saw him at the same time. "Holy shit, girl! Is that who I think it is?" he whisper-shouted, grabbing my arm.

"It sure is," I said, marveling at seeing Joe Kingsley in person but also wondering why I was so surprised when sightings of him were quite commonplace in the city and in the Hamptons. In fact, almost everyone I knew had encountered him at some point.

But this was *my* first time, and apparently the same was true for Curtis, because he sighed and said, "He's even hotter in person. Look at those legs. I *can't* handle it."

"I know," I said, squinting into the sun, then shielding my eyes to get a better look. He was wearing black athletic shorts, a gray sweatshirt, and a rainbow-striped beanie, complete with a big red pom-pom. It was equal parts adorable and absurd.

"And I love Thursday," Curtis said.

"Who?"

"His dog. That's the name of his dog."

"Oh," I said, nodding, thinking that there was no bit of celebrity trivia that Curtis didn't know.

We kept staring as Joe flung a Frisbee toward the ocean and Thursday bounded after it. He leaped into the air, narrowly missing before frantically paddling into the surf as Joe clapped, either caught up in the moment or aware that he had an audience. The latter seemed more likely.

"Mercy," Curtis breathed. "That's the *sexiest* man to ever walk the Earth. Dead or alive."

"Dead men can't walk," I said, blowing my nose. I was starting to catch a cold.

Curtis pushed my hand away from my face, then blended the

makeup around my nose with an egg-shaped sponge before turning back to gawk at Joe.

"I wonder if he's still with Margaret Braswell—"

"Margaret Braswell?" I said, remembering the petite brunette Joe had dated when he was at Harvard. I hadn't heard her name in years. "I thought he was dating Phoebe Mills?"

"God, girl. Keep up. He got back together with Margaret ages ago."

"Oh. I didn't know," I said, memories returning of my Joe Kingsley stalking days. How much those pictures of him had brought me comfort, especially that one of him on the beach with the shark's tooth necklace. I smiled to myself, thinking how incredible it was that we were both here now, in the Hamptons. My thirteen-year-old self wouldn't have believed it.

Suddenly, Joe turned and tossed the Frisbee again, this time away from the shoreline, in our direction. It sailed through the air, landing just feet away from us.

"Oh my God," Curtis said. "He did that on purpose."

"No, he didn't," I said as Thursday ran toward us, and Joe followed him.

"He *so* did," Curtis hissed under his breath, barely able to contain his excitement. "He wants to meet you."

"You just said he's dating Margaret?"

"So what? Maybe they just broke up. Or . . . maybe they're about to break up. If you get my drift."

"Whatever," I said, rolling my eyes, as Thursday bypassed the Frisbee and trotted over to our chairs.

Curtis kneeled to pet him, saying, "Good boy, Thursday! The best boy, aren't you?"

"You're shameless," I added under my breath, shaking my head as Joe caught up to his dog.

"Get over here, you rascal," Joe said. He then looked up at us and said, "Gosh, I'm sorry. He never listens!"

"Don't be sorry. He's adorable!" Curtis gushed. "What's his name?"

Shameless, I thought again, as Joe told him what he already knew.

"Thursday! What a cute name! How'd you come up with that?"

"'Cause I adopted him on a Thursday," Joe said. "And it's the best day of the week. You have the whole weekend to look forward to."

"Oh my God. Today's Thursday!" Curtis said. "What are the chances?"

"About one in seven," I deadpanned.

Joe laughed, his face lighting up, then looked directly into my eyes. I held his gaze, feeling a little light-headed. I'd met celebrities before, but no one near this famous—or handsome. Overwhelmed, I had to glance away for a second. When I looked back his way, he was still staring at me.

"I'm Joe, by the way," he said, extending his arm.

I gave him a half smile, then shook his hand. "I'm Cate. And this is Curtis."

"It's great to meet you both," he said, nodding earnestly.

"Oh, my goodness. Same," Curtis said. "I'm a big fan. Huge."

"Thanks, man," Joe mumbled. A fleeting but unmistakably uncomfortable look crossed his face. "So . . . what are you guys working on today? A movie?"

"No. It's a campaign for Calvin Klein," Curtis said, though we technically weren't supposed to be divulging any details of the shoot. "Cate is our talent. I'm sure you recognize her?"

I rolled my eyes and said, "I'm sure he *doesn't.*"

"Actually," Joe said, staring at me with a look of deep concentration. "You *do* look familiar."

"Yeah, right," I said.

He wouldn't have been the first person to recognize me. But it was almost always girls or gay men, with an occasional creeper thrown in.

"I'm serious," Joe continued, his face becoming more earnest by the second. "You look *really* familiar." He squinted a little and then said, "Wait. Are you on a billboard near LaGuardia?"

"Oh my God, yes! She is!" Curtis said.

Joe looked smug as he gave me a wink. "Yep. I knew it. I never forget a face. Not one as pretty as yours, anyway."

It was the kind of line that usually sounded cheesy, but Joe's delivery was so sincere that it disarmed me, and I could feel my heart flutter a little as I thanked him.

"So where are you from?" Joe asked me.

"New Jersey."

"Whereabouts?"

"Montclair."

"You live there now?"

I shook my head and said, "No. Not since high school. I live in the city."

Joe nodded and said, "And how long have you been modeling?"

"Since I was sixteen," I said, wondering if he was really trying to discern whether I had gone to college. It was something a lot of people tried to figure out by asking the same sorts of questions.

"But she's way more than just a pretty face," Curtis chimed in.

I shot him a look to tone it down, but he ignored it and continued to promote me. "She's a whole mood . . . and nobody has more style. . . . She could be the next Anna Wintour. Only not as mean."

"*Maybe* as mean," I said with a smile, hoping to shut Curtis up.

Joe laughed, then bit his lip and lowered his voice. "Well. I'll keep my eye out for you, for sure."

He seemed to be flirting with me, and I suddenly felt weak—butterflies-in-my-stomach and clammy-hands weak. I told myself to get a grip. Joe was just a charming guy—everyone knew that—and any second, he would move on with his dog and his day and his life.

But as the minutes passed, he stayed so focused, locked in on me, asking me more questions. Meanwhile, Thursday panted at our feet and Curtis fussed with his makeup kit, humming Whitney Houston's "How Will I Know."

"Well, I guess I should let you get back to work," he said after another few minutes of small talk.

"Yeah," I said, glancing over at the crew—who were clearly getting restless.

"Maybe I'll see you around . . . at Bubby's or The Odeon," he said, two of the places I'd mentioned when he asked where I liked to hang out.

"Yeah. Maybe."

"Hopefully," he said, staring into my eyes again, his face so serious.

As he held my gaze, I felt the strangest sensation. A connection. It was almost as if I'd known him in another life—or at least for a long time in this one. I reminded myself that everyone probably felt this way when meeting Joe—that it was a function of his fame, along with all the photographs we'd seen of him over the years. We *felt* like we knew him, but that was obviously only one-sided, illusory.

A few seconds later, Joe asked for my phone number, saying

he'd love to get together sometime. Before I could answer, Curtis was handing over one of his business cards, my name and number written on the back.

"Thanks, man," Joe said, grinning at Curtis. Then his face grew serious again as he gazed back at me, holding the card up. "So I can call you?" he said.

"Sure . . . why not?" I said with a little shrug, doing my best to play it cool, telling myself that the chances of him actually calling were remote at best.

CHAPTER 9

Joe

It took more self-discipline than I'd ever used in my life, but I took Berry's advice, and I didn't call Cate. It was torture. I told myself that the feeling would pass, but I couldn't put her out of my mind. I found myself looking for her in the city. Ideally, I wanted to see her in the flesh, but I scoured billboards, sides of buses, and subway placards, too. Once, I even picked up a *Vogue* magazine, flipping through the pages, hoping to come across her photo.

About a month later, Margaret and I went to The Odeon for dinner. Just after we finished eating, I got up to go to the men's room. After I'd taken a few steps, it crossed my mind that the check might come when I was gone, and I hated for Margaret to pay for anything. I didn't make much more than she did, and her trust fund was likely the same size as mine, but my mom had ingrained in me never to let a girl pay. So, I turned back to the table, removed my wallet from my back pocket, and handed it to her, telling her to use my credit card.

"I can get this one, Joe," she said.

But I shook my head and insisted. Big mistake. When I got

back to the table, I saw her face and instantly suspected what had happened.

"What's wrong?" I asked, hoping that I was wrong.

But Margaret cleared her throat and said, "I swear I wasn't snooping. . . . I was looking for your credit card—"

I nodded, believing this. My wallet was a mess, just like my desk, my apartment, everything in my life. I braced myself as she held up that damn business card. "But I found this."

I nodded, reminding myself that I hadn't done anything wrong.

"What is it?" she said.

"It's a makeup artist."

"Why do you have a makeup artist's card?"

I swallowed, telling myself not to lie, that the cover-up is always worse than the crime. "It's a guy I met on the beach. He was at a photo shoot," I said.

She stared at me a beat, then flipped it over and read aloud: "Cate Cooper."

My stomach fluttered hearing her name, but I said nothing, waiting.

"Who is she?" Margaret finally asked, answering the question I'd wondered in the prior weeks about whether Cate was famous. I guess this was my answer, though not necessarily conclusive. Margaret was often clueless about pop culture.

"She's . . . a girl . . . who was with that makeup artist. . . ."

Margaret nodded, staring into my eyes. She was never one to be jealous or suspicious—not even of Phoebe, whom we'd crossed paths with at a recent event—but she seemed to be both now. Or maybe it was just my guilty conscience.

"Did you ask for her number?" she said.

I hesitated, then told the truth, once again. "Yes," I said.

"Why?"

"Oh, I don't know. . . . She was nice . . . cool . . . you know. . . ." I said, now completely flustered.

"Is she a model?" Margaret asked, looking so hurt.

"Yes," I said. "But I never called her."

She nodded slowly, as if taking this fact into consideration. "And when did you get this number? A long time ago?"

It felt like a trap. If I got it a long time ago and still had it, that didn't look good. If I got it recently, that, too, was a problem. Once again, I went with the truth. "It was that weekend you were at a conference, and I was in the Hamptons with Berry."

"Was Berry with you? When you met her?"

I shook my head.

"Does she know you got this?"

"Um . . . yeah," I said. "I mentioned it."

"And what did she say about it?" she said, the questions now rapid-fire.

"She told me not to call her."

"She didn't approve?"

I nodded, my face getting hotter. "What does it matter what Berry thought? Or when I got the card? The point is, I didn't call her—"

"Then why do you still have this? In your wallet?"

I shrugged and told her I didn't know.

She stared at me for what felt like a long time, then put the card on the table, with the "Cate" side up. She looked at it for a few seconds before sliding it across the table at me.

"Well, it's not too late," Margaret said.

I shook my head, picked up the card, and tore it in half, feeling a strange pang.

Margaret was stone-faced for several seconds before she took a deep breath and said, "Look, Joe . . . I don't think I can do this."

"Do what?" I said.

"Be with you."

I laughed nervously and said, "Because of a girl's phone number? Who I didn't even call?"

"Because of a lot of things," she said. "It's just too much. . . . Being with you . . . it's too hard."

"Wait. Is this about the *Post*?" I said, referencing the article they'd just run listing "Five things you might not have known about Margaret Braswell." All five facts were positive—or at least neutral—but she still loathed the attention.

"Yes and no . . . I'm just not very good at this. . . ." Her voice trailed off.

"Yes, you are," I said. "The press loves you."

"Until they don't," she said—which was pretty damn insightful, par for the course for Margaret. She paused, then said, "Joe . . . I know you're going to run for office one day . . . and the attention on you will only get more intense. . . ."

"No way," I said. "How many times do I have to tell you that I don't want that?"

She stared at me, her expression changing. "Okay, Joe. Tell me . . . what *do* you want?"

"I'm fine being a lawyer," I said. "For now."

"For now," she echoed, as if I'd just confirmed her point.

I started to say something defensive, but stopped myself, doubling down. "Yes. For *now*. I mean . . . I don't think I have to have everything mapped out in my early thirties, do I?"

She took a deep breath, as if gathering all her reserves. "Here's the thing, Joe. I don't think you know what you want. Or *who* you want."

"That's not true, Margaret," I said.

She stared back at me.

"I want *you*," I said, at that moment meaning it.

Margaret shook her head. "You don't know who you want

because you don't know who you *are*. The whole world thinks they know you . . . but you don't even know yourself."

I could tell she wasn't trying to be mean—Margaret was never mean—but her words still cut me.

"I'll figure that out," I said. "Soon. I promise I will, Mags. You can help me."

Margaret shook her head, looking so sad. "I don't think I can help you, Joe."

I forced a smile. "Wait. Are you saying I'm a lost cause?"

Margaret didn't take the bait. "No. I'm saying that you have to do this on your own. For yourself. It has to come from within."

"Okay. Yes. You're right," I said. "It *will* come from within. I'm close to a breakthrough here. . . ."

"Good," she said. "I really hope that's true." Her eyes filled with tears, which killed me. I can't stand when *any* girl is sad, but seeing Margaret cry was the absolute worst.

"Don't cry, Mags. Please," I said. "Just give me a little more time. I *love* you."

"I love you, too, Joe," she told me. "And I always will. But I can't do this anymore. I need to move on. I'm sorry."

I KNOW I could have fought to keep Margaret. I could have gone out and bought her a diamond ring the very next day. She would have said yes. I know she would have. At the very least, I could have smoothed things over, reassured her, bought myself a little more time. Instead, I just let her quietly slip away, acquiescing to her decision. In doing so, I likely only proved her theory about me not being in control of my own life. Once again, I had chosen the path of least resistance.

My mom was devastated and also angry, accusing me of suffering from Peter Pan syndrome. But I insisted that it had been

Margaret's doing, almost convincing myself of the same. Then, about a week later, Margaret came by to pick up the things that she had left at my place. We arranged for her to do it when I wasn't home, but somehow the press caught on and stalked her as she loaded bags into the trunk of her car.

In the photos, she looked distraught—like she'd been crying for days—which confirmed everyone's narrative that I had broken her heart. Deep down, I knew they were right, and I'd never felt so guilty—way too guilty to track down the very girl who had upset Margaret in the first place.

ALMOST A YEAR later, Margaret called me out of the blue. My stomach lurched a bit hearing her voice, and I felt that weird emotion you have when someone you once knew so well now feels like a stranger.

After catching up for a few moments about our families and jobs, she told me that she had some news—and she wanted me to hear it from her first.

"Okay," I said, expecting her to tell me she was moving out of the city, something I knew she had wanted to do. Maybe she was even returning to Africa. "What's up?"

"I'm engaged," she said.

"Engaged in *what*?" I asked, confused.

"Engaged to be *married,* Joe."

I was stunned, and for some reason, my pride felt a little hurt, too. But I played it off, pretending to take it in stride as I asked her who the lucky guy was. Did I know him?

"Yes. You know him."

"I do? Who is it?"

"Toby," she said.

I only knew one Toby, and there was no way she was marrying

that guy. A classmate from Harvard, Toby Davis was brilliant but socially awkward as hell. "Toby who?"

Margaret sighed, then said, "*Our* Toby."

"He's not *my* Toby," I said with a laugh, trying to cover for the fact that I was feeling territorial.

"Joe. Stop it."

"Okay. Sorry," I said. "But wow."

"Wow *what*?" she said, her voice uncharacteristically challenging.

"I'm just surprised. . . ." I said, knowing I was being a little unkind. "We used to make fun of him. How he followed you around like a puppy dog."

"Well. We were wrong about him. . . . He's amazing . . . and doing really exciting things," she said.

It felt like a dig, especially when she launched into this whole spiel about his PhD in molecular biology and his dream of finding a cure for cancer.

"Well. I guess we were right about *one* thing," I quipped, doing my damnedest to be a good sport.

"What's that?" she said.

"That dude really *is* smarter than me," I said, hoping I didn't sound bitter.

She didn't refute my statement, which made me feel worse— and even more stupid. I also couldn't help feeling that I'd been duped into thinking that Margaret loved me more than she really had.

"Are you okay?" she said.

"Oh yeah," I said. "Totally. This is great news. Congratulations, Mags."

"Thank you, Joe."

"Give Toby my best as well. He's a very lucky guy."

"Don't, Joe—"

"What? It's true. Good for him."

"Okay, Joe," she said with a sigh. "I just wanted you to know—and hear it from me—"

"Yeah. Yeah. Thanks, Margaret. I appreciate it. . . ."

"You're welcome."

"So, have you set a wedding date? Will I be invited?" I said with a nervous laugh.

"No date yet. And I don't know about the invite. . . ." she said. "Toby wants us all to be friends . . . but I'm not sure I can do that—"

"Yeah. Well. Either way. This is great news. Really great. I'm glad you're happy."

"Do you mean that, Joe?" she said.

"Of course," I said, my tone softening.

"How about you? Are *you* happy?" she asked.

"Oh, you know me," I said with a laugh. "Happy enough."

CHAPTER 10

Cate

Just as I expected, Joe didn't call after that day on the beach. I think Curtis, who had already begun to plan my wedding makeup, was more upset than I was. I was definitely disappointed, but told myself that it was a much-needed reality check and a great reminder not to get my hopes up. What had I been thinking, anyway? Obviously, Joe Kingsley was from a different world— and it seemed pretty clear that he had gone home and concluded the same. My work might put me on private beaches in the Hamptons, and in proximity to a certain class of people, but that didn't mean I actually *belonged* with them.

It was probably a blessing in disguise. I knew Joe had a reputation for being a bit of a playboy, and I had no interest in being his flavor of the month. A fling with a man like him could only break my heart, something I had so diligently avoided.

When I shared all of this with Curtis, he gave me his usual speech about how I was not a second-class citizen just because I hadn't grown up with a silver spoon. He also reminded me that Joe had dated "that train wreck Phoebe Mills."

"Gee, Curtis. Are you trying to say that I'm a train wreck, too?" I said, smiling.

"Oh my God! No!" Curtis said, objecting a little too much. "I'm saying that I saw what I saw. That man was drawn to you. Like a moth to a flame."

"Uh-huh," I said, thinking that Curtis might be right about our attraction, but that there was still a massive difference between wanting to *sleep* with someone and wanting to *date* them. Joe clearly had no interest in the latter, and apparently not enough interest in the former to even make a phone call.

A few weeks later, my theory was confirmed when I saw in the tabloids that Joe *was*, in fact, still dating his college girlfriend. I couldn't decide whether that made him a bad guy for getting my number in the first place—or a good guy for not having called me. In the end, it didn't really make a difference, but I found myself perusing more of those magazine articles, searching for clues in the photos. I was especially interested in the ones of Joe and Margaret doing all their preppy activities: sailing, skiing, rare-book browsing. It made me a little ill, but I refused, on principle, to be jealous of a woman with an uninspired bob haircut who wore Fair Isle sweaters and pearls, sometimes at the same time.

What I *was* jealous of, though, was the respect that came with Margaret Braswell's credentials, from her Harvard degree to her work in the Peace Corps to her noble teaching profession. There was no way I could compete with a woman like that. It made me think a bit more than I usually would about who I wanted to be, other than just a survivor. As Daisy had told me years before, my modeling days were numbered, and it was clear that my mom was never going to leave Chip, no matter how much money I made or help I offered. The end game had changed, and it was time to make a move. For myself.

—

THAT FALL, AN opportunity came along when Wilbur Swift, an up-and-coming British fashion designer whom I'd befriended during his Burberry days, offered me a role at his new label. I said yes, quitting modeling for what I hoped would be for good.

Initially, Wilbur hired me to work on the creative side, but he ultimately moved me to sales, praising my people skills and deciding that I should have a more "visible role." As I traveled back and forth between our Madison Avenue store and our flagship in Sloane Square, he had me working with our most prominent clientele. I styled socialites and actors, dressing them for parties and weddings and charity balls, as well as editorial shoots and red-carpet appearances. It was a pay cut from modeling but a huge step up in my quality of life, and I felt more respected and valued than I had before. Don't get me wrong, I still had massive insecurities about my lack of a formal education, but by that time, I had seen enough of the world and been around enough wealthy, high-profile people to know how to fake it. I think it also helped that I began to develop relationships with some of my clients and to see that no matter how rich or successful someone was, they still had problems. As the expression goes: more money, more problems. I didn't think that was true—they were just different problems.

I found myself remembering my high-school days in Montclair—when I'd used clothes to feel better about myself—and how I'd ultimately created a new identity—or at least masked my real one. I channeled that energy when dressing my clients, especially the ones who seemed depressed or worried about something. I'd usher them into my dressing room, sit them down on a comfortable chair, and hand them an espresso or a glass of champagne. Then we'd have a chat—and I'd ask them questions about what they were looking for. Sometimes they didn't know. But I'd find out, putting them at ease before assembling a great outfit. The moment when they looked into the mirror and smiled filled me with satisfaction and a sense of purpose. There was so much that was shallow about the fashion industry—but it could also be transformative.

ABOUT SIX MONTHS into my gig, Wilbur and I were flying from New York to London together, enjoying cocktails in first class, when he asked me, out of the blue, who would be my dream client. Without hesitation, I said Princess Diana. In the middle of divorcing Prince Charles, she was technically no longer in the British royal family, but that didn't diminish her star power in any way whatsoever.

"Dream *male* client?" Wilbur asked.

I shrugged, finding men's fashion significantly less interesting, then said, "I don't know. Robert Redford . . . Paul Newman . . . maybe Brad Pitt."

Wilbur took a sip of his Kir Royale (he traveled with his own crème de cassis, adding it to the airline champagne). "What about Joe Kingsley?" he asked.

My heart skipped a beat as I shrugged, squeezing more lime into my gin and tonic, feeling relieved that Joe hadn't crossed my mind for a while.

"Yeah. He'd be up there, too, I guess."

"Cate," Wilbur said, smiling and shaking his head. "Why in *God's* name didn't you tell me that you know Joe Kingsley?"

"What?"

"I ran into him at a party—he told me he knows you. You're my director of *celebrity* sales, and you don't mention that you know the most famous man in the world?"

"Well, first of all, I don't *know* him. Not like that," I said. "And second of all, there are plenty of men more famous than he is."

"Such as?"

"I don't know . . . plenty of people."

"Name them."

"As I said: Robert Redford, Paul Newman, Brad Pitt."

"Rubbish," Wilbur said. "Nobody knows those guys' parents. Or cares about their *baby* pictures."

"So what?" I said. "All that means is that those guys are self-made—they came to fame later in life—whereas Joe is famous because he was born into a rich family. He was famous at *birth*."

"Exactly," Wilbur said, as if I'd proven a point for him.

"That's not impressive," I said. "He hasn't accomplished anything on his own."

"Well, neither has Diana. All she did was marry into a family."

"Touché," I said.

"So?" Wilbur said. "Why didn't you tell me you knew him?"

"Because I don't really. We just met once. In passing. It wasn't a big deal."

"Well, you made an impression on *him*," Wilbur said, smirking.

"How do you know that?" I asked, a little perturbed with myself for feeling flattered.

"Because he told me, girl! He told me how you two met in the Hamptons . . . on the beach. . . . He said he lost your number, but he somehow knew we worked together . . . and he wants to come in for an appointment."

"Oh. Cool," I said, nodding and doing my best to feign professional nonchalance. "What's he looking for? Casual stuff? Business attire? Black tie?"

Wilbur grinned. "He didn't mention *clothing*. But he *did* ask me whether you were single."

"And?" I said, getting a funny feeling in my stomach.

"And I told him you were."

"Oh my *God,* Wilbur. You know I have a boyfriend," I said.

I'd been seeing a British soccer player named Arlo Smith for a couple of months. Jocks weren't really my type, but with tattoos and spiky hair, Arlo had something of a rock-and-roll vibe that I loved. We had fun together, and things were going well.

"You're going to turn down Joe for a third-rate footballer?" Wilbur said.

"Wow, Wilbur. Don't be such a snob."

"Guilty as charged. I *am* a snob."

"Well, I'm *not,*" I said, reaching for my lavender eye mask, ready to recline my seat and doze off. "And I'm happy to sell Joe Kingsley a boatload of clothes. But I'm not entertaining any of the rest of this."

"The rest of what?"

"You know what."

"And whyever not?"

"Because," I said, feeling resolute. "I don't need that kind of nonsense in my life."

ABOUT TEN DAYS later, Joe strolled into our new SoHo store right in the middle of a busy trunk show. I spotted him out of the corner of my eye but was with a client and pretended I hadn't seen him. For more than thirty minutes he hovered nearby, turning down help from my sales associate, clearly waiting for me.

When I was finally free, he tentatively approached me and said, "Hi there, Cate."

"Oh. Hi, Joe," I said with a bright but detached smile. "Are you here for the trunk show?"

Joe put his hands in his pockets, shuffled his feet a little, then said, "Um. Well . . . I'm here to see *you,* actually."

I laughed and said, "Well, that's a shame. I would rather you be here for the trunk show. It's amazing."

"Well, yeah. That, too," Joe said with a shy smile. "Will you show it to me? Please?"

I gave him a brisk nod, then launched into my sales spiel, pretending he was just another client with a lot of money. It was a professional opportunity. Nothing more. Joe listened intently, and when I suggested he try a few things on, he agreed.

"Lovely," I said, ushering him over to a fitting room, intentionally choosing the smaller of the two available.

Over the next hour, Joe tried on various items that I selected while I waited outside for him, along with Yolanda, our seamstress. Every time the door opened, and he walked out and stood in front of the floor-to-ceiling mirror, I felt a little breathless. His body was made for clothes, but it occurred to me that I didn't often see him dressed so nicely. At one point, he said as much, fiddling with the lapel on a jacket and asking if it looked right.

"Yes," I said. "I don't even think you need any tailoring. Do you, Yolanda?"

"No. He's perfect," she said, all starry-eyed.

"Yes. *It's* perfect," I said, correcting her little slip.

IN THE END, Joe decided on a navy suit, two sport coats, three shirts, an orange necktie, and a pair of tan driving moccasins. As I rang him up, I gave him my usual post-sales reassurance about spending a lot of money. *You did really well. You got some great, versatile pieces. I think you're going to be really happy with these.*

Joe thanked me and agreed. I walked him to the door, thinking I was in the clear. But at the last second, he said, "So look, Cate. I wanted to say something."

"Yes?" I said, keeping it light.

"I just wanted to say that . . . I'm really sorry I never called you."

I gave him a blank stare, pretending to be confused.

"You know. After we met . . ." he said. "That day on the beach."

"Oh. That. Yes," I said, waving him off. "No worries."

"I wanted to—so badly—but the timing wasn't right. . . ."

"Hmm," I said, nodding, thinking of Margaret.

"But it is *now*," he told me.

"Oh, it *is*, is it?" I said with a laugh, thinking that he obviously meant *his* timing.

"Yes," he said, missing my point. "So do you think . . . maybe . . . I could take you to dinner some—"

"I'm sorry," I said, cutting him off. "But I'm dating someone now."

"Oh, okay . . . I wasn't sure. . . . Wilbur said it wasn't serious."

"Well, Wilbur doesn't know everything about my personal life."

"Oh, yeah. Of course," Joe said.

I nodded and gave him a close-lipped smile.

He hesitated, then said, "Yeah . . . so, um, what about lunch? Could you do lunch? Or coffee? Or take a walk in the park?"

Feeling both empowered and determined, I told him that probably wasn't a good idea. "But I'll tell you what," I added, now just toying with him. "If you want to give me your number, I can be in touch if things with this guy ever change."

Joe grinned, then reached into his wallet for his business card. He handed it to me and said, "That sounds great. I'm feeling pretty hopeful."

"Oh? And why's that?" I said, my voice sounding surprisingly flirty.

"'Cause you just called him 'this guy,' " he said. "Not a good sign for the ol' boy."

"And you're assuming you'd be my next choice?" I said, playing it coy and careful.

"What can I say?" Joe grinned. "I'm an optimist."

THAT EVENING, CURTIS came over with Thai takeout. I gave him and Elna the update, and they had opposite reactions, as usual.

"He had his chance," Elna said, rolling her eyes.

"He was dating someone!" Curtis said.

"Well, now *she* is. And Arlo is a great guy," Elna said.

"I know . . . but Joe is so gorgeous," Curtis said.

"He's *too* good-looking," Elna said. "Guys like that are trouble."

"He's not a 'guy like that,' " Curtis said. "He's *Joe Kingsley*. An American *icon*. If you grew up here, you'd understand."

"Something tells me Black folks in this country might also disagree with this icon notion," Elna said.

"She has a point, Curtis. At the end of the day, he's just another rich white guy. What's he actually done to be so famous?"

"He's famous because he's Joe friggin' Kingsley," said Curtis, the master of circular reasoning. "That's why."

"Stop encouraging this shit," Elna said. "It's not good for her. She's happy with Arlo."

"Arlo's her boy toy," Curtis said. "He's not her final destination."

I listened as they argued back and forth for a few minutes and then said, "Isn't anyone going to ask if *I* have any interest in Joe?"

"Well? Do you?" Elna said.

"No," I said. "I do not."

"Ha," Elna said, gloating at Curtis.

"She's lying, Elna," he said, shaking his head. "I don't know if she's lying to *us* or to *herself,* but either way, she's *definitely* lying. Everyone is interested in Joe Kingsley."

THE FOLLOWING DAY, I received a bouquet of red roses at the store, along with a note. It read:

> Roses are red,
> violets are blue.
> He waits for her call,
> 'cause patience is a virtue.

It wasn't signed, but I knew who it was from, and I have to admit it got to me. No part of me wanted to break up with Arlo, and I wasn't about to cheat on him, but I found myself thinking of loopholes, ways I could call Joe and still be on the up-and-up. Maybe we *could* be friends. I could almost picture it, the two of us hanging out in coffee shops, or going to Knicks games, maybe even attending an occasional event when he couldn't find a proper date. I imagined that Arlo would be cool with it—that Joe would win him over, just as I would win over Joe's next girlfriend. We could be *When Harry Met Sally* without all the sexual tension and confusion.

Deep down, though, I knew I was just rationalizing, and that I couldn't hang out with Joe, even as friends. I also knew that he'd move on to someone else soon enough.

But the following week, I received another flower arrangement at the store—even more spectacular than the first. He raised his game on the poem, too, this time offering a limerick:

There once was a girl named Cate.

Around her he couldn't think straight.

She sold him some pants while he begged for a chance,

Then prayed that she'd go on one date.

I cracked up, then found his business card in his file, calling him on the spot.

"You're nuts," I said, grinning into the phone.

"What do you mean?" he said, playing dumb.

"The flowers. And this ridiculous limerick—" I said.

"You didn't like my poetry?"

"It's ludicrous," I said. "And you bought more than a pair of pants."

"No doubt," he said. "I broke the damn bank in that store."

I smiled, then said, "How are you enjoying your new clothes?"

"I love them. . . . I'm actually wearing my loafers right now. They're very comfortable."

"Good," I said. "I'm glad you're happy."

"I'd be happier if you went on a date with me."

"Yeah . . . well . . . I still have a boyfriend," I said, feeling a wistful pang, wishing I could say yes. "But maybe we *could* do something, as friends . . . like that lunch you mentioned?"

"Hell, yeah! When? Tonight?"

I told him that the last time I checked lunch didn't happen at night—and that I already had plans anyway.

"Okay. How about tomorrow? The day after?"

"I really can't," I said. "I'm leaving for Fashion Week . . . and I still have so much to do to get ready."

"Where are you going?"

"Paris."

"Awesome. I love Paris. Where are you staying?"

"At the Bristol."

"Hmm . . . Maybe I'll show up and say hi."

I laughed and said, "You'll just hop on a plane and head over to Paris, huh?"

"I might. . . . You never know," he said. "Would you have dinner with me? Or lunch? If I flew to Paris?"

"I don't know," I said, smiling into the phone.

"But you're not saying no?"

I shook my head, now full-on grinning. "I guess you'll have to fly to Paris and find out."

THREE DAYS LATER, when I checked in to the Bristol, the lady at the front desk handed me an envelope with my name written on the front, informing me that it was from a gentleman guest. I nodded and thanked her, thinking it was probably from Wilbur. But the look of restrained glee on her face made me wonder.

There's no way, I told myself as I declined the bellman's offer to help with my bag and took the elevator up to the tenth floor, eyeing the envelope the whole way. When I got to my room, I started to open it but felt so foolishly hopeful that I made myself put it down on the bed and wait a little longer.

I went to work unpacking and getting organized for the week. It was a ritual that never got old, especially when I was in an upscale hotel. I arranged my makeup and toiletries in the marble bathroom; hung my dresses and skirts in the closet; filled the dresser drawers with my knits, nightgowns, and underwear; lined my shoes against one wall; and placed my handbags, clutches, and belts on the ottoman at the foot of the bed. Last, I put my jewelry in the safe, setting the code to 3005, my childhood apartment number in Hackensack.

At that point, I sat on the bed and picked up the envelope, feeling a bit more in control. It probably wasn't from Joe any-

way, and even if it was, I didn't have to get swept up in one of
his grand romantic gestures. I owed him exactly nothing. But as
I opened the letter and saw his initials at the bottom of the
page, I could feel my heart beating faster. Then I scanned up to
read:

> Dear Cate, I know you're going to be very busy this week,
> but I took my chances that you might have an opening in
> your schedule. I'm in Room 1010 if you want to reach
> me. If I don't hear from you, no worries. Paris is never a
> bad idea. Fondly, JSK

I put the letter back down on the bed as it started to sink in
that Joe was not only in Paris but also *in* my hotel, and *on* my
floor—which I didn't believe for one second was a coincidence. It
was just further evidence that he could get anything he wanted.
Whether a room in a sold-out hotel or a girl. *Any* girl. Honestly,
my mind was a little blown, but I wasn't sure whether to be flattered by his effort or suspicious of his intentions. I ruled out the
former, telling myself there was no way he'd come just to see me.
At the very least, he had a backup plan—another woman he could
call and wine and dine. His spontaneous trip to Paris wasn't romantic—it was about the thrill of the chase, and the fact that he
couldn't take no for an answer. The second he got what he
wanted—which undoubtedly was sex—he'd move on to his next
conquest. I'd been down this road before, just never with stakes
this high or a man this famous. I told myself it was all the same
thing, though, and as long as I knew the deal up front and didn't
cross any lines, I could play along with his game. So I picked up
the phone and dialed his room.

Joe answered on the first ring, saying a cheerful hello.

My heart pounding, I said, "Hey, Joe. It's Cate."

"Cate!" he said. "You got my note! I'm so glad to hear from you!"

"Uh-huh," I said, cool as can be. "And what brings you to Paris?"

"Umm . . . I'm here to see you. . . . I mean, I was hoping to take you to dinner," he said, sounding the slightest bit flustered.

"So, you really rolled the dice with that one."

"What can I say? I live on the edge."

"You sure do."

"Well? Are you free at all?" he asked.

"Well, let's see. . . . I'm pretty booked this week—but I'm free tonight if you are?"

"I am!" he said. "And I'd *love* to have dinner with you. Where would you like to go?"

"How about Epicure? Right downstairs?" I said, thinking the hotel restaurant seemed like less of a date than going out on the town.

"Perfect. I'll make a reservation," he said. "How does seven sound?"

"Make it eight," I said, figuring I might as well make him wait an extra hour.

A LONG NAP and a cold shower later, I was standing before my closet in a plush white towel, a second one wrapped around my head, debating what to wear to dinner with Joe Kingsley. Obviously I wanted to look good, but I didn't want to flatter him by trying too hard, either. I also wanted to reinforce the point that I was a serious professional woman—and that he was crashing my business trip. In that vein, I contemplated my go-to camel-colored pencil skirt, which I could pair with a black cashmere sweater or a crisp white blouse. Then again, I didn't have to be quite so but-

toned up. I could just as easily play his game while looking a bit
sexy, which might be more satisfying, especially when it came time
to reject him.

Ultimately, I opted for a clingy but still understated black
sheath dress—a sample from our new collection—and four-inch
strappy stilettos that would put me at his height, maybe slightly
taller. I kept my jewelry simple, wearing only diamond stud earrings and a slim gold cuff bracelet, and pulled my hair back in a
low, tight chignon. Finally, I did my makeup with a light hand—as
usual—just a little concealer and powder, along with black mascara and my signature red lipstick.

Glancing at the clock, I saw that I still had a few minutes to kill
before I hit the "fashionably late" window, so I sat down to call
Arlo, who was in Brazil for a soccer match. I was prepared to
tell him the truth—that I was having dinner with a pushy client
who happened to be Joe Kingsley—but felt a little relieved when
he didn't answer his phone. I would tell him later, no big deal, I
told myself as I gathered up my room key, lipstick, and compact.
I stashed them all in my small black clutch, then headed out the
door.

A moment later, I was off the elevator and walking toward the
restaurant. As I gave myself a final pep talk about not, under any
circumstances, falling for Joe Kingsley, I spotted him standing by
the maître d's podium in his new Wilbur suit and was freshly
overcome by how handsome he was. I stopped in my tracks and
took a deep breath just as he looked up and saw me. His face lit
up, and I saw him mouth an unmistakable *wow* as I walked the
rest of the way to him at a confident runway pace.

"Wow," he repeated in a whisper when I reached him. "Hello,
Cate."

"Hello, Joe," I said with only a hint of a smile.

He hesitated, then placed one hand on the small of my back,

the other on my shoulder, and gave me a double-cheek kiss, which can feel a little pretentious coming from an American. But I decided it worked in this case, perhaps because we were in Paris—or maybe because he was Joe Kingsley, after all. American royalty.

"You look stunning," he said.

I thanked him, debating whether to return the compliment. I decided that he'd heard it enough and simply said, "I like your suit."

"Thanks," he said with a broad grin. "It's new."

A few seconds later the maître d' politely interjected with a greeting, then escorted us to a secluded table overlooking the hotel's interior courtyard. I could feel a few stares along the way and had a flashback to my own first Joe Kingsley sighting, on the beach. I felt a little sheepish remembering how giddy I'd been.

"*Finally*," Joe said, once we were seated and settled and alone. He leaned over the table, staring into my eyes.

"Finally *what*?" I asked.

"Finally we're on a *date*." He smiled, and I saw a dimple in his left cheek that I'd never noticed in photographs of him.

"It's *not* a date," I said, shaking my head.

"Oh, it's a date, Cate."

"Look at you and your little rhymes," I said, trying not to smile.

"Hey, I gotta stick with what works. My poetry got us here."

I tilted my head and said, "Is that what you think?"

"Yes," he said, chuckling some more. "I think that limerick did you in."

"Oh, it did me in, all right," I said, rolling my eyes.

"Admit it . . . you loved it," he said.

I gave him a close-lipped smile and shook my head.

"You're lucky I didn't hit you with one of my world-famous haikus. You'd have melted on the spot."

I crossed my arms and said, "Try me."

Joe cleared his throat, then put his elbows on the table, resting his chin on his clasped hands. He stared out over the courtyard, appearing deep in thought. After a few seconds, he turned back to me, cleared his throat again, then began reciting in the deep voice of a Shakespearean actor, "He came to Paris . . . just to look in her blue eyes . . . by the candlelight."

"Not bad," I said, laughing. "Corny as hell, but not bad."

"It might be corny, but it's true," he said, looking so unbelievably earnest that I almost believed he really *had* come all this way just to see me.

I started to respond but was saved by our waiter, who arrived to give us a rundown of the menu and wine list. Joe responded in clumsy French, asking a few questions before I took over, in much better French, ordering a bottle of Burgundy and informing our waiter that we needed another few minutes to peruse the menu.

When we were alone, Joe said, "Your French is *so* good."

"Thanks."

"Did you take it in school?"

"No. I took Spanish. I just picked it up from my modeling days. I did a lot of work here."

"Wow. That's so impressive. I'm terrible with languages. I took, like, ten years of French and it's still horrible."

"It really *is*," I said with a laugh, thinking that it was actually a little surprising—and refreshing—as I would have pegged Joe as the kind of guy who would never risk embarrassment and only do things that he knew he was really good at.

Over the next two hours, as we ordered and ate and finished our bottle of wine, Joe continued to surprise me. He was so full of contradictions. On the one hand, he was bold and brash and adventurous, talking about how much he loved flying his airplane and heli-skiing and windsurfing. On the other hand, he seemed introspective and thoughtful and kind—almost gentle. I noticed, for example, that he always made eye contact with the busboy, thanking him every time he refilled our water glasses even when Joe was in midsentence. He didn't seem to put himself above anyone, and his humility verged on self-deprecation as he told me about his grades in college—and how he'd failed the bar not once but *twice*.

Of course, I knew this already, remembering the embarrassing headlines, but I played dumb and said, "Oh. Wow. That must have sucked."

"Yeah. The first time wasn't *that* bad. . . . I mean, it was a huge buzzkill and hassle. But it happens. . . . The second time, though?" He shook his head and smiled, like it was a fond memory. "That really did *suck*."

"Well, at least you can laugh at yourself," I said.

"Yeah, I try. But my mom didn't think it was too funny."

Picturing Dottie Kingsley, I winced and said, "*Ohh*. Yeah. I bet not."

"She was *beside* herself."

"Why? Is it that big of a deal?" I said, feeling a little defensive about my own academic record. "You can take the bar exam as many times as you want, right?"

"Yeah," he said. "You *can* . . . but let's just say that that's not expected of a *Kingsley*." He said his last name in an exaggerated, snobbish voice.

"Yeah. I guess not," I said, thinking it had never occurred to me that it might be kind of a drag to have super successful parents or a famous name. I had also never considered that there was any sort of silver lining to having an abusive stepfather and an arguably not so great mother. I mean, hell, simply by having become a functioning member of society I was something of a success story.

"So, after all of that, do you like being a lawyer?" I asked, wanting to stay off the subject of my own life.

Joe appeared to ponder this question, taking a sip of wine. "Yes and no. Working in the DA's office can be fun . . . but it can be demoralizing. I may quit soon."

"And do what?"

"Oh, I don't know. I need to figure that out," he said, giving me a look that messed me up a little inside.

I held his gaze, resisting the urge to look away, but said nothing.

"And what about you?" he said.

"What about me?"

"Do you feel like your life is . . . on track?"

"My *life*?" I said with a laugh. "That's a pretty broad question."

"Okay. Your work?"

"It's good, I guess."

"And how about your relationship?"

I hesitated just long enough to have given him my true answer, then tried to recover. "Passion is overrated."

"You don't believe that, do you?"

"Yes," I said. "I do. And I've found that it's better to keep your expectations low in life. About everything."

"Damn," Joe said, shaking his head. "That's kind of depressing."

I shrugged and said, "Not to me."

"Were your expectations low for me? Tonight?"

I smiled and said, "Yes. Very."

"So I surpassed them?" he asked, his face all lit up.

"Un peu," I said, lowering my voice and giving him my most seductive look. "Mais cela reste à voir."

CHAPTER 11

Joe

It wasn't the first time a beautiful woman had shot me down. In many of those cases, though, they were simply playing hard to get. I didn't mind jumping through an occasional hoop, but ironically, the women who played the most games usually turned out to be the least interesting. Every once in a while, though, I'd come across a woman who really *was* elusive. Cate fell into that category.

When I tracked her down at the store where she worked, she was very polite and pleasant, helping me buy a bunch of nice clothes. But I couldn't really read her, and when I got up the nerve to finally ask her out, she told me she had a boyfriend. It was a boundary I almost always respected, and a line I *never* crossed if the woman was in a serious relationship, but with Cate, I got the distinct impression she was using him as an excuse—perhaps making him up altogether.

So I put on a full-court press, sending her flowers and writing her poems and then *really* going out on a limb by booking a last-minute flight to Paris, where she was headed for a work trip. The whole thing was pretty over-the-top, and in the back of my mind, I was worried that it might backfire and put her off entirely. But I decided I had nothing to lose other than my pride, which I didn't really care about, and a few days of work, which I cared even *less* about. After I'd been assigned yet another drug case involving an African American teenager being charged as an adult for selling pot, Gary's words were weighing heavily on me, and I was about an inch away from resigning anyhow.

As it turned out, the transatlantic gamble paid off. Cate finally relented, agreeing to meet me for dinner. I was super stoked, especially when I saw her walking toward me in her hot black dress and high heels. I have to admit I can be as shallow as the next guy.

But as we sat together by candlelight, talking for hours over a bottle of fine wine and French cuisine, I could feel a shift, along with a tightness in my chest that I only get when I start to really like someone. I learned that like me, Cate was an only child who had lost her father at a young age, but we didn't dwell on the subject—or anything too heavy. Instead, we kept things light, talking mostly about our work and travel. She'd been all over the world during her modeling days, and I found her stories fascinating. I loved the way she talked with her hands and threw her head back when she laughed and wasn't afraid to reach across the table and touch my arm when she was making a point. She was so engaging—and then there was something unpredictable about her, too, something that kept me off-balance in the best possible way. At one moment, she'd be teasing me as if we'd been friends for years; in the next, she would sort of pull back and stare at me with those aloof, ice-blue eyes, completely unbothered by long stretches of silence. I'd fumble around to fill them so that our time together wouldn't end.

When I finally walked her to her room to say good night, it crossed my mind that I might, for the first time, be in over my head with a woman. The thought of it thrilled me.

—

I STAYED IN Paris three more nights, slipping notes under Cate's door every morning, wishing her a good day. I knew she'd be mostly tied up with work, but I still hoped that I might see her again before I left. Meanwhile, I kept a low profile, lounging about my room, watching movies and catching up on sleep. When I did venture out, I stayed off the beaten path. One morning, I rented a bicycle and rode all over Montmartre, discovering the coolest little cobblestone squares and colorful art deco buildings and hidden cafés and art galleries and bookshops. I'd always had a thing about used and rare books, which was a little strange given that I didn't read much. I always intended to, and often I included reading among my New Year's resolutions, but somehow I never got around to finishing the books I collected, or in some cases even *starting* them. My favorite discovery, though, was a quaint shop specializing in vintage handbags and silk scarves. I immediately thought of Cate, and decided I wanted to buy her something. For over an hour, I agonized about my selection, finally settling on a mostly blue "brides de gala" Hermès scarf from the fifties. As the shop owner told me about its history, and how the design had been reimagined several times over the decades, I pictured how pretty it would look on Cate.

ON MY FINAL night in Paris, just as I was giving up on hearing from her, she called my room and asked what I was doing.

"Oh, nothing much," I said, feeling hopeful that she might want to see me. "Just hanging out . . . watching a movie."

"What're you watching?"

"*Braveheart*. For about the fourth time," I said, wondering whether that made me cheesy or romantic in her eyes.

She laughed, indicating that it was more likely the former, then said, "Do you want some company?"

"I'd love some," I said, feeling so excited. "My room or yours?"

"Mine, please," she said without hesitating.

"Cool. When should I come by?"

"Now's good," she said. "Unless you want to finish *Brave-heart?*"

"Nah," I said, smiling. "I already know what happens."

CHAPTER 12

Cate

As hard as I tried, I couldn't get Joe out of my mind after our nondate date. I continued to believe that pursuing him—or, more accurately, letting him pursue me—was a bad idea in the long run. But after three nights of knowing he was right down the hall, wanting to see me and even putting sweet notes under my door, I could feel myself caving to his persistence, even asking myself what would it hurt to kiss him one time? After all, he *was* Joe Kingsley. It would be quite the notch in my belt. Guys did this sort of thing all the time. Why couldn't I do the same? If I just played along with his antics, I could forever say that I had kissed Joe Kingsley, my preteen crush and an American icon.

I decided it was just too good to pass up, but that I needed to break up with Arlo first. I called him and cut right to the chase. To paraphrase, I told him that it had been a good run, but it wasn't really working for me anymore. I blamed our schedules and busy travel and not living in the same city.

"Besides, we don't have all that much in common. I don't even know the rules of soccer," I said, feeling a stab of guilt that I'd never gone to watch him play in person.

"Yeah. But at least I never had to worry you were a groupie," he said in his cute Liverpool accent.

"Ha! That's certainly true," I said, smiling into the phone.

"So . . . do you think we can still be friends?" he asked. "Grab a pint when you're back in town?"

"Of course," I said, though I really couldn't see a friendship continuing, especially given that we had better sex than we did conversation.

"Friends with *benefits*?" he said, clearly thinking along the same lines.

"We'll see," I said, on the fence. On the one hand, it was sort of the ideal setup. I could go do whatever I wanted with Joe, guilt-free, and still hang out with Arlo. On the other hand, I loved a good, clean break. Either way, I had successfully extricated myself from another relationship, and I felt the usual sense of relief that came with that.

As I said goodbye and hung up the phone, it crossed my mind to just call it a night and not bother with Joe. But his magnetic pull was apparently too great, because the next thing I knew, I was calling his room, then inviting him down to mine.

Moments later, he was standing in my doorway, grinning at me. His hair was messy, as if he'd been sleeping, and he was wearing khaki shorts, a faded T-shirt, and those white terry-cloth hotel slippers that I didn't think anyone actually ever put on.

I smiled back at him—it was impossible not to—and told him to come on in, motioning toward the only chair in the room. He took a few steps forward, pausing to give me a kiss on the cheek— only one cheek this time. As I closed the door behind him, I noticed he was carrying a small bag with a fancy pastel logo. Maybe he'd picked up a box of chocolates in the gift shop, I thought, as that seemed like something out of his cliché flowers-and-poetry playbook.

"Cute slippers," I said as he sat, putting the bag at his feet.

"Thanks. But be forewarned: don't ever try to take them home with you. I made that mistake once."

"You stole the slippers?" I said, mildly amused, as I sat on the side of my bed, facing him.

"No! I thought they were free—you know, like the shoe polish and the nail kit—but they charged me an arm and a leg for them."

I laughed, then asked what he'd been up to for the past few days.

"Oh, you know," he said, running his hand through his hair and messing it up even more. "Lots of napping . . . watching movies . . . I went on a few bike rides and did a little exploring and shopping." He paused and gave me a shy smile—or at least a smile *pretending* to be shy—and added, "Mostly I was just hoping to hear from you."

"Yeah, right," I said, rolling my eyes and waving him off.

"It's the truth," he said, his eyebrows knitting earnestly together, "whether you believe it or not."

I stared at him, deciding that I actually *did* believe him—which was dangerous. It was one thing to kiss him; it was another to start imagining that he might like me. I couldn't let that happen. I had to stay in control. With that renewed resolve, I scooted back on the bed and leaned against the headboard, my legs stretched out straight and crossed at the ankles. I was wearing cashmere drawstring shorts and a matching tank, so I had lots of skin showing, and could feel his eyes on me. I knew exactly what I was doing—and the effect it was having.

Sure enough, he took a deep breath and said, "God, Cate . . . You look *so* good."

I thanked him, then patted the spot next to me on the bed. "Would you rather come over here and talk?"

"I'd love to. . . . Can I take my slippers off first?" he said with a smile.

I laughed and said, "Please do."

He kicked them off, then stood and came over to the bed, bringing his paper bag with him. "I got you a present," he said, climbing up next to me, looking so proud of himself.

"You did, huh?" I said, sitting cross-legged as I turned to face him.

"Yep," he said, handing it to me.

I reached inside and pulled out a flat, square box that felt too light to be candy. I gently shook it, listening to the rustling sound of tissue paper, and said, "What is it?"

"Open it," he said, now beaming.

Feeling self-conscious, I removed the lid of the box and peeled back the tissue, finding the most beautiful cobalt blue and poppy red scarf, its design unmistakably Hermès.

"Oh, *wow,*" I said, running my hand over the silk, surprised by how lavish a gift it was. "It's gorgeous."

"You really like it?"

"Yes," I said, picking it up by one corner and unfurling it in the air before laying it out flat on the bed. "I love it."

"It's vintage . . . from the sixties. . . . I found it in the coolest little store—that's why it's not in an orange box," he said.

I smiled, resisting the urge to say, *Yeah, I was pretty sure Joe Kingsley didn't go for a knockoff.*

"I'm not quite sure of your style yet, but it seemed like you," he said, his voice soft.

My heart skipped a beat at his use of the word *yet,* and I told him again that I loved it. "I've always had a thing for scarves," I added.

"Oh good," he said. "And the color? I almost went with a

black and white one because you seem to wear more neutral colors?"

I told him that was true, surprised that he'd noticed, but that I liked pops of color, especially when it came to accessories.

"Yes. Like your lipstick," he said, staring at my mouth.

Butterflies filled my stomach as I gazed back down at the scarf, tracing the pattern with my finger before folding it diagonally in half, then putting it over my head. There were so many ways to wear a scarf—and I'd tried them all—but this time, I went with a seventies hippie style, tying two corners back at the nape of my neck and leaving the third free, my hair spilling down my back and shoulders.

"So chic," he said, leaning back on his elbow and staring over at me.

I smiled, reaching up to unknot and restyle the scarf, now tying it under my chin.

"Oh, I *love* that look," he said. "It's like Grace Kelly . . . in a convertible cruising along the French Riviera."

I smiled, thinking that it was also a signature Dottie Kingsley look, as he said, "You actually remind me of Grace Kelly."

"What?" I said, laughing. "We look absolutely *nothing* alike."

"I know. But the way you carry yourself," he said. "You're so . . . I don't know . . . elegant."

I resisted the urge to say something self-deprecating, having learned that this tactic gets you nowhere in life. Instead, I thanked him and slipped the scarf off my head, folding it neatly and returning it to the box.

A few seconds passed before he started to smirk at me. "So. Did you dump that dude yet?"

"That *dude*?"

"Yeah."

"His name is Arlo," I said, hesitating. "And yes. As a matter of fact, I did."

"You *did*?" he said, sitting up, suddenly very alert. "When?"

"About thirty minutes ago," I said, feeling bold. "Right before I called you."

"Really?"

"Yes."

"Why? Because you dig me?" he said with a laugh.

"I wouldn't go that far."

He smiled and said, "But you do like me a *little*. . . . Right?"

"Yes. A little," I said, then went out on another long limb. "Enough to kiss you. Once."

"Just once?" Joe said.

"Yep." I nodded. "One and done. You know—a 'what happens in Paris stays in Paris' type thing."

"But what if I want to kiss you back in New York, too?" he said, leaning in closer, staring at my mouth again.

"Let's not get ahead of ourselves," I said, biting my lip.

He moved even closer, his face now inches from mine. I could see his chest rising and falling under his T-shirt as he reached over and touched my face, then cupped my cheek, before sliding his hand to the back of my neck. He pulled me closer to him as I inhaled a scent that I would later learn was Dior's Eau Sauvage— the same cologne his father had worn.

Our foreheads touched first, then our noses, and as I closed my eyes, I could feel his warm breath on my face. One dizzying second later, his lips were grazing mine in the softest, lightest whisper of a kiss. It could barely even count as a kiss. But I *wanted* it to count. Because it was perfect.

The perfect first kiss.

No—the *only* kiss.

My heart racing, I pulled away and caught my breath and said, "There. One kiss. That's all."

He shook his head and said, "Just one more?"

I tried to say no, but I couldn't. Instead, I nodded, in a complete daze, as he took me in his arms and lowered me to the bed and kissed me again and again and *again,* leaving absolutely no doubt in my mind that this wasn't just a Paris thing.

SURE ENOUGH, WHEN I returned to my apartment in New York three days later, there was a message from Joe on my answering machine. I couldn't quite believe it as I listened to him ramble, telling me he missed me and "please call me back the second you come home. The *very* second."

I smiled, hit by a wave of excitement. I'd been trying not to obsess. But I could feel myself starting to fall for him. Reminding myself that this was a really bad idea, I picked up the phone and called him anyway.

"Cate!" he shouted into the phone when he heard my voice. "It's about time! When did you get back?"

I considered telling him I'd been home for a while but decided there was no point in playing games. Whatever was going to happen would happen, and it was probably better to just get the show on the road.

"Just now," I said.

"As in—this very second?"

"Yes. You told me to call you the second I got back, didn't you?" I said in a playful voice.

"Atta girl," he said. "When can I see you?"

"When do you *want* to see me?"

"Now?"

I laughed and said, "How about tomorrow?"

"That would be awesome," he said. "What should we do?"

"Something low-key," I said, feeling exhausted and jet-lagged—but also hedging my bets.

"Okay. I could come to your place? We could rent a movie and order in?"

"Umm . . . I don't know. . . . I have a roommate," I said.

Elna was out of town, but I didn't want him to come to my apartment regardless.

"She's welcome to join us . . . you know, for a little while," he said with a chuckle.

"I don't know," I said, waffling. "I kind of don't want her to know I'm hanging out with you."

"Why not?" he said. "She doesn't like me?"

"She doesn't know you," I said. "But she doesn't like the *idea* of you."

"Why not?" he said, sounding a little hurt.

"I think you could guess the reasons."

"Hmm . . . Well, do *you* like the idea of me?"

"The jury's still out," I said with a smile.

He laughed and said, "Damn. You really don't sugarcoat anything, do you?"

"Nope," I said. "What's the point?"

"I agree. I like that."

A few seconds passed before he said, "Okay . . . well, how about you come over to my place tomorrow? I'll make you dinner."

"You can cook?"

"Not really. But I can get takeout and transfer it to plates and pretend I made it."

"Nah," I said with a laugh. "Remember. There's no need to fake anything with me."

—

THE FOLLOWING EVENING after work, I went home to shower and change before heading down to Joe's. I was glad Elna was away, which meant I didn't have to answer any questions about where I was going. As much as I confided in her, I wasn't ready for that. When I got out of the shower, I cranked up my music, opened a bottle of Amstel Light, and blew my hair out, flat-ironing it pin-straight and parting it in the middle. Going for a feminine but laid-back feel, I put on a vintage silk Miu Miu dress with a brown and white floral print and nude slingbacks with low block Prada heels.

At that point, I was on autopilot and could have been getting ready for any date, but by the time I got into my taxi, I was keenly aware that I was headed to the apartment of *Joe Kingsley,* a man with the highest possible pedigree who was way, *way* out of my league. If not an absolute fact, it was a statement that 99.9 per-cent of the world would agree with—and as we got closer to his SoHo address, I could feel myself start to panic. What in the world was I thinking, anyway? How did I think this was going to end other than badly?

I told myself there was no point in second-guessing my deci-sion—it would be too dramatic and weird to cancel last minute. Better to just view the whole thing as an experiment. See how far we could get before he realized what I knew to be true. Or maybe he already *did* know. It was suspicious—or at a minimum noteworthy—that Joe had yet to ask any real details about my family or educational background, simply accepting my vague and very misleading comments about "still finishing up my degree." It was tempting to believe that those topics had simply slipped through the cracks, but I knew better. Guys like Joe always came out of the gate with that question: *Where did you go to school?* In most instances they meant college, though the boarding school types cared about high school, too. And if you went to a public school, you sure as shit better be from an upscale suburb. It was bizarrely consistent. I also knew those queries were usually just a ruse—disguised as casual conversation when they were really trying to discern my social status. In other words: Was I a working-class girl who had used modeling to pull myself up by my boot-straps? Or did I come from a "good family" who had insisted that I also go to college?

The fact that Joe hadn't really pressed me on the subject meant one of three things: (1) I'd successfully misled him into making the wrong assumptions; (2) He knew the truth about me—on some level—and liked me anyway; or (3) He wasn't analyzing any of that because all he really wanted was a fling. The last one seemed the most likely, I concluded as we turned onto a block that felt quintessentially SoHo—hip but a little grungy—with cobblestone streets and prewar warehouses converted to apart-ments. I paid my fare and got out of the cab, looking around, half expecting to see the paparazzi lurking in the shadows. But there was no sign that Joe—or anyone of import—lived in the gray build-ing before me. There wasn't even a doorman. I climbed the stairs, scanning the buzzers, looking for Joe's name, somehow knowing that his wouldn't be labeled.

I took a chance and hit the only unmarked apartment number, holding my breath, waiting. A few seconds later, Joe's voice came back fuzzy over the intercom. "Hello?"

"Hi. It's me," I said, my heart starting to race.

"Hey! Come on in! Take the elevator to the fourth floor!" he said, buzzing me in.

I took another deep breath, reminding myself that I really had nothing to lose so long as I kept my expectations low, then opened the heavy front door. I made my way through the spartan, empty lobby, then took a small elevator up to the fourth floor. When the doors opened, Joe was standing right there, waiting for me with a huge smile. Thursday was at his side, wagging his tail and attempting to jump on me as Joe held him back and reprimanded him.

"It's fine," I said, petting him, remembering that day on the beach. "Thursday and I go way back."

"I guess that's true!" Joe laughed. He was looking as handsome as I'd ever seen him, dressed casually, wearing faded blue jeans, a cream Henley, and black and white Adidas sneakers, the laces loosely tied.

"So . . . hi," he said with a cute little laugh, then gave me a big hug.

"Hi," I said, hugging him back, inhaling his cologne, which already felt familiar.

We separated and he stared at me with a goofy grin. "You look amazing. *Wow*."

"Thank you," I said feeling shy, attempting to pet Thursday again. Joe intercepted my hand, then led me down the hall to his apartment. Though he'd mentioned living in a loft, I was still a little blown away by how dramatic and cavernous it was. With floor-to-ceiling steel-framed windows, exposed brick walls, and a completely open floor plan, the space was very cool, but also a bit *cold,* and I couldn't decide whether I loved or hated it. As I walked the whole way into the room, putting my bag on his mammoth brown leather sectional, I decided that I wouldn't want to live in a place like this—I preferred cozy spaces—but that it was nice to visit. Perfect for a one-to-several-night stand.

"What do you think?" Joe asked.

"It's great," I said, glancing at him, "for a bachelor pad."

"*Ouch,*" he said. "Maybe you can help me spruce it up some? I need some more end tables and lamps and stuff."

I smiled and said, "You don't need my help."

"Yes, I do," he said. "You have great taste. And I want you to like it here."

"You do, huh?" I said, raising my eyebrows, nonchalantly flirting. "Why's that?"

"Because I like *you*," he said. "And I want you to be comfortable here . . . so you keep coming back."

Before I could respond, he put his arms around my waist and gave me a kiss. "I told you it wasn't a 'one and done,'" he whispered.

My heart racing again, I thought, *Shit. You sure did.*

"Okay. Now that that's settled . . . are you hungry?"

"A little," I said, thinking that I never really knew how to answer that question. Maybe it was a by-product of modeling for so many years—but I'd trained myself not to think about food—unless I was downright ravenous.

"Well, as you know, I can't cook. But I do epic appetizers," he said, gesturing over to his kitchen. "Wanna see?"

I nodded as we took a long stroll to the other side of the room, where he'd laid out a banquet-size platter. It was loaded with wheels of cheese and little rows of crackers and rolled-up meats and enough dried fruit to choke a horse.

"Impressive," I said.

"Wait. Is that impressive as in *impressive*? Or impressive *for a bachelor*?"

I gazed down at the board, pretending to scrutinize his work, then said, "I'd say it's impressive on an absolute basis."

"Yesss," he said, pumping his fist in the air like he'd just sunk the winning shot of a basketball game. "Now. Can I get you a drink?"

"Sure," I said, leaning on the counter.

"Beer? Wine? Or I can make you a cocktail? My bartending skills are legit, too."

I smiled and told him that I'd love a glass of wine.

"Red or white?"

"Whatever's open."

He shook his head and said, "Nope. I'm opening one for you. For *us*. Please choose."

"Okay," I said, nodding. "I'd love a glass of red, please."

Joe gave me a brisk bartender's nod as he rubbed his palms together, then walked over to a small built-in wine refrigerator, scanning the bottles and selecting one from the bottom row. I watched as he used an old-school corkscrew to open the bottle, took two stemmed glasses from a cabinet, and carefully poured our glasses, wiping the side of the bottle with a dish towel. He returned to the island to hand me the slightly fuller glass, standing at the corner of the counter, perpendicular to me.

I thanked him as he raised his glass in the air and looked in my eyes. "To our *third* date."

"But who's counting?" I said, clinking my glass against his.

"*I* am," he said as we both took a sip. "I'm sentimental like that."

"Are you?"

"Well," he said. "About things that matter."

I bit my lip, feeling myself start to blush and wishing my fair skin didn't so easily give me away.

"I haven't stopped thinking about you since Paris," Joe said.

My stomach fluttered, but I played it cool. "Yes," I said. "Paris was nice."

"*You're* nice," he said, putting his hand over mine, which was resting on the counter, next to my glass.

"Actually, I'm not all that nice," I said, trying not to smile.

He stared at me a beat, then said, "You know who you remind me of?"

"Uh-oh. Do I want to know?"

"Okay. This is kind of random . . . but that woman Billy Joel sings about—"

"The waitress who practices politics while the businessman slowly gets stoned?" I laughed.

He smiled and said, "No. 'She's Always a Woman.'"

I tried to remember the lyrics to that song, and as some of the more colorful lines came to me, I said, "Wait. The one about the cruel, lying woman who will cut you and laugh while you're bleeding?"

He smiled and said, "Not that part. I was thinking more of how you are in such control." He stared at me stone-faced for several seconds before softly singing: *Ohhh, she takes care of herself, she can wait if she wants.*

I played along. "You got me. Both of those things are true," I said.

"You really are a mystery," he said.

I rolled my eyes and said, "No, I'm really not."

"Okay, then tell me some things," he said. "About *you.*"

I felt myself tensing up a little, as I said, "What do you want to know?"

He took a deep breath, then exhaled even harder, appearing deep in thought. "Okay," he said. "Who do you love most in the world?"

I laughed and said, "That's a strange question."

"Is it?"

"Yes," I said. "What kind of love are we talking here?"

"*Love.* In its purest form."

"I have no idea how to answer that—"

"Yes, you do."

"No, I don't. . . . Who do *you* love the most?"

"Okay. Well, my grandmother is first. Hands down. Second is my mother," he said, ticking them off on his fingers. "Third is my friend Berry. Fourth is my cousin Peter. Fifth is my uncle Mark—Peter's dad." He gave me a smug smile and said, "Easy."

"Oh my God," I said, laughing. "That's so weird."

"What's weird about it?"

"That you can *rank* everyone in your life—with no hesitation whatsoever. . . . Who does that?"

"*I* do," he said.

"Okay. Well, tell me this," I said, feeling bold. "Where did your last girlfriend fit into that equation?"

"Then or now, in real time?"

Intrigued that she might still be in the mix, I said *now*.

"I don't know . . . pretty far down. Maybe somewhere in the twenties or thirties?"

I laughed, thinking that I couldn't name thirty people I loved—or even liked a lot.

"So, you're still friends?" I said.

"Sort of . . . We don't talk . . . but I guess I still consider her a friend."

"What's she up to?"

"She's engaged," he said, shrugging. "Teaching in Brooklyn."

Making a mental note to ask Curtis if he knew anything about Margaret's fiancé, I nodded and said, "Okay. What about *then*? When you were together?"

"Hmm. That's a tough question," Joe said, staring into the distance for a few seconds before looking back at me. "At her peak, she was probably tied with Uncle Mark."

"She never got higher than tied for *fifth*?" I said, laughing. "Ouch."

Joe laughed, then said, "Hold up. Wait a sec! I see what you're doing here. You flipped this shit around—you got me talking about myself—"

I shrugged, gave him a half smile, and said, "Sorry that I can't rank everyone in my life."

"Okay, I'll make it easier for you. Who's your best friend? Can you answer that?"

"Elna," I said.

"Is she the roommate who doesn't like me?"

"The *idea* of you," I said. "And yes."

"Okay. And who's next?"

"I don't know. Probably Curtis—the guy you met on the beach, the day you got my number and then never called—"

"Jeez!" he said, laughing. "Will you ever let me live that down?"

"Probably not," I said. "And third would be Wendy. A high-school friend."

"What's Wendy like?"

I shrugged and said, "Oh, I don't know . . . she's a lot of fun, outgoing . . . a little loud. She was the head of the cheerleading team in high school. That type."

Joe nodded and asked whether I had been a cheerleader, too.

"What do you think?" I asked, poker-faced.

"Well . . . you were a model . . . *sooo* . . ."

"Not the same at *all*," I said. "Models don't have to be cheerful. . . . Elna isn't cheerful. Nor am I."

"So Elna's a model?"

I nodded.

"That's how you met?"

I nodded again.

"And what about Wendy? What does she do?"

"She's a stay-at-home mom," I said, thinking that I could never quite decide whether Wendy's life sounded boring or pleasant. It depended on the day.

"Do you like her husband?"

I shrugged and said he was fine. "He's a lawyer like her dad. Sort of vanilla. Nice enough."

He smiled and said, "Am I vanilla?"

I thought for a second, then said, "No. You're *sweet* . . . but not vanilla."

He smiled, then pulled me into his arms and gave me a very *nonvanilla* kiss.

A COUPLE HOURS later, after we'd snacked on Joe's cheese board, polished off the bottle of wine, and made out on the sofa, he took me back to his dimly lit bedroom and laid me across his bed and kissed me some more. I had a good buzz going but was still perfectly clear-eyed and very certain of how I wanted the night to end. Having sex with Joe felt inevitable—a foregone conclusion. It was going to be now or later, so it might as well be now.

With that decision made, I took charge, standing up, reaching back to unfasten the hook-and-eye closure of my dress, then shimmying out of it. The streetlights softly illuminated his room, and I could feel him watching me in my matching lace underwear as I pulled back the covers and crawled into his bed between the crispest, coolest sheets.

When I finally met his gaze, I saw a look on his face that went beyond lust and approached awe. It had the effect of making me feel more brazen.

"My God, Cate. You're gorgeous," he said, yet he didn't make a move. He just lay there on top of the covers, frozen on his side, restrained and respectful.

"Come here," I said, my heart pounding in my chest.

"Hmm?"

"Take your clothes off and come here," I said more explicitly, lifting the covers, showing him my body, tempting him.

"Are you sure I should do that?" he whispered.

"Yes," I said, nodding. "Very sure."

Joe took a few deep breaths, then sat up and did what I asked. Now it was my turn to watch as he undressed. As a model, I'd been around plenty of good-looking men with beautiful bodies— and Arlo's was as rock hard and chiseled as any of them—but something about Joe's body was different. Better. Maybe it was the hair on his chest—which I loved. Maybe it was the knowledge that it was Joe. I thought of that poster on my wall, suddenly re-membering a moment that I'd either forgotten or repressed. My first orgasm happened while I stared up at it, fantasizing that it was Joe who was touching me. I had no idea what I was doing— and had only read about sex in Judy Blume's novel *Forever,* which didn't cover the nitty-gritty of orgasms. But I figured it out that night. For a second, the memory embarrassed me. But then, a switch flipped in the other direction, and I felt even more turned on. Powerful, even.

A moment later, wearing only boxers, Joe had found me under the covers. He lay beside me, kissing me even more hungrily than he had in Paris or on his sofa earlier, pausing only to reach around and unhook my bra, pulling it off me, then tossing it to the side of the bed. I wrapped my arms back around him and sighed, as we lay skin to skin for the first time. It crossed my mind that this might be enough for now—it felt that good—but the thought didn't last long, as his hands started moving all over my body, everywhere he could reach. That went on for a while until he rolled me over and kissed my breasts and stomach. He tried to move his face lower, but I stopped him, grabbing his shoulders, telling him to come back to me. When he did, I slid my hands down his back, dipping them past the elastic waistband of his boxers. "Take these off, too," I whispered. "Please."

He groaned a little in response but obliged my request. When his boxers were off, I laid my cheek on his chest, gazing down at him—*all* of him—then touched him for the first time. As I listened to his breathing, I stroked him as softly as I could, watching him grow even harder.

"God, Cate," he said with a low moan.

I slid my thong off, then took his hand and guided it down between my legs.

"Damn," he said, his breathing now heavy. "You're *so* wet."

"You made me this way," I whispered as his fingers moved in circles in the exact right place, which only I had ever been able to find.

Then I pulled him back on top of me, kissing his neck, arching my back, and spreading my legs. "I want you," I said.

"Oh, my God, I know," he groaned.

"I mean it. Right now. I want you—"

"Are you sure—" he said, staring into my eyes.

"Very sure," I said, my heart pounding.

Looking as nervous as I felt, he nodded, then reached over to open the drawer of his nightstand, pulling out a condom. He quickly put it on, his hands trembling.

I spread my legs a little more, then reached down to slowly guide him inside me. Like our first kiss, everything felt like slow motion. His touch was light and lingering and impossibly good. He teased me for a long time. Then, when I couldn't stand it another second, I wrapped my legs around him and dug my fingers into his back and pulled him all the way inside me. And then I knew that there was absolutely, positively no turning back.

CHAPTER 13

Joe

By the time Cate and I had sex for the first time, I knew I was going to fall in love with her. Our chemistry was *that* good. Then again, maybe the sex was incredible because I already had developed such strong feelings for her. Like a "chicken and egg type" thing. Who knows which it was, but over the next few weeks, I became addicted to her. She was so damn *gorgeous,* but it was much more than that. I loved her air of mystery, and the way she was willing to call me out on my bullshit. I loved the way she was so strong one minute—and quietly vulnerable the next. I loved the way she looked at me and how she touched me and the sound of her voice and the way she laughed and the smell of her skin. Not only her perfume, but her actual *skin,* especially after we really went at it and she started to sweat. She drove me crazy. Like a drug I couldn't get enough of. Even in the satiated aftermath of sex, when I would have rolled away from other women, secretly wishing I could just snap my fingers and be alone, I found myself wanting *more* of Cate. Holding her in my arms and stroking her hair, I'd ask what she was thinking.

"Nothing," she'd usually murmur, my go-to answer in the past when I got the same question.

"You have to be thinking *something*," I'd say.

It was something I'd been told in the past, which I now under-stood as a statement of mild frustration. At that point, Cate would normally shush me or ignore me. The not knowing was a little unsettling. At the same time, the mystery of what was going on in that beautiful head of hers drew me in more.

Meanwhile, she insisted that we keep our relationship a secret—though she didn't call it a relationship, or label it at all. She refused to go out in public together, except for one time when I convinced her to meet me in the very back corner of a movie theater so we could see an indie film my old buddy Charlie Vance had produced. We ended up missing a good bit of the second half when she decided to go down on me. Afterward, she got herself together and whispered goodbye.

"You're leaving? Before it's over?"

"You can tell me what happens," she whispered. "It's too risky to leave together."

As if it hadn't been risky to wrap her lips around my dick.

"Okay," I said, knowing that she made the rules. "Can I see you later? Please?"

She shook her head and said, "Let's quit while we're ahead. I have a gut feeling that the paparazzi will be waiting for you."

I nodded, because I actually had the same feeling; I just didn't care. But Cate did, so that was that. It was unprecedented. Most girls *wanted* to be seen with me, and with them, it had usually felt like a test I had to pass. In other words: did I like them enough to go public with the relationship? That was always the question. I think even Margaret, who loathed the press and the spotlight, at times felt that the media validated us.

But Cate didn't need validation—from me or anyone else. I let our loose status quo ride for another few weeks, biding my time, then tentatively brought it up again.

"Have you told anyone you're seeing me?" I asked, as we sat on my sofa eating Chinese delivery and drinking Sapporos that she'd picked up from the bodega near my house.

Without looking at me, she shrugged, as if I hadn't just asked her a yes-or-no question.

I laughed and said, "Well?"

"I may have mentioned it to Elna," she said.

"You *may* have?"

"Yeah. I sorta had to," she said. "She asked who I'd been hanging out with, and why I always came home in the middle of the night . . . so . . . yeah . . . I told her it was you. . . ." Her voice trailed off.

"And? What did she say?"

"Not much," Cate said, shrugging again. "But she agreed that I shouldn't get busted being seen with you."

"And why's that, exactly?" I said, staring at her profile.

She put her chopsticks down and looked back at me. "Because I don't want or need that kind of drama. I know you're used to it, but I'm not."

I nodded, feeling a little hurt. She was basically telling me that I wasn't worth the trouble. "So . . . let me ask you a question. . . ."

She made her usual mmm-hmmm sound, like she was amenable, but a little bored.

"If you liked me more, would I be worth the drama?"

Cate smirked, glanced my way, and said, "Maybe."

"Damn," I said, pretending to pout.

"Oh, poor baby. Did I hurt your feelings?" she said teasingly.

"A little," I said, as she softened the blow by crawling onto my lap.

"No, I didn't," she said.

"Yes, you did," I said, loving the attention.

She put her arms around my neck, then straddled me, pushing

me against the back of the sofa with the weight of her body before nuzzling the side of my face with her nose.

"C'mon, Joe. It's better this way."

"What way?"

"*This* way," she said, kissing me. "Just the two of us."

I nodded, because it sounded nice when she put it that way. More intimate, in the way things always are when there's a secret involved.

"So, I guess that means you won't go to the Proust Ball with me?" I said, pointing down at the invitation that had just arrived in the mail.

"I don't do *balls*," she said.

"But I need a date."

"I'm sure you can scrounge one up."

"You wouldn't be jealous? If I went with another woman?"

Her jaw tensed for one hopeful second. But then she shrugged, shook her head, and said, "No. I don't do jealousy, either."

"You never get jealous?"

"No," she said. "What's the point? It doesn't change anything."

"Damn," I said.

There really was no one like her.

ABOUT TWO WEEKS later, I decided to try again. We'd just made love and were lying naked in my bed when I said, "I'm starving. What do you say we go to El Teddy's?"

"Can't we just order?"

"El Teddy's doesn't deliver," I said.

"Well, we can do takeout, then. Want me to pick it up? I don't mind."

"Why can't we just go?" I said.

"You know why."

"C'mon, Cate. What are you scared of?"

"Who said I'm scared?" she fired back. "I'm not scared."

"Then why can't we go out?"

She sighed and said, "We've been over this."

"But I want to sit at a table with you, and let a server bring us food . . . and we can't get margaritas to *go*," I said.

She hesitated, and I could tell I was making slight progress. But then she shook her head, kissed my cheek, and said, "Not tonight, Joe."

"Why not? What's wrong with tonight?"

"Because," she said. "I didn't bring any of my stuff. . . ."

"What stuff?"

"Stuff to shower and get ready . . . my toiletries and makeup."

"You can use my toiletries. And you don't need makeup," I continued. "You're a natural beauty."

"Mmm-hmm."

"Is that a yes?"

"No. It's not a yes."

"C'mon. I can call ahead and ask for a private table. Nobody will see us—"

"Yeah, right," she said with a laugh. "Like you can just go incognito somewhere."

"I can sometimes. I did in Paris. Nobody knew I was in Paris."

"I'm sure *someone* knew."

"Well, the press didn't . . . and the press won't be at El Teddy's, either."

"How do you know?"

"Because it's a neighborhood joint," I said, running my fingers through her silky hair. "It's low-key. Nobody gives a shit. And besides . . . it's time."

"Why?" she said. "Why is it time?"

"Because we've been together for almost two months."

"No, we haven't."

"If you count Paris, we have. And you haven't let me take you out one time here. . . . All we do is have sex in my apartment."

"And you're *complaining* about that?" she said with a laugh. "Isn't that a dream scenario for most guys?"

"Maybe. For most guys. And maybe for me in the past," I said, being as honest as I could, as if candor could somehow help my case. "But, Cate . . . I really like you. . . ." My voice trailed off as I felt a surge of unfamiliar nervousness that only grew when she didn't reply.

"Say something," I said in a low voice.

She sighed and said, "I really like you, too. You know that."

I smiled, feeling like a puppy who had just done a trick and gotten a treat. "How much do you like me?"

"A solid amount."

"Enough to go drink some margaritas with me? In *public*?"

She let out a long sigh, pretending to be deep in thought. "Okay. Yes. I like you exactly *that* much. No more and no less."

I perked up, hoping there wasn't a catch. "So, you'll go?"

"Okay. Fine. I'll go."

"As in—right now?"

"Well, we should probably put some clothes on first," she said.

I laughed. "You think that's necessary?"

"Yeah," she said. "Call me crazy, but something tells me that people *would* notice if Joe Kingsley walked into El Teddy's in his birthday suit."

CHAPTER 14

Cate

After I slept with Joe that first time, the floodgates opened.
We saw each other nearly every day, but always in secret,
at my insistence. I told him that I didn't want any drama—and
that was true.

What I *didn't* tell him was that I knew his interest in me had a
shelf life, and I believed that whatever spell I'd managed to cast
over him would be broken the second people found out about
us—and the truth about me. There was no way that his feelings
for me could withstand the scrutiny of his inner circle, let alone
the tabloid press and millions of people obsessed with the Kingsley family. Eventually, it would be pointed out to him—or he
would otherwise figure out—that we just weren't compatible in
any real way. In the meantime, our secret also felt like an insurance policy against public humiliation. I might very well fall in
love with Joe, but I wasn't going to let the whole world watch me
crash and burn when the inevitable happened.

For days, which then turned into weeks, I remained vigilant.
Other than Elna, I didn't tell anyone about Joe. Not Curtis or
Wendy or even my mom when I took her to lunch for her birth-

day and knew the news would make the best gift, even better than the diamond cross necklace I'd given her. I just couldn't take the chance that Chip would find out and somehow try to sabotage me. It was sad—tragic—that his abuse rendered my relationship with my mom so superficial, even strained. If he weren't in the picture, I truly think I would have been sharing everything with her. She would have been the first call I made when Joe and I met on the beach, and when he showed up in Paris. But I'd long since learned that I could only be so close to her and that there was really nothing I could do until she was ready to leave him. You simply can't help someone who doesn't want to be helped.

Meanwhile, I was super careful with the paparazzi who occasionally lingered outside Joe's building. Whenever I spotted anyone even vaguely suspicious, I'd walk on by, returning only when the coast was completely clear. Sometimes I'd just head home for good, which had the added benefit of driving Joe crazy. It's not that I wanted to play mind games with him, but I was keenly aware of keeping a level playing field. So no matter what I was feeling, which was getting to be quite a lot, I did my best to appear blasé. It was the only way to protect myself.

I think the concept of a completely clandestine relationship intrigued Joe at first, as he mentioned several times that our hiding felt romantic. He also loved getting one over on the tabloid press. Based on stories he'd told me, his relationship with the paparazzi could get contentious, but even when it didn't, Joe still wanted to win the cat-and-mouse game.

A cynical part of me wondered if Joe liked skipping all the wining and dining and going straight to the bedroom. I mean, what guy wouldn't like having no-strings-attached sex, especially if you knew the relationship couldn't go anywhere?

Eventually, though, he started pressuring me to go out in public with him. It was reassuring, evidence that he really did like me, but I still dragged my feet, wanting to live in our limbo fantasyland for as long as I could.

Then, one night, when he begged to take me out to dinner, I finally relented. As we left his apartment and walked openly through the streets of SoHo and then into Tribeca, I was more than a little apprehensive, hyperaware of all the double takes and outright stares. At one point, I even trailed a few steps behind him, just to play it safe.

"What are you doing back there?" Joe said, laughing, seemingly oblivious to the attention that followed him everywhere.

I shooed him ahead, but he insisted on waiting for me. Even after I caught up, though, I tried to appear as if I wasn't really with him. But by the time we'd settled into a back corner of the restaurant with chips and salsa and a pitcher of margaritas, I could feel myself start to relax. Joe must have noticed the change because he reached for my hand across the table, giving it a little squeeze.

"See?" he said. "Look at us. Totally under the radar."

I glanced around and had to admit that he was right. The restaurant was packed, but nobody was paying any attention to us. It was an advantage of a trendy downtown spot; the crowd was too hip to stare at a celebrity.

"So, what do you think about doing this more often?"

"Going out to dinner?"

"Yes. And just—making things official."

"And what does that entail?" I said. "A press release?"

I was making a joke, but apparently it wasn't such a far-fetched concept. "Well, not a *press* release per se," he said. "But maybe a statement of some kind . . ."

"Wait. Seriously?" I said, nervously reaching for a chip.

"Well, yeah," he said. "You know, we could just issue a brief statement confirming our relationship."

"And why is that necessary?"

"It's not *necessary*. We can always stick to 'no comment' if you prefer . . . but sometimes silence backfires."

"How so?"

"People draw their own conclusions about what's going on."

I swallowed, feeling a wave of nervousness, and suddenly wishing we were just back in his apartment, hunkered down on the sofa, still playing make-believe.

"Look. I really don't care what anyone thinks," he continued. "I just want to be able to *do* things with you."

"We have been doing things," I said with a knowing smile.

He smiled back at me and said, "Yes. And I've greatly enjoyed those things. Believe me. But I'd like to do other stuff, too. Go to dinner and events and parties and ball games."

I nodded, listening, thinking.

"I want to take you to the Hamptons for the weekend. And go on *vacations* . . . and I want to meet your friends and family. Especially your mother . . . Have you told her about me?"

"She's heard of you," I said, smiling at him.

He laughed, then said, "You know what I mean. . . . Have you told her about *us*?"

I shook my head.

"Well, I want to meet her . . . and I want you to meet my mother, too."

My stomach turned a somersault as I tried to decide which scenario I dreaded more.

"So what do you think?"

"I don't know, Joe—"

"Okay, I don't want to rush you . . . but can we at least stop hiding? And just tell everyone the truth?"

I lowered my voice and leaned toward him. "You mean that we've been fucking for two months? *That* truth?" I said, mostly

just to throw cold water on my feelings. But I think I was also
testing him.

"Jesus, Cate," Joe said with a laugh. "Do you have to say it
that way?"

I shrugged and said, "Well. Isn't that what we've been doing?"

"No," he said, reaching for my hand. "We've been making
love."

I rolled my eyes and pulled my hand away, saying, "Ugh. Please
don't ever use that expression again."

He laughed, then said, "Okay. Well, regardless of what we call
it—I don't kiss and tell. . . ."

"Bullshit," I said with a smile.

"I don't!"

I took a sip of my margarita, then licked some of the salt from
the rim of my glass. "So, you're telling me that you *never* talked
to your guy friends about what it was like to fuck Phoebe Mills?"

"Ugh! Stop saying that word!"

"Okay, fine. What it was like to *have sex* with Phoebe Mills?"

He blushed and looked away.

"Yep. That's what I thought."

"Okay. You got me there," Joe said. "But that wasn't a real
relationship."

"What was it, then?"

"It was mostly *just* sex. I mean, we did have fun together,
but . . ."

I gave him a "gotcha" smile.

"Don't look at me like that," he said.

"I'm not looking at you like anything," I said.

"Yes, you are. Do you think less of me?"

"No. Why would I? You think I've never had 'just sex' before?
With no strings attached?" I said.

"I don't know," he said, looking intrigued. "Have you?"

I nodded and said yes, of course I had.

"Wait. Is that what we've been doing?" he said with a look on his face that I couldn't read. "Are you using me for sex?"

"Yes," I said, raising my glass. "Sex and margaritas."

Joe smiled and said, "C'mon. Be serious. Are we . . . a couple?"

My heart was now racing, and all I wanted to do was say yes. Instead, I said, "I thought we weren't doing labels."

"It's time for labels, Cate," he said, giving me one of his smoldering stares, which further undid me. "Are you my girlfriend?"

I took a deep breath, reminding myself that there was no way this was going to end well. But I still nodded, feeling my first wave of hopefulness that maybe we could be somewhat of a normal couple, at least for a little while.

EARLY THE FOLLOWING morning, after rolling out of Joe's bed to head home and shower for work, I was ambushed right outside his building by a beefy man in a black leather jacket. For one disorienting second, I actually thought I was being mugged. Then I saw that his weapon was a camera and realized, too late, that I was under a different kind of assault. Blinded by a flash, I raised my purse to my face and bolted down the block, debating between the subway—which had been my original plan—and a taxi, which would make a cleaner getaway but was more uncertain at this hour. I opted for the latter, praying that I'd get lucky and find one.

As I swiftly walked to the corner, the guy kept perfect pace, at one point even circling in front of me, shooting me straight on as he ran *backward,* taunting me.

Hey, honey, what's your name? Click, click. *Can you give me a sexy smile?* Click, click. *How long have you been fucking Joe?* Click, click. *Are you a whore?* Click, click, click.

It was ironic—since I had used the word *fucking* last night—

and I suddenly realized that on some level I'd been trying to pre-empt what others might say about it. If I said it first, it would hurt less. But hearing him say it still felt degrading, and it didn't help that people were staring at me as the cameraman and I bobbed and weaved all over the sidewalk. At one point, I tripped and al-most fell, stumbling into a gray-haired man in a suit—who had the nerve to shoot me a look of disgust—mumbling that I needed to watch where I was going. As if he couldn't plainly see that I was being pursued.

When I got to the intersection, I stepped out into the street, frantically searching for a taxi as the guy kept taking pictures and firing off rude questions. It was unbelievable how relentless he was, but what shocked me more was that not a single person stepped in to help. Instead, they just kept coming and going in the crosswalks around me.

Finally, a lone Good Samaritan who was out for a morning jog intervened. She was young and petite but had a fierce expression, and I watched with awe and gratitude as she stepped between me and the cameraman, yelling at him to leave me alone. It was just enough interference to allow me to flag down a taxi.

Sliding into the backseat, I gave the driver my address, realiz-ing I was in a full sweat and on the verge of tears.

"Are you okay, miss?" he asked as we made eye contact in the rearview mirror.

"Yes, thank you. I'm fine," I said, wiping my eyes and catching my breath, all the while thinking, *Holy shit.*

As we made our way uptown, I told myself that I had probably overreacted—that nothing truly terrible had happened. Yes, a sleazy photographer seemed to know what was going on between Joe and me—and was now in possession of what were certainly hideous photos. But what could he really do with them? Who would want to publish those without more concrete proof that I was tied to

Joe? And even if they did make their way into a tabloid, so what? I hadn't committed a crime. Joe and I were both single adults, and we'd only done what a million other single adults in the city had done the night before. What was the worst that could happen?

By the time I got back to my apartment, I'd talked myself off the ledge enough to call Joe and fill him in. But I left out some of the details, including the word *whore*.

"Oh, Cate. I'm sorry, baby," he said.

He had never called me *baby* before, and I was surprised by how much it comforted me.

"It's not your fault," I said.

"Yeah, it is," he said. "I should have gone to get a cab with you."

"You offered," I said—because he always did. "Anyway, that would have made it worse."

"Maybe," Joe said. "But I still wish I had been there for you. I've been dealing with these assholes my whole life. At the very least, I should have prepped you better."

"How would you have done that?" I asked.

"I don't know—there are just some tips. . . ."

"Such as?"

"Such as . . . never run."

"Why not?"

"'Cause it's like running from a bear. It just amps everything up and makes it worse. You have to stay calm. Pretend they're not there. . . . Plus, you don't want them to think you're flustered. They get off on that. Pictures sell for a higher price if you look pissed or upset . . . which is why they talk shit. You just have to ignore them."

"Okay," I said, taking mental notes, but thinking that was probably easier said than done. "Well, I just wanted to let you know. . . ."

He must have heard the reluctance in my voice, because he said my name as a worried question. "Cate?"

"Yeah?"

"Don't be scared," he said.

"I'm not scared," I said, lying through my teeth.

THAT NIGHT, I returned home from work to the strong aroma of pot and the sound of Elna and Curtis laughing in the living room. As I put my bag and keys down in the kitchen, I rounded the corner and saw them both sprawled out on the sofa in a cloud of smoke, watching a Mary J. Blige video on BET. Elna's bong sat on the coffee table between them, along with a box of Wheat Thins and an empty container of hummus. Clearly, they'd been at it for a while.

"Ahhhh. There she is," Curtis said, glancing up at me.

"Yep. There she is," Elna echoed.

"Hey, guys," I said with a substantial sigh as I kicked off my heels and plopped down on a floor pillow on the other side of our coffee table.

Curtis ignored me, staring at Elna. "Does our girl here know how much trouble she's in?"

Elna smirked, then shrugged. "I don't think she does . . . but maybe. . . . Always hard to tell with her."

It was one of their favorite schticks, talking about me as if I weren't in the room, though to be fair, we all did it to one another.

I rolled my eyes and shot Elna an accusatory look. "So you told him?"

"Lady," Curtis said, waving his finger in my face. "She didn't tell me *shit*. You're on freaking Page *Six*!"

My stomach dropped just as I noticed the newspaper on the

coffee table. Sure enough, Curtis held it up and waved it in my face. "Extra, extra! Read all about it!'

I pushed his hand away and groaned. "Do I even want to see it?"

Elna gave me a glazed look, then slid the bong across the coffee table toward me. "Well, you might want to hit this first."

"Shit. Is it that bad?" I said, refusing the bong and reaching for the paper instead.

"I mean—" Elna said as Curtis held it out of my reach. "It's not that bad—"

I groaned, then said, "Okay, gimme that thing."

Curtis shook his head and patted the spot on the sofa next to him. "No. You come here. I can't stop looking at him."

"*Him?*" I said, getting up and moving over to the sofa. "There's a picture of Joe?"

"Yep," Curtis said. "Looking fine as hell."

As I sat down, squeezing between my friends, I saw the headline—JOE KINGSLEY'S NEW FLING—along with three photographs laid out sequentially. The first was a medium-range shot, taken last night, of Joe and me walking into his building. He was holding the door open for me, one hand on the small of my back— which wasn't terribly incriminating. But the *second* shot—a close-up of me in broad daylight, *leaving* Joe's building, wearing the same jeans and top, with messy hair and a bewildered, busted look on my face—told a different story. In the third photo, I was standing on the corner, holding my purse up to my face. The caption spelled everything out for less discerning readers: *Former model Cate Cooper takes "walk of shame" after steamy night with Joe Kingsley.*

"Ugh," I said, putting my head in my hands. "Unreal."

"I'll tell you what's *unreal*," Curtis said, pausing dramatically.

"What's unreal is that I had to read about this in the paper! Why didn't you tell me? What is going on here?"

"Okay. Calm down," I said, then summarized the order of events as succinctly as I could. I told him that I'd been seeing Joe since Fashion Week and hadn't told him sooner because I didn't quite believe it was going to last, and I didn't want to get his hopes up.

"Well, they're up! *Way* up!" Curtis said. "I'll never forget the way he looked at you on the beach that day. How serious is this, anyway?"

I hesitated, then told him the truth. "I don't know. I mean, he called me his girlfriend last night—but . . . I can't imagine that it'll last for much longer."

"Yes, it will!" Curtis said. "And remember—I call dibs on your wedding makeup."

I shook my head and said, "See? That's the reason I didn't tell you—"

"She has a point," Elna said.

"I'm serious, Curtis. No more wedding talk! That's not going to happen."

"Okay. Well, how about just *regular* everyday makeup?" he said, tapping his finger on the middle photo. "If you're going to be in the tabloids, we're really going to have to up your game."

"Jeez, Curtis! I didn't know I was going to be *photographed*! This guy totally ambushed me."

"Clearly," he said, cracking himself—and Elna—up.

"Stop it, guys," I said as our phone started to ring.

Elna answered it, made a few seconds of small talk, then handed it to me, mouthing, *It's your mother.*

"Oh, God," I whispered. "Does she know?"

Elna put her hand over the receiver and said, "Well, it was sort of hard to understand her through all the hyperventilating, but yeah . . . I'm pretty sure she knows."

Bracing myself, I took the phone and said hello as my mom began firing off giddy questions: *Is it true? Did you spend the night with Joe Kingsley? What's going on? Chip said you're on Page Six!*

I confirmed that the statements were true, feeling certain that Chip had found a way to disparage me to my mom.

Sure enough, the next words out of her mouth were "Chip said it was a one-night stand?"

I bit my lip, now feeling hurt and defensive in addition to everything else. Of course my mom believed Chip's negative spin. In the end, she would always choose him over me. Always. But pride still made me come back at her. "No, Mom. It wasn't a one-night stand. We're seeing each other," I said, walking a fine line between defending myself and dangerously overblowing my relationship with Joe.

"Oh, wow. That's incredible!" she said. "Have you met Dottie?"

"No."

"Are you going to?"

"I don't know, Mom. I doubt it. We'll probably break up soon—"

"Can I please meet him before you do?" she said, clearly having no faith in my staying power.

"I don't know, Mom," I said again, just wanting to get off the phone.

"C'mon, Cate! You *know* how much I love the Kingsleys."

"I know, Mom. But he's a real person," I said, trying to put into words what I had grappled with over the past couple of months.

"I know he's a real person," she said. "What does that even mean?"

"It means he's not who you think he is. . . . He's just a regular guy."

"Well, according to *People* magazine, he's also the Sexiest Man Alive."

I sighed and said, "Mom. *Please*."

"Okay. But do you think I could get my picture taken with him? At some point?"

"We'll see," I said, thinking that at the rate she was going, there was no way I'd let her get anywhere near him.

CHAPTER 15

Joe

A few nights after the paparazzi busted Cate leaving my apartment, I went to dinner with my cousin Peter, his fiancée, Genevieve, and Berry. I'd invited Cate to join us, but she'd turned me down—for the third day in a row—alluding to not wanting a repeat of the paparazzi incident.

"So, who's the latest model?" Berry asked me just after our drinks were brought to the table. It was the first time I'd ever kept her in the dark about anything significant in my life, and I wasn't even sure why I had, other than a general feeling of protectiveness toward Cate. This question confirmed my instinct—and I felt annoyed.

"I thought you didn't read the *Post*?" I said.

"I don't. It's trash," she said. "I saw it over someone's shoulder on the subway."

"Likely story," I said as Peter and Genevieve listened with amused expressions. "Just admit it—you stalk me."

"You wish," Berry said, taking a sip of her wine. "So . . . what's the deal? Is it just a fling?"

"No," I said. "It's not 'just a fling.' As a matter of fact, I've been seeing her for two months."

"Wow. Two *whole* months?"

"Yes," I said, ignoring her sarcasm. *"Exclusively."*

"Aww," Genevieve said in her usual sweet voice. "Good for you, Joey."

"Okay," Berry said. "So. Tell us about her."

"Her name's Cate Cooper," I said, overcome with the warm, tingly feeling that Cate always gave me. "She's amazing."

Berry stared back at me and said, "Where did you meet?"

"In the Hamptons." I hesitated and then said, "She's the one you told me *not* to date."

"I did?" Berry said.

"Yeah. About a year ago. I met her while she was working on the beach. Remember?"

"Oh. Yeah. *That* model."

"Former model. She retired."

"And what does she do now?"

"She works with Wilbur Swift."

"Who?" Berry said.

"Wilbur Swift, the fashion designer?" Genevieve said.

I nodded.

"Never heard of him," Berry said.

Genevieve filled Berry in. "You'd love his stuff. His designs are so clean and minimalistic." She turned to Peter and said, "You know that navy dress I have with the white piping?"

"The one you wore to Laura's shower?" he said, referring to our cousin's baby shower—which was months ago. It was *so* Peter to keep track of such details.

Genevieve nodded, looking proud of her attentive fiancé.

With Wilbur now legitimized, I shot Berry a smug smile, then turned in my chair, kicking one leg out to the side of the table and pointing down at my loafer. "These are Wilbur driving mocs. Soft as butter. My new favorites. Anyway. Cate is Wilbur's right-hand *woman*. . . . She has impeccable style—and she's just really . . . cool," I said, wishing I had the words to capture her essence. "And yes, she sold me these."

Berry nodded, then said, "Interesting. So, where'd she go to college?"

I stared at her and shook my head. "Look, Berry. I know what you're doing here, and I'm not going for it," I said.

"What?" she said, all wide-eyed innocence.

"Can you stop being a snob for, like, one second?"

"I am *not* a snob," she said, truly believing what she was saying. "I'm just asking *basic* questions. It's pretty standard to ask where someone went to college."

"Nah. Good try. That's a coded, elitist question. And you know it. You sound like my mother," I said, getting worked up. I looked at Peter and said, "Doesn't she?"

Always the diplomat, Peter shrugged and said, "Oh, I don't know, Joe. She's just asking where the girl went to school. It's not like she asked what *country club* she belongs to—or what her father does for a living."

"Yeah. For real, Joe," Berry said. "What *should* I be asking you?"

"I don't know—stuff like . . . what we like to do together. Whether she's *nice*."

"Oh, I *know* what you like to do together," she said, rolling her eyes. "And so does everyone else who reads the *Post*. But I'll play along. Is she *nice*?"

I smiled, shook my head, and said, "Actually? No. Not especially."

Genevieve laughed and said, "Wait. Seriously?"

"Well, she's not a *bitch* or anything . . . but she's not one of those overly nicey-nice girls. She's not fake. *Nothing* about Cate is fake."

Berry raised her eyebrows and said, "Nothing? A model without a boob job?"

I shook my head and said, "Okay, Ber. Now you're just being a bitch."

"Okay, sorry," Berry said, her expression softening a bit. "When can we meet her?"

"Only when I can trust you to be polite to her," I said.

"I'm always polite!"

I resisted the urge to remind her about Nicole—and some of the other times she'd been less than pleasant with women I liked—and said, "We also have to get through this initial paparazzi situation."

"Meaning what?" Peter said.

"Meaning she just got stalked and is now a little skittish. . . . Cate hates drama."

"And she's dating *you*?" Peter laughed. "Good luck with that, man."

"Exactly," Berry said. "And also, fun fact: women who go around saying they hate drama secretly *love* drama."

"That's pretty accurate, actually," Genevieve said.

"Well, tell me, Ber," I said. "Do *you* hate drama?"

"You know I do," she said, walking right into my trap, as I knew she would.

"So then—you actually *secretly* love it?"

"No," Berry said. "But here's the difference. I don't go around dating the world's most famous bachelor and then complaining when my picture is in the paper. And you'll forgive me if I don't entirely buy that a model—or a former model, whatever—hates photographers and attention."

Peter frowned, then said to Berry, "I have to agree with Joe on this one. You can't assume she loves drama or attention because of her former profession—or because she's dating Joe."

"Exactly! As hard as it might be for you to believe, Berry . . . Cate is actually dating me *despite* my name . . . and stuff like this, right here, is why she didn't want to join us."

"You invited her?" Berry said, looking surprised.

"Of course I invited her. She's my *girlfriend*. I'm falling in love with her," I blurted out, my heart racing.

"Whoa!" Peter said, moving his chair back with exaggerated surprise, then looking at the girls. "Did you hear what the world's most eligible bachelor just said?"

"I sure did," Genevieve said, clasping her hands and bringing them to her heart. "Do you mean that, Joe?"

Without flinching, I said yes, then looked right at Berry. "And I'm going to need you to trust me—and give her the benefit of the doubt for a change."

Berry stared back at me for a few seconds, then asked, "How serious is this? Is she . . . *marriage* material?"

I took a sip of my wine and answered a different question than the one she seemed to be asking. "Well, if by 'marriage material,' you mean someone I can see myself marrying? . . . Then the answer is yes," I said. "She absolutely is."

THE FOLLOWING MORNING my mother called, playing dumb, waiting for me to tell her the news that she obviously had already heard from Berry. I played dumb right back, forcing her hand.

"Oh. And I hear you're in love?" she finally said after some small talk. Her tone was neutral, but I knew better.

"Yep. Seems that way," I said, bristling.

"And she works in fashion?"

"Yes," I said. "She has incredible style. She works with Wilbur Swift. You know him, right?"

"Vaguely," she said. "So, Joseph, would you say she is more like Phoebe or Margaret?"

I bit my tongue—and *not* figuratively—then said, "I'm not sure I understand that question, Mom. She's not like either of them. She's her own person." I paused, then added, "Like we all are."

"Yes," my mother said. "I suppose that's true. . . . Well. When can I meet her?"

"Soon," I said.

"How soon?"

"As soon as I convince her that her life won't suck with me in it," I said. Then I told my mother that I really had to go.

CHAPTER 16

Cate

In the days following my debut in the tabloids, I fielded countless phone calls and emails from friends and acquaintances who had either seen the *Post* or heard about it. Everyone wanted to know what the deal was with Joe. I told them that we were seeing each other, but that it wasn't serious. We were just having fun. It added up, of course, because that's how the world saw him. He was the ultimate good-time guy.

Meanwhile, I kept a low profile. I was too nervous to risk getting caught again, and I told Joe I just needed a few days to regroup. On our fourth night apart, he invited me out with some of his friends and family. I declined, opting instead for my paparazzi-free living room with Elna and Curtis. At the end of the night, he called me from what sounded like a pay phone at a bar.

"Where are you?" I asked.

"Brother Jimmy's," he said.

"Which one?"

"The one on Second Ave."

"Oh," I said, feeling excited that he was so close to my apartment.

"Can I come over? I need to see you. Please?" he said, sounding a little bit drunk. Maybe a *lot* drunk.

My mind ticked through the calculations—the risk of getting busted versus the considerable reward of seeing him—but decided that it was better to be safe than sorry. "I don't think that's a good idea," I said.

"Aw, c'mon. Why not?"

"Because it's late."

"It's not *that* late."

"Still. It'll look like a booty call," I said.

"That's ridiculous. You're my girlfriend," he said. "It's not a *booty* call."

I sighed, thinking that was easy for *him* to say when he wasn't the one getting called a whore.

We talked in circles for a few seconds before I said, "Look, Joe. If you were photographed coming to my place at this hour, exactly *no one* would construe that as you missing your *girlfriend*."

He sighed, then said, "Okay. Well, can I come see you in the morning? Can we hang out for a little while?"

"I really can't," I said. "I have to be at work early."

"What about after work?"

"Maybe. I just don't know."

He hesitated, then said, "Cate, what's going on here? If we're going to be together, we have to actually be together."

"I know. . . ."

"So, what's the deal? Are you trying to break up with me? Already?"

"Not yet," I said.

"Ouch."

"I'm just kidding," I said with a laugh. "But the other day really shook me. And right now I just want to hunker down and avoid some slimeball photographer chasing me down the street calling me a whore."

"Oh, Cate. *Shit*," Joe said. "He called you that?"

"Yeah," I said. "He did."

"Okay. Look. This is what I was trying to tell you . . ." he said, suddenly sounding sober—and very serious. "This is why we need to step out and establish ourselves as a real couple. The sneaking around is backfiring. We have nothing to hide."

"What do you mean 'step out'? What does that entail?"

"Well. It could be any number of things. We could go to an event together. Do the whole red-carpet drill. Pose and smile, arm in arm."

"I don't know about an event," I said, imagining all the conversations I'd have to have with haughty philanthropist types.

"Okay. We can just go out to dinner . . . the two of us . . . and tip off a photographer as to where we are."

"You mean—*cooperate* with the paparazzi?" I said, the mere thought filling me with disgust.

"Yeah. But it would be on our terms."

"How do we do that?"

"Well . . . One of the guys—Eduardo's his name—has been following me for years. . . . But he's less offensive than the others. . . . I know he'd do it for us. . . . Then we can plant an official statement—"

"An official statement?" I said, my heart skipping a beat. "What do you mean?"

"You know . . . something like 'A source close to Joe Kingsley confirms that the two have been in an exclusive relationship for several months now.' That type of thing . . . which will run alongside our photo."

"Have you done that before?" I said, thinking of Margaret—and the girls before her.

"No."

"Then why are you doing it now?"

"Because I wanna protect you."

"Do I need more protection than the others?" I asked, thinking that there was no way anyone had name-called Margaret—a Harvard-educated blue blood with a *bob*.

"No," Joe said. "You're actually tougher than any girl I've ever been with."

"So why, then?" I pressed.

"Because," Joe said, "I'm crazy about you, Cate. And I want this to work. More than anything. And if this will help us be together, I want to do it. That's why."

It was so hard to believe what he was telling me, but, somehow, I did.

THAT FRIDAY EVENING, after agonizing about what to wear to dinner, I walked out of my apartment wearing a little black Yohji Yamamoto dress, black slingbacks, and red lipstick. It had been a full week since I'd seen Joe's face, and my heart skipped a beat when I saw him smiling at me through the backseat window of a shiny black town car.

I quickly opened the door before he could get out and do it for me, sliding in beside him. "Hey," I said, feeling oddly shy.

"Hi, there," he said in a low voice. "You look *fantastic*."

"You do, too," I said, noticing he was wearing the same Wilbur ensemble he'd worn in Paris.

We stared at each other for a few more seconds before Joe turned to tell the driver we were all set.

As we pulled away from the curb, I asked him where we were going, as he'd wanted it to be a surprise.

"Aureole," he said. "I wanted to take you somewhere a bit

more imaginative . . . but it was tough to get a reservation on such late notice."

"*You* had trouble getting a reservation?" I said. "That seems unlikely."

"I didn't use my own name, dippy."

I laughed, then said, "So. What name did you use?"

"Myles Savage."

I laughed and said, "How'd you come up with that?"

"It's a guy I prosecuted," he said. "Who I liked a lot."

"But you prosecuted him anyway?"

"Had to. But I may or may not have fumbled in my closing argument," he said with a wink.

I smiled. Joe had previously confided that he sometimes blew a case on purpose when he didn't think justice was exactly being served.

"So how do you feel?" he asked.

"A little nervous," I said. "But happy."

"Good. Me too," Joe said, grinning, before leaning over and giving me a light kiss on the cheek.

A few minutes later, we turned onto Sixty-first Street. Joe finally let go of my hand as we pulled up to the restaurant. I'd been there once before, back in my Calvin Klein days, and I winced remembering how I'd embarrassed myself by eating the fuzzy-hair layer of the artichoke heart. I'd come a very long way since then, but I still didn't belong here with Joe. I pushed the thought out of my head as the driver started to get out of the car.

"It's okay, man," Joe said. "Stay put. I got this."

"Are you sure, Mr. Kingsley?" the driver said.

Joe said he was sure, then pointed out my window to a man smoking a cigarette on the sidewalk just a few doors down from the restaurant. "There he is," Joe said. "My guy. Eduardo."

I nodded, my stomach churning, then checked my lipstick in my compact. It looked fine, but I touched it up anyway, stalling.

"You ready?" he said.

I nodded.

Joe smiled and gave me a thumbs-up before getting out of the car on the street side, then slowly circling around to my door, giving Eduardo time to get in position. The second he opened my door, the car was bathed in camera flashes. As Joe reached down for my hand, I gave it to him, stepping as elegantly as I could out of the car and onto the curb, which is always tough to do in a dress and heels, especially while being blinded.

The next few seconds were, as much as I hate to admit it, a bit of an adrenaline rush—so different from the last time I'd been photographed on the street. This time, it felt more like modeling. Plus, I was ready, and I was with my boyfriend, who was always doing chivalrous things, like putting his hand on my back, guiding me toward the front door of the restaurant, murmuring for me to watch my step. I still didn't believe in fairy tales—or that this story was going to have a happy ending. But in that moment, I couldn't help feeling a little bit like Cinderella.

Right as we got to the door, Joe paused, his hand still on my back, then turned to look at me and smile. I don't think he was staging a final shot. It seemed more like he wanted to reassure me that we'd made it through the gauntlet. In any case, I smiled back at him as the camera flashed one more time.

It would be the image we chose the next day, in a secret meeting with Eduardo right before he sold exclusive rights to *People* magazine for two hundred thousand dollars. He gave us half, which Joe and I donated to the Kingsley Foundation. It boggled my mind that anyone would pay that much money for one *photograph*. But what really blew my mind was everything that came after the issue hit the stands.

CHAPTER 17

Joe

The minute the *People* magazine issue landed, and the world saw that dazzling photo of Cate walking into Aureole on my arm, she became a full-blown sensation—and not my latest fling. The paparazzi camped outside her apartment and the Wilbur Swift store, following her all over the city, while reporters and morning shows blew up her answering machine with requests for interviews.

I could tell Cate hated everything about the attention, but she handled it with grace, following my advice about not running or trying to hide and instead just going about her business. She attributed all the hoopla (as she called it) to the quote in the *People* article from a "Kingsley insider" confirming a "committed relationship." Obviously, that whipped some folks up, but I told her it was more than that. After all, the press and public had never been this frenzied over Margaret.

When I pointed that out to Cate one night, she looked surprised. "And why is that?"

"Because she's not you," I said, thinking that Margaret was the type of girl everyone expected me to be with—but Cate was the kind of girl everyone wished they could be. "And, I mean—

have you seen yourself?" I smirked, putting one palm on her ass as we stood at my stove together, making pasta.

"C'mon. Be serious," she said, brushing off my compliment along with my hand. "Do you think it's because we're such an unlikely match?"

"Unlikely? How so?"

"You know," she said, looking a little uncomfortable. "We have pretty different backgrounds."

"They're not *that* different," I said.

"Compared to you and Margaret, they're pretty different," she said.

I shrugged, wishing I hadn't brought up Margaret in the first place and vowing not to do it again. "Oh, I forgot to tell you! My mother saw the *People* magazine," I said, changing the subject.

"She did?"

"Yeah. I guess her hairdresser showed her or something. . . . Anyway, she told me you appeared to have 'understated elegance.'"

"That's nice," she said.

"Yeah. She really wants to meet you," I said, testing a noodle and determining that it was ready. "And that's far from a given. Believe me."

Cate looked thoughtful, then asked if my mother had ever met Phoebe.

"Nah," I said, as I turned off the burner and put on my oven mitt.

"Why not?" Cate asked, following me to the sink as I poured the pasta into a colander.

"Because I knew my mother wouldn't like her."

"And why is that?"

"Because Phoebe lacked substance," I said.

"How so?" Cate pressed.

"I don't know. . . . She was just a little shallow. She only really cared about fame and money and her designer goods," I said, remembering how she was always shamelessly trying to get freebies.

"I like designer goods, too," Cate said with a shrug. "I mean . . . I work for a *fashion* designer."

I shook my head and said, "It's not the same thing."

"If you say so . . ." she said, her voice trailing off.

"Yes. I say so. And my mother will agree," I said. "She's going to love you."

Cate looked down, blushing. "Even though I didn't go to college?"

I obviously knew she hadn't gone, but it was the first time she'd ever said the words aloud, and I hated that she looked so embarrassed.

"Cate. You had a different path. You're self-taught and self-made. You've traveled the world. Shit, you speak fluent French. That's more impressive."

"More impressive than what? A Harvard degree?" she said. "I don't think so. . . ."

"Well, *I* do," I said. "And I know my mother. Can she be a snob? Yes. Absolutely she can. But she knows substance when she sees it. And more than anything, she values strength of character and authenticity, and you are drowning in both."

Cate gave me a small smile, looking dubious, then said, "Okay. But there's something else I need to tell you. . . ."

"What's that?" I said.

She bit her lip and took a deep breath. "It's really embarrassing."

"You can tell me," I said softly. "Whatever it is . . ."

She swallowed, then met my gaze, her cheeks an even deeper shade of pink. "Well, in addition to, um, not going to college . . . I actually . . . didn't finish high school. . . ."

"Oh," I said. It wasn't at all what I expected—and I had to admit, I could see why she was so embarrassed—but I did my best to reassure her. "That's okay, honey. Who you are matters to me—not how much formal schooling you've had. You can be educated without degrees."

She shook her head, looking so miserable, like she might cry. "I don't know, Joe. I really don't think your mother will see it that way."

"Yes. She will. She knows that some of the world's most successful people . . . didn't finish high school," I said, stumbling a bit as I did my best to avoid the words *dropped out.*

"Name one," she said. "From this century."

"I can't come up with examples like that . . . but there are plenty. . . . Pretty sure John Travolta's one. . . . And my mom loves that guy. She saw *Grease,* like, ten times. It's the first video she bought when we got our VCR."

"So because your mother likes *Grease* she's going to be okay with me being a high-school dropout? I don't think so," Cate said, but at least she was smiling. "Your family represents pedigree and good upbringing to the vast majority of people in this country. I hardly think your mother is going to be okay with this."

"Look. You left home for a bigger opportunity, right?"

"Well . . . yeah . . . among other things . . ."

I wanted to ask about those other things but assumed it was money and didn't want to make her more uncomfortable. "Well, how is that different from Travolta?"

"He's a tad bit more successful than I am."

"He's more famous. Not more successful."

"Oh my God, Joe. Be serious," she said with a laugh. "Yes, he is!"

"Okay," I said, trying another angle. "Do you regret your career in modeling? All the experiences you had because of it?"

She hesitated, then said, "Well . . . yes and no . . ."

"Hey! The answer better be no!" I said. "We wouldn't have met if you weren't a model."

She nodded, then said, "I know. I've thought of that . . . and I really was able to see the world because of that job. Places I never otherwise would have gone. But still . . . everyone should graduate from high school."

"Okay . . . so go get your GED," I said with a shrug. "It's never too late to go to college, either, if that's what you want. And if you don't, that's fine, too. You have a great career and you're smart as hell. At the end of the day, it's really just a piece of paper. . . ."

"Again. I really don't think your mother will agree."

"Yes, she will. It'll all be fine."

"Are you going to tell her?"

"I don't think it's necessary to make some big announcement. But if it comes up, we tell the truth. And if she doesn't like it—"

"Which she *won't*—"

"Then her loss," I said, raising my voice a little.

"You don't mean that," she said.

"Yes, I do," I said. "I absolutely do."

She stared at me for a few seconds before thanking me in a whisper.

I shook my head, then said. "You don't have to thank me. That's just basic shit. . . . Loyalty 101."

"Maybe," she said with a small smile. "But I can still thank you."

CHAPTER 18

Cate

In our deal with Eduardo and *People,* selling them exclusive rights to our photograph, they agreed to play by our rules and print only what we wanted them to print. Which is to say the most basic information about me. Name, age, hometown, job title, and a reference to the fact that I had once been an Elite model. And, of course, there was a quote from a fake Kingsley insider declaring us an official item.

Joe's plan worked to a T. Our relationship was legitimized overnight—hell, *I* was legitimized—and it was impossible not to find that gratifying, and, if I admit, a little exciting.

Of course, the elevation to Joe's legitimate girlfriend came with a price, as everything in life does. I was no longer anonymous—which was one of the things I'd always loved about the city. I mourned my sudden loss of the privacy that I'd taken for granted for so long, even during the peak of my modeling career. I'd never been a known name like Cindy, Christie, or Elle.

I was maybe being a little paranoid, but I felt as if I was constantly being watched—on the subway, in the park, everywhere. Even when I wasn't, I feared that I would be at any second. I could never let my guard down, and it was physically and mentally draining to know that I was always one headline away from being exposed as an impostor. As in: HIGH-SCHOOL DROPOUT DUPES AMERICA'S PRINCE.

I decided I needed to tell Joe the truth about not finishing high school before the press found out first, so I worked up the courage one night as we made dinner in his kitchen. The fleeting look of shock on his face crushed me, though he quickly recovered, saying all the right things. It was a painful, mortifying couple of minutes, but it also felt like a weight had been lifted. I was so relieved, in fact, that it crossed my mind to confide everything about Chip's abuse and my real reasons for leaving home. Ultimately, though, I decided against that, just as I had with Wendy in high school. I'd rather be judged than pitied, especially because I understood that the latter doesn't necessarily immunize one from the former.

A few days later, Joe invited me to the Hamptons for the upcoming weekend. His mother and Berry were going to be there, and he wanted me to meet them. I said yes, trying not to overthink things, which was difficult to do when Curtis kept peppering me with giddy questions.

"What are you going to take as a hostess gift?" he asked me a couple of days before our departure as the two of us hung out at my place.

"I don't know," I said. The thought hadn't crossed my mind— which worried me. What else could I be forgetting?

"Well, you need to nail that."

I nodded, then said, "I can't go wrong with a nice bottle of wine, can I?"

"Yes, ma'am, you most certainly can go wrong with a bottle of wine. Depending on the bottle," Curtis said. "Besides, wine as a hostess gift is a cliché."

"Sometimes things are cliché for a reason," I said. "Wine feels like a safe choice."

"It's not the time to be safe," Curtis said, shaking his head and pacing around my bedroom. "You're having a moment, and you need to seize it. *Amplify* it. Make a statement."

"Alrighty, then," I said. "How about a bottle of champagne?"

"Too presumptuous."

"A bottle of pastis?"

"Too French."

"Dottie's half French."

"But *you're* not. So it's pandering . . . and can we please think beyond alcohol."

"Okay. How about a nice scented candle?"

"Ugh. A candle? That's more cliché than wine. And anyway, scents are too personal."

I sighed and asked for his suggestion, which I should have just done to begin with.

"I don't know. . . . But it needs to be expensive . . . yet not come *off* as obviously expensive. Like one of those home goods that catches your eye . . . until you pick it up and get sticker shock."

I nodded, thinking that it was the reverse of the usual rule of thumb—to have something look more expensive than it was.

"Think ABC Carpet & Home—*not* Barneys or Tiffany," he said.

"Well, yeah. Obviously not *Tiffany*," I said, picturing the absurd overkill of showing up with a blue box and white silk ribbon.

"It can't be a known brand, but it needs to signal *luxury* . . . like a fabulous serape-stripe Turkish robe that's chic enough to double as a poolside cover-up."

I laughed, amused by his specificity. "Oh, sure. The serape-stripe Turkish robe, of course."

Curtis sat on my bed and smoothed the bedcovers around him, ignoring me. "We need to think high-end lifestyle here, for sure . . . Slim Aarons . . . Babe Paley . . . Bunny Mellon. . . ."

"Or, say, Dottie Kingsley?"

"Oh my God, *yes*. Yes! Good point," he said, pressing one hand to his temple. "Can you *believe* this is happening?"

"Nothing is *happening*," I said, though I knew what he meant.

"Well, it's *about* to happen," Curtis said. "It's *on*, girl."

I laughed, but couldn't help feeling a little excited, too.

"Now, let's see . . . what bag will you be packing?"

"Are we talking about my *suitcase*?"

"Yes," he said. "But you know you can't take an actual *suitcase*, right?"

"I can't?" I said, glancing over at the carry-on-size roller bag I'd already pulled from my closet.

He followed my eyes and looked horrified. "That thing?" he asked, pointing. "No way."

"What in the world, Curtis? It's a basic black bag!"

"Still. No," he said. "You'll look like a flight attendant."

"What's wrong with being a flight attendant?" I said, shifting into my defensive, contrarian mode.

"Oh, stop. You know what I mean. There's nothing wrong with being a flight attendant. Nor is there anything wrong with a basic black suitcase," Curtis said. "But it's the wrong look. . . . You're not going on a business trip. You're *weekending*."

I gave him a pointed look, then said, "Please never use that as a verb again."

"But that's what you're doing. You're *weekending*," he repeated with extra panache. "In the Hamptons. With the Kingsleys. So you're going to need a satchel of some sort."

"A *satchel*?" I laughed.

"Soft luggage. Like a Louis Vuitton duffel. Or a brown leather bag, well worn with a beautiful patina. Like it's been all around the world."

"That suitcase *has* been around the world—and I hardly have time to get a leather bag patinaed in the next few days," I said.

"Yeah. No. I'm sorry. That thing is depressingly pedestrian. What else do you have? Anything with a patrician vibe?"

I laughed. "You're absurd."

"Okay, how about a duffel?"

"Sorry. No."

"You don't own a single *duffel*?"

"Not the kind of duffel you're talking about."

"What kind is it?"

"An L.L.Bean tote bag," I said, thinking of the one that Wendy's mother had given me long ago.

Curtis pursed his lips, thinking. "I think we can work with that. . . . The large size?"

I nodded.

"And what's the accent color?"

"Navy."

"Okay . . . and is it monogrammed?"

"Yes," I said.

"Even better."

"Okay," I said, amused. "But please explain to me why on earth you think L.L.Bean is better than a Tumi suitcase?"

"Because you need to go high or low. Old-money types love the price-point extremes. . . . They either drive a brand-new Mercedes or a beat-up Volkswagen. . . . They wear a Rolex or a Timex . . . and they resist any sort of upgrade on their electronics because 'Hey, this one still works!' It's reverse snobbery. New money equals new shit."

"Wow," I said, thinking of Joe's stubborn loyalty to vinyl and cassettes over CDs. "That's really true."

"Yeah," Curtis said. "Stick with me, kid. I know what I'm doing here."

THAT SATURDAY MORNING, Joe picked me up just before sunrise with Thursday in tow. To my great amusement, he was driving an old Jeep Wagoneer with seventies wood paneling. Smiling to myself, I put my L.L.Bean tote in the backseat, along with a gift bag containing Curtis's choice of a linen robe, then climbed into the car next to Joe.

He beamed at me and said, "Don't you look cute."

"Thanks," I said with a laugh, thinking that no one ever called me cute.

"And look—we *match*," he said, giving me a once-over as he patted my leg.

I nodded—we *were* both wearing denim and white, but the similarities stopped there. Possibly overthinking what was appropriate for a beach weekend with Dottie Kingsley, I'd worn a sleeveless silk blouse, flared jeans, and leather slides, whereas Joe had on old Levi's, a dingy T-shirt, and red high-top sneakers.

"Nice shoes," I said.

"You don't like Chuck Taylors?" he asked, pretending to be wounded before checking his rearview mirror and putting his car in drive.

"Not particularly," I said. "Especially when they're *red*."

Joe laughed, then said, "Well, my mother hates them, too."

"Is that why you wore them?" I asked.

He laughed and handed me one of two coffee cups in the console between us. "Here you go. Three creams, no sugar."

"Aw. You're the best." I gave him a quick kiss, then leaned back in my seat, getting comfortable.

Joe drove down Second Avenue, one hand on the steering wheel, the other fiddling with the radio dial. He landed on John Mellencamp singing "Wild Night" and immediately joined in, belting out the lyrics. It was a little loud for so early in the morning, but his enthusiasm was infectious. I looked out my window and smiled, feeling a contentment that bordered on excitement. Getting out of the city was always a thrill, especially in the summertime when you were with a guy you liked. *Really* liked. Life was good, I told myself, and a few minutes later, as we merged onto the Long Island Expressway, I was singing along, too.

The next two hours passed quickly, as Joe and I laughed and talked and listened to music. Occasionally I'd feel myself start to fret about the introductions to come, but for the most part, I kept my anxiety at bay. I wasn't one to put my foot in my mouth—I was too circumspect for such missteps. It was all going to be fine. Or maybe it wasn't. Either way, I would survive.

BY THE TIME we reached the windmill at Halsey Lane, the effects of my pep talk to myself had expired, and the high of our road trip was replaced by a sinking dread. To be fair, it was the effect the Hamptons always had on me, even when I wasn't headed there to meet Dottie Kingsley. It could be really fun—and was undeniably beautiful—but it was also exhausting. Everywhere you looked, there were bankers and lawyers and PR types, and, yes, models, all jockeying for position, frantically trying to figure out where to go, what to wear, and how to gain entry to the hottest restaurants, clubs, and parties. Like one big casting call. Even though I had opted out of the scene years ago, and my memories of all those pretentious White Parties were in the distant past, there was no way to pretend that I wasn't now headed into the biggest audition of my life.

As we pulled down a residential road marked PRIVATE, Joe waved to a man sitting in a Buick, reading a newspaper. He slowed to a stop, wound down his window, and yelled, "What's up, Hank?"

"Same old! Good to see you, Joe!"

Joe waved again, then kept driving, telling me that Hank had been with his family for years.

"Is he a security guard?" I asked.

"He does it all. Handyman. Gardener. Gatekeeper," Joe said as we reached the end of the road and the entrance to the Kingsley driveway.

Joe turned on to it, but I couldn't see anything, the property screened by tall privacy hedges.

"Here we go," Joe said, pulling through an open gate. "Home, sweet home."

Conjuring images from my mother's old magazines, I knew it would be impressive. But as the sprawling waterfront property came into view, I caught my breath. It was so much more spectacular in person, the way photographed landmarks often are. The "Kingsley compound" comprised three buildings, all gleaming white clapboard. The main house was a mansion by any measure. It had a wide front porch and green-and-white striped awning and managed to be both grand and charming at once. It was flanked by two smaller buildings, which Joe said were the pool house and guest cottage.

"Wow. It's beautiful," I said, overwhelmed by the explosion of color—the impeccable green lawn, the pink roses climbing white trellises, the purple hydrangeas blooming all over the yard, and the backdrop of vivid blue sky and sea meeting on the horizon.

"Yeah. It's pretty special," Joe said as he parked, acknowledging that even he realized this wasn't your typical *Hamptons* beautiful.

His voice and smile were both soft, nearly reverent, and I couldn't help thinking of his father and the weight of his family's history, especially as I looked up and saw an American flag flying from a pole in the center of the lawn.

"When was it built?" I asked, wanting to know, but also stalling, not quite ready to get out of the car.

"Nineteen ten," he said. "My grandfather built it."

"He did?" I said, impressed.

"Well, no." Joe chuckled. "He *had* it built."

"Oh, yes, of course," I said. "And now your whole family shares it?"

"Yeah," Joe said.

"How does that work with all the cousins?" I asked, still stalling. "Are there sign-ups for certain weekends?"

"Not really," Joe said. He opened his door, stepping onto the crushed seashell drive, then letting Thursday out of the car. "We just sort of make it work. It's more fun when we're all here together anyway."

I smiled to myself, amused by the notion of making a massive waterfront estate in the Hamptons "work," then reluctantly opened my door while Joe retrieved our bags from the backseat. I tried to take my own, but he wouldn't let me, so I followed him and Thursday down the path instead, then climbed the stairs leading up to the porch of the main house. When we got to the door, Joe motioned for me to go in first, both of his hands full.

I took a breath and opened the door, holding it for Joe. The foyer was dimly lit with a faded floral wallpaper that surprised me until I remembered Curtis's theory. These people had nothing to prove.

"Hell-oooo?" Joe called out, dropping our bags at the foot of a wide staircase that turned ninety degrees at midflight. When nobody replied, he mumbled that they must be out back, then led me down a long hallway, passing two large rooms filled with dark antiques, sun-faded upholstered furniture, and wall-to-wall bookcases. Other than in a library, I'd never seen so many books.

As we reached the back porch, I got unexpected goosebumps from both the sweeping view and the fresh realization that I was here, in this famed setting. Tucked into a vast green lawn the length and width of a football field was a turquoise pool surrounded by stone decking, a tennis court lined with more hedges, and gorgeous formal gardens. Beyond the manicured perfection was the curved, rugged shoreline and an endless stretch of sparkling water dotted with colorful boats, the sails of which Joe would later refer to as spinnakers, a word I loved the sound of.

"There they are!" Joe said, pointing to a row of white Adirondack chairs in the far corner of the yard, two of them occupied.

My stomach dropped a little in anticipation as Joe cupped his mouth with his hands, then belted out a hello. Dottie and Berry turned and waved, then stood in unison and began slowly walking toward us as Thursday raced around the yard. Berry trailed one step behind Dottie, and I thought of the Queen of England, wondering if this family followed similar protocol. As they approached the porch, I could see they were both wearing shift dresses— Dottie's lemon yellow and Berry's a mix of pastel blues and pinks—and I fleetingly questioned my outfit. I reminded myself I needed to be me—it was the only way.

"C'mon," Joe said, taking my hand, leading me down the porch steps and across the lawn. His grip was firmer than usual, as if he could tell that I was nervous. Or maybe *he* was.

"Well, you made good time!" Dottie said as she neared us. I instantly recognized her voice, from where, I wasn't sure. Maybe it was a documentary or an episode of *60 Minutes* that my mom had forced me to watch. It was surreal, being here in front of a woman whom I was just meeting, yet felt like I knew so much about.

"Yes. I think it was a record!" Joe said, squeezing my hand.

"I hope you weren't speeding," his mother said, as we closed the gap.

"Only a little bit!" Joe said, grinning.

He let go of my hand, then gave his mother a formal hug and kiss on the cheek. I waited for him to do the same with Berry, but instead he reached out and mussed her hair. She pushed his hand away and laughed, and I could instantly feel their close rapport.

"Mother and Berry . . . this is Cate," Joe said. "Cate, this is my mother and Berry."

I pushed my sunglasses up onto my hair, headband style, but instantly regretted it, both because the sun was now in my eyes and because Dottie and Berry kept their glasses on. Not wanting to fidget or appear nervous, I lived with my decision, squinting into the sun as Dottie gracefully extended her slender arm to shake my hand.

"Cate," she said, making my name its own sentence. Her fingers were delicate and birdlike, her skin oddly cool given all the sunlight. "How do you do?"

For some reason, the wording of her simple question flustered me, and I stumbled over my reply. "I'm well, thank you. . . . It's so nice to meet you . . . both of you," I said, shifting my gaze to Berry.

"The pleasure is all ours," Dottie said in a tone that went along with her handshake. Not quite aloof, but close. Her oversize glasses were dark, covering much of her face, but I could still make out her chiseled cheekbones, which Joe had inherited. Like the estate itself, she was more striking in person and almost formidable, despite her small stature.

"Yes," Berry said in a cheerful voice, stepping forward to give me a quick hug. "We've heard *so* much about you, Cate."

"Likewise," I said, a word I don't think I'd ever used before. "Thank you for the invitation, Mrs. Kingsley. Your home is so *lovely*." It was another word I seldom used.

Dottie nodded in response, as if I'd just stated a fact rather than given her a compliment, then said, "We're so pleased you could come for a visit. . . . Shall we go in? Are you hungry after your drive?"

What was the polite answer—yes or no? Fortunately, Joe chimed in for us, announcing that he was starving.

As we all made our way back into the house, I braced myself for a formal brunch served in the dining room on a table set with silver and crystal. I was both surprised and relieved to find that we were eating on a farmhouse table just off the kitchen, with simple place settings and some baked goods, fruit, and a pitcher of orange juice that looked freshly squeezed.

"There's a fresh pot of coffee in the kitchen," Berry said.

"And I can put the kettle on if you prefer tea?" Dottie said, looking at me.

I politely declined both as we all went to the table, sat down, and began serving ourselves. No one spoke for an awkward moment. Then Dottie turned to me and smiled.

"So, Cate, Joe tells us you grew up in Montclair?" she said, using her fork, European style, to pierce a strawberry half.

"Yes," I said.

"That's a lovely town," she said. "Do your parents still live there?"

"Yes," I said. "Well, my mother and stepfather."

"I see," she said. "And your father?"

"He actually passed away when I was quite young."

"Oh, I'm so sorry," Dottie said, cutting her eyes to her son as if to say he should have warned her.

"Thank you," I said, looking down, wondering if I should acknowledge her loss as well. Or Berry's, for that matter, as Joe had told me that she'd lost both of her parents in a plane crash. But I decided that it was better to move on from the gruesome accidents that united us.

Apparently, Berry felt the same because she quickly changed the subject. "Joe tells us that you work in fashion," she said as she spread cream cheese on her bagel half.

It was more of a statement than a question, but I answered it anyway. "Yes," I said, nodding. "I do."

"I'm sorry—I forgot the designer's name?" she said.

"Wilbur Swift," I said.

"That's right. Sorry. I'm clueless about fashion—much to Dottie's horror."

"Oh, Berry," Dottie said, shaking her head. "You know that's not true."

"That I'm clueless or that you're horrified?" Berry said with a laugh.

"Neither is true! . . . Now, *Joe* is another story," Dottie said.

"Heey, now! I resent that!" Joe said, pretending to be offended, but looking oddly proud of himself.

Dottie ignored him and looked at me. "Cate, I do hope you'll be able to assist him on that front."

"I'm trying, Mrs. Kingsley," I said, playing along.

Joe laughed and accused us of being jealous of his style.

"*What* style?" Berry said.

The two sparred for a few seconds, sounding like brother and sister, before Dottie cut in. "And how is *your* job going, Joe?" she said, eyebrows raised.

Joe avoided her gaze, taking a huge bite of a donut. "It's okay," he said with a shrug, powdered sugar on his lower lip.

Dottie stared back at him. "Just . . . *okay*?"

"Yeah," Joe said. "I'm thinking of requesting a transfer to another division. Maybe white-collar crime."

"Why white-collar crime?" she asked. "Is it more prestigious than doing drugs?"

"Yeah. Well, Mother, doing drugs isn't prestigious at all," Joe deadpanned. "In fact, there is quite a stigma attached to it."

"Oh, Joseph," Dottie said, waving him off. "You know what I meant. Would this be a promotion?"

"No, Mother," he said, speaking slowly, his jaw tensing. "It wouldn't be a promotion. It's just a different division. . . . I'm tired of prosecuting petty drug offenses that, for the most part, seem racially motivated. Gary agrees."

Dottie nodded and said, "Would it be better in terms of making political connections? Ultimately running for office?"

Joe shrugged, and Dottie said, "What do you think, Cate?"

"About moving to white-collar crime?" I said, meeting her gaze, wondering why I felt so nervous.

Dottie shook her head and said, "No. About Joe running for office one day?"

I could feel everyone staring at me as I stumbled over my reply. "Umm. I don't know," I said. "I mean . . . I think he'd make a great . . . politician . . . you know . . . if that's what he wants to do."

"Key word being *if*," Joe mumbled.

Dottie pretended not to hear him as she kept staring at me. "Yes. I agree, Cate," she said. "I think he'd be wonderful. He has so much to offer—and could really make a difference."

For a few seconds, the mood at the table seemed a little awkward. Then Berry righted the ship, chatting breezily about Joe's cousin Peter's recent engagement and the spring wedding he and his fiancée, Genevieve, were planning in her hometown of Annapolis, Maryland. I listened, wondering if I'd be attending. I could only hope that I would.

AFTER BRUNCH, JOE and I went to our respective bedrooms to freshen up and change into swimsuits. I wasn't exactly sure of our agenda, only that we were going out on his boat, and that it was just the two of us. I'd been on boats before, but only the extremes— either yachts for modeling shoots or tacky river cruises with tour guides telling bad jokes amid nauseating gasoline fumes. So I wasn't exactly sure what to expect or what to wear. I played it safe, changing into a tankini with a cover-up and a pair of leather sandals. Then, deciding I looked a bit too bland, I pulled the Hermès scarf Joe had given me out of my bag, folded it in half, and wrapped it around my head, tying a double knot under my ponytail.

When I finally opened my door, Joe was waiting for me in the hall.

"Hey, baby," he said, grinning at me. "I like your scarf."

"Why, thank you," I said, reaching up to touch it. "This hot guy gave it to me in Paris."

"Wow." He grinned again. "He must *really* like you, huh?"

"Seems that way," I said.

IT TOOK SOME time to get to the marina, and even longer to get Joe's boat freed from the dock. It reminded me of snow skiing— the one time I went, I couldn't *believe* all the effort that was required just to get onto the slopes. It didn't seem worth the trouble, and it kept crossing my mind that I'd rather be sitting on the beach with a good book.

Once Joe and I were out on the sparkling water, though, with an ocean breeze on our faces, it all made sense, and I almost understood why these people loved their boats as much as they did. It really was exhilarating, and my heart raced as Joe revved his engine and sped toward the horizon under the brightest blue sky painted with thin, wispy clouds.

As gorgeous as the views were—in every direction—it was hard to take my eyes off Joe. I don't think I'd ever seen him look sexier than he did driving his boat, one hand on the steering wheel, the other reaching up to keep his backward baseball cap in place as he took sharp turns in the water, showing off. Gripping the top of the windshield on the center console, I yelled for him to slow down, but he only laughed and went faster as we got wet from the sea spray. I rationally knew we weren't in any real danger—that Joe knew what he was doing—but there were moments I still felt a little scared. It was the *good* kind of scared, though. An adrenaline rush from the beautiful world and this beautiful man.

After Joe got the speed out of his system, we turned around, heading toward the shore. I thought maybe we were going back to the dock, but instead we puttered up and down a series of peaceful inlets. Along the way Joe occasionally let me steer as he told stories. Some were about his father and grandfather, family lore passed down to him. But he also shared his own memories, which ranged from simple and sweet to outlandish and braggadocious. There was even one tale of a near-death experience involving kayaking in a storm. I listened, marveling over both his stupidity and his bravery. I was especially fascinated by the reaction from his mother and Berry; his mother had been terrified, and Berry only angry. It was a dynamic I could perfectly picture after having met them.

As if reading my mind, Joe suddenly asked what I thought about them.

"I *love* them," I blurted out. It was a bit of an overstatement, yet still felt sincere, perhaps because my heart felt so full.

Joe looked relieved. "You *do*?"

"Yes. Berry's really sweet." I hesitated, then added, "Honestly, I didn't expect that. I knew she'd be nice, but I thought she would be a bit . . . *harder* on me."

Joe nodded, not bothering to play dumb, which I appreciated. "Yes. She can be very protective . . . but I could tell she loved you, too."

I smiled and told him that made me happy.

"And what about my mother? Do you see what I mean about her? She didn't last twenty minutes without grilling me about running for office. It's relentless."

"Yeah," I said. "But she just wants the best for you—and thinks that you could use your name to make a difference. You really would make a great public servant."

"Oh, I like that description," Joe said. "It sounds better than politician . . . and you really think so?"

"Yes. You genuinely care about people. You care about the cases you prosecute and you care about why defendants find themselves in situations that lead them to commit crimes," I said, feeling a wave of pride in him. He was such a good person. "I love that about you."

"Wow. That's really nice. Thank you," he said as we entered the most picturesque cove. The shore was rocky, and the water like glass. For the next few minutes, we idled along, taking in the scenery. Then Joe cut the engine and announced that this was the perfect spot for a picnic. He walked around the console to the front of the boat, reached for the anchor, and tossed it into the water. I watched as he quickly and expertly tied some fancy nautical knot, thinking what a turn-on it was when a man was so good at something.

He glanced up, catching me staring at him, and smiled. "What?"

"I was wondering whether you were a Boy Scout."

Joe laughed and said, "What were you *really* thinking?"

I swallowed, feeling myself blush as I put my hand on his tanned forearm and said, "Okay, yes. I was thinking that watching you tie a knot is kind of sexy."

Joe laughed.

I smiled as he moved to the back of the boat, spread a towel on the floorboards, and asked me to join him. I sat down, watching as he got to work unpacking a small cooler.

"When did you put this together?" I asked, impressed with his organization.

"I didn't. I begged Berry to pick it up from a store in town," he said, opening a bottle of chilled white wine with a corkscrew and pouring it into plastic cups. He handed me one, then took his sunglasses off, hitching them on the collar of his shirt.

"To us," he said, raising his cup with a soulful expression.

"To us," I repeated, tapping the edge of my cup against his.

For the next thirty minutes or so, we sipped wine and ate grapes and cheese and crackers and little cucumber sandwiches, talking and laughing.

At some point, my buzz kicked in, the talking turned into kissing, then full-on making out.

"Is this safe?" I whispered at one point as he slid his hand under my swimsuit top, then pulled it up and kissed one breast while he palmed the other.

"Yes," he said. "It's totally private back here."

"What about long-range cameras?" I said, thinking of all the celebrities who had been photographed topless on vacations.

"There's nobody out here, babe," he said, now taking my hand and pressing it against his erection.

He let out a low moan that made me wetter than I already was, and I knew then what was going to happen. Sure enough, Joe laid me on my back, pulling down my bathing suit bottom. He slid one finger slowly inside me, then took it out even more slowly before putting it in his mouth. Then he went down on me.

It was so good—*too* good—and I begged him to stop even as I held on to his head, my hands running through his hair. Then, just as I was on the brink of exploding, he pulled down his swim trunks, climbed on top of me, and slowly entered me.

"How?" he whispered when he was the whole way in. "How is it *this* perfect?"

"Because it's us," I said, breathless.

"Yes. Because. It's. Us," he said, thrusting inside me with each word as the boat began to sway, then rock, water slapping against the sides.

I stared up at the sky, watching the clouds drift along, feeling completely helpless as Joe talked to me in a low voice, telling me that I was his. I belonged to him. He belonged to me. His voice in my ear made me come so fast and hard, and as I dug my hands into his back, he came, too, saying my name over and over.

Afterward, we lay there together for the longest time, sweating and catching our breath. The sun was hot, but there was a breeze, and we both fell asleep. I'm not sure how much time passed, but when we woke up, we put our suits back on. Then Joe sat up and said it was time for a swim.

"Wait," I said. "Aren't there sharks?"

He laughed and said, "Tons. But I'm brave like that."

I couldn't tell if he was joking. "Seriously! Tell me, Joe!" I said, as he stood at the back of the boat, preparing to jump into the water. "Are there sharks?"

"I've never seen a shark in *this* cove," he said. "But you never know. There's a first time for everything!"

Wondering if it was the first time he'd had sex in this boat, I stood and moved toward him, then looked nervously down into the water. I couldn't see the bottom. "How deep is it?"

"About ten feet," he said. A second later, he was diving in. As he swam just below the surface, I admired the lines of his body. When he finally emerged, he shook the water from his hair, grinning up at me. "Get in here!" he said. "It feels *so* good."

It was something people always claimed after jumping into cold water; I wasn't buying it. "I'll pass," I said.

"You're not going to swim?" he asked.

It was the last thing I wanted to do. Beyond the fact that I knew it would be cold, I didn't want to embarrass myself. I knew how to swim, but barely—and had a distinct memory of failing a water treading test in the swim unit of ninth-grade gym class. I couldn't believe how exhausting it had been to simply stay afloat.

But Joe kept begging me, and I didn't want to be *that* girl. So I asked if there was a ladder.

"A ladder?" He laughed, doing a backstroke behind the boat. "There is no ladder, baby. Just jump in."

"Well, then how would I get back into the boat?"

"There's a little swim platform back here. See?" he said.

I looked down and nodded.

"C'mon. Just get in. *Now.*"

I could tell then that he wasn't going to give up, so I took a deep breath and climbed over the back of the boat, then slowly eased myself down onto the teak platform that was like a little bench just above the ocean surface. Dangling my legs into the cold water, I kicked them, hoping that this would be enough to appease Joe. I didn't want to confess to another shortcoming. But he swam over to me, grabbed my calves, and tried to pull me in.

At that point, I panicked and blurted out the truth. "Joe, no! I can't swim!"

His smile turned to surprise, then concern. "You can't *swim*?" he said, now half out of the water, his arms on either side of my thighs.

"Well, I can a little bit," I said. "But not very well. And I just . . . I don't like deep water."

"Well, we need to fix that, baby," he said.

I nodded, so embarrassed, as Joe heaved himself out of the water onto the platform beside me and said, "Everyone needs to know how to swim. It's just not safe—"

"It's safe if I stay away from the water," I said, cutting him off with a smile.

"But, Cate," he said. "Don't you love it out here?"

I nodded and said that I did, very much.

"So, we'll get you lessons. Or I can teach you. Hell. Why don't we start now?"

I shook my head, starting to panic, knowing how persuasive he could be. "Not today. Please? Another day. Soon."

"Okay," he said. "We should probably start in a pool anyway."

"Yes. Definitely a pool. Where I can see the bottom. And there are no sharks."

Joe climbed back into the boat, then pulled me up after him. He grabbed a fresh towel and wrapped it around me, even though he was the wet one.

"I'm sorry—" I said.

"For *what*?"

"That I can't swim," I said.

"Whatever," Joe said, shaking his head. "You're exactly what I want."

I nodded, feeling a little better, remembering what we'd just done.

"Cate?" Joe whispered, cupping my face.

"Yes?" I said.

"I love you," he whispered into my ear.

I inhaled, too overwhelmed with emotion to exhale, let alone speak, but finally found my breath and voice. "I love you, too," I whispered back.

He leaned down and gave me a long, slow kiss that felt like a seal on our joint declaration.

And just like that, for the very first time, I began to imagine a future with Joe.

CHAPTER 19

Joe

It was the most beautiful, sunny day, perfect for Cate's first spin in my boat. I was on a complete high as I showed her all around (and showed off some, too). Then, just when I thought things couldn't get any better, we anchored in a quiet cove and made love on the water before falling asleep in each other's arms. When we woke up, I went swimming, burning off nervous energy, because I knew that it was time to tell her. I couldn't wait another day.

Back in the boat, I finally said it: *I love you*. Just like that. I could see in her eyes that she felt the same, but I still felt as if my heart might explode in my chest as she said the words back to me.

WHEN WE GOT home, Cate and I found Berry on the back porch playing solitaire at a small square table we called our "puzzle table." Right away, I could tell she was in some sort of a mood, as she barely looked up from her cards, curtly answering my questions about her day ("it was fine") and my mother's whereabouts ("she's resting"). It was very uncomfortable and a little rude.

A few more seconds passed before Cate quietly excused herself, saying she was going upstairs to shower. As she slipped into the house, it crossed my mind to follow her and reassure her that Berry just got melancholy sometimes—and that when she did, she could come across as dismissive. But a small, paranoid part of me worried that I'd done something to upset her. Had I not been appreciative enough about the picnic lunch she'd picked up for me? Should I have asked her to join us on the boat? I sat down beside her, waiting for her to look up.

When she didn't, I cleared my throat and said, "Are you winning?"

Berry nodded, and in the next few seconds, she finished the game in a flurry of activity. I watched as she swept up the cards and began to shuffle, her eyes still down.

"Okay, Berry. What's going on?" I asked in a quiet voice. "Did something happen today?"

"Yes," she said, finally meeting my gaze. "You could say that."

"And? Do you care to share it with me?" I said, trying to be patient but feeling the first hint of annoyance. It turned into full-on aggravation when she just shrugged.

Berry let out a weary sigh, as if I were the one testing *her* patience, then motioned for me to close the door. I leaned back in my chair, pushing it shut. Then I crossed my arms over my chest, waiting.

Several more seconds passed before she said, "Did you know that she grew up obsessed with you?"

I stared back at her, completely confused. "What are you talking about? Who's *she*?"

"Cate," Berry hissed under her breath. "She had a *poster* of you in her bedroom. Up on her wall. She and her mother were both obsessed with you. Still are."

"That's nuts," I said, my voice low and even, though I could feel my heart starting to race.

"Sorry. But it's *true*," Berry said.

"How the hell do you know?" I snapped.

"It's in the *National Enquirer*."

"Are you *kidding* me?" I said, my voice louder. "The *National Enquirer*?! When did you start reading tabloids?"

"It's a quote from Cate's own *mother*."

"And the *National Enquirer* never makes up quotes?"

"There are pictures, too. Of Cate's mother with her Kingsley memorabilia. You have to see it."

"First of all, I'm not looking at that shit," I said. "Second of all, I'd bet a thousand bucks that they lied or twisted the truth or somehow tricked her mother into saying it. And third of all, even if it's true, and Cate had a life-size poster of me in her room as a kid, so what? What does that have to do with our relationship now?"

Berry stared at me, blinking, a self-righteous look on her face. "Well, let me ask you this, Joe."

I stared back at her, waiting.

"Did she ever tell you any of this?" she asked.

"You're assuming it's true!"

"I saw photographs!"

"Of Cate's room when she was a child?"

"No. But of her mother and all the memorabilia. Did she ever mention that backstory?"

"Backstory? You mean that her mother collects shit? Like a lot of Americans? I mean, my father *was* a war hero, you know?"

"But *you* weren't."

"Yeah, Berry. I got that. Thanks."

"Oh, c'mon, Joe. We're not playing that game right now—"

"That game?" I said. "Wow. Okay. Got it."

"We aren't talking about your father right now, Joe! We're talking about the fact that she grew up obsessed with *you*. And had pictures of you in her room. Did she tell you any of that?"

"No, that hasn't come up, Berry. We have other things to talk about, fortunately."

"And you don't think this is a significant omission on her part?"

"No," I said. "I really don't."

"So you aren't at all suspicious?"

"*Suspicious?* Of what?"

"Of her intentions."

"Her intentions? She loves me!"

"Well, yes, I gathered that. . . . Clearly she was on a mission—"

"Whatever, Berry! We met *randomly*. I walked by her on the friggin' beach. I went up to *her*. . . . If anything, I was the one on a mission. She turned me down for the longest time. I flew to Paris to take her out, for goodness' sakes."

Berry stared back at me, shaking her head.

"I *did*," I said. "That's what happened. Those are the facts."

"Well, clearly it was an effective strategy on her part," she said. "Playing hard to get or whatever."

"She wasn't playing hard to get. . . . She *was* hard to get. . . . She was reluctant to go out with me."

Berry rolled her eyes. "Yeah, right."

"She *was*, Berry! She had a boyfriend."

"She had a *boyfriend*?" she said, as if this were yet another piece of pivotal evidence. "I didn't know that."

"I'm sorry I didn't fill you in on her entire dating history, along with all the details of her childhood."

Berry blinked. "Did she cheat on him?"

"No. She broke up with him, and then went out with me," I said, fudging the time line a bit. "Why are you making such a big deal out of this?"

"Are you actually trying to tell me that you don't see this poster thing as a red flag?"

"No," I said, ready to die on the sword. "I don't."

"So, this woman—Cate's mother—has a Kingsley obsession, and she raises her daughter to feel the same. And then, years later, she just happens to fall in love with you . . . for *you*?"

"Is that really so hard for you to believe? That someone would love me?"

"That's not what I'm saying, and you know it."

"Then what are you saying?"

"I'm saying it's oddly coincidental that she grew up with this crush on you . . . and is now *dating* you. . . . And for the record, Dottie agrees."

"Oh, for Christ's sakes, Berry! You showed my *mother* a *National Enquirer* article smearing my girlfriend? Really?"

"We just want what's best for you, Joe. We just want you to be careful. You can be too trusting—"

"Don't tell me to be careful!" I shouted at her. "It's condescending and insulting."

She started to say something about always having my back and being on my side, but I was no longer listening. Instead, I got up and walked back into the house, slamming the porch door as I went.

If Berry wanted to talk about *sides,* I could pick a side. In fact, I already had.

A MINUTE LATER I was outside Cate's door. I knocked once, then walked in before she could answer and saw her standing by the window, wrapped in a towel. She looked so beautiful, and for one second, I forgot my anger. Then she asked if Berry was okay—and I knew in that instant that we had to go. We couldn't stay here.

I took a deep breath and said, "Not really. But it's sort of a long story. I'll tell you everything in the car. . . . I want to go—"

"Go where?" she said, walking over to me, finger combing her wet hair.

"Back to the city."

Frowning, she said, "Wait. What? You want to go home?"

"Yeah."

"Why? What happened?"

"I'll tell you in the car. Just trust me. We need to go."

ABOUT TEN MINUTES later, Cate and I were both changed, packed up, and in the car, with Thursday and our bags in the backseat. Fortunately for my mother's and Berry's sakes, I didn't see them as we left the house. Otherwise, there might have been a scene—which they couldn't stand. They much preferred to talk shit behind people's backs.

As Cate and I got on the main road, it occurred to me that in leaving I was ratcheting up the drama. I also knew I was being hotheaded and stubborn. But it felt like my only choice. I had to stand up for the woman I loved. What Berry had implied about her was so unbelievably unfair, and I wasn't going to hang around and take it.

Several minutes of silence passed before Cate spoke. "Do you want to tell me what's going on?"

It was the last thing I felt like doing, but I knew I had to tell her the truth. We were a team, and that was how it was going to be.

I gripped the steering wheel, took a deep breath, and said,

"Apparently there was a hit job about you in the *National Enquirer*."

"Oh, God," she whispered. "What did it say?"

"I didn't see it. But Berry said there's some quote from your mother," I said, glancing at her.

Cate looked horrified. "My *mother*?"

"Yeah. But they make stuff up all the time. Including quotes."

"What did my mother say? What was the quote?"

"Her *alleged* quote . . ." I said, glancing over at her face and seeing her expression of pure anguish.

"Joe. Just tell me."

I slowly inhaled, filling my lungs to capacity, before blowing out. "She allegedly said that you had a poster of me in your room when you were a kid . . . and that she collected stuff about my family. . . ."

"Shit. *Unreal*," she said, under her breath, as if talking to herself. She turned to look out her window so that I could no longer see her face.

"I know," I said. "It *is* unreal. That's what I told Berry . . . that I don't believe any of it."

"Actually," Cate said in a small voice, still staring out her window. "It *is* true. I *did* have a poster of you in my room. A long time ago."

My heart sank—not because I saw this as a red flag, but because I knew so many other people would. Hell, my own best friend and my mother did.

"I'm sorry," she said. "I should have told you."

"It's okay," I said, though I did wish that Cate had told me about it first. I hated learning anything about her secondhand like this. "This doesn't change anything."

"I feel like it does," she said.

"No, it doesn't. It *really* doesn't. You were just a kid. . . . And anyway, I'm flattered. You had good taste."

"Stop it, Joe. You're not *flattered*. It probably seems so creepy—"

"No, it doesn't. I swear—"

I kept glancing at her, but she wouldn't look my way, so I suddenly veered off the main road, turning down a side street. I pulled over to the curb in front of a random house and parked the car.

"Please, Cate," I said, shifting in my seat to stare at her. "Please look at me."

It took a few more seconds, but she finally met my gaze. Her cheeks were bright red, and she looked like she was on the verge of tears.

"Oh, honey," I said. "Don't be upset."

"I can't help it, Joe."

"Okay. But can you just . . . talk to me?"

"I don't know what to say."

"Tell me how you're feeling. . . ."

"How do you *think* I'm feeling?" she said, her voice breaking up. "How would *you* feel if your mother talked to the *National Enquirer* about you?"

"Awful," I said. "I'd feel awful."

"Yes. That's the word for it."

"But I'm sure she didn't mean any harm. I'm sure she thought she was just sharing a cute story," I said. "And it *is* cute."

"Stop it," she said, closing her eyes and pressing both hands to her temples. "It's not cute. It's *mortifying*. And it gives the totally wrong impression."

"Not to me."

"It does to Berry. And your mother."

"Who cares?"

"*I* care. And so do you. I know you do."

"I care about you way more."

"What did Berry say?" she asked.

I shook my head and sighed. "She's just protective of me. That's all."

"Tell me what she said, Joe. Please."

I sighed again, then said, "She called it a 'red flag.' "

"*Shit*," Cate whispered, biting her lip. "She thinks I'm some kind of star fucker—"

"Don't say that—"

"Gold digger—"

"Stop. No."

Cate closed her eyes and shook her head.

"Look, Cate. She doesn't know you," I said. "She'll come around. I told her it was a load of crap. And honestly, I probably should have stayed and talked through everything. But I just got pissed—"

"Did your mother see the article?"

"Yeah," I said. "Berry showed it to her."

"Does she think it's a red flag, too?"

"I don't really know. I didn't see her before we left."

Cate nodded, then asked a question that broke my heart. "Are you embarrassed to be with me?"

"No!" I said as forcefully as I could. "I'm proud to be with you. *So* proud. And I couldn't care less what the tabloids say. I left to make a point. I'm sick of Berry and my mother getting involved in my life, and I'm not putting up with this crap anymore. These stupid concerns about my name and reputation and appearances and what people think . . . It's all just nonsense. . . . I just want to be happy. And you make me happy."

Cate hesitated, then stared into my eyes, and said, "You make me happy, too, Joe. . . . But—"

"But *nothing*," I said. "Please don't let this affect us. Please."

"Okay," she said. "I'll try not to."

I took off my seatbelt and leaned over to give her a big hug. She hugged me back, but whispered in my ear that she was sorry.

"Don't be, baby. You didn't do anything."

"Okay," she said as we separated. "But I'm going to kill my mother."

I shook my head and said, "No. It's not her fault, either. The tabloids manipulate people all the time. We just need to talk to her and explain, so that this doesn't happen again. . . . We need to protect her."

"I'll talk to her," Cate said.

"No. *We* will," I said. "We're in this together, Cate. Me and you."

CHAPTER 20

Cate

I f someone had told me to brainstorm worst-case scenarios, I'm not sure I could have come up with anything more horrible than my own mother selling me out to the *National Enquirer*. Giving any sort of interview would have been bad, but my mom took it to another level, announcing to the world that I had grown up with a huge crush on Joe and that she had fueled that interest with her own lifelong Kingsley obsession. Of course, it also happened to be the *truth,* which made it so much worse. There was nothing I could deny when Joe told me about it.

Instead, I fumbled my way through the humiliating confession. For a moment, I wondered whether it would be the end of us. I could easily imagine that Joe would be so turned off by it all that I'd lose him. Instead, he sweetly insisted that he was flattered—and all his wrath seemed directed Berry's way. I was a little touched by how chivalrous he was being, but the fact that he felt the need to so fiercely defend my honor, making the unilateral decision to leave the Hamptons, only made me more embarrassed.

For most of the ride home, I was too distraught to talk. I stared out my window, my mind racing with paranoid thoughts that I was reluctant to put into words.

But as we approached Manhattan, I turned to him and said, "Are you sure you aren't a little upset with me?"

Joe looked surprised by the question, which was something of a comfort. "Yes, I'm sure. Why would I be upset with you?"

"I don't know. . . . Because of the poster."

"A poster you had when you were a little girl?"

"A poster I didn't tell you about."

"That's not important," he said. "It's trivial."

"Then why did we leave in such a hurry? If you aren't upset?"

"You asked if I was upset with *you*. And I'm not. But I *am* upset with Berry. And my mother."

"Why? It's not their fault that my mom spoke to a tabloid." I was playing devil's advocate—but also trying to understand exactly what had gone down, as well as the intimate dynamic among the three of them.

Joe hesitated, frowning out the front window as if deep in thought. "I really don't see why Berry felt the need to read that crap when she had just met you herself. Especially because she's the first one to rail on the tabloids."

"Well, isn't that kind of natural?" I said, trying so hard to be fair. "I feel like I might take a peek, too, you know?"

"Fair enough, I guess. But she didn't have to buy it, bring it home, and show it to my mother."

"Okay. But why not just laugh it off and move on? Instead of storming out?"

"Because they drew false conclusions—that you'd been some superfan stalking me. It's absurd."

"But if it's so absurd, why get so pissed? Doesn't that just give her accusations credence? What if the tabloid said I was an alien? Without a belly button?"

Joe smiled. "Holy cow. Where do you come up with this stuff?"

I shrugged, then said, "Well? If the article had said that, would you have left in a huff?"

"It depends," Joe said. "If Berry believed it? Maybe."

I shook my head and said, "I don't think so. I think you would have laughed in her face and moved right on."

"So what are you trying to say?"

"I'm saying—that maybe you're not just upset with what Berry thinks. . . . Maybe you're upset because, deep down, you think it, too."

"That's not true," Joe said a little too quickly.

"Okay . . . but did you really feel that I needed such staunch defending?"

"*Needed?* No. I don't think you *needed* it. But I think you *deserved* it. It's not fair what she was implying about you—"

"I know it's not," I said, so appreciating his loyalty and steadfast sense of justice. Hell, basic fairness. "But I still don't want you fighting with your family because of me."

Joe shook his head and said, "I'm not fighting with my family because of *you*. I'm fighting because of *them*. Their attitude . . . their judgment . . . and that has really nothing to do with you. It's been going on for years, on a myriad of topics. And I had to draw a line in the sand."

"Thank you," I said—because I hadn't said it yet.

He shook his head and said, "Don't thank me. It's so basic. You'd do the same for me, wouldn't you?"

"Yes. Of course I would."

"Okay, then. Please don't worry. I got this. They'll come around."

I nodded, trusting him, fighting my instinct to run and hide.

"So. My place or yours?" he asked.

"Mine," I said. "It's closer."

WHEN WE WALKED into my apartment, Elna came out of her bedroom with a look of surprise and confusion.

"Hey! What are you doing back?" She fixed her eyes on me as if Joe were invisible.

"Change of plans," I said, then segued right into an introduction, thinking that it was a little crazy that they hadn't yet met. "Elna, this is Joe. Joe, this is Elna."

They exchanged pleasantries, then Joe asked if he could use the bathroom.

"Of course," I said, pointing down the hall to my room. "You can use mine."

He nodded, then quickly left with our bags. Elna watched his back until he turned in to my room, then whispered, "What the heck is going on?"

I gave her the rundown, embarrassed all over again. Elna was predictably indignant and appalled on my behalf yet managed to soothe me a little.

"If Joe's got your back, who cares what anyone else thinks?"

"*I* care—"

"Well, *don't*," she said.

I nodded, just as Joe returned, and Elna immediately addressed the elephant in the room.

"Cate told me what happened. That was really awesome of you to defend her," she said. "Thank you for doing that."

Joe nodded and slid his arm around my waist. "Of course. *Always.*"

I reluctantly smiled, as Elna suggested we sit down. "Can I pour you guys a stiff drink? I think you need one."

"Okay," Joe said. "Twist my arm."

"Cate?" Elna said.

"I'll take one, too. Or maybe just a shot," I said with a laugh before leading Joe over to the sofa.

I was kidding, but a minute later, Elna returned with a small plastic tray. On it were three bottles of Amstel Light, already opened, and three mismatched souvenir shot glasses of a golden brown liquor.

"I was kidding about the shot!" I said, though it suddenly seemed like a good idea.

Elna shrugged and said, "Kidding or not, I think this situation calls for tequila, don't you, Joe?"

He smiled and said, "Absolutely."

She put the tray down, and said, "We don't have limes, but should I get some salt?"

"Nah," Joe said. "Let's keep it simple."

"I like your style," she said as she handed him a "Big Apple" glass, gave me one with a British flag, and took a Vegas glass for herself.

"To having shitty mothers!" she said, raising her glass. "And lest you think I'm not in the club, Joe, mine is the shittiest of them all!"

I was taken aback that she'd just gone there with Dottie. "Joe's mother isn't shitty," I said.

"Neither is yours," Joe said to me. "But they both messed up."

He then raised his glass. I followed suit, and the three of us threw back our tequila, returning the glasses to the tray in unison.

"So. Do you guys think I should call my mom?" I asked, glancing at the cordless phone resting on the end table next to me.

"Are you sure you're ready for that?" Joe said in a gentle voice.

I nodded, thinking the shot had helped.

"Okay," he said. "But don't be too hard on her. She just made a mistake."

"I disagree," Elna said. "This was more than a *mistake*. It was totally unacceptable." She shifted her gaze to me and said, "Let her *have* it."

"Whoa," Joe said with a chuckle. "Elna, remind me never to get on your bad side!"

"Just don't get on *Cate's* bad side, and you and I will be just fine." Elna was smiling, like it was a joke, but I knew better, and I could tell Joe did, too.

He gave her a solemn nod, then said, "I promise."

I took a deep breath, picked up the phone, and dialed my old home number. As I listened to it ring, I visualized the seventies green wall phone in the kitchen, willing my mom to answer it before Chip could pick it up. Instead, I heard his loathsome voice in my ear: *Toledano residence.*

"Hi, Chip. It's Cate," I said as calmly as I could, even as every muscle in my body tensed. "Is my mother there?"

"Yes. But she can't come to the phone right now."

My jaw clenched tighter. It was possible that she really *wasn't* available, but it was far more likely that she was standing right there, and he just wanted to control the situation.

"Okay," I said. "Will you please tell her to call me as soon as possible? I need to discuss something with her."

"Discuss *what*?"

I took a breath and said, "Were you aware that my mother talked to the *National Enquirer*?"

"Yep. I am aware," Chip said proudly.

In that second, I knew he'd had his hand in this. Hell, he probably called the paper himself.

I took a deep breath to steady myself, but my voice still shook as I said, "So how much did they pay you?"

"Oh, it was a nice little chunk of change," Chip gloated.

I bit my lip so hard it hurt as my mind raced for a retort.

"Well, that wasn't very smart of you," I finally said. "If you had held out just a little longer, maybe a few more months, until Joe and I were even *more* serious than we are now, that information would have been worth a lot more."

Satisfying silence filled the airwaves.

"And also, fun fact: everyone knows the *National Enquirer* doesn't pay as much as, say, *People* magazine. But, oh well! Live and learn—"

Before I could finish my sentence, Chip had hung up on me, confirming my victory. I put the phone down and exhaled.

Elna spoke first. "Chip?"

I nodded.

"He's such a *dick*," she said.

"Yeah," I said, still processing everything. For one second, I felt better about my mom, even a little guilty that I had rushed to judgment. But she still shared the blame, as Elna always said about her. At most, she'd been a coconspirator; at the least, she hadn't defended me. She never did.

I glanced at Joe, who looked confused and concerned. "Was that your stepfather?" he said.

"Yes. That was my mom's *husband*. And Elna's right. He's a dick."

I knew I was in tricky territory—and that the last thing I wanted to do was air more of my family's dirty laundry. So I stopped there.

I think Elna must have sensed that Joe didn't know the truth about how I'd grown up because she quickly changed the subject. "Okay. Screw him. What should we do tonight? Can I be your third wheel?"

"Absolutely!" Joe said so enthusiastically that it warmed my heart.

"Should we call Curtis, too?" I said.

"Yes! Call Curtis," Joe said.

"Sure," Elna said, then smiled at Joe. "But warning: he probably *still* has a poster of you on his bedroom wall."

Joe laughed and a feeling of relief washed over me. Yes, my mom had let me down, and Joe's mother and Berry sucked, too. But those weren't things that either of us could control, and they certainly weren't reasons to throw in the towel on our relationship. If anything, I could feel those things bringing us closer together, and I was reminded of what I already knew. That Elna and Curtis were more my family than my actual flesh and blood were. That you can make your *own* family.

I called Curtis, filling him in on everything, including Elna's joke at his expense. He laughed, then said he'd be right over.

Over the next thirty minutes, Elna, Joe, and I finished our beers, chatting about lighthearted topics, telling Joe funny stories about Curtis. The stage was perfectly set by the time he waltzed into the living room, sat down beside Joe, and whipped out his ancient autograph book. I knew that he was just going along with the fanboy shtick, and that the book mostly contained signatures from Disney characters that he'd gathered as a kid. Honestly, it felt a bit too close for comfort to the posters-on-my-wall story line, but I bit my tongue and let Curtis be himself. I watched as he flipped open his book and handed it to Joe, along with a ballpoint pen clipped to one of the pages.

"First things first," he said, crossing his legs. "Can I please have your autograph? I'm your biggest fan—"

Elna shook her head and laughed.

"Jesus, Curtis," I said. "You don't think I've been embarrassed enough today?"

"Oh, stop!" Joe said, swatting my leg, laughing. "I'm flattered! Should I sign here on this page?"

"Yes, please. Right under Mickey's signature."

"Mickey Mantle?" Joe said.

"No, sir," Curtis said. "Mickey *Mouse.*"

Joe's eyes widened. "Wait. Hold up. You've met *Mickey Mouse?*"

"I sure have," Curtis said, sitting up straighter. "And Minnie, Pluto, Donald, and Daisy."

"How 'bout Goofy?" Joe said.

"Yes, Goofy, too."

Joe nodded, pretending to be impressed. "Where'd you run into them? Disney World? Or Land?"

"Neither. We met at the Philly Spectrum. Summer of 'seventy-four. Disney on Ice. I still get chills thinking about it," Curtis said. "Life highlight for sure. This is second."

Joe laughed and scribbled his autograph right under Mickey's, then shut the book with authority. He put it down on the coffee table in front of a beaming Curtis.

"So," Curtis said, pointing at our empty shot glasses. "It looks like I'm behind."

Joe nodded and said, "Yeah, man. Catch up."

"Okay. But I don't do shots alone. Firm policy."

"Fair," Joe said. "I'll re-up."

"Cate and El?" Curtis asked, getting to his feet.

"Might as well," I said as Elna nodded.

A few seconds later, we were all doing shots, opening more beers, and playing Curtis's favorite drinking game, Never Have I Ever. It was the grown-up version of Truth or Dare, and potentially as dangerous, especially with Curtis asking the questions. He started out easy, saying, "Never have I ever picked up a hitch-hiker."

As Joe took a sip of his beer, I knew not to be fooled. Curtis was just getting started.

"Did the person freak out when they realized it was *you*?" he asked.

Joe laughed and said, "Nah. He was cool."

"Unlike *you*," I said to Curtis.

He shrugged, then raised the stakes. "Okay. Never have I ever . . . snooped through the stuff of someone I was dating."

This time, only Curtis drank. As we all jokingly shamed him, he said, "But I always end up confessing!"

"Do you confess because you feel guilty or because you saw something that pissed you off so much you couldn't keep it to yourself?" I asked, knowing the answer.

He made a face at me, then said, "Okay. Your turn, Joe."

"No, man," he said. "You're on a roll here."

Curtis smiled, then said, "Okay. Never have I ever . . . had a one-night stand."

"Define one-night stand," Joe said.

Curtis laughed. "Well, that's a yes if I ever heard one."

"For real, though," Joe said, as I leaned in, so curious about his answer. "Definitions on this totally vary. Is it when you sleep with someone once, then never again after that? Or when you sleep with someone on the *night* you meet them and then never again?"

"The second one," Curtis said. "I think the term implies that it not only happened just once, but that it was also *impulsive*. Like on the same day you met."

"Okay, then. Phew. I'm in the clear," Joe said. While Curtis and Elna drank, I came up with a legal loophole: I'd had sex with a guy I'd met one night—but *after* the clock struck twelve. Hence two separate days. No drink for me.

"Okay. Never have I ever cheated," Curtis said.

Elna unabashedly drank; Curtis proudly abstained; and Joe

sheepishly grimaced, then asked for clarification. "On a test? Or in a relationship?"

"Either one," Curtis said, as I waited, staring Joe down.

Joe took a sip of beer.

"Which one was it?" I asked. "A test or a girl?"

"I don't have to answer that! He said *either*—"

"Okay. Well, then . . . Never have I ever cheated on a girlfriend," I said, crossing my arms and staring at him.

"Dang," Joe said, then drank again.

"Talk about red flags," I said, smiling.

"Stop that! It only happened once. And I was young! In high school!" Joe said. "And anyway, you cheated, too, Cate!"

"Never!"

"Yes, you did!" he said, then asked Curtis and Elna for their take on the Arlo situation and our first dinner in Paris.

"That wasn't a date!" I said in protest.

"Yes, it was," Curtis said. "Drink."

"Oh, whatever," I said, taking a long drink.

The game went on for a while, turning more outlandish and risqué.

Never have I ever had a friend with benefits.

Never have I ever joined the mile-high club.

Never have I ever gone down on someone in a taxi . . . or a movie theater.

Before I knew it, we were all pretty lit. I reminded Joe that our last meal had been hours and hours ago, on the boat, and suggested that we order some food.

"Nah, let's go out," he said. "Anyone in the mood for a nice steak?"

"*Yesss!*" Curtis said.

Joe started rattling off the names of high-end steak houses as Elna shook her head. "We'll never get a reservation this late."

Curtis and I made eye contact, and I could tell he was thinking what I was thinking—that any restaurant would bump Joe's party to the top of its walk-in list. I had the feeling Joe was thinking it, too—and that it embarrassed him.

"You're right, Elna," he said. "How about a burger and beer at a dive bar?"

"Even better," Curtis said, putting his boots back on.

The paparazzi crossed my mind, but I was tipsy enough not to care. Let them take pictures of us. Let them talk shit about me. I was with my people, and nothing else mattered.

Less than twenty minutes later, the four of us were walking into a random Irish pub on Second Avenue. I'd passed it many times but had never been inside. It was one of the things I loved about the city—there was always something new to discover. As my eyes adjusted to the dim lighting, I could see that the clientele was older, mostly male, and a little rough around the edges. The best part was that they were vastly more interested in the boxing match on the small screen above the bar than the fact that Joe Kingsley was in their presence. We crammed into a small booth, ordered a pitcher of beer and more fried food than we could possibly eat.

At some point, we got up and played songs on the jukebox in the back of the bar, singing and dancing to upbeat classics like "Sweet Home Alabama" and "Brown Eyed Girl" while mingling with some of the rowdier regulars. The last thing I really remember was Joe cutting in between me and an old Irish guy. He pretended to be jealous, then kissed me right in front of everyone. It was a very far cry from dinner with Dottie Kingsley in the Hamptons— not at all the way we thought the weekend would turn out. But in some ways—really *most* ways—it was even better.

CHAPTER 21

Joe

Over the next few days, my mother and Berry both left multiple messages on my answering machine, apologizing and pleading with me to call. I ignored them, and I must say, it felt good to take a stand.

At first, I could tell Cate appreciated my loyalty, and that it made her feel a little better about the whole incident, but as the days passed, she seemed to grow uneasy and encouraged me to make peace.

"They said they were sorry," she reminded me one night as we were getting ready for bed.

"They were half-assed apologies at best," I said.

"But they *were* apologies."

I pointed out that her mother had apologized, too, but that Cate was still angry at her.

"That's totally different," she said.

"How so?"

"Because my mother's defense is that she didn't 'say anything bad.'"

"Well, she has a point."

"No, she doesn't! And you *know* it, Joe. Talking to the tabloids about me—or us—is not okay. Ever."

"Yes, but shouldn't her *intentions* count for something?"

She stared at me, deep in thought. "Well, your mother and Berry had good intentions, too. They were just looking out for you."

"At *your* expense," I said.

"But I'm fine," she said. "You're *way* more upset about it than I am."

I wasn't sure if that was true, so I mumbled something about it being the principle. Which it was. I was sick and tired of my mother and Berry getting away with this stuff.

"Don't get me started about 'the principle.' My mother sold information about me to the *National* freaking *Enquirer*. She's the reason we're in this situation in the first place."

"No," I said, shaking my head. "I've been in this situation since I was born. My mother cares more about appearances than she does about me. And Berry just hops right on board with it."

"Okay," Cate said. "We're going in circles."

I nodded.

"So," she said, crossing her arms. "What do you say we make a little deal?"

"And what would *that* look like?" I said. I'd be screwed if she were my opposing counsel.

"If you make up with your mother—*and* Berry—then I'll take you home to meet mine."

I smiled because I knew she had me. "Okay," I finally said. "You've got yourself a deal."

A FEW DAYS later, I had to make a big opening argument as co-counsel in a murder trial. Cate took off work to come and watch me—which I found really touching. It was the first time she'd seen me in action, and I nailed it, if I do say so myself, probably because I knew she was there. My grandmother showed up as well, the two of them running into each other in the courtroom hallway, each recognizing the other from photos, then sitting together in the gallery. It was the best feeling in the world when I looked over and saw my two favorite people, side by side.

Afterward, my grandmother took us to dinner at Harry's of Hanover Square. She and Cate hit it off right away, drinking martinis and talking like a couple of chatty schoolgirls. I knew they'd get along, but I was surprised by how relaxed they both were as they bonded over their love of old Hollywood actresses and films. They agreed that there was no one better than Ingrid Bergman in *Casablanca,* but they seemed equally obsessed with Katharine Hepburn, praising her roles in *The Philadelphia Story* and *Guess Who's Coming to Dinner* (they apparently both had a thing for Sidney Poitier).

"I love how outspoken and unconventional Katharine Hepburn is," Cate said.

"Yes—and cantankerous with the press," Gary said, laughing. "She has no time for their nonsense."

I waited for Gary to tell Cate that she and Katharine were actually pretty good friends, but she didn't, likely not wanting to name-drop.

"You know . . . she wore pants in public long before most women would have dared to do so," my grandmother added instead.

"Not before you did, Gary!" I said.

"We're talking about Hollywood, Joe," my grandmother said, always so modest. "She's a trailblazer in that world—"

"Yeah," I said. "And you're the *original* trailblazer!"

My grandmother attempted to deflect again, but Cate returned to the subject, asking about Gary's work for women's suffrage. Her probing questions led to a long, lively discussion about politics, really the first time I'd ever heard Cate talk about the subject beyond telling me who she voted for in the '92 election. She was so at ease with Gary, way more than she had been with my mother and Berry, although to be fair, Cate never really had the chance to talk with them.

On that subject, I went out on a limb toward the end of dinner, telling my grandmother about our disastrous trip to the Hamptons. She sided with me, as I knew she would, and showed Cate the appropriate amount of empathy. I wasn't sure what Cate's reaction would be to my raising the subject—she was usually so private—but she chimed right in, filling in the gaps of the story, blaming her own mother more than mine.

I shook my head, debating the point, then told my grandmother about our deal. That we were going to let both our mothers—and Berry—off the hook.

"I think that's the right result," Gary said, nodding. "You have to remember—people generally do the best they can."

Cate leaned in, listening. "What if their best is abysmal? And I'm speaking of my mother now. Not his."

"Well," Gary said. "At that point, we have to work even harder to show them grace and forgiveness."

As Cate earnestly nodded, I smiled and said, "But, Gary, why is your best so much better than everyone else's? Huh?"

"It's not," my grandmother said. "We just see eye to eye, Joey."

"Always have," I said.

"And I can tell the two of you do as well," my grandmother said.

"Yeah, we do, Gary," I said, nodding, then smiling over at Cate. "We really do."

—

THE NEXT DAY, I called my mother and asked if I could come over after work to talk.

"Of course," she said. "What time?"

"Six?"

"Perfect. Would you like to stay for dinner?"

"No, thank you. I just want to talk. It shouldn't take long," I said.

"Certainly," she said.

"Great. Do you mind if I ask Berry to come, too? I'd love to talk to the two of you together."

"Of course. Then I'll see you both tonight."

I RAN INTO Berry in the lobby of my mother's building. We were both soaking wet, caught in an unexpected summer downpour, which gave us something to talk about on the elevator ride up-stairs. We walked into the foyer, and my mother ran to fetch us towels.

After drying off the best I could, I walked straight into the liv-ing room, all business, taking my usual spot on the sofa. My mother followed.

"Can I get you a drink?" she asked as Berry ducked into the powder room.

"Yes, please," I said. "I'll take a bourbon. Neat."

She nodded, then walked past the baby grand piano, over to the bar cart, surveying the bottles. "Is Knob Creek okay?" she said, glancing back at me. "It's all I have. Uncle Mark finished the last of the Blanton's."

"Whatever's fine, Mom," I said.

"Would you like a drink, dear?" my mother asked Berry when she joined us in the living room.

Berry declined, sitting on the far end of the sofa, an awkward gap between us. No one spoke until my mother returned with my bourbon—and a martini for herself. She handed me my glass, hovering over me.

"Thank you," I said, looking up at her.

"You're welcome," she said, finally settling in her armchair.

As I took my first sip of bourbon, I got a strange feeling of déjà vu. I realized it was more of a flashback to the week of my eighteenth birthday, when the two of them had ambushed me with their lecture on Nicole. This time, though, the tables had turned. Clearing my throat, I began to speak.

"What happened in the Hamptons can't *ever* happen again," I said as boldly and clearly as I could.

"Joseph—" my mother said.

I held up my hand and said, "Please. Let me finish."

My mother's eyebrows rose with surprise, but she only nodded, falling silent while I continued *my* lecture.

"I can't make either of you like Cate," I said. "Nor can I force either of you to approve of her. In fact, I know you do not. Cate doesn't have the pedigree you've always felt was important. Not even *close*. She didn't go to college, and before you read about it in the press, I should tell you—she never graduated from high school."

I paused, letting this information sink in, almost enjoying the shock they tried to mask with wide-eyed nods.

"That's fine," my mother said, her eyes flicking over at Berry.

"I know you don't think that's *fine*, Mother," I said. "I know you're *both* judging her right now . . . and I know you both think she's not good enough for me. That I should be with someone more like Margaret."

I paused, daring them to deny it, relieved when they didn't.

"But if you want a relationship with us—with *me*—you're going to need to keep those opinions to yourself," I continued, now on a roll. "Because I don't care what *anyone* thinks of Cate. Not the two of you. Not the press. *No one.* My opinion of Cate is the only one that matters here. And I happen to think she is the most amazing woman I've ever met. She's strong and independent and completely self-made. She's also *brilliant* . . . and as worldly as any girl I ever met at Harvard—and much more authentic."

I stopped abruptly, remembering that this wasn't a sales pitch or a closing argument in a legal case. I didn't need to convince them of anything; I just had to make it clear what I wasn't going to tolerate moving forward.

"So yeah. That's all," I said. "Please keep your two cents to yourselves. Because I love Cate. And she is here to stay."

Silence filled the room, but I made myself sit in it, waiting, until Berry finally cleared her throat and said, "You're right, Joe. I'm sorry."

Floored, I stared back at her, unable to remember a single time in the twenty years I'd known her that she'd simply apologized with no strings or explanations or *but*s.

"Thank you," I said, nodding.

"I'm sorry, too," my mother said. "We were just worried about you—"

"That's no excuse," I said.

"I know," my mother said, looking down.

"I'm in love—and I'm really happy."

"And we're happy for you," she said.

"Yes," Berry said, nodding. "And just so you know—*liking* her was never the issue."

"No," my mother said. "She's *lovely*—"

"The issue was simply—"

I shook my head and cut Berry off. "There *is* no issue. Remember?"

Berry sighed and said, "Yes. And we are doing our best to apologize. We are *truly* sorry."

I took a swig of bourbon, swallowed, then finally let them off the hook. "Okay," I said with a curt nod. "Apology accepted."

My mother gave me a close-lipped smile, but she looked like she might cry. It crossed my mind that she was probably upset about the high-school diploma thing, not the way she'd made Cate feel. But it was a start.

"Okay," I said, draining my whiskey. "I better get going."

"Already?" My mother's face fell. "You just got here!"

"I'm sorry," I said, steeling myself for any guilt trips. "But I have dinner plans with Cate." I put my glass on the coffee table rather than taking it to the sink the way I usually would.

"Oh," my mother said, looking a little wistful. "Well, have fun."

"Yes," Berry echoed. "Have fun. Please tell her we said hello."

"Will do," I said with a brisk nod. Then I stood and saw myself to the door.

I MAY HAVE gone a little overboard with my messaging, but the mission was accomplished. In the next few days, Berry called and invited Cate to lunch, and my mother sent her a note, apologizing for the way things had turned out in the Hamptons and saying that she hoped we would return soon. I happened to be at Cate's place when she received it—so we read it together.

"Oh, my. What did you say to her?" Cate asked me. She looked concerned, but also touched.

"I told her how it's going to be. Both her and Berry."

I waited for her to ask more questions, but she just slid the note back into the envelope and put it down on her kitchen table.

"You know what this means, right?" I finally said.

"What?" she asked.

I pulled her into my arms and whispered in her ear, "It means . . . that it's your turn."

"My turn for what?" she said with a shiver.

"Your turn to make nice," I said, then kissed her forehead. "With your mother."

She made a noncommittal sound, so I put my hand under her chin and made her look me in the eye.

"C'mon, Cate," I said, my voice as stern as I could make it. "We had a deal. You promised."

"I know. I'm working on it."

"What does that mean?"

"It means. I'm trying to set something up. . . ."

"Have you called your mother?"

"Yes."

"And?"

"She invited us to dinner."

"She *did*? When?"

"This weekend. Saturday night."

I grinned and said, "That's fantastic."

"I haven't said yes yet."

"Why not?"

"Because I hate Chip. And I don't want to see him. Or be in his house."

"Okay. Well . . . we could have dinner in the city? The three of us?"

"No," she quickly said. "She doesn't like to drive—"

"We could send a car for her?"

She shook her head. "No. That'll cause a problem with Chip. Trust me."

I hesitated, then said, "Can I make a suggestion?"

She nodded.

"Let's just meet this challenge head-on."

She nodded again.

"You got my back—and I got yours," I said.

THAT SATURDAY, I picked Cate up late in the afternoon, and the two of us set out for Montclair. I could tell she was nervous, so at one point I reached over to put my hand on her thigh. "Can we have a positive attitude here? This'll be fun!"

"Yeah. You don't know Chip. . . . It won't be fun. But I did invite Wendy . . . as a buffer."

"Oh, cool," I said. "I'm excited to meet her."

"Yeah," she said, sounding so glum.

"Positive attitude!" I said. "I'm sure it'll be fine."

"It *could* be fine . . . or it could be horrible . . . depending."

"Depending on what?"

"On Chip's mood. On how much he's had to drink. On the weather. Who knows?"

I was really starting to hate the sound of this guy, but figured Cate was probably exaggerating. "It'll be fine," I said again, patting her leg, then turning on the radio.

About thirty minutes later, we arrived in Montclair. It was one of those Jersey suburbs with a great, family-friendly reputation, but it was even prettier than I'd expected. As we drove through the quaint downtown area, lined with shops, restaurants, and an old theater, I made a comment about it seeming like an idyllic place to grow up.

"For some, maybe," she said under her breath.

"You didn't like it?"

"The town is fine," she said with a shrug, then pointed out my next right turn.

"Just *fine*? What didn't you like about it? Too small? I always wished I grew up in a small town," I said, babbling a little in my attempt to keep things upbeat.

"The town is great. I just didn't like my *home,*" she said.

I glanced at her, struck by how sad the statement was, and it suddenly occurred to me that she may have grown up on the "wrong side of the tracks," so to speak. But a few turns later, we arrived on her quiet, tree-lined street. The homes were modest, but perfectly respectable, and I felt a sense of relief. Not for my sake—but for hers.

"It's that one," she said, pointing at a narrow two-story house with white aluminum siding and green shutters. The lawn appeared freshly mowed and watered, and the simple landscaping was as neat as could be, like a child's drawing. Whistling, I showed off my expert parallel parking skills, wedging my car into a tight spot along the curb.

"And voilà!" I said, turning off the engine.

"Yep," Cate said. "Here goes nothing."

I laughed and said, "Hey! What happened to that positive attitude we talked about?"

She rolled her eyes and said she'd try, making no move to get out of the car until I came around to open her door. As she stepped onto the sidewalk, I put my hand on her back and walked beside her toward the front porch. The house was only a few feet from the street, so within seconds we were at the door. Oddly enough, Cate rang the doorbell, her mother immediately appearing. She was attractive, and I could tell she had been very beautiful as a younger woman, though her skin was now weathered, like she was a smoker or a sun worshipper.

"Oh, hi! You're here! Come in! Come in!" she said, beaming at us through the screen door before Cate pulled it open.

I smiled and said hello, then wiped my feet on the doormat even though I knew my shoes were clean. Cate walked in first, hugging her mom and fielding a few questions about our drive, as I trailed behind. Once inside, I did a quick scan of the foyer, noting the gray linoleum floor with an elaborate pattern and a framed painting of the Virgin Mary hanging on the wall.

"Mom, this is Joe. Joe, this is my mom . . . Jan," Cate said.

"It's so nice to meet you, Mrs. Toledano," I said.

"Oh, please call me Jan," she said, staring up at me with a starstruck expression that I'd seen many times before.

I started to shake her hand, then changed my mind, leaning down to give her a quick, awkward hug.

"Goodness, you're tall," she said, blushing and letting out a high, nervous laugh. "And more handsome in person. My goodness gracious."

"*Mom,*" Cate said under her breath, looking mortified. "*Stop* it."

I laughed and waved Cate off. "Don't tell your mother to stop! She's being nice," I said. "Thank you, Mrs. Toledano."

She smiled at me as Cate peered up the staircase. "Is Chip home?"

"Not yet," Jan said. "But he should be back any minute. Wendy's coming, too! But she can't stay. . . . Oh, goodness, my manners! Come in! Sit down!"

I smiled, then followed Cate and her mother down a short hall, past the kitchen, and into the very *brown* family room. The wall-to-wall carpet was brown; the sofa was brown; the coffee table was brown; the heavy curtains, closed and blocking out any natural light, were brown.

Cate and I sat next to each other on the sofa as her mother

offered us something to drink, rattling off an extensive beverage list, which included not only water, beer, wine, and Coke, but also Crystal Light, Mountain Dew, and milk.

"Milk, Mom?" Cate said, shaking her head. "He's not twelve."

I laughed and said, "She didn't say *chocolate* milk."

"Exactly," her mother said.

I pretended to contemplate this option, then told her I'd take a beer.

"We have two kinds," she said. "Rolling Rock in a can and a Heineken in a bottle. I'm assuming you'd rather have the bottle?"

"Actually, I'll take the Rolling Rock," I said.

"In a glass?"

"The can is fine," I said.

"Do a glass, Mom," Cate said.

Her mother nodded, then asked if she wanted anything. Cate shook her head.

"Okay, then! Be back in a jiffy."

While we waited, I took Cate's hand and squeezed it. "She's very nice," I whispered.

"Thank you," Cate whispered back, giving me a small smile.

A moment later, Cate's mom returned with my beer.

"So, ladies . . . I'm drinking alone, I see?" I said with a laugh.

Jan said she was sorry, looking genuinely worried.

I told her I was only kidding, but she still popped back up, returning to her chair with a glass of white wine. Holding it in her lap, she said, "Well, I know Cate is going to be upset at me for saying this—but I just *have* to—"

"*Mom*—"

"C'mon. Let her—" I said, smiling.

Jan looked at Cate and said, "Can I?"

"Oh, whatever," Cate said with a sigh.

Jan turned back to me and said, "Well, I was just going to

say . . . that I can't *believe* you're sitting here in our house right now. And that you're dating *my* daughter. It's just incredible. I loved your father—and I've been following you since the day you were born—"

"Okay, Mom. That's enough," Cate interjected. "He gets the point."

"Well, thank you. Truly. It's really nice of you to say all that," I said. "And it means a lot to me that you cared about my father. He certainly did so much to make people proud."

"Yes, he did. He *really* did. Your grandfather, too. And your grandmother, Sylvia? What a pioneer! I just *love* her!"

"*Mom.* You don't even *know* her—"

"Joe gets what I'm trying to say—"

"Yes, I do, Jan. And I appreciate it. So much . . ." I hesitated, then took the direct approach. "I know Cate gave you a hard time about the *National Enquirer,* but I thought it was really sweet. I love that your girl had my poster on her bedroom wall."

"Oh my God," Cate said under her breath, burying her face in her hands.

"See, Cate?" Jan said, jubilant. "I told you it wasn't a big deal!"

"It really wasn't," I said, trying to make them both feel better at once.

Jan looked relieved. "Well, thank you for saying that . . . but it won't happen again. Cate explained to me how the media is—I didn't know. I thought it was okay so long as you didn't say anything bad. Which I would *never.*"

"Yes. The tabloids are a slimy lot. They will twist what you say. Hell, they'll make *up* what you say. You have to be careful, and it's usually better to say nothing."

"I know," she said, nodding earnestly. "Lesson learned. It won't happen again. I *promise.*"

"Well, thank you. But I'm mostly worried about *you*, Jan. I just want you and Cate to be safe," I said, draping my arm around Cate's shoulders.

"Gosh," she said. "That is very sweet."

"I mean it."

"Thank you, Joe."

The doorbell rang, interrupting our lovefest.

"Oh, that must be Wendy!" Jan said.

A second later, a cute brunette burst into the room.

"Hello! Hello! Hello!" Wendy said, giving Jan a big hug.

She was definitely the cheerleader personality that Cate had described, peppy and bubbly, bouncing on her toes as she made her way over to us. Cate and I both stood, and Wendy embraced her for an unusually long time.

"I've missed you so much!" she said.

It seemed a little over the top given how close they lived to each other—but genuine.

The second they separated, Wendy turned to face me, giving me a toothy grin. "Hi! You must be Joe!" she said, extending her arm to shake my hand. "I'm Wendy! It's so wonderful to finally meet you. Cate's been hiding you. For too long. From her *best* friend."

"I haven't been *hiding* him," Cate said. "We've just been laying low."

"Well, better late than never!" Wendy said. She flipped her dark hair behind her shoulders, then turned and bounced back over to the chair next to Jan, sitting, smoothing her short skirt and crossing her very tanned legs.

"So, tell me. What's new with you guys?" Cate looked at Jan first, then Wendy.

They both shrugged in response and Cate asked about Gabby.

Wendy's eyes lit up as she talked about her young daughter at length. Her stories were a little dull, but her chattiness alleviated any pressure on me to make small talk. It also seemed to lighten Cate's mood, Wendy's cheerfulness feeling like an antidote to the brown shag carpet.

About a half hour of mostly Wendy talking later, Jan asked if we were hungry. "I made some onion dip," she said. "It's in the fridge. I could bring it out?"

"Well, sadly, I have to get going soon," Wendy said.

"Already?" Jan said.

"I know. I wish I didn't have to! But Matt is incapable of putting Gabby down for a nap, let alone bedtime." She turned to me and told me how wonderful it was to meet me.

"Thank you for coming," Cate said.

"Of course! I had to meet your new beau!" she said, beaming at me.

I smiled and said, "Let's get together again soon."

Before Wendy could answer, we heard footsteps in the foyer. A second later, Chip appeared. I stood up to shake his hand, but he refused to look at me, issuing a blanket hello instead.

Jan announced that she was going to get him a beer, then scurried off to the kitchen.

Wendy broke the silence. "How have you been, Mr. Toledano?" she asked. "Fighting the good fight out there?"

It was the right thing to say, apparently, because Chip smiled, nodded, and said, "Trying to! . . . How have you been, Wendy?"

"Great, thanks!" she said, then filled him in on her husband and daughter as Jan returned and handed him his beer.

I watched the whole thing unfold, marveling that someone could be in a room this long without acknowledging two of the four people in it. It was awkward and weird and rude as hell, and I felt myself getting angry on Cate's behalf.

Wendy obviously picked up on the vibe, too, because she said, "So, Mr. Toledano, have you met Joe?"

Chip said no, then looked over at me and nodded. "Hello."

"Hi," I said back. "Thanks for having me."

"No problem."

"Well, I better go," Wendy said, finally looking a little uncomfortable, too.

Jan and Cate both started to stand, but Wendy shook her head and said, "Nobody get up! I know my way! . . . Cate, call me soon! Love you!"

"Love you, too," Cate said, her voice strained.

As soon as Wendy was gone, we all transferred to the dining room for Jan's onion dip, followed by a lasagna dinner served with garlic bread and a salad. All the while, Chip's passive-aggressive bullshit and bad manners continued. Not once did he address Cate directly, thank his wife for preparing our meal, or ask me a single question. In fact, all of his actions seemed designed to show me that he didn't know or care who I was. Obviously, I didn't need my ego stroked—and certainly not by the likes of him—but it became too much when he asked where my parents lived.

Cate's foot found mine under the table, her toe pressing into mine, as I cleared my throat and said, "My dad's dead."

"Sorry to hear that."

"*Chip,*" Jan said, looking horrified. "You know who his father is. Joseph Kingsley, Jr."

Chip stared at me with a blank expression, then shrugged as if to say *Never heard of him*. It was so absurd that I shook my head and laughed bitterly. He could slight me all he wanted—but not my father.

"What's so funny?" Chip asked.

"Nothing," I said, shaking my head, still smiling.

"Seems like you're amused about something?" he said, staring me down, clearly trying to intimidate me. "What is it?"

"Well, it's certainly not my dead father," I said, gazing back at him, poker-faced.

"Okay. Well, look. We better get going," Cate said, standing, picking up her plate, then stacking it with mine, silverware on top. She turned and marched to the kitchen, and I heard a clang as she dropped everything into the sink. A second later she was back, crossing her arms, telling me again that it was time to go. Meanwhile, Chip kept eating.

"But I made dessert," her mother said.

"They said they had to go, Jan," Chip said.

"I know, but—"

"But what?" he said. "What don't you get?"

She opened her mouth to reply, then closed it.

"We'll do dessert another time, Jan," I said, getting to my feet. "At my place."

"Oh, that would be wonderful," she said. "And I'd love to meet your mother."

"She'd love to meet you, too. You'll have to come to the city soon," I said, then added how much I thought they would have in common, and that she should also come out to the Hamptons.

At that point, I was just trying to piss Chip off. My tactic seemed to work because he got up from the table without a word, walked out of the room, then headed up the stairs.

Looking distraught, Jan rushed after him.

"See? See what I mean?" Cate whispered. "He's a *menace*. A goddamn menace."

I put my arm around her, kissed her forehead, and whispered, "I know. C'mon. Let's get out of here."

She nodded, and the two of us walked to the door. Then, just as we were about to leave, we heard Chip yelling from upstairs.

Cate closed her eyes and shook her head. She then turned

around and looked up the staircase as Chip shouted. His words were unintelligible, but it didn't sound good.

"Damn. Is she okay?" I said, now worried in addition to everything else I was already feeling.

Cate shook her head. I stared at her, putting all the pieces of the puzzle together. Looking back, I feel stupid that it had taken me so long to process what was happening in that house. Chip was more than an asshole—he was a *wife beater*.

"Should I go up there?" I asked Cate.

"No," she answered quickly. "That's a really bad idea. . . . I'll go. . . ."

Jan suddenly appeared at the top of the stairs, descending them quickly. When she got to the bottom, she forced a smile and mumbled, "Sorry about that. He's just in one of his moods. His job is so stressful—"

"Mom," Cate hissed under her breath. "Quit making excuses for him."

"I'm not—I just . . . It will be fine." She smiled again, bigger this time, but I could see the fear in her eyes, along with a telltale red mark on her right arm.

CHAPTER 22

Cate

"Mom, please, *please* come with us," I pleaded under my breath as we stood by the front door.

"I can't, honey," she whispered, shaking her head.

"Yes, you *can*, Mom," I said, doing my best to stay calm. "He's going to hurt you."

"No . . . I can smooth this over," she said.

I shifted my gaze to Joe and could see his shock, along with fear. It was something I'd never seen on his face. Joe was never afraid. Of *anything*.

"Jan—I know it's none of my business—" he said, his voice low but strong.

It was what people always said, and it wasn't true.

"Yes, it *is* our business," I said, cutting him off. "We need to get her out of here. *Now.*"

"Oh, Catie," she said in her Stepford Wife voice. "I'll be fine. I promise."

"No, Mom," I said, feeling increasingly frantic. "It's time. It's way past time. Please. Let us help you. Go get in the car."

Before she could reply, Chip was charging down the stairs. "What the hell are you all whispering about?"

I fought against my ingrained instinct to cower, finding the courage to reach out for my mom's hand. "She's coming with us," I said, staring Chip dead in the eye. "That's what we're whispering about."

"The hell she is!" Chip said, grabbing my mom's other wrist and yanking her as hard as he could, like she was the rope in a game of tug-of-war.

Joe put his hands in the air, palms out, his shoulders squared to Chip. "Whoa! C'mon, man! Let her go! Calm down!"

Chip's eyes narrowed as he dropped my mom's arm and took a slow, dramatic step toward Joe. "You. Pompous. *Prick,*" Chip said. "Don't you *dare* tell me what to do."

"C'mon, man. I'm not telling you what to do. I'm just—I just want *everyone* to calm down."

"Get the hell out of my house!" Chip said. "And take your little gold-digging tramp with you."

I held my breath in horror and humiliation as Joe squinted at Chip. "What did you just say?" he said.

"Did I *stutter*?" Chip asked.

"Apologize," Joe said, the two men nose to nose. "Right now. Or—"

"Or *what*?" Chip said.

"Or else . . . you're going to have a real problem on your hands!" Joe said.

Chip shrugged with a smirk. "If that's what you want. Let's go, pretty boy." He shoved his way past my mom and me, then walked out the door, taking a few strides onto the front lawn before turning to face the house. "I'm waiting!" he taunted, his arms crossed.

Joe took a step toward the door, but I blocked his path with my body, and said, "Don't, Joe. He's not worth it."

Joe shook his head. "I'm not going to let him talk about you like that, Cate! No way!"

"And I'm not going to let you fight him," I said, picturing a scene on the front lawn, along with tomorrow's headlines. I turned to my mom for one last-ditch, frantic effort. "And, Mom, I'm begging *you*. . . . If you ever cared about me, if you love me at all, you'll go get in the car and leave that man, once and for all."

She stared back at me like a wounded, disoriented animal, then whispered, "I can't." Her eyes looked blank. "And you both need to go."

In that second, something died inside me, and I gave up, once and for all. "Okay, Mom," I said, disgust drowning out every other emotion. "Have it your way. . . . Goodbye and good luck. Let's go, Joe."

I turned and walked out the door, past Chip, and straight to the car. To my relief, Joe followed me, even as Chip continued to taunt him: *"That's what I thought, pretty boy!"*

Joe started to open my car door, but I told him that I could do it myself, and a second later, he was sitting beside me, starting the engine. As he pulled away from the curb, his headlights illuminated the little house that had once been my mother's dream. And in that second, I silently vowed that I would never return to this place again, *so help me God.*

JOE HELD MY hand the whole way home, but we both said very little. I could tell he was in shock, and maybe I was, too. Obviously, I'd seen Chip abuse my mom a thousand times, but watching it unfold with a witness—with *Joe*—was a new kind of trauma for me. Or maybe it was the *same* trauma, just a different level of shame. None of my usual mechanisms of denial were going to work this time. Joe had seen where I came from, and there was no taking it back.

He took me to his place without even asking. I was glad, as I might have told him I wanted to be alone but realized I did not. When we got inside his dark apartment, he turned on a few lights, greeted Thursday, then pulled me to him, giving me a long hug. When we finally separated, I braced myself for a line of questioning and felt relieved when he said only, "Why don't you go take a shower while I walk the dog?"

"Okay," I said.

He kissed my forehead before I turned and walked to his bedroom, then his bathroom, closing the door before slowly removing my clothes. I started to look in the mirror, then stopped, embarrassed by my own reflection. I told myself that I'd done nothing wrong, but I still felt a wave of intense guilt and shame as I stepped into the shower. It was the best place to cry, but that night, no tears came.

About twenty minutes later, I finally got out of the shower, toweled myself off, and wrapped myself in Joe's chenille robe. I walked out to the living room and found him sitting on the sofa in his favorite green-and-blue plaid pajama bottoms. On the coffee table were two mugs of tea, the bags still steeping, along with a plate of buttered toast cut on the diagonal.

"I put a little honey in your tea," he said with a small smile.

When I didn't smile back, he said, "I'm sorry. I don't know what to say. . . ."

"You don't have to say anything."

"Should we call and check on your mother?"

"No," I said, shaking my head.

"Okay. Just come sit with me?" He patted the sofa beside him.

I sat beside him as he handed me my warm mug, steam still rising from it. I brought it to my lips without taking a sip, then turned my eyes to him and said, "Do you think we could pretend this didn't happen?"

He looked surprised, his eyebrows raised. "I don't know, Cate. . . ."

"Please?"

He sighed, ran his hand through his hair, then nodded. "For tonight, yes . . . we can pretend. But not forever."

I took what I could get, the two of us drinking our tea in silence.

"You should eat something," he said at one point, gesturing toward the toast.

I shook my head and said I wasn't hungry, remembering why I had been so thin in high school.

After a while, my eyelids grew heavy, the chamomile working its magic. The next thing I knew, Joe was gently shaking me awake. "C'mon, honey," he said, pulling me to my feet. "Let's go to bed."

CHAPTER 23

Joe

As upsetting as our visit to Montclair was, I think it brought Cate and me closer. I certainly understood her better than I had before, so many things crystallizing, including her motivation to drop out of high school and move to the city. I also got why she had always resisted romantic relationships, doing her best to keep men at arm's length, the way she had with me in the beginning. Even now, she didn't want to talk about what had happened with her mother and Chip, and whenever I tried to broach the subject, she would shut down. I decided I should leave it alone for a while, giving her time to work through what she was feeling.

About two weeks later, I tried again.

"Cate, can I ask you something? About your mother and Chip?" I asked, just after we'd made love. She was lying in my arms, and I felt her body tense.

"Okay," she said, sounding more than a little reluctant.

"Growing up . . . did you ever try to get help? Like from a teacher or counselor or Wendy's parents?"

"No," she said.

"Why not?"

"I was too afraid."

I wrapped my arms more tightly around her, then said, "Afraid that he'd hurt you and your mom?"

"Not me. But her. And he *would* have," she said. "For sure."

"Did he ever hit you?"

"No," I said. "For the most part it was just verbal abuse. But I always felt that he was one trigger away from smacking me around, too. I think he held that over my mom's head as another way to control her. If she didn't play ball, I was next."

"*Damn*," I said under my breath, feeling a fresh surge of rage toward Chip. Honestly, I was afraid of what I might do to him if I ever saw him again.

"And anyway," Cate said. "If I had told? Nothing would have happened to him. He would have denied it. Called me a liar. It would have been my word against his. And he's a cop—"

"But people would have seen the cuts and bruises," I said, feeling nauseous. "They'd have to believe you."

"No they wouldn't, Joe," she said. "That's not how this stuff works. My mom would have denied it and given everyone her bullshit about falling down the steps . . . and at that point, what could anyone do? They can't *make* her admit it."

"Yeah," I said with a sigh. It was a pattern I'd seen and heard about, both anecdotally and in the course of my job. It was probably why my colleagues who worked on domestic violence cases seemed to burn out the quickest, not to mention the social workers, who did the really soul-crushing work.

"Plus, if I'm totally honest—" Cate hesitated. "It wasn't just the fear of Chip. It was also a fear of what people would think of my mom and me. I know that sounds bizarre. . . . It does to me, too, now that I'm older and away from it."

"What do you mean? They'd just think you were victims . . . of something terrible."

"Yeah," she said. "Exactly. But I didn't want to be a victim. I was ashamed." She was silent for several seconds, then lowered her voice and said, "On some level, I still am."

"Oh, Cate. You have *nothing* to be ashamed of!"

"I know that *rationally*," she said. "But it always felt like a social class thing to me—"

"That's not true," I said as emphatically as I could. "Domestic violence doesn't discriminate."

"I know that *now*. But as a kid—I couldn't see it. And I just felt so powerless. I think I internalized a lot of things that Chip was telling me. . . . That I was dumb. That I'd never amount to anything. It was hard not to feel . . . worthless."

"When did that change?" I said. "As soon as you left home?"

She didn't answer right away, but I could hear her breathing— and also feel her chest rising and falling against mine. "It took a long time. A *very* long time," she finally said. "And sometimes . . . I can still hear him . . . and I still believe him."

"Oh my God, Cate, no. You're *so* amazing—"

"I'm really not, though, Joe. You always say that. And I appreciate it—I really do. I love that you see me that way. But if I were amazing, I would have gotten my mom out of this situation."

"You just said yourself it's not that easy—"

"I know, but I still feel like I failed her," she said. "Elna disagrees—she blames my mom so much."

"For not leaving on her own?"

"Exactly. On some level, I think she's right. I believe all that stuff about how we are each the captain of our own ship or whatever. That you can't help someone who doesn't want to be helped. But she's my mother, you know?"

"I know," I said, kissing her forehead. "I feel like we should try to do *something*. We could report him. . . . It would be his word against *ours*—he'd lose that battle."

"Yes. But at what cost? What would he do to my mom?"

"We could get a restraining order—"

"Like *those* work."

"We could get her full-time security—"

"Believe me, I've thought about all of that. Every few months, I hatch a new plan. But the other night? . . . Something snapped inside me, and I started to think that Elna really is right. How could my mom do this to herself? How could she have let me live that way? I mean, God . . . I think about having children . . . I just can't imagine allowing someone to treat my child that way."

"I know, baby . . . I think a lot about that stuff, too, lately. Having kids," I said, stroking her hair. "And how I want to do things differently than my mother."

"Yeah. But I feel like she's done a pretty good job. You've turned out really well. And it doesn't seem like you should have," she said. I could tell she was smiling, but also serious.

"I know. She's a good mother. She really is. But sometimes I resent all the Kingsley pressure and hype. I'm not going to do that to my kid—" I thought for a second, then added, "Of course, with my mediocre accomplishments, some of that pressure will be diluted."

I laughed, but Cate didn't. "Don't, Joe," she said. "Don't put yourself down. I don't know a better man."

"Wow," I said. "Do you mean that?"

"Of course I do."

She tilted her head up and gave me a soft, soulful kiss that made my heart explode.

THE REST OF the summer passed both blissfully and uneventfully. There was no further drama with our families, in part because we limited contact with both. Cate called to check on her mother now and then but didn't make any attempts to see her and I didn't pressure her. In the back of my mind, I fantasized about a rescue or revenge mission, but for now I safeguarded Cate's mental health and prioritized our relationship.

Meanwhile, Cate acclimated to her growing fame. She still despised and feared the paparazzi, and we erred on the side of keeping a low profile, but we weren't in hiding, either. We freely went to restaurants and bars, Broadway shows and baseball games. We even attended the occasional benefit or gala or fundraiser together, the sort of boring events I'd been saying no to for months. For a shy person, Cate was a natural at working a room and could turn on her charisma like a light switch. One moment, she'd be sitting anxiously in the back of a town car, dreading the function to come, and in the next, she was dazzling celebrities and politicians.

The key to her charm, I think, was that she was always so authentically herself. Despite her insecurities, she never overcompensated by trying to impress anyone, nor did she try to hide behind me. Instead, she mingled on her own, deflecting the fawning that came with being my girlfriend while showing genuine interest in others. Nobody could accuse her of being my arm candy. If anything, I could feel myself becoming dependent on *her*. I couldn't stand to be away from her, and even accompanied her on a few of her business trips to London.

Yet as intense and all-consuming as our relationship was, it never felt unhealthy or obsessive. Before her, I had believed that passion came with a price. That you had to choose between being madly in love and being at peace. With Cate, I had both, and it was magic.

As SUMMER FADED into fall and Cate and I entered our third season together, I decided it was time to get a ring—that I couldn't wait any longer to officially begin our life together. I wasn't sure what our future would look like, but I knew we would define it together—*our* way.

I didn't think it was a good idea to ask her mother for her hand in marriage, but an old-fashioned part of me wanted to ask *someone*. So I invited Elna to lunch, the two of us meeting at Rao's in East Harlem, one of my favorite spots.

Just to be on the safe side, I brought a stack of file folders with me, spreading them out on the table between us so it would look like a working lunch. The last thing I needed was for the tabloids to accuse me of cheating on Cate with a model.

Elna laughed, clearly aware of what I was doing, then said, "Nice props."

"One can never be too careful."

"No," Elna said. "One cannot."

"So," I said, smiling. "I think you might know why we're here."

"Yes," she said. "I think I might."

"I'm going to ask Cate to marry me."

"That's wonderful," she said, but the look on her face was so inscrutable that it worried me.

"You think so?"

"Yes. I do."

"Then why aren't you smiling?"

"Because I'm thinking . . . this is heavy stuff. Cate's life will change. I mean, it already *has*—but it will *really* change. Forever."

I swallowed, feeling nervous. The conversation wasn't going exactly the way I'd hoped. "Yeah. That's kind of the idea of marriage," I said, forcing a smile. "Life will change for both of us. Hopefully for the better."

"Yes," she said, nodding. "Hopefully."

"Okay, Elna. You're scaring me here," I said.

"I don't mean to scare you," she said, her expression softening a little. "I'm happy for you. For *both* of you."

"So I have your blessing?"

She smiled. "Yes, of course you do."

I gave a sigh of relief, then said, "Do you think she'll say yes?"

"I think it's very likely," Elna said.

"But not a sure thing?"

"Nothing's a sure thing with Cate," she said. "I think you know that by now."

I nodded, then asked if she'd help me pick out a ring.

"Oh, shit," Elna said, shaking her head and laughing. "I was hoping you wouldn't ask me that. . . . I have *no* idea what to tell you."

"Are you serious?" I asked. "Isn't that something girls discuss?"

"Maybe most girls . . . but not us."

"Shit," I said. "So . . . no guesses on her favorite cut of diamond?"

"Well, I'd say something classic . . . but not too predictable or boring."

"Is a round cut boring or classic?" I asked.

"I'd say it's classic. But I don't know . . . maybe a little boring, too?"

"Okay," I said, laughing. "You *do* realize that you're *zero* help here, right?"

She smiled and shrugged. "I told you. It's not my thing."

"Would Curtis know?"

"Probably. But you can't ask Curtis! He can't keep a secret to save his life."

"Okay. What about Wendy?"

Elna made a face. "I'm not a huge Wendy fan, but it's actually not a bad idea. . . . I feel like it's the kind of thing she'd have discussed with Cate—"

"Do you think you could get me her number?"

"Yes," she said. "Just be careful. Wendy's the type to parlay you asking her ring advice into taking the credit for your entire marriage—and acting like she's your best friend forever."

"Yeah. But I already have a best friend," I said, grinning. "And I'm fixin' to marry her."

THAT EVENING, I called Wendy and asked if she was coming into the city anytime soon, that I'd love to meet up with her for coffee.

"Sure! How's tomorrow?" she said.

"Great," I said. "Please don't tell Cate that we spoke."

"Mum's the word," she said.

The following afternoon, we met in a coffee shop near Madison Square Park. I cut right to the chase. "I need some ring advice," I said.

"Oh my gosh! This is *so* exciting!" Her voice was loud, and I caught the barista glancing over at us.

I didn't know Wendy well enough to shush her, but I leaned toward her and lowered my voice, hoping she'd get the hint. "Yeah. I'm so excited. But this is obviously a huge secret. Nobody can know about this conversation."

"Of *course* not!" she said, sitting up as straight as she could. "And I'm so honored that you'd come to me. Truly. This is amazing. Thrilling."

I didn't burst her bubble by telling her that I'd asked Elna first. I just said, "I know how close you and Cate are—and how long you've known her."

"Yes. Cate is like a sister to me," Wendy said, tearing up.

"Truly. I just love her to pieces, and I'm so happy she's getting the fairy tale—and Prince Charming—that she deserves."

I nodded and smiled but was starting to feel slightly uncomfortable. There was something about the words *fairy tale* and *Prince Charming* that came off as slightly condescending toward Cate. I told myself I was being too critical and pressed onward. "So . . . thoughts on the ring?"

"Well, let's see . . . I know Cate loves mine," Wendy said. She put her hand on the table, then stared down at a mammoth rectangular stone that looked more like glass than a diamond.

"It's very pretty," I said, though the last thing I was going to do was copy Wendy's ring.

"Thank you. My husband did a great job. It's an emerald cut. Fun fact: less than three percent of the world's diamonds are emerald cut. So, they're the rarest . . . which makes them the most expensive. . . ."

I nodded and smiled.

"Oh—and good news. Cate tried it on once, and it fit her to perfection. So, we know her ring size is a six and a half!" Her voice was loud again, and this time I put my finger to my lips.

"Oops! Sorry," she said.

"It's okay. We just want to be careful."

"Oh, totally."

"So. She's never mentioned her favorite cut?"

"*Hmm*," Wendy said. "Would you believe that I can't recall a single instance? Which is so strange. I mean—I had mine picked out by the time I had my first kiss!"

I nodded, glad that Cate wasn't like that, even though it made my project trickier.

"My only advice?" Wendy said with a smirk.

"What's that?" I said.

"Go big or go home, ya know?" She laughed, then said, "Also, don't do a pear, marquis, or God forbid, heart-shaped. Barf."

"Thank you," I said, nodding and smiling. "This is all very helpful."

"It's my pleasure. And I couldn't be more thrilled for her! I mean—*gah*! Who would have *thunk* it! Talk about a *Cinderella* story."

"Well, that's sweet. But I'm the lucky one," I said.

Wendy nodded, looking earnest. "Yes. You really are. And she'll love whatever you give her."

"I hope so."

"Hey, this is just a thought, but did you ever think about a family ring? Like an heirloom of some kind?"

"Yeah . . . I have . . . But I don't know . . . I think Cate and I like the idea of a fresh start," I said, thinking that both of us wanted to escape the story lines of our pasts.

Incidentally, I also was a little ready to escape Wendy. I could tell her heart was in the right place, and that she was genuinely happy for Cate. But I still left the coffee shop feeling slightly uneasy.

By the time I got home, it hit me. Cate wouldn't have wanted me to poll her friends about the ring. She'd want me to pick it out myself, completely on my own. Even if I got it wrong, it would be right.

ABOUT A WEEK later, I put on a baseball cap and sunglasses, made sure I wasn't being followed, and walked into Harry Winston for my after-hours appointment with an older gentleman named Horace. I knew I'd be paying more than I would in the diamond district, but it felt right and romantic.

Horace immediately put me at ease with both his knowledge and his discretion, giving me a full tutorial on diamonds while assuring me that there would be no leaks. After we'd covered those basics, he asked me to tell him about Cate.

"Well, she's wonderful," I said. "But I assume you're asking about her taste in jewelry?"

"Yes," Horace said. "Tell me about her style."

"She actually doesn't wear much jewelry," I said, describing the few pieces that she wore on a regular basis. Her Cartier watch was the only real staple, along with two pairs of stud earrings—diamonds and pearls—which she rotated. Other than that, she just wore an occasional gold bracelet.

"I see. Lovely," Horace said, nodding approvingly. "It sounds like she's quite understated . . . a minimalist."

"Yes!" I said, knowing that I was beaming. "That's exactly the word for it! She's a minimalist. She sparkles, but she isn't flashy."

"Understood," Horace said. "Well, you've come to the right place, Mr. Kingsley."

I smiled, more excited by the second.

For the next hour, the two of us looked at diamonds of every shape and color, including a yellow one. They were all beautiful, but nothing seemed quite right for Cate. Then Horace mentioned an eternity band, and I perked up, intrigued by the name.

"What's that?"

Horace told me it was a ring with uniform stones that went the whole way around the band, pointing out an example in a glass case.

"Are they considered classic?"

"Very," Horace said, explaining that eternity bands traced back four thousand years to the ancient Egyptians, who were said to offer them as tokens of eternal love and life.

"Oh, wow. I love that."

"Yes. They're really beautiful. I must tell you, though. It's highly unusual to go that route for an engagement ring. The eternity design is more common for a wedding or anniversary band. Most ladies prefer one significant stone for their engagement ring—"

"Yes. But Cate isn't like most ladies," I said.

"Yes. I'm quite sure she is not," Horace said.

"I really like this idea," I said, the wheels turning in my mind. "What if we mixed in another stone, too? Like alternated between a color and a diamond?"

"We could certainly do that. If you go that route, I'd recommend emeralds or sapphires. They are very sturdy stones."

"I love the idea of sapphires," I said. "To match her eyes."

"Hmm. Yes. A diamond and sapphire eternity band," Horace said, nodding. "That would be beautiful."

"Would it still sparkle? I want a lot of sparkle."

Horace nodded. "Indeed it would. For more sparkle, I would recommend round stones. It will be stunning and unique."

"Yes. That's what I want. Stunning and unique. Like Cate."

"Well, we will make that happen for you, Mr. Kingsley."

"Joe," I said, grinning. "Please call me Joe."

Horace smiled and said, "We will make that happen for you, Joe."

"Thank you," I said. "How long will it take?"

"Are you in a hurry?"

"Yes," I said. "I actually am."

"I'll have it ready in a week."

CHAPTER 24

Cate

Taking Joe home to meet my mom and Chip had been painful for a lot of reasons. I was obviously mortified and ashamed by the contrast between his family and mine. I was also filled with guilt and resentment toward my mom. And then there was pure, burning hatred for Chip that I hadn't allowed myself to unearth for some time.

But over the next few days and weeks, the whole ordeal became strangely cathartic, too. I was relieved that Joe knew the truth about Chip, as it felt like the last bit of me that I hadn't shared. In some ways, it wasn't unlike my memory of confiding in Elna, although the risk felt a bit greater with Joe—or at least more embarrassing. After all, friends don't generally leave you when they discover the skeletons in your closet, but high-profile boyfriends from socially elite families very well might.

But Joe didn't leave—and he wasn't at all paternalistic, either. He understood the nuances at play, and I discovered that the reward in telling him was as great as the risk I'd felt. Whether he knew it or not, his reaction to my confession felt like a huge breakthrough, both for us as a couple and for me personally. In a weird way, I felt truly understood—and safe—for the first time in my life.

Meanwhile, as my confidence in our relationship grew, so did the spotlight on us. It was as if the world could sense that we were more in love than ever, though more likely it was just that we were stepping out together with greater frequency, the paparazzi be damned. I did my best to ignore the circus. And when I did somehow catch wind of a negative headline, I took it with a grain of salt.

Harder to ignore, though, were the increased demands on my time. My client list exploded, everyone wanting to wear Wilbur and work with me. Invites for luncheons and parties and galas poured in. Fashion magazines asked me to pose on their covers. Other designers sent me endless freebies, begging me to wear their clothes and shoes and jewelry and handbags. I mostly turned them down, as it felt wrong—and like a conflict of interest, given Wilbur. But when I did accept them, the items immediately sold out. According to Curtis, who was positively giddy about my rising fame, the tabloids had dubbed the phenomenon the "Cate effect." He also claimed that women were starting to emulate my minimalistic style, forgoing tanning beds in favor of pale skin and ditching their layered "Rachel 'dos" for long, straight hair. My longtime colorist, Miguel, informed me that he now was booked months in advance, as people had figured out who was responsible for my pale blond highlights.

One night as Curtis was doing my makeup for an event that Joe and I were attending, he told me his clients all wanted to know what color lipstick I wore.

I smiled and said, "Do you tell them it's called 'red'?"

"They know *that*," Curtis said with a laugh. "They want to know the exact brand and shade. They want to know what lip liner you use. They want to know what moisturizer you use. They want to know *everything* about you. You're becoming a fashion *icon,*" he said, applying blush to the apples of my cheeks. "And once I do your wedding makeup, you're going to make *me* a star, too."

I laughed his comment off, but Curtis doggedly remained on the topic. "When do you think he'll pop the question?" he asked.

"Calm down," I said. "We've only been together seven months."

"And? You never talk about it?"

"No," I said.

It was the truth, though we did reference the *distant* future, even discussing baby names at one point. Not surprisingly, Joe said he didn't want to have a "Joseph the Fourth"—that he'd want our son to have his own identity—but that he liked the name Sylvia for a girl, after his grandmother.

"What about you?" Joe had asked, looking a little shy. "What names do you like?"

I shrugged, then told him that I'd never given the subject much thought, but I did like offbeat, one-syllable boy names like Finn and Tate and Quill.

"Oh, I *love* Finn," he said.

Of course, I didn't tell Curtis about *that* conversation. There was no point in feeding the monster.

THAT COLUMBUS DAY weekend, Joe and I were set to go to the Hamptons with Peter and Genevieve. The four of us had gotten together for dinner or drinks several times, and I really enjoyed their company. Peter reminded me a lot of Joe, although more serious, and Genevieve was very fun to talk to. She showed genuine interest in my world of fashion, and we'd discovered that Genevieve's stylist, Amy Silver, was one of my favorite clients.

At the last minute, though, Peter, a banker at Goldman Sachs, got called in to work. I was a little disappointed, as I'd been looking forward to bonding with Genevieve, but I was also happy for the downtime with Joe. It had been a particularly frenetic week for both of us, and the idea of taking long walks on the beach with Thursday, curling up by the fire, and sleeping in sounded so appealing. I could tell Joe felt the same and worried that he was a little out of sorts about something. I didn't press, though, figuring he'd bring it up when he was ready.

Sure enough, about thirty minutes into our drive out east, he cleared his throat and said, "So, I wanna talk to you about something."

"Okay?" I said, feeling a little nervous, hoping it wasn't anything bad.

"I know I talk about quitting my job all the time," he said, shooting me a pensive look before returning his eyes to the road. "But I think I'm ready to give my notice."

"That's great, honey!" I said. "Do you have ideas about what's next?"

He took a deep breath, then said, "Well . . . how would you feel if I actually did run for office?"

"Are you serious?" I said, staring at him.

Joe nodded.

"Wow," I said. "Which office?"

"Congress," he said. "The House of Representatives."

"Wow," I said again, getting chills at the thought. "Tell me more."

"Well . . . you know that big meeting I had the other day? The one I was nervous about?"

"Yes?"

"Well, it was with Judith Hope," he said.

"Should I know that name?"

"She's the chairperson of the New York State Democratic Committee. And she's trying to convince me to run for Congress. . . . What do you think?"

"Well, what do *you* think? I thought you didn't want this?"

"I didn't . . . but I don't know. Maybe I could do some good. More good than I'm doing now . . ."

"What does your mother say?" I asked.

"I haven't talked to her about it."

"Have you talked to your grandmother?"

He shook his head and said, "No, honey. I wanted to talk to you first."

"Oh, wow," I said, feeling honored—and also overwhelmed by the responsibility.

"Do you think I'd be any good at it?" he said.

"I think you'd be awesome," I said. "But I want you to be happy."

"*You* make me happy."

"You make me happy, too . . . but I'm talking about your *job*."

"You're more important to me than my job—"

"Joe!" I said with a laugh. "Focus!"

"Okay. Sorry," he said, smiling. "I'm trying."

"Do you think this might be something you really want? Or would you be doing it because you're Joe Kingsley and people expect it of you?" I asked.

"I don't know. . . . I'd say neither. I think if I did it—I'd be doing it because I think I have an obligation to help as many people as I can."

"That's a great answer," I said.

"And so long as you're by my side, I think we can accomplish some big things . . . not that I would expect you to give up your career to be some congressman's wife or anything like that."

"Actually, I think it might be time for me to make a change, too," I said. Some of my recent thoughts about work were suddenly crystallizing in my head.

"Why do you say that?" he asked. "I thought you loved your job?"

"I do. In some ways. I mean . . . I love some of my clients. But for the most part, it's not all that fulfilling. At the end of the day, I sell clothes to rich people."

"It's way more than that—and you know it. Wilbur depends on you. You're doing so much for his brand. From a business perspective. From a sales perspective. From a creative perspective."

"Thank you, Joe," I said. "But *you're* actually doing more for his brand than I am."

"I am not! I bought a few things back in February," he said, being his cute literal self. Or maybe he was just being self-deprecating. Sometimes it was hard to tell.

"Joe, look. I know I'm good at my job. But the bottom line is, the fact that I'm dating you has moved more Wilbur product than my sales acumen. And I'm just not sure that's tenable for much longer," I said, choosing my words with care.

"What's that mean?" he asked, looking worried.

I took a deep breath and said, "The core of my job is sales and catering to high-end clients, and it's really tough to do that now that I'm in the press so much."

"Why?" he asked.

"Because it's a service-oriented business, and wealthy people expect—and want—to be the center of attention. The dynamic doesn't work if I'm someone they see in the tabloids. They don't like it . . . or, sometimes, they like it too much. . . . But no matter what, it almost always creates this weird dynamic. It just doesn't work."

"Shit," he said. "I'm sorry—"

"Please don't say you're sorry. Otherwise, I'm not going to want to tell you stuff."

"Okay . . . I'm sorry—I mean I won't . . . I just hate this. And I feel guilty."

"Please don't. It's not like that. I promise," I said. "I think I just need a change. Change is good, right?"

Joe nodded, then asked if I wanted to stay in the fashion industry.

I said I didn't know, thinking there wasn't much else that I was qualified to do.

"Would you . . . I don't know . . . maybe want to go back to school?" Joe asked, giving me a sideways glance. "There are so many options in the city. NYU. Fordham. Columbia. The New School or Parsons. With your work experience, you could get in anywhere."

I smiled and tried to make a joke, asking if he'd be willing to write me a recommendation. "I bet a letter from Joe Kingsley would greatly improve my chances."

"C'mon, Cate," he said. "Be serious! Would you want to go back to school?"

"Maybe," I said. "Maybe at night."

"At *night*? I'd never see you!"

"Well, I have to earn a living," I said.

"True. But you could move in with me."

"I'd still need a job."

"No, you don't. I could support you."

"No, thank you," I said, feeling embarrassed. "I don't want to be supported by my boyfriend."

"Okay. Well . . . you could work for my campaign? For a salary?"

"So, you'd be my boss?" I said, making a point.

"No. We'd be part of a team," he said. "And I'd be running on a platform we both cared about."

"Which is what, exactly?" I asked.

"I don't know," he said. "I just know that I'd want to help people. We can sort the rest of the details out later. Together."

I looked at him, thinking that he sounded more than a little naïve. But it wasn't a bad start for someone who'd felt so stuck. And I really liked the part about being together.

THE WEATHER FORECAST for most of the weekend looked menacing, and the sky was already turning gray. As soon as we arrived at the house, Joe suggested we walk Thursday while we still could. I agreed that it was a good idea, so we took our suitcases upstairs and quickly changed into sweats and sneakers. On our way out the door, Joe made a stop in the mudroom, grabbing a tennis ball for Thursday, then riffling through a basket containing a motley mix of baseball caps and other hats. I spotted the rainbow-striped knit cap that he'd worn the day we met.

"I remember this one," I said, plucking it from the pile, wondering if he knew its significance.

He gave me a cute little grin, confirming that he did. "I'm gonna wear it again. . . ."

I laughed and called it absurd.

"Do you want a hat? It's getting cold out there. . . ."

"Okay," I said, taking the elastic band from my ponytail and shaking my hair loose before choosing a white, ribbed wool hat. I put it on and, channeling my modeling days, gave Joe a faux pouty look.

He smiled and pulled me into a hug, whispering that he loved me. He didn't say those words a lot, so it meant something every time. I told him that I loved him, too, feeling so happy.

We left the house via the back porch, following Thursday, who raced to the fence at the edge of the property, wagging his tail, waiting for us to catch up. A moment later, Joe was unlatching the gate, the three of us making our way down the wooden walkway, past the dunes covered with sea grass. Where the boards met the sand, Joe and I paused, taking in the view. That first glimpse of the ocean got me every time. There was nothing like it, no matter the weather. In some ways, I liked it even better on days like this one.

"Which way?" Joe said.

I glanced in one direction, then the other, pointing toward the northeast, where the sky looked slightly less ominous. Joe nodded in agreement as Thursday ran to the water's edge, barking and chasing a seagull.

We began to stroll, finding that sweet spot of wet packed sand that was hard enough to walk on but not in range of waves. We laughed at Thursday's antics but didn't talk much, falling into a contented zone of quiet togetherness. A good bit of time and distance passed, though it was hard to measure either on the beach, before Joe asked what I was thinking.

I'd just been replaying our conversation about his potential congressional run, and I answered him honestly.

"Does that stress you out?"

"No."

"Not even a little?"

"Nothing stresses me out right now," I said. "Except the sky," I added, looking up just as thunder rumbled in the distance. It was getting darker and windier, too.

"Should we head back?"

"Maybe," I said. I remembered hearing once that you were more likely to get struck by lightning on the beach. I asked Joe if this was true, and he nodded.

"Yeah," he said. "Not because of the water—just because you're the shortest path from the sky to the ground."

"Yikes," I said, stopping in my tracks.

"But I'm taller, so you're still safe," Joe said, pulling me into his arms.

"Not if you're hugging me," I said, playfully pushing him away.

Joe assured me that *nobody* was going to get struck by lightning, hugging me again. I nestled against him, thinking there was nowhere in the world I'd rather be.

After a few seconds, he released me and said, "You know where we are right now?"

"No. Where?" I said, looking around.

"We're about fifty yards from where we met," he said, pointing up the shoreline.

"Oh, my goodness," I said with a sigh, remembering. I smiled and said, "You were shameless that day."

"I was?" Joe said, laughing. Clearly, he knew exactly what I meant.

"Using your poor dog to meet some random girl on the beach," I said.

Joe grinned back at me. "A guy's gotta do what a guy's gotta do."

"And look at you now," I said. "Still wearing the same ridiculous hat."

"Hey!" Joe said, pretending to be offended. "What's so ridiculous about it?"

"Everything," I said, smiling. "You look like a court jester."

He laughed and said, "No, I don't! Jester hats have three points. And jingle bells."

"Fine," I said. "But it's still ridiculous."

He reached up, grabbed the cherry red pom-pom on top, and pulled the hat off, depositing it on the beach. "Is that better?"

"Much," I said, as Thursday plucked the hat from the sand and made off with it.

"Good dog," I yelled after him. "Get rid of that thing."

When I turned back to Joe, he was looking at me with the oddest expression.

"Are you okay?" I said.

He nodded, but I could tell he was breathing funny, like he might cry.

"Joe. What's wrong?" I asked.

He bit his lip, then ran his hand through his longer than usual hair. "Nothing," he said. "Everything is perfect."

Then, suddenly, he dropped to one knee, reached into his pocket, and pulled out a ring. Though it was perfectly obvious what was happening, I was still in a state of disbelief. He looked up at me and said my name in a whispered question. *Cate?*

"Yes?" I said, my heart pounding in my chest, tears filling my eyes.

He began to talk. His voice was low and his speech rapid as he told me how much he loved me and that he'd never met anyone like me and that he wanted to spend his life with me. He said some other things, too, but I couldn't focus on his words. It was as if my tear-blurred vision also affected my ability to hear. Or maybe my heart was just beating too loudly.

"Catherine Cooper," I heard him say at the end of his speech. "Will you marry me?"

I opened my mouth to answer, but my yes caught in my throat, and I could only nod. He reached for my left hand and slipped a delicate band onto my finger. Sparkling with sapphires and diamonds, it fit me perfectly.

"It's gorgeous," I breathed, fighting back more tears and then deciding that I didn't have to.

"*You're* gorgeous," he said, beaming up at me, just as the skies opened.

"Come here," I said, and pulled him up to hug him.

"I love you, Cate," he whispered in my ear, the words sounding better than they ever had.

"I love you, too, Joe," I whispered back.

"Forever?" he asked.

"Forever and ever," I said. Just then, Thursday returned with Joe's hat, clearly wanting in on the action.

"Hey there, good boy!" Joe said. "She said yes! She's stuck with us now."

He stooped down, pried Thursday's mouth open, and removed the slobbery, sandy hat, promptly putting it back on his head.

"I guess I'm stuck with that hat, too, huh?" I said, smiling up at him.

He nodded, holding my gaze for the longest time before kissing me softly in the falling rain.

CHAPTER 25

Joe

My original plan had been to take Cate to Paris and reenact our first date, popping the question at the table overlooking the courtyard at Le Bristol. But given our hectic work schedules, I knew it might be weeks before we could both pull off a trip to France, and there was no way I could wait that long. Besides, I worried that a trip to Paris might tip her off about what was coming, and the romantic in me wanted to surprise her.

My next idea was to take a sunset cruise aboard my boat—which I hadn't yet dry-docked for the season—and propose to Cate in the cove where we'd made love. It would be a little chilly this time of year, especially out on the water, but we could bundle up. I ran the idea by Peter and Genevieve. Not only did the plan meet with their approval, but they offered to help me execute it. Basically, we'd all head out east for the weekend, and while Cate and I took the boat out, they'd be back home, setting up a romantic dinner for two with lots of candles and roses. Genevieve balked a bit on the roses, calling them clichéd and cheesy. Peter argued that I *was* cheesy—and that Cate should know what she was in for.

"Fine," Genevieve relented. "But let's do pink, not red."

"No way," I said. "Cate hates pink."

"No. She doesn't *wear* pink. But she likes it on other people."

"How do you know?"

"We've discussed it."

"When? How did that come up?"

"You don't believe me?"

"Yeah, I believe you. I just wanna know the context."

She laughed and asked why.

"Because I want to know everything about her," I said.

Genevieve looked at Peter and said, "Gosh. He's *obsessed*. Are you this obsessed with me?"

There was only one answer to this, and Peter gave it to her, laughing. "Of course I am."

Genevieve turned back to me and said, "The context was the pink bridesmaid dress she had to wear for her friend's wedding—a dress she detested."

"See?" I said. "I told you—"

Genevieve cut me off. "Nope. She definitely said she likes pink on some people—just not on her. She specifically mentioned Marilyn Monroe's dress in *Gentlemen Prefer Blondes*."

"Yeah. She loves those old movies," I said, nodding.

"God. You really *are* obsessed," she said, looking at me this time and shaking her head.

I grinned and said yes, guilty as charged.

UNFORTUNATELY, OUR ELABORATE plan was foiled by two things: Peter got called in to work, and the weather forecast was filled with rain. Genevieve suggested we wait until the next weekend, but I told them I would wing it alone. I didn't want to wait. Cate and I would drive up Saturday morning, spend a relaxing day together, and unwind from all the pressure we'd both been under at work. Then, just after nightfall, I'd build a fire, open a bottle of champagne, and pop the question. Afterward, and assuming she said yes, we would celebrate at a nice restaurant, or if Cate wasn't in the mood to go out, we could stay in and cook together. It would all work out—and Cate actually wasn't the kind of girl who needed rose petals scattered at her feet.

On Saturday morning, Cate, Thursday, and I were on the road by nine. All I could think about was the ring, especially as we talked about the future. I told her about my meeting that week with the Democratic state party chairwoman and how she was trying to convince me to run for Congress, and Cate told me that she was thinking of leaving her job as well. It was all a bit overwhelming and nerve-racking, but I told myself that it would work out. We would figure things out together; I just needed her to say yes.

The closer we got to the Hamptons, the more excited and jittery I became. I didn't know how I would get through the whole day but knew I needed some exercise, and suggested we take Thursday for a walk on the beach before it started to rain.

"Sure," Cate said.

As we unpacked and changed, I eyed my sneaker where the ring was hidden. I told myself I needed to wait until later, but the second Cate went into the bathroom, I reached into the shoe, opened the black velvet box, and stuffed the ring in the pocket of my sweats. Just in case the moment was right, I wanted to be ready.

As it turned out, that moment came about a mile down the beach, with Thursday at our side, close to the spot where we met. Fighting the worst nerves of my life, I worked up the courage to drop to one knee, reach into my pocket, and pull out the ring. My mind was spinning as I tried to remember all the parts of the speech I'd been practicing in my head for days. I have no idea if I sounded eloquent or like a blathering idiot. All I recall with any clarity is the way she looked down at me and nodded, her eyes filling with tears.

I felt almost drunk as we walked back to the house in the pouring rain, pumped full of the best kind of adrenaline. Meanwhile, the wind picked up and the waves turned dark gray and choppy. When we were almost back to our yard, there was an electric flash in the sky followed immediately by a deafening clap of thunder. Cate screamed while Thursday began barking his head off, and the three of us took off in a mad sprint back to the house. By the time we arrived at the back porch, we were drenched, and a weird combination of cold and sweaty. Stripping our soaked clothing off, we laughed, then ran naked upstairs to the bathroom, heading straight into the shower.

From there, the images are seared into my brain. Kissing Cate under the hot water. Pressing her against the black-and-white tile wall. Slowly entering her, then thrusting harder until she called out my name. And most of all, the way she looked at me afterward, her blue eyes sparkling, just like the ring on her finger.

CHAPTER 26

Cate

That stormy weekend in the Hamptons, Joe and I talked endlessly about the future. He made the final decision to quit his job, and I resolved to get my GED, attend college, and help with his campaign.

We also decided to keep our engagement a secret from the press. To that end, I would wear my ring on my right hand and deny its significance—which would be more believable because of the ring's nontraditional design. We called a few close friends and family with our news, including Elna, Wendy, Peter, and Genevieve, who already knew of Joe's plans, along with his grandmother, mother, Berry, and Curtis, swearing them all to secrecy. Sadly, I did not call my own mother. With Chip in the picture, it just wasn't safe for her to know. In the back of my mind, I wondered if we could even invite her to our wedding. When I mentioned this to Joe over coffee on Sunday morning, he looked horrified.

"What? Your mother *has* to be there," he said. "We'll find a way to get her there safely without him."

"I don't know if that's possible. It might be too risky," I said, envisioning Chip calling the media and blowing everything up. Or worse.

"We can do it," Joe said, stirring more sugar into his mug. "Don't worry about that."

"Or . . . we could just elope?" I said.

"Is that what you want?"

I hesitated because in some ways it always had been what I wanted, even before I knew I would be marrying into the highest-profile family imaginable. There were just too many things missing in my life for a traditional wedding, including a father to walk me down the aisle. Weddings also cost a fortune. I had some money saved, but it still felt like a waste. "Well, eloping sure would be easier," I finally said.

"Forget about what's *easier*," he said. "Is that what you *want*?"

I sighed, then shook my head and said no, mostly because I knew that wasn't what *he* wanted—and I didn't think it was fair to him to have any of my issues cloud our decision. That wasn't the way to start a life together.

"Good. Because I want to see you walking down the aisle. So badly."

I smiled. "Okay. But I don't want a *huge* wedding, either," I said, thinking of Wendy and Genevieve and how the planning sometimes seemed to take away from the underlying sentiment of marriage.

"I agree. I'd rather have something small," Joe said.

"Will your mother be okay with that?"

"She'll have to be," he said. "It's *our* wedding."

I smiled.

"So . . . what do you envision?" he asked.

"I don't know," I said, looking down at my gorgeous ring, feeling overwhelmed. I looked back up at Joe and said, "Something intimate and very private."

He gazed into my eyes and said, "Go on."

"Well . . . let's see," I said. "I picture just two attendants. A best man and maid of honor."

"Elna and Peter?"

"Yes. Elna and Peter," I said, thinking Wendy might be hurt, but she'd get over it.

"Will we be in a church or outside?" he asked, like a little boy at story time.

"Either one. But maybe a church would be nice," I said, thinking that it would also eliminate the possibility of the paparazzi filming our ceremony from a helicopter. We wouldn't have to worry about weather, either.

"Where is this church?"

"Somewhere remote and secluded . . . maybe a small wooden chapel with only a few pews inside," I said. That would be the last place anyone would suspect that Joe Kingsley would marry.

"Ohhh, yes. I like that. A lot . . . What else?" he said, his expression growing softer by the second.

"Well . . . let's see. . . . We'll exchange vows after dark . . . by candlelight . . . because there might not be any electricity in our little church."

Joe closed his eyes and inhaled. "Yes. Candles covering the altar."

"Yes. *Filling* the church . . ." I said. "And the pastor might need a flashlight, too. To read from the Bible."

His eyes still closed, Joe said, "What's the season? Summer?"

"Maybe," I said, imagining a warm breeze coming through the open windows of the church, rustling my bouquet and hair. Or maybe there would be a chill in the air. I'd always loved the idea of a winter wedding with snow falling outside. I could wear a faux-fur stole and long gloves. "Any season could work."

Joe opened his eyes. "Will there be music?"

"Yes. Of course. But nothing elaborate or loud. No organ. Maybe a vocalist or a violinist."

"What about a harp?"

I laughed and said, "No. There won't be room for a harp. The church is too small."

"Will you wear white?" he asked, looking hopeful, perhaps because he'd recently overheard me telling Genevieve that I loved untraditional wedding gowns—whether short or with color.

"Yes. I'll wear white," I said—because it was clearly what he wanted. "But I can't tell you anything else about my dress. It's bad luck."

I smiled, picturing a sheath gown and a simple veil. Maybe just a crown of flowers in my hair.

"Will I wear a tux?"

"No," I said. "It won't be that formal."

"Ah, right . . . So just a suit?"

"Yes. A dark suit. Perfectly cut."

"How about the one I bought from you?"

I nodded and said yes that would be perfect, along with a pale blue or silver necktie, perhaps with a hint of shimmer.

Joe stood up from the table and came around to pull me to my feet. "Tell me about our first kiss . . . as husband and wife," he said, as his arms encircled my waist.

"It will be perfect," I said, gazing up at him. "Not too short, not too long. Just right."

"Should we practice?"

"Yes. That's a good idea," I said, closing my eyes. I felt his warm breath on my face and his lips brushing softly against mine.

"Like that?" he whispered.

"Mmm. That's close," I said. "But I think we should try again."

He kissed me a second time, a little longer and harder. "Like that?"

"Oh. Yes," I said. "*Exactly* like that."

THE NEXT COUPLE of months were, quite simply, the happiest of my life. It was also the first time I can ever remember truly enjoying the holidays—at least since I was a little girl, before Chip came on the scene. Joe and I put all of our planning for the future on a brief pause and went full throttle on all the romantic activities that I'd always wistfully watched other couples do.

We went to see the Christmas tree lighting at Rockefeller Center and the Rockettes at Radio City Music Hall. We ice-skated at Wollman Rink and went sledding on Pilgrim Hill. We had tea at the Pierre and hot chocolate at Junior's. We wandered the toy aisles at F.A.O. Schwarz and perused the elaborate winter wonderlands behind the department store windows, from Macy's to Saks to Lord & Taylor—which Joe referred to as the pièce de résistance of window displays. There was something so endearing about how much he embraced it all, including activities that many denigrated as touristy. Nothing was beneath him, and I fell more in love with every passing day.

AS WE ROLLED into the new year, Joe finally resigned from his job and began quietly putting together his campaign team. Meanwhile, I signed up for the GED exam, ordered college brochures, and gave my notice to Wilbur. It was a bittersweet moment. As sad as Wilbur said he was to lose me, he seemed to understand that my current role with the company was no longer feasible. He was over the moon when I told him that Joe and I were engaged.

As we sat in his swanky corner office, I cleared my throat and asked the question that had been on my mind. "Will you make my gown?"

Wilbur's jaw dropped, and it took a second for him to speak. "Are you serious?"

"Yes," I said, smiling. "I'm serious."

"Are you sure? There are way bigger designers out there—"

"I want you. Just say yes."

"My goodness, yes. *Yes!* . . . It would be the greatest honor!"

Wilbur was prone to exaggeration, but as he pressed his hand to his heart and blinked back tears, I could tell he meant it.

"Thank you," I said.

"No. Thank *you*," he said, immediately standing and pacing around his desk the way he always did when he was excited about a project. "So tell me. When and where will your wedding take place?"

I cleared my throat and said we were thinking about June or July—so as not to preempt Peter and Genevieve's spring wedding— and that we had chosen a small, historic church on Shelter Island called Union Chapel in the Grove.

"Oh, I love Shelter Island!" Wilbur said.

"Me too. Joe took me there over New Year's," I said, thinking of the romantic weekend we had spent at the Ram's Head Inn, a bed-and-breakfast looking out over Peconic Bay. I told Wilbur how we'd accidentally stumbled upon the little chapel on the western bank of the island. It had been established as a Methodist prayer hall back in 1875.

"How perfectly quaint," Wilbur said.

I smiled and said, "Yes. That's what we're going for. Cozy and understated and private . . . so all of this is top secret."

"Of course! I swear," Wilbur said, holding up his right hand and placing his left on an imaginary Bible. "You know discretion is my middle name."

I smiled.

"Do you have a florist? A caterer? Where will the reception be held?"

"We're not sure yet. We've only made a few calls to the inn and the church. That's as far as we've gotten—"

"Oh, honey. You've made calls? This is going to leak *so* fast," Wilbur said, looking worried.

I shook my head and told him about our aliases—Sylvia and Dean Bristol—after his grandmother, my father, and the Parisian hotel where we first kissed.

"I *love* it," Wilbur said, sitting back down at his desk. He pulled a sketchbook out of the top drawer and flipped it open to a blank page. Then he grabbed a sharpened pencil from a pewter cup next to his computer and gazed over at me. "So, let's talk about the dress. What are you thinking?"

I smiled and said, "Well. You know my taste as well as I do."

"Yes," he said. "Elegant, streamlined simplicity."

"Yes. I want simple. No lace or beading or other embellishments."

Wilbur nodded. "Sleeveless?"

"Yes. But not strapless."

"Spaghetti straps?"

"Yes," I said. "Maybe a silk slip dress, cut on the bias? Floor length but no train."

Wilbur nodded, his pencil flying over the page as he began one of his infamous croquis drawings.

After a few seconds, he looked up and said, "Veil or no veil?"

"Veil, I think," I said. "And maybe long white gloves? For a hint of glamour?"

"Oh, *heavens,* yes . . . and your bouquet?"

"Lilies of the valley," I said. "They're Joe's favorite—and his mother carried them when she got married."

"Fabulous," he said. "A nod to the Kingsley tradition."

"Yes," I said. "But we really want to do things our way—"

"Yes," he said. "A modern-day Cinderella."

I laughed and asked if that made him my fairy godfather.

"Bibbidi-bobbidi-boo," Wilbur said, waving his pencil like a wand.

FROM THAT VERY first sketch, my gown—and our wedding plans—came together quickly and covertly. We used our aliases whenever possible—and when it wasn't possible, we had vendors sign ironclad confidentiality agreements. All the while, my happy streak continued.

More striking than my feelings of happiness, though, was the complete absence of self-doubt and my usual relentless brand of cynicism. For once, I wasn't waiting for the other shoe to drop. Why had I always kept my expectations so low? I wondered. How could I have believed that true love didn't exist in the world—or that somehow I wasn't worthy of it? With Joe at my side, and his ring on my left hand (or my right when I was out in public), nothing could stop us.

Or so I thought until that cold but sunny March morning in the park.

I had just completed my two-loop jog around the Reservoir and was doing my usual stretching by the South Gate House when I saw a man approaching me. I'm not great at remembering faces, but I could have sworn I'd seen his before. He had an unusually full head of golden hair given his middle age—and combined with his strong jawline, blue eyes, and weathered skin, he gave me a Robert Redford vibe. A downtrodden version of Robert Redford, that is, wearing a baggy olive-green sweatsuit.

As he got closer, he kept his eyes on me, and I grew uneasy.

There was no sign of a camera, but I suspected that he might be a reporter. Then again, I was wearing my standard park disguise of oversize sunglasses and one of Joe's wool caps. I'd even tucked my ponytail into the back of my fleece jacket, as I'd learned it was my hair that typically gave me away. So it was a long shot that any-one would recognize me—unless he'd followed me from my place.

I told myself I was just being paranoid, that he was probably only innocently people-watching the way a lot of New Yorkers did. Sure enough, he stopped a few feet away from me, then leaned on the chain-link fence that Joe always referred to as a blight on the park and stared out over the water. Clearly, he was minding his own business, and I needed to do the same.

I finished my stretching, then walked past him, my thoughts moving on to my to-do list for the day. But no sooner was he gone from my mind than he reappeared out of the corner of my eye, walking alongside me in perfect lockstep. At that point, I got a chill. He was *definitely* following me. The only question was whether he was a reporter—or some sort of stalker.

My heart pounding in my ears, I began to run. He did the same, then called out my name. *Cate. Please stop. I just want to talk to you. Please.*

His voice was low and calm, and there was something about the way he said *please* that defused my fear, replacing it with run-of-the-mill annoyance.

I stopped, turned, and looked him straight in the eye. "Stop following me!" I demanded. "Now!"

"I'm sorry," he said. "I need to talk to you. Just for a minute. *Please.*"

I shook my head, but he kept talking. "It's not what you think. It's not about Joe or anything like that," he said.

"Then what's it about?" I asked, my hands now on my hips.

"Can we sit down? Please?" he said, pointing over at a bench. "I promise I only need five minutes—"

I hesitated, wanting to say no. But my curiosity got the better of me, along with his blue eyes. They looked kind. I reminded myself that Ted Bundy had kind blue eyes, too, but still said, "Fine. Five minutes."

He thanked me, then walked over to the bench, sitting on one end. I followed him, sitting on the other end, waiting for him to speak. I glanced at my watch, letting him know that he was on the clock.

Meanwhile, he crossed his legs, then uncrossed them, like he couldn't quite get comfortable. Or maybe he was just stalling. Another few seconds passed as he pulled a pack of cigarettes and a lighter out of his pocket and offered me one.

I shook my head.

"Is it okay if I smoke?" he asked, sounding really nervous— and not at all predatory.

I relaxed a bit more, then shrugged and said go ahead, watching as he lit his cigarette, took a long, slow drag, then exhaled.

"Okay. Do you mind telling me who the hell you are?" I said, waving away the smoke.

"You really don't know?" he said, meeting my gaze.

"No clue," I said, though he really did look eerily familiar. "Have we met?"

Silence stretched between us as I stared at him, waiting.

"Yes, Cate," he finally said. "I'm your father."

Bolting up from the bench like it was on fire, I took a few steps away from it, then glared down at him, something snapping inside me. "You're a real sicko, you know that?"

"Cate—"

"Nice try," I said. "My father died when I was three years old."

He shook his head. "No, Cate. I didn't die. . . . Shit . . . is that what your mother told you?"

"Yes. That's what she told me," I said, my voice shaking, my world spinning. "Because that's what happened. My father was in a car accident. He's dead. You are *not* my father."

"Yes, I am, Cate," he said, nodding, a desperate look on his face. He dropped his cigarette and crushed it out in the dirt at his feet, then looked at me again. "I *was* in a car accident—an accident that I caused. I'd been drinking and driving . . . and I . . . I killed a man and his pregnant wife. I got charged with three murders . . . and I went to prison. For twenty-two years. I just got out—"

I shook my head, thinking that there was no way—no *possible* way. But as he stared back at me, I remembered where I had seen his eyes. They were the eyes from the photograph. The only one I had of my father.

"Oh my God," I heard myself say. My knees buckled, and I collapsed back onto the bench.

The next few minutes were like a dream, his voice coming in and out. He talked about the letters and birthday cards he had sent me from prison and how they came back as undeliverable. He told me about his grief and guilt. How not a day went by that he didn't think about that couple and their unborn baby. He talked about finding God, and praying for forgiveness, and living for the day when he could see me again.

Hot tears streamed down my face as anger bubbled up from deep within me. Anger at him for drinking and driving and killing people. Anger at Chip for taking his place. Anger at my mother for lying to me all these years. "Why didn't she tell me?" I said. "Why?"

"I don't know, honey."

"Don't call me that," I said.

"I'm sorry. . . ."

I took a few gulps of air, then said, "Does my mother know you're out of prison?"

He nodded. "Yes. I found her first—"

"And?"

"And it didn't go well. She begged me not to look for you."

"Why?" I said, although I knew *exactly* why. To cover for herself and her lies. I wondered if Chip even knew the truth. I bet not—or he would have rubbed this in my face long ago.

But this man gave me a different answer. "Because of Joe—and your beautiful life. She didn't want me to ruin things."

"She told you about Joe?"

"No. I saw her in the *National Enquirer*. A buddy of mine recognized her—and showed me. . . . That's how I tracked her down. . . ."

I closed my eyes as the bitter, shameful reality sank in. It was worse than I'd ever thought. Joe was a Harvard alum running for Congress with a father who had died an American hero. I was a high-school dropout with a father who had taken three lives and spent most of his life in prison. This was *so* much worse than Chip; Chip had never murdered anyone. And he wasn't my *blood*.

I thought of what the tabloids would say about me when they found out. What Joe's *mother* would say. It was too much—*way* too much—and every feeling of self-doubt and inadequacy I'd ever known came rushing back. Joe was too good for me, plain and simple, and even if he could get over the horrible truth about where I came from, I knew that I never would.

"I have to go," I said, getting to my feet again.

"Cate—" he pleaded, staring up at me, his own tears spilling. "I'm so sorry I wasn't there for you—"

"Sorry won't bring those people back."

"I know. God, I know . . . but I have atoned as much as possible for what I did. And the victims' families have forgiven me. I just hope you can, too—"

"You've been gone my whole life. My *whole* life."

"I know. But you're still a young woman. . . . It's not too late—"

I shook my head and backed slowly away from him. I didn't want to hear another word. "Yes, it is. It's *way* too late."

"Cate. You're the only thing I've ever truly cared about. I'm your father—"

"No! You're not my father. I don't have a father," I said. "Or a mother. You are both dead to me."

Then I turned and ran away from him as fast as I possibly could.

CHAPTER 27

Joe

For several months after Cate and I got engaged, everything was so damn good. Exciting and hopeful and just *wonderful*. I realized that beyond how much I loved her, being with her also allowed me to escape being a Kingsley, at least in part. Our relationship was the first thing in my life that didn't feel foisted upon me—like Harvard, and law school, and my respectable job as a prosecutor. Even the campaign felt like another weight on my shoulders, a burden of my legacy. But with Cate by my side, that pressure felt manageable. She kept telling me that I could do it. That she was proud of me. That I didn't have to be my father, but that I was more than the free-spirited, risk-taking lightweight persona I'd always tried to hide behind.

Then, suddenly and overnight, everything changed. That was my perception, anyway, though maybe it had happened more gradually, and I'd just been too busy with my campaign to notice.

I'd returned from Peter's bachelor party in Miami, his wedding only two weeks away. My flight landed around two, and I called Cate the second I walked in my door from LaGuardia. It had only been forty-eight hours since I'd seen her, but I missed her a crazy amount.

Elna answered their phone, and after we chatted a few seconds, she put Cate on.

"Hey! Where've you been?" I asked her. "I tried you twice yesterday. Did you get my messages?"

She said yes. Nothing more.

"Are you okay?"

"I'm fine. Just a little under the weather . . ."

"Oh, shoot. Do you think it's the flu? It's going around."

"No," she said. "It's mostly just a headache."

"A migraine?" I asked, familiar with those from my mother's spells over the years.

"I'm not sure," she said, sounding both vague and distant.

"Okay. Well, can I bring you anything? Meds or soup?"

"No. I'll be fine," she said. "I just need to lie down."

"Okay," I said. "Check in with me later, okay?"

"Will do," she said, then quickly hung up.

LATER THAT NIGHT, when I hadn't heard back from Cate, it crossed my mind that she could be mad about Peter's bachelor party. She hadn't asked any questions, but I was sure she assumed strippers were involved—which they had been. In the scheme of bachelor parties, it had been on the tame side—just the standard antics in a hotel suite—but I was still feeling guilty, wishing that we had taken a sailing trip instead.

At the risk of interrupting her sleep, I called Cate back. She answered on the first ring, sounding wide awake.

Wondering why she hadn't called me, I asked her how she was feeling.

"Pretty much the same," she said, her voice as flat as it had been on the first call.

"Oh . . . Well, I'm sorry to bother you again—but I was just worried . . . are you upset with me about the weekend?"

"The weekend?"

"I mean—the stripper stuff . . . It's all so stupid . . . but harmless. And I just wanted you to know that nothing happened."

"Jeez, Joe," she said. "I would *hope* nothing happened."

Feeling a little stupid, I said, "Yeah. Totally . . . I didn't even get a lap dance. In case you were wondering."

"I wasn't. But thanks," she said with a little laugh that I couldn't read.

"Okay . . . so you're sure you're not upset with me?"

"Yeah. I'm sure."

"And nothing's wrong?"

She hesitated, then said, "No. Not really."

"Not *really*?"

She sighed, then said, "I just have a lot on my mind."

"What's on your mind?" I said, getting increasingly worried.

"You know. Everything. The wedding. The campaign . . . It's a lot. . . . I'm just not sure we can pull this off—"

"Pull the campaign off?" I asked her—because not a day went by that I didn't think about throwing in the towel before I'd even declared my candidacy. I had no experience, and beyond how worrisome that was, I wasn't even sure what I stood for. At times, I even felt paranoid that I was just being manipulated, used for my name. Much like at my job in the DA's office, everyone involved in the campaign had an agenda, but instead of being one cog in the whole operation, I was now in the eye of the storm.

"Not the campaign," Cate said. "I meant the wedding."

"The wedding?" I asked. "Did something happen? Did the press find out?"

"No. But I'm sure they will. Maybe we should put the wedding on hold so you can focus on your campaign?"

"No way," I said. "Marrying you is my top priority."

"But—"

"But what?"

"I don't know. . . ." she said, her voice trailing off. "Nothing, I guess."

"Cate. Please talk to me. Tell me what's on your mind. Have I not been helping enough with the planning?" I asked, suddenly sure that was it. The past few weeks had been incredibly hectic as I'd been bombarded with endless administrative tasks, from hiring staff to filing paperwork to gearing up for fundraising. And then there was the matter of Valentine's Day, which she'd told me she hated and wanted to ignore. I'd believed her, but maybe it had been one of those tricks. A test that I'd failed. My mind was spinning as I waited for her to answer.

"I just don't know that the timing is right. . . . I don't know if it makes sense to plan a wedding while our lives are in such flux. . . . And, really, what's the rush?"

"There's no rush. But I also don't see the point in waiting. And the longer we wait, the more likely the media will find out."

"Yeah," she said. "But if they *do* find out, there will be a complete circus at the same time you're announcing your run."

"Okay. So you want to wait until after the election? Is that what you're saying?"

"Yeah. I guess."

"What about moving in with me? Do you want to put that on hold, too?"

I held my breath, praying she'd say no. Instead, she sighed and said, "I don't know. Maybe. You know your mother hates the idea—"

"I don't care—" I said, getting upset.

"Okay, Joe," she said. "I'm just feeling a little overwhelmed. That's all . . . and this headache—I just want to go back to sleep. Is that okay?"

"Of course, honey," I said.

I told myself to be patient—that her mood would pass. But I felt a knot in my stomach as I hung up the phone.

FOR THE NEXT few days, it was more of the same. Cate kept blowing me off and making up excuses until I finally told her I was coming over to see her. Right now.

"I'm about to go for a run," she said, evading me once again.

"Where?"

"At the Reservoir."

"Can I meet you there?"

She hesitated, then gave me some excuse about how the paparazzi were more likely to recognize her if she was with me. But I was determined to see her, already lacing up my Nikes.

A minute later, I was out the door, hightailing it up to the park. When I got to the Reservoir, I began walking clockwise against the foot traffic, searching for her. About half a loop around, I spotted her running toward me. Wearing all black, she looked so strong—her pace faster than usual.

She didn't see me until she was right on me, but as soon as she did, she gave me a smile. It was a good sign.

"Fancy seeing you here!" I said, grinning at her.

She rolled her eyes and shook her head. "You're too much," she said, leaning down to put her hands on her knees and catch her breath.

"I had to see you," I said.

She stood up straight, then stared into my eyes, her expression impossible to read. "Well. Here I am."

"Yes. A sight for sore eyes . . . Mind if I join you?"

"Do I have a choice?" she said with a laugh.

I smiled back at her and said no.

"Well. Come on, then," she said, jogging away from me and motioning over her shoulder for me to join her.

I took a deep breath, then reversed direction, catching up to her. For the next twenty minutes or so, we ran in silence as I struggled to keep up with her. At one point, she suddenly stopped, abruptly swerving off the path. She then plopped down onto the ground and began to stretch. I followed her, sitting cross-legged in the grass beside her, waiting for her to say something.

When she didn't, I cleared my throat and said, "Okay, Cate. What's going on? You're not yourself."

"I told you. I'm just feeling overwhelmed," she said, avoiding my gaze as she spread her legs in a V shape and touched her nose to one knee, then the other.

"Are you getting cold feet?" I asked her point-blank.

"I wouldn't say cold feet," she said, waffling. "I just think we're moving . . . a little fast."

"Okay. We can slow it down . . . if that's what you really want."

She nodded. "Yeah. I just think we should do that for now. You need to focus on your campaign. Give it your all. You can't have any distractions right now."

"You're not a distraction."

"Weddings are a distraction," she said. "Look at Peter and Genevieve. They're consumed. . . ."

"We aren't having that kind of wedding."

"Still. If the media finds out . . ."

"Would you rather just elope?"

"Joe. Stop!" she said. "I told you what I wanted! I want to wait! You're not listening!"

"Okay, honey," I said, putting my hand on her leg. "Calm down."

She pushed my hand away and said, "Don't tell me to calm down! I hate when you do that!"

I looked at her, surprised, because I couldn't remember a single instance when I'd ever told her to calm down. I almost pointed this out but decided that probably wasn't a good idea. Instead, I just apologized.

"Don't be sorry," she said. "Just stop all of this."

"All of what?"

"The clamoring and nagging . . . I just need a little space."

"From me?"

"From everything!" she said, her voice rising, as I caught a woman staring at us. Her face lit up as she pointed us out to her friend.

"Shhh," I said, looking down at the ground. "People are look-ing—"

"Don't shush me! And of *course* they're looking! You came to the park when I told you not to!"

"I came to the park because you refused to see me," I said, my worry morphing into frustration with a tinge of anger.

"Exactly. I refused to see you because I didn't want to see you. Get how that works?" she said, her voice icy.

"Jeez," I said. "Why are you being such a jerk?"

"I'm not being a jerk, Joe! I told you I wanted to go for a run alone, and you showed up anyway! That's selfish as hell. It's not always about you!" she yelled, getting to her feet and glaring down at me.

"Dammit, Cate," I said, standing and facing her. "I know it's not about me. I'm trying to—"

"What?" she yelled. "What, exactly, are you trying to do?"

"I'm trying to talk to you. I'm worried about you," I said.

"Well, don't be! I'm fine! I was fine before you. I'm fine now. And I'll be fine—" She stopped abruptly, and so did my heart.

"Finish your sentence," I said.

She shook her head.

"Come on, Cate. Go ahead and tell me. What were you going to say?"

"Nothing," she said, clearly lying. Then she shook her head and turned to go.

I grabbed her arm and said, "That you'll be fine *after* me? Is that what you were going to say?"

She pulled away and said, "No. I was just going to say that I'll *always* be fine."

"No, you weren't," I said. "That's not what you were going to say."

She bit her lip, shook her head, then said, "Okay, Joe. You want to push this?"

"Yes," I said. "I do."

"Fine," she said, her eyes flashing with anger.

I waited a few seconds, then watched with shock as she took off her ring and shoved it into my chest. "I can't do this."

"What?" I said, backing up, horrified.

"Take the ring, Joe," she said, giving me a steely gaze.

"No," I said, shaking my head. "Don't do this—"

"Take it, Joe. *Now.*"

I kept shaking my head, then began to beg. *Please don't do this. Please.*

But she clearly wasn't listening. Instead, she dropped the ring on the ground, then turned and walked away.

CHAPTER 28

Cate

'm not sure where the photographer was hiding or how long-range his camera lens was, but he caught every second of our fight in the park—on *video,* no less—including the part after I left, when Joe sat back down on the ground and cried, his face in his hands.

I never actually saw the video, but Elna and Curtis and Wendy did, along with everyone else and their mother, after the film and photographs were sold to *Entertainment Tonight* and dozens of other outlets. I asked my friends to give it to me straight—and they did, reading aloud the headlines, ranging from HUNK DUMPED to CATE HATE to the simple and succinct IT'S OVER!

It was the biggest shitshow to date, proving once again that bad news outsells good. The only silver lining was that things finally seemed black and white. Our caught-on-camera fight crystallized my gut feeling that I couldn't marry Joe. If the press went this crazy over a fight in the park, I couldn't imagine what they'd do when they discovered the truth about my father. It would be unbearable for everyone involved, not to mention the damage it would do to Joe's image and political career and relationship with his mother. Bottom line, the tabloids got it right, for once.

It *was* over.

Meanwhile, I hid from the world as photographers staked out my apartment and my phone rang off the hook. I screened my calls, ignoring everyone, including Joe, who left several pleas on my answering machine.

The only time I picked up was when I heard my mother's voice droning on about how sad she was to see that Joe and I were in a fight. Overcome by rage, I grabbed the phone with one hand as Elna held my other.

"Don't ever call me again," I said, my voice low and steady.

"Cate? Is that you?"

"Yes," I said, closing my eyes, determined. "And listen carefully—because this will be the last time you ever hear my voice."

"What in the world is going on? I'm so confused—"

"Really, Mom? Are you *really* going to sit there and play dumb with me?"

Silence filled the airwaves.

"I met *Dean,* Mom," I said. "In the park. Too bad the paparazzi didn't get a video of *that,* although I'm sure it's only a matter of time before they break that news, too—"

"Oh, Catie . . . I'm so sorry—I just wanted to protect you. . . ."

"Bullshit, Mom! That's the biggest load of crap I've ever heard. You have *never* protected me. Never! Not once in your life."

"Catie. Please. I've tried—"

"No, Mom. If you wanted to protect me, you would've left Chip. You wouldn't have married him in the first place. I grew up with a monster who completely eviscerated my self-esteem because you, Mom, are a coward. A selfish coward," I said, my voice now shaking.

Elna was still holding my hand and squeezed it as hard as she could.

"I'm sorry," my mother sobbed into the phone.

"How could you lie to me like this? About my own father? How?"

"Cate, please! Try to understand. You were a little girl. A baby. I didn't want you growing up knowing that your father was in prison—"

"So you tell me he's *dead*? How about a nicer lie, like, say, he moved to Africa to feed starving people?"

I was mostly being sarcastic, but my mother missed it, saying, "But then you'd have hope that he'd come back."

"Well, surprise! He *did* come back!"

"He wasn't supposed to," she said. "They said life with no parole."

"Oh, for fuck's sake, Mom! Do you hear yourself?"

"You were so little—"

"Okay, well, what about when I grew up? When I was a teen-ager? When I left home? It never crossed your mind to sit me down and tell me the truth?"

"A million times," she said, sobbing. "But—I couldn't—"

"WHY NOT?" I screamed, pulling my hand away from Elna as I stood up and began pacing around the room.

"Because. Then Chip would have known . . . and he would have . . ."

"He would have WHAT, Mom?"

"He would have gone berserk. . . ."

"Berserk like throwing cat shit around my room—or berserk like breaking your collarbone? Or something else?"

"Cate. Stop. Please."

As I listened to my mother sobbing, doing her best to justify the unjustifiable, I felt any last trace of residual compassion I'd ever had for her disappear.

"I mean it, Mom. I'm done. Please don't ever call me again."

I hung up before she could respond, then promptly crawled back in bed, where I pretty much remained for the next three days, except when Elna made me get up to shower or eat.

On the fourth day, Elna and Curtis staged a mini-intervention in my bedroom.

"Cate, you can't hide like this forever," Elna began. "You have to face the world."

"And you have to talk to Joe," Curtis added. "He's left so many messages. He's called both of us—"

"What have you told him?" I asked, sitting up in bed.

"Nothing," he said. "I swear."

"Elna?"

"He hasn't. We haven't. But you have to talk to him."

"There's nothing to talk about. It's over. I gave him back the ring."

"Okay, look," Elna said. "If you don't want to marry him, that's fine—"

"No, it's not!" Curtis chimed in.

"Yes, it *is*, Curtis," Elna said in her most stern voice. "But even if she doesn't marry him, she owes him an explanation about why she's doing this."

"Why *is* she doing this?" Curtis asked her.

I sighed because I'd explained it to him several times already. My father was an ex-con who was responsible for the deaths of three human beings. I said it again.

"But *you* didn't do anything," Curtis said. "You didn't even know any of that—"

"Nobody will believe that I didn't know," I said. "I told Joe he was dead."

"You thought he *was* dead! Joe will believe you. You're not a liar, Cate. He knows that."

"It's just too much," I said, thinking of the things I *had* kept from him along the way. "And Dottie and Berry will *never* believe it. Never."

"But it's the truth—" Curtis said.

"Sometimes the truth doesn't matter. Do you know anything about politics? The Kingsley family?"

"They've had scandals before," Curtis said. "You've heard the rumors about his father cheating, haven't you?"

"Those are just rumors," I said. "Joe doesn't believe them."

"Where there's smoke there's fire," Curtis said.

"Are you *seriously* comparing infidelity to murder?"

"It wasn't murder," Curtis said. "It was a tragedy—and yes, it was criminal—but none of this is a reason for you *not* to marry the love of your life."

"Elna?" I said, turning to her. "Will you please explain this to him?"

Elna cleared her throat and said, "I think you're missing the point, Curtis. It's not that her father's crimes are the reason not to marry Joe. And it's not whether Joe will believe that she didn't know . . . because I, for one, think he will believe her. . . . It's that Cate sees this as further proof that she can't live the Kingsley life."

"But she *can*!" Curtis said.

"But maybe she doesn't want to—" Elna said.

"She doesn't want to marry the hottest guy in the universe who is madly in love with her and treats her like absolute gold?" he said.

"Maybe she doesn't want the pressure that comes with that. The constant scrutiny. The feeling—misguided though it is—that she isn't good enough."

I nodded and said, "Yes. All of that. Thank you, El."

"But you love him," Curtis said. "Doesn't love conquer all?"

"No," I said. "It doesn't. And besides—if I truly love him, I need to let him go. He'll be better off without me."

"I don't believe that," Curtis said. "And neither do you. I know you don't."

"Yes, I do! Elna, help me out here. . . ."

Elna sighed and said, "I can't help you. This isn't for me to decide. Or Curtis. Or the press or Dottie or Joe. You have to figure it out for yourself."

I sighed and told her that I already had.

"Fine," Elna said. "Fair enough. But you still have to get up, get dressed, and get on with your life."

I nodded, knowing she was right.

"And you have to go talk to Joe," she added. "You have to tell him what's up. You don't have to marry him, but you owe him an explanation."

"I can't tell him the truth," I said, adamant. "He'll just try to convince me it's okay . . . that he understands . . . that we'll make it work."

"Because it *will* work!" Curtis said.

"But I don't want it to anymore. I don't. I don't want this," I said, now crying.

Elna put her hand on my arm and told me to calm down.

I nodded, taking a breath.

"Just go talk to him, Cate. Tell him a modified version of the truth. Tell him *something*."

"Oh my God, that poor man," Curtis said.

"He'll be fine," I said, as sickening images of Joe with other women filled my head. "He'll move on fast."

"That's not fair," Curtis said, shaking his head. "Just because he's a Kingsley doesn't mean he can't have a broken heart."

"He'll be fine," I said again, wondering if I ever would be.

CHAPTER 29

Joe

It was our first big fight. Really our *only* fight since we'd been together. Yet the whole world, including my friends and family and my entire campaign team, saw a close-up video of it.

I did my best to downplay it to everyone, laughing it off as another example of the media blowing things way out of proportion. Yes, we'd had a spat, I told them, but we'd quickly made up. Everything would be fine.

Berry was the only one who got the full truth, and I leaned on her just like old times. We analyzed the fight, along with everything that had happened since Cate and I got engaged, searching for clues. We were both baffled, but Berry concluded that I'd done nothing wrong, and that it had to be something internal with Cate. I just needed to be patient, she said, and give her a little time and space.

I did my best to follow Berry's advice, showing as much restraint as I could—which didn't amount to much. I left multiple messages on Cate's machine, and called her friends, too. I just wanted to remind her how much I loved her and that I missed her.

But four torturous days passed, and the phone never rang. By Sunday morning, I was in a state of utter despair. It didn't help that it was raining, and I loved rainy days with Cate. All I wanted to do was curl up under a blanket with the woman I loved. I tried to be productive and distract myself, pretending that it was already Monday. I called my staff, went into the office to work on donor lists, then hit the gym for a harder than usual workout. Nothing made me feel better, so I called Berry and convinced her to come day-drink with me.

Within thirty minutes, she was on my doorstep with a bottle of wine, a pizza, and an old photo album she'd recently unearthed from her aunt's apartment.

"It's five o'clock somewhere, right?" she said.

"Hell, yeah, it is," I said, grinning at her. "Come on in."

For the next few hours, Berry and I pored through old photos, some of them dating back to junior high, and listened to CDs from that nostalgic era, a soundtrack of our friendship. Meanwhile, the wine flowed. Berry wasn't a big drinker, but she kept pretty good pace with me that afternoon, probably sensing that that's what I needed. A dear old drinking buddy.

I did my best not to talk about Cate, because by that point there was nothing new to say. But eventually Berry brought her up.

"If she doesn't contact you before Peter's wedding this weekend, it's over," she declared. "Even if she comes back to you, it's over. You can't take her back."

I nodded, listening, craving clarity, even if it meant Berry's rules and deadlines.

"By the wedding, do you mean the actual ceremony on Saturday—or Thursday, when we're flying down?"

"Thursday," she said, so definite. "She knows when your flights are."

"Okay," I said, nodding. That gave Cate four more days. Surely she wouldn't blow me off for that long. "And tell me why this is the cutoff?" I asked.

"Because it's one thing to do this when only you and I know what's going on; it's another thing to let you go to that wedding by yourself."

I nodded. "Go on."

"You're the best man, Joe. She knows what Peter's wedding means to you and your family . . . and if she lets you go into that weekend solo, where you're going to have to field questions from a few hundred people, she's a heartless bitch."

"Whoa," I said. "That's a little over the top."

"Is it?"

"What happened to 'she might be going through something'?"

"I'm quite sure she *is* going through something," Berry said. "But that doesn't give her carte blanche to do whatever the hell she wants to you."

I nodded as Berry kept going.

"You've given her everything. This girl—without even a high-school degree—"

"Berry—don't go there—"

"Well, it's true!"

"That has nothing to do with *anything*."

"The hell it doesn't," Berry said. "Look, Joe. Like it or not, you're a pretty big fucking prize—and she's an unemployed high-school dropout."

"She had to quit her job because of *me*."

"Regardless. What in the world is she thinking? It makes absolutely no sense. And beyond the fact that it's totally crazy, it's also cruel."

"Cruel?"

"Yes, Joe. It's cruel."

I nodded. Because it suddenly seemed that way to me, too. "Okay. So, if she doesn't call me by Thursday, it's over," I said, getting a little fired up.

"Yes. Over."

Berry stared at me a long time, and said, "It's getting late, and I'm drunk. I better go."

"No!" I said, reaching for her hand, panicking. I didn't want to be alone. "It's only eight o'clock. Stay longer. Stay the night. Please, Ber? You can have my bed. I'll take the couch."

Berry laughed and said, "That's all you need. For the paparazzi to catch me leaving here tomorrow morning."

"I guess," I said, feeling a wave of pure sorrow.

Berry must have been able to tell because she said, "It's going to be okay, Joe. Just give her a little more time."

"But what if she never calls?" I said, staring down at our empty pizza box. "What if I never talk to her again?"

"Well, then . . . it wasn't meant to be."

I stared at her, my head fuzzy from wine. I suddenly recalled one of our first conversations about her parents and how some people had the heartlessness to say that "things happen for a reason." It was crap, she had said, insisting that the universe was pure, brutal chaos. "I thought you didn't believe in that stuff," I finally said.

"What stuff?"

"Fate and destiny type stuff," I said.

"I didn't used to," Berry said, resting her head on my shoulder. "But lately . . . I'm not so sure. . . ."

"What's changed?"

"It's not about what's *changed*," she said, her speech a little slurred. "It's about what *hasn't* changed."

"I don't get it."

Berry turned and looked up at me, tears in her eyes.

"Oh, shit, Berry," I said. "Why are you crying?"

"I'm not," she said, wiping her eyes with two tight fists.

"C'mon. Talk to me. What's wrong?"

"I don't know."

"Yes, you do."

"I'm just sad."

"Why? Tell me."

She took a few deep breaths, then said, "I'm sad because . . . because I miss my parents. After all these years, I still miss them. . . ."

"I know, Ber—" I said, taking both of her hands in mine.

"And I'm sad because *you're* sad—and I hate it when you're sad," she said, now talking quickly. "And I'm sad because I'm nearing my mid-thirties, and I'm still single without a prospect in sight."

Berry's dating life—or more typically, her *lack* of a dating life—was something we never really discussed. At times, I even convinced myself that it didn't matter to her. She had a great career and more friends than anyone I knew. I said as much, but she shook her head, her chin trembling.

"Face it, Joe. I'm alone. And this isn't a pity party. It's just a fact."

"You're not alone," I said. "You have me."

"Not since Cate," she said. "And we both know that the only reason I'm over here tonight is because she's being a psycho *bitch*—"

I tensed up, confused by competing loyalties.

Berry sniffed and wiped her nose on her sleeve. "Sorry. I shouldn't have said that."

"It's okay," I said.

"No, it's not. I don't want this to be me versus her. I want you to make up, and I want to be her friend. But Joe, I'm also not going to let her treat you like shit. And it's taken everything I have not to call her and give her a piece of my mind."

"Aww," I said, feeing touched, even though I was glad she

hadn't done it. "That's really nice—but I don't think that's a smart move."

Berry smiled through her tears and said, "Don't worry . . . but can you promise me one thing?"

"Anything."

"Promise me that things won't ever change with our friendship. No matter what. No matter who you end up with."

"I promise," I said. "And, shit, if Cate leaves me for good, maybe you and I should get married."

I waited for Berry to laugh—or tell me how ridiculous that was. Instead, her eyes welled with tears.

She shook her head and whispered, "Don't say that."

My smile faded as I said, "Sorry. It was just a joke."

"I know—but just . . . don't," she said, one tear rolling down her cheek.

"Is it really that horrid of a notion?" I asked, making one last attempt at humor.

Berry bit her lip and shook her head, "No, Joe," she said, her chin trembling. "I'd marry you tomorrow if I could."

I froze, thinking I must have heard her wrong, that the alcohol was playing tricks on me, but she kept talking. "I've been in love with you since the seventh grade," she said.

I opened my mouth, but nothing came out. Instead, I put my arms around her and pulled her against my chest. "Shit, Berry," I said, kissing the top of her head.

"Yeah," she said. "Tell me about it."

My mind racing and clouded at once, I whispered, "I love you, too, Berry. But—"

"Joe. Stop. I know. I know you don't feel that way. I know you're in love with her. But I needed to tell you. After all these years—I just needed to tell you."

I nodded, now tearing up a little, too. "I'm glad you did."

"You are?"

"Yes," I said. "And I promise that nothing—and *no one*—will ever change how close we are."

Then, as if on cue, the phone rang. I think we both knew, even before I answered, that it was Cate.

CHAPTER 30

Cate

That Sunday evening, less than a week before Peter and Genevieve's wedding, I made the final, painful decision to follow my head over my heart. As much as I loved Joe, we didn't belong together. It wasn't going to work. Breaking up with him was the only way—and I needed to do it before the press got wind of the story about my father. It was only a matter of time, and I couldn't wait for that bomb to go off in Joe's life.

So I picked up the phone and called him. It rang a few times before he answered.

"Hi," I said, my heart racing. "It's me."

"Hi, Cate," he said, sounding so tired and sad.

"Do you think I could come over? To talk?"

"Of course," he said. "I'm dying to talk to you."

"Can I come now?"

He hesitated, then said, "Well, Berry's here right now, actually."

Feeling relieved that I could put the conversation off another night, I said, "Okay. What about sometime tomorrow?"

"Wait," he said. "Can you hold on one second?"

I said yes, then listened to the muffled sounds of voices. When he came back on, he said, "Now's good, actually. Berry's about to leave."

"Are you sure?"

"Yeah," he said. "I'll see you soon."

FIVE MINUTES LATER, I was in a cab, headed downtown. The traffic was light—standard for a Sunday night—and I arrived in SoHo in record time. As I slid out of the taxi, I spotted Berry sitting on the steps of Joe's building, wearing a long, puffy black coat and red Hunter rain boots.

"Hi," she said when I got close to her. Her expression was inscrutable, but I could somehow tell she wasn't happy with me. That she'd been waiting for me.

"Hi," I said, now standing right in front of her, my hand on the railing.

"Are you going to break his heart?" she said, still seated.

I stared at her, speechless.

"Wow . . . You're really going to end it. . . . Aren't you?"

I couldn't make myself answer the yes-no question, so I stammered my way through an explanation. "I—I just don't think we're right for each other—" I said.

Berry's expression darkened even more. "Then why did you accept the ring in the first place?" she asked in a steely voice.

"I don't know. . . . It was a mistake," I said, feeling so flustered and guilty. "I shouldn't have."

She nodded, her jaw clenched, and I braced myself for her to tell me off. Instead, her voice came back quiet and even. "That's correct. You shouldn't have. It's not right to play with someone's heart like that."

"I wasn't doing that, Berry. I loved him—I still love him. . . . I just don't think we are right—"

"Okay, whatever, Cate. I don't need to hear all of this. . . . I just wanted to say that he has a family wedding this weekend. And it's a really big deal. And he needs you to go with him. He needs the support."

I stared at her, taking this in, thinking that I needed to just rip off the Band-Aid. For his sake *and* mine.

Berry continued. "If you don't go . . . you're going to ruin the weekend for him."

"It won't ruin the weekend," I said.

"For Joe it will. It absolutely will. He'll be too sad to fake being happy for his own cousin. And he's the best man, Cate. Everyone will be looking at him, feeling sorry for him, asking him questions about where you are. Including the bride and groom."

I nodded noncommittally, thinking it over. The possibility of my absence negatively affecting Peter and Genevieve's wedding had never occurred to me. If anything, I thought everyone would be better off just getting the show on the road with their regularly scheduled Kingsley programming. "But . . . I don't want to be a distraction," I said.

"You'll be *more* of a distraction if you aren't there," she said. "Besides, it's rude. He RSVPed for two."

"I'm sure he can find another date," I said, instantly regretting the snide way I sounded. It wasn't fair.

Berry made a scoffing sound. "He's Joe *Kingsley*. He can't just bring some random date to his cousin's wedding. That's worse than going alone. Oh my God. You really have no idea the pressure he's under, do you? Do you even care?"

I suddenly wanted to explain that that was *exactly* why I was breaking up with him. But it wasn't worth it—she wouldn't get it. How could she possibly? Instead, I took a deep breath and said, "I'll talk to him. I'll give him the option. But I'm not going to lie about my decision. My mind is made up."

Berry shook her head and mumbled something under her breath that sounded like *I knew you were trouble.*

"Excuse me?" I said, staring her down, suddenly so angry—and even more sure I couldn't be part of Joe's world. *Their* world.

She looked me dead in the eye. "I said . . . *I. Knew. You. Were. Trouble.*"

"Yeah," I replied, my heart shutting down a little bit more. "I'm quite sure you did. So that should make you very happy, Berry. You get to be right about me. Congrats."

Berry opened her mouth to answer, but I stepped around her, determined to have the last word. Then I used my key to unlock the front door of Joe's building for what was sure to be the last time.

CHAPTER 31

Joe

Twenty minutes after Berry left my apartment, Cate knocked on my door.

I opened it, forced a smile, and said, "Did you lose your key?"

She held it up and said, "No. It's right here. . . . I wasn't sure if I should use it—"

I smiled again and said, "I'm just glad you're here. Come on in."

She took two steps into my apartment, then stopped like she'd never been there before. I contemplated giving her a quick hug but decided against it. Instead, I turned and motioned her toward the kitchen. She followed me, and when we got there, she put the key down on the island. It was a bad sign, and my stomach dropped.

"You're giving it back?"

She nodded, staring down at it.

"Okay, then," I said. "I see where this is headed."

She lifted her chin, which started to tremble, then said, "I'm sorry, Joe. For everything—"

"Oh my God, Cate. Are you *really* breaking up with me?"

"I just don't think we're right together—"

I cut her off and said, "Stop with the vague bullshit. Just give it to me straight. Is it over?"

She nodded, her eyes filling with tears.

"Fuck," I said, my head spinning and my heart racing. "Is it someone else? Arlo?"

"*No*," she said. She looked sufficiently horrified to put my mind at ease on that one point.

"Okay, then. What's changed? Did I do something wrong?"

"No, Joe. It's nothing like that. You didn't do anything."

"Then why? There's got to be a reason."

"It's not just *one* thing. . . ."

"C'mon, Cate," I said. "Please don't give me that 'it's complicated' bullshit. I need a reason."

"I just don't think we're compatible long-term."

"How are we not compatible? We get along so well! We never fight," I said.

"We just aren't."

I let out a frustrated sigh, then said, "So is this one of those 'you like the thermostat up and I like it down' type things? Or more like: you don't want kids and are afraid to tell me?"

"It's neither of those things. . . . It's a lot of things. . . ."

"Name one."

"Well," she said, crossing her arms. "You're a Kingsley . . . and I'm . . . far from that."

"Well, that's a good thing, dummy," I said, attempting a smile. "Because if you were a Kingsley, then that *would* be a problem."

She forced a smile in return, then looked down at the counter again.

"Seriously, Cate. I'm going to need you to be a little more specific here," I said. "I need a reason."

"*Reasons*," she said.

"Name them."

She sighed, then said, "I didn't even finish high school. . . ."

"You're fixing that. What else?"

"My mom and Chip—"

"Wait," I said. "Did something happen?"

"Not that I'm aware of," she said with a shrug. "But what if it does? It could hurt your career."

"No, it couldn't."

"Yes, it could, Joe. Don't be naïve. Chip could find a way. Besides, it's just so embarrassing. . . . My background doesn't go with yours. You belong with someone more like you—"

I suddenly felt squeamish, remembering what Berry had just confessed to me and wondering if Cate had some kind of women's intuition. If that was the case, maybe she felt guilty—like she was in Berry's way. It also occurred to me that maybe Berry or my mother had said something to Cate. Maybe one of them had actually told her that she needed to do this.

Feeling dizzy, I said, "Is this about Berry? Or my mother? Did one of them say something to you?"

She shook her head. "This is my decision, Joe. Not theirs."

I let out a weary sigh, rubbed my eyes with my hands, and said, "Can we go to counseling? Would that help?"

"No," she said. "I don't think so."

I nodded, unwilling to give up, but knowing that I probably didn't have a choice. Cate knew her own mind; it was one of the things I loved about her.

I stared at her, overwhelmed by heartbreak, as she took a deep breath and said, "I did want to ask you something . . . and I'm sure you'll think it's a bad idea. . . . But if you want, I can still go to the wedding with you?"

"Really? You'd still come with me?" I asked. Relief washed over me, not only because I wanted her to be there, but because I still had an opening. A chance to change her mind.

She nodded and said, "Yeah. If you want me to."

"Of *course* I do."

"Are you sure?"

"I'm positive."

She nodded, then said, "What do we tell people? If they ask about the fight in the park?"

"Nobody will ask," I said. "It's none of their business, and we don't owe anyone an explanation."

"Okay," she said, nodding.

"Will you wear my ring?" I asked.

She froze up, then said, "I don't know, Joe."

"Please?"

"Okay," she said with a sigh.

Before she could change her mind again, I turned and went to my bedroom, fished the ring out of my top dresser drawer, and ran back to the kitchen.

"Here," I said, handing it to her.

She gave me the saddest look, then took it and slipped it onto her right hand. I would have preferred the left, but it was better than nothing. I was back in the game, and I felt a dash of hope that I could win her back over the course of the weekend. For now, less was more, and I would focus on logistics. Take charge.

That's when I got the idea to take my plane. Fly her down. Cate wasn't a girl who got caught up in luxury, but I figured it couldn't hurt.

"So, listen," I said as casually as I could. "I think I'm gonna fly myself down to Annapolis. . . . Do you want a lift?"

Cate looked surprised. "In your plane?"

"Yeah."

"But we already booked flights—"

"I know. But I thought this would be more fun. Plus, we can avoid the crowds and paparazzi," I said, keeping my voice breezy.

"Have you ever flown that far?" she asked, chewing on her lower lip, looking worried.

"It's not far at all. It's a quick, easy flight. And Peter said the weather is looking beautiful this weekend," I added. "Honestly, it's a piece of cake."

"Won't your mother and Berry be worried?"

"Probably. But tough," I said, making a point, just in case the two of them had anything to do with Cate's change of heart.

"Okay," she said, nodding. "What time would we go?"

"It's obviously flexible. But I'm thinking we could leave the city around two or three. Get to the airport by four. Take off shortly after that. That way we'll be landing right at sunset. It will be beautiful."

She hesitated a few more seconds, looking down at her ring, as she twisted it twice around her finger. Then she looked back up at me, gave me a slight smile, and nodded. "Okay," she said. "That sounds nice. Thank you, Joe."

CHAPTER 32

Cate

After I agreed to go to Peter and Genevieve's wedding with Joe, I tried to put my emotions on hold, telling myself I just needed to get through the week without overthinking things. It was impossible not to be sad, knowing what would be coming afterward, but one thing at a time.

For the next three days, I pretended that I was only headed to a modeling shoot—and prepped accordingly, just like the old days. I got my eyebrows waxed, my highlights touched up, and my nails done. Then, on the evening before we left, I went to Bergdorf and bought a black off-the-shoulder, silk crepe dress from Rive Gauche, the ready-to-wear line from Yves Saint Laurent.

Curtis, who insisted on going shopping with me and was still in denial about the breakup, pushed back on the idea of my wearing black. He said that black was a downer for a spring wedding by the water, and the dress was way too "drapey" for my body.

"It looks like a potato sack," he said.

I told him that was the point. The dress hit the right understated note, and the less people noticed me, the better.

"Because you don't want to upstage the bride?" Curtis eagerly asked.

I rolled my eyes but smiled, thinking that everyone should have a cheerleader as big as Curtis. "No, honey. Because I'm on the way out the door. Better to blend into the woodwork," I said, thinking that I also needed to avoid the wedding photographer, lest I end up in too many of Genevieve's photos.

Curtis stuffed his fingers into his ears, closed his eyes, and shouted, "I can't hear you! I can't hear you!"

I waited until he was finished, then said, "You're ridiculous."

"No, *you're* ridiculous. And I refuse to believe I won't be doing your wedding makeup later this year."

"Wait a second. Is this about my relationship ending—or you not getting to do my wedding makeup?" I smiled, determined to keep the mood light—or at least not heavy.

"Both," he said. "Oh! That reminds me—I picked up a new MAC lipstick for you. It's called Russian Roulette. You'll love it."

"Well, the name feels somehow appropriate, but I'm not wearing red lipstick this weekend."

"Why not?"

"I told you. I'm going for understated. Neutral."

"Red *is* a neutral."

"Still. It's too bold."

"C'mon, Cate. If you're going to insist on black, can you please just do a red lip?"

"I'm not sure why you care so much. But sure. Whatever," I said, throwing him a bone.

"Personally, I *don't* care," Curtis said with a smile. "But Joe loves your red lipstick."

THE PLAN WAS to meet at Joe's place at two, then ride out to the Essex County Airport together. But around noon, he called and told me that his meeting was running late, and that it might make

more sense to link up at the airport. I told him that was no problem, then asked what time I should arrive.

"Let's say four," he said.

"Okay," I said, knowing that for Joe, that meant closer to five.
"As long as we're not flying in the dark," I added, starting to get
a little anxious about the flight. Like a lot of people, I had a thing
about small planes, and it didn't help that I knew how much his
mother and Berry feared his flying.

"Daylight savings, baby! Sunset's not till seven-something," he
said. "We'll be fine."

"Okay," I said. "I'll see you at four."

As PREDICTED, JOE jogged into the terminal a few minutes past
five.

"I'm so sorry I'm late!" he said, out of breath. "The traffic was
insane."

"It's fine," I said, closing my magazine. I stood up and put on
a soothing face.

"Man—" he said, shaking his head.

"What?"

"Nothing . . . It's just . . . you're a sight for sore eyes. It's been
a long time."

My stomach fluttered a little—because I loved seeing his face,
too. But I played it off with a laugh and said, "I just saw you four
nights ago."

"Yeah. But I was drunk as shit four nights ago."

"You were?" I said, suddenly wondering if Berry had been
drinking, too. I'd replayed our conversation many times, feeling
both guilty and angry about everything she'd said—and *not* said.

"Yeah," he said with a shrug.

"Well, I'm glad you're not 'drunk as shit' *now*."

Joe laughed, but the second the words were out of my mouth, I thought of my father and what he'd done, and felt a wave of nausea. Drunk driving—or flying—was nothing to joke about.

I pushed those thoughts away as two men escorted us out to the tarmac. The older, obsequious one was in a suit and tie; the younger guy, in an orange vest, carried my bag.

"What do you think?" Joe asked, beaming proudly as we approached his red and white plane. I knew, from hearing him talk about it, that it was a Piper Saratoga.

"It's very pretty," I said, wondering if that was the proper adjective for a plane. "Or should I say handsome?"

Joe chuckled and said, "Pretty. She's definitely a girl."

"How can you tell?" I asked, playing along.

"'Cause she's *that* beautiful," he said with an amorous sigh.

I smiled, but I could feel myself getting more nervous by the second. The plane looked smaller than I'd expected—and decidedly less sturdy—almost like a toy plane with low, skinny wings and a three-blade propeller in front.

As I watched the orange-vest man take Joe's duffel from him, then climb a rinky-dink staircase and load both of our bags onto the plane, it crossed my mind to abort the mission. Fear of flying was the perfect excuse. And bonus: his mother would be on my side. I wondered if she even knew what he was up to today.

I played it out in my head, thinking that it would be embarrassing, but so what? I reminded myself that the game was over; I didn't have to pretend to be the cool, adventurous, fearless girl anymore. If anything, it was better to give Joe something to talk to his next girlfriend about. I could hear him now, telling her how skittish I'd been about everything. Boats, swimming, skiing, airplanes. All the stuff he loved.

But I knew what would happen if I backed out. Joe would stay with me, and I'd be messing things up for him. We'd have to re-book commercial flights and wouldn't be able to get to Maryland until tomorrow morning, which meant he would miss his round of groomsmen's golf. I had no choice but to suck it up.

Trying to make light conversation, I asked, "How many passengers does *she* hold?"

"Six!" he said with the proudest grin. "But it's just two today, babe!"

"So . . . no copilot?" I asked, though I already knew the answer. Joe had told me before that the plane was certified for a single pilot—and since he'd passed his final flight test, he always flew solo.

"No. I don't need one. This is a cinch," he said, shifting his gaze from the plane to me. "You're not worried, are you?"

"No," I lied.

The man in the suit, who had been pretending that he wasn't listening to us, now turned around and said to me, "This is a very high-performance aircraft, miss. It can practically fly itself."

I smiled, relaxing a little as Joe said to the man, "You forgot the part about me being a hell of a pilot!"

The man laughed and said, "Yes. The very best, sir."

"Monty, if you call me sir one more time . . ." Joe said, raising his fist in jest.

"Sorry, Joe. Habit."

Joe smiled and whistled, looking up. "Blue skies the whole way to Annapolis!"

At that point, we were at the foot of the stairs, and Joe motioned for me to climb aboard. "Ladies first!" he said.

I took a breath and climbed the few steps up, ducking into the plane when I got to the top. The cabin was tight and stuffy.

"Have a great flight!" the two men yelled up at us in unison, waving.

I waved back as Joe bellowed out a thank-you. Then he pulled up the stairs, latching the door shut. Still crouched down, I asked him where I should sit.

"Next to me!" he said, pointing to the copilot's seat.

I sat down and put on my seatbelt, watching as Joe went over a meticulous checklist, talking to himself as he fiddled around with levers and buttons and various laminated papers. After several minutes, he put on a headset, flipped on a radio, and started talking to the control tower, rattling off letters and numbers. Joe was the most competent man I'd ever met, and I felt a sharp pang, wondering how I could possibly give him up.

After a few more exchanges with the tower, Joe turned to me and offered me my own headset. "You want to put this on?"

"Do I need to?"

He smiled and said, "Only if you want to listen in."

"Sure," I said, nodding and taking the headset. "Is there anything else I should know?"

"The life vests are right behind us," he said, pointing over his shoulder. "Under the first-row seats."

"No other safety features?" I asked. "Oxygen? Stuff like that?"

Joe gave me a reassuring smile and said, "There's no need for oxygen, honey. We won't be going that high. Just sit back, relax, and enjoy the ride. And the view!"

I nodded, putting on my headset and forcing a smile back.

He gave me a final thumbs-up, then turned on the engine, still flipping switches. A few seconds later, he began to drive, steering the plane toward the runway, where we waited in line behind two other planes. I watched as they took off and we crept closer to the front of the line.

Then it was our turn. Joe's face lit up more and more as the noise of the engine and the propeller got louder and louder, groaning and whirring at once, until we were finally taking off, surging

up and into the air. It was terrifying but also exhilarating, reminding me of the time Joe took me out on his boat.

As we gained altitude, the vibrations and noise lessened, and I
felt myself start to relax. It was smooth sailing through bright
blue skies, the sun still well above the horizon. I wondered what I
had been so worried about. It really was a piece of cake for Joe,
and at one point, he even flipped open a tin of Altoids and offered
me one. I smiled, shook my head, and pointed at the sky as if to
say *stay focused*. He nodded, looking back at the horizon.

As we cruised along, I began to daydream, thinking of all our
happy times together, refusing to contemplate the end. Not yet. At
some point, the droning of the propellers, the warm sunlight, and
all the vibrations of the plane lulled me to sleep.

I'm not sure how much time passed, but when I woke up, the
sun was beginning to set and we were approaching a body of
water that must have been the Chesapeake. The view was breath-
taking. We were getting close. As I sat up in my seat, Joe looked
over and smiled at me. I smiled back, feeling a wave of pure love.
I told myself to stay in the moment—to cherish this time together.

Then, suddenly, the engine made a weird sputtering sound. In
the next second, I saw smoke outside my window. I glanced over
at Joe, praying that he'd appear calm. Instead, I saw panic etched
all over his face and watched as he began frantically flipping
switches and talking adamantly over the radio. I didn't follow
what he was saying, but it didn't sound good, nor did the loud
bang that followed.

Joe jumped and screamed *fuck* as our propeller slowed, then
ground to a sickening stop. Meanwhile, the plane quickly lost altitude, dropping and gliding while Joe continued to steer and ma-
neuver. "Don't worry! We'll be okay!" he yelled without looking
at me.

I nodded, believing him. He could do it; he could do *anything*. But we kept falling, and Joe looked more terrified by the second. My heart pounding in my ears and my throat constricting, I closed my eyes. Fearing that this was the end, the Kingsley curse crossed my mind. It was something Joe and I had never talked about—something I dismissed as ridiculous. In every family there was tragedy, especially in a big family like Joe's. Yet here we were.

When I opened my eyes, Joe was looking at me, shouting, "We've lost power! We gotta land on the water!"

Terrified and now starting to hyperventilate, I stared at him and nodded.

Seconds felt like hours as Joe kept yelling into his mic, sweat pouring down his forehead and cheeks. I began to pray, then silently recite the Lord's Prayer—at least the words I could remember. *Thy Kingdom come, thy will be done* echoed in my head until I heard Joe begin to shout.

Mayday! Mayday! Mayday!

It was a word I'd only ever heard in movies, and I suddenly understood what people meant by an "out-of-body experience." I felt as if I were somewhere else, watching a disaster unfold, and I could only vaguely hear the man on the other end of the radio who was trying to help Joe land his plane on the water.

A second later, static filled the airwaves and the radio went silent. We were on our own.

"Fuck!" Joe yelled, ripping off his headset and throwing it to the floor between us. From there, his lips were moving, but I couldn't hear what he was saying, and I wondered whether he was coaching himself or praying.

"Grab the life jacket behind the seat," Joe yelled at one point, his eyes still on the horizon.

Feeling paralyzed, I couldn't move.

"*Now,* Cate! Life preserver! Now!"

I took my seatbelt off and followed his instructions, grabbing my life jacket and putting it on, my hands shaking.

"Sit down! Head down! Brace for impact!" Joe yelled.

I got back in my seat while we continued to sink, gliding downward, careening toward the water. I realized we were going to crash and maybe—*probably*—die. Meanwhile, Joe kept steering, concentrating, swearing. His lips never stopped moving.

In those final few seconds before we crashed, the cabin was eerily quiet, and my thoughts scattered. I pictured my mother and then my father, forgiving them both. I saw Elna, then Curtis and Wendy. Mostly, though, I saw Joe and me together, a hundred scenes and memories flashing through my mind.

Then we hit the water. I screamed and closed my eyes, but we didn't die. Instead, the belly of the plane skipped across the surface, once, twice, three times. Unscathed. It felt like a miracle. Then we hit the fourth time, and the wing on Joe's side dipped into the water, and we were thrown violently sideways. Water surrounded us, and instantly began seeping in everywhere. I looked over at Joe and saw blood on his forehead, his eyes closed.

I screamed his name, but he didn't answer or open his eyes. He couldn't hear me. *Nobody* could hear me. I was alone. I told myself that I had to calm down and focus, that I didn't have much time. The plane began taking on more water, and I could feel us sinking. I took off my seatbelt, then reached over and unlatched Joe's. I shook him, trying to wake him up, still calling his name. He was breathing, but motionless, and didn't respond. I pulled him free from his belt with all my strength, then stood and reached for the latch to open the door. I heard it click, but it didn't open, so I kicked it as hard as I could and it finally released, more water pouring in. I scrambled back to Joe, dragged him from his seat, and pulled his body toward the door. The water in the cabin was now knee-deep, which helped me get him to the door, as by then he was floating. I looked out, straight into the Chesapeake, which was still rushing into the plane. We had to get out—or sink with the plane. It really was sink or swim. I pulled the cord on my life jacket, relieved when it inflated. Then I took a final deep breath and paddled out into the freezing water, pulling Joe behind me.

It was almost dark by then, and so hard to see with waves hitting my face. I looked around and noticed that one wing of the airplane had broken off and was floating nearby. Shivering uncontrollably, I struggled to swim over to it while barely holding Joe's head above water. After a few strokes, I was exhausted, and it suddenly felt hopeless. The wing was too far away, and I was getting numb. I told myself I had to keep going. I had no choice. Somehow, I got us there, reaching out to grab the wing with one arm, gripping Joe's head with the other. As I turned to look back, I watched the plane disappear, becoming completely submerged in the bay.

The next few minutes got colder and darker and more hopeless, and I began sobbing as uncontrollably as I was shivering. It was the end, and I knew it. I told Joe that I loved him, hoping he could somehow hear me.

At some point, I was completely numb—so numb I could no longer feel the cold. Then, just as I started to fall asleep, I heard an engine in the distance. I tried to yell but couldn't—I was too exhausted. I had no voice—and no free hands to wave. So, I just prayed they would find us. The last thing I remembered was an incredibly bright light shining in my eyes.

DAYS LATER, I would learn exactly the way things happened. How Joe's Mayday to the tower was relayed to the Coast Guard, who immediately dispatched a boat to save us. At the same time, witnesses saw our crash landing, and news reporters were immediately on the scene, our rescue broadcast all over the country and world.

But that night, when Dottie rushed into my hospital room, I was unaware of any of that. I pictured a much different scenario—that she'd been quietly summoned from her hotel in Annapolis, the public unaware of the accident.

"Oh, darling," she said, her heels click-clacking on the floor as she crossed over to my bedside. "Thank God you're okay!"

I caught the nurse staring at us for a beat before she closed the door, giving us privacy, and it suddenly occurred to me that Dottie and I had never been completely alone before. I'd also never seen her so disheveled, including in the photos taken the day her husband died. Her hair was mussed, her eye makeup smudged, and her lips bare.

"Have you seen Joe?" I asked. My voice was hoarse and sluggish, like it wasn't my own.

"Yes, dear. I've seen him. He's going to be fine. Just fine," she said in a soothing voice. Nurses had told me the same, but I'd feared they weren't telling me the truth—and I knew there was no way Dottie would lie to me about her son. I felt a final surge of relief.

"Can I see him?"

"Soon," she said. "They're keeping you both overnight—out of an abundance of caution. Joe got a pretty good knock on the head."

"I know," I said, welling up with tears, remembering everything.

Dottie reached out and patted the heavy heated blankets that were pulled up and tucked around my chin. "Sweetheart, he's fine. I promise."

I nodded, blinking back tears. She swallowed, then added, "Thanks to you, Cate. You saved his life."

"No," I said, shaking my head. "He saved *mine*. That landing . . . I don't know how he did it. I thought we were going to die."

"Cate," she said, her voice suddenly strong. "He *would* have died without you. The Coast Guard told me what happened . . . how you were holding on to him."

I felt my chin quiver, tears streaming down my cheeks.

"Shh—shh, sweetie. Please don't cry," she said. She reached into her handbag, pulled out a handkerchief, and dabbed my cheeks.

"I'm sorry," I said, sniffling, pulling my arms out from under the blankets, taking the handkerchief, and wiping my nose. "I shouldn't have let him fly. . . ."

"Nobody can stop Joe from doing what he wants," she said, smiling through her own tears. "Not even you."

I nodded and said, "I know."

We sat in silence for several long seconds before Dottie cleared her throat and said, "You can't leave him, Cate."

I stared at her, wondering what, exactly, she knew. She spelled it out for me. "Berry told me you were coming to the wedding just to be nice . . . before you end things for good. . . ."

"I love him so much," I said. It felt like the truest statement I'd ever uttered until my next one. "But I just want what's best for him."

"I know you do, honey," she said. "And I hope you can see that you *are* what's best for him."

Thinking of my father, and that horrible accident from long ago, I shook my head and said, "I don't think so, Dottie. I wish I were . . . but I don't think so."

"Yes. You are," she said, nodding emphatically. "You *are*."

"There are things you don't know . . ." I said, my voice trailing off.

Dottie pressed her lips together, inhaled through her nose, then sat on the edge of my bed, taking my hand in hers. Her skin was cool, just like it was that day in the Hamptons when she shook my hand in her backyard. It felt like a lifetime ago.

"Cate," she said, gazing down at me. "I need to tell you something—and I want you to listen very carefully."

I nodded, blinking, waiting.

After several more seconds of silence, she said, "I know about your father. I know about his prison sentence and that he's out now."

Stunned, I asked her how she knew.

She took a deep breath, then said, "Your mother told me everything."

"My *mother*? When?"

"After your argument with Joe in the park. She assumed it was about this. . . . She couldn't get ahold of you—so she came to my apartment."

I stared at her in disbelief. It was so much to process. "I didn't know about my father until just recently. I thought he was dead," I finally said, wanting her to know that I hadn't lied to Joe.

"I know. Your mother told me that, too."

"Does Joe know?" I asked.

"No," she said. "I didn't think it was right to tell him for you. It's your story to share."

"Thank you," I said, too emotional and exhausted and overwhelmed to muster anything else.

"Joe's right," she said, looking into my eyes. "You're a good person. And I pray that you will marry my son. I want you to be his wife, and I want you to be my daughter-in-law. My *daughter*."

The moment felt like a miracle—the second of the night.

"You do?" I said, getting choked up.

"Yes. I do," Dottie said. "Cate, you saved his life. I'll never be able to thank you enough."

"You just did," I said, smiling through my tears.

CHAPTER 33

Joe

Everyone wanted to know what I was thinking in those final moments before we smashed into the Chesapeake Bay. *What went through your mind?* That's how people usually worded the question, and by the looks on their faces, I think they were hoping for some sort of deep existential answer.

The truth is, I wasn't thinking about the meaning of life—and I never contemplated the possibility of death. There were no prayers of any kind. God didn't enter my mind at all. It wasn't that I didn't believe in Him—because I did and do—but there wasn't time for that. Instead, I focused on my training, trying to remember everything I had been taught about ditching an airplane in an emergency landing. *Touch down at the slowest possible speed, at the lowest possible rate of descent. . . . Keep the wings trimmed to the surface of the water rather than the horizon. . . . If two swells differ in height, land on the higher one. . . . Ditch into the wind. . . . The more whitecaps, the greater the wind. . . . It's easy to misjudge altitude by up to fifty feet, especially at twilight. . . . Avoid the face of the swell at any cost.*

Beyond those basics, I was only worried about Cate. She couldn't swim that well, and the water was going to be freezing cold, and we wouldn't have long to get to safety. I wanted to hit the pause button and reassure her that everything was going to be okay. We were going to be fine. I was going to protect her at any cost.

The funny thing is, all my thoughts and optimism would have been exactly the same had we both been killed. I would've been wrong, of course, but I would never have *known* that I was wrong. In a strange way, that realization, one that first came to me in the morning, when I was still in the hospital, brought me closer to my father. I tried to tell myself that his final human emotion wasn't fear, but some variation of the same gritty faith that I'd felt. I told myself that I was more like him than I thought.

In my wildest dreams, though, I never would have imagined the turn things would take. That I would hit my head and be knocked unconscious. That Cate would be on her own. That she would have to find the superhuman strength and courage and wherewithal to get us out of that broken plane before it sank to the bottom of the bay. That she'd then have to keep my head above the water, somehow get us both over to the wing—when she could barely swim in the best conditions—and hold on for dear life, fighting exhaustion and hypothermia. In other words, I never fathomed that *Cate* would have to save *me*.

It makes me almost cry every time I think about it. How scared and alone she must have felt in that dark, cold water without any help from the person who got her into the situation, the man who was supposed to protect her.

"I'm so sorry," I told Cate in the early morning hours after the accident, crying as I held her in my arms. We'd both been treated, and a nurse, along with my mother, had wheeled her into my room, so we could talk alone. "I'll never forgive myself for letting this happen to you."

"Oh, Joe. It's okay, honey. I'm fine," she said, crying, too. "We're both fine. We made it, baby."

"I know. But I left you all alone," I said, wiping away tears.

"But I wasn't alone," she whispered, holding me so tight, the two of us lying side by side in my bed. "I was with you. I held on because of *you*. I wasn't going to let you go."

"*God,* Cate," I said under my breath, thinking that I'd never felt so loved in my whole life.

I also felt a fresh wave of faith, just like the feeling I had when I was trying to land that plane. This time, though, it was about Cate and me. And I just knew we were going to be okay. No matter what the future held, we were going to be okay.

Cate

It's been twenty years since Joe and I nearly lost our lives in the freezing cold waters of the Chesapeake Bay. The nightmares have mostly subsided, but not a week goes by that I don't remember the feeling of almost losing Joe.

For a long time, I wanted to erase those memories completely, along with the trauma of Chip and my childhood. With the help of a wonderful therapist, though, I have come to realize that those things are a part of who I am—as a woman, a wife, and a mother. What doesn't kill you makes you stronger, they say, and I believe that's true. Maybe if I hadn't been forced to survive Chip, I wouldn't have been able to save Joe. And surely surviving that crash helped me do what I eventually did: sit down with Barbara Walters and tell her—and the whole world—about the domestic violence I'd grown up with.

As terrifying as that was, it was also empowering. Liberating. Because, as it turns out, the truth really *does* set you free. It set my mom free, too, as she finally left Chip and that house in Montclair. She now lives in an apartment in Murray Hill and works on the nonprofit that Joe and I founded to help women like her.

Perhaps more incredible than her escape, she and Dean became close friends, maybe because they both understood redemption and second chances.

I've learned so much about those things, too, but to me, life is less about overcoming adversity and more about the power of gratitude. On this anniversary of our plane crash, I am feeling particularly thankful. Joe and I are with our kids in our favorite place, our second home on Shelter Island, not far from the church where we married in a small ceremony before thirty-five of our loved ones, including Berry, who is now one of my closest friends.

At thirteen, Sylvie and Finn are old enough for quality conversation, yet too young to want to escape us, and Joe and I aren't taking this sweet spot of their childhood for granted. As we finish eating, Finn clears the dishes without being asked, while Sylvie reaches for her phone, which has become her appendage. They are as close as I've ever seen boy-girl twins, but opposites in virtually every way. Finn is more like I am—fair-skinned, towheaded, and even-tempered—while Sylvie is a loud, lovable, dark-eyed clone of Joe. A daddy's girl to the core.

I watch her now, holding up her phone, posing for a selfie. She raises her brows and puckers her lips, faux-animated and frozen for one second before resuming her furtive tapping, sending, scrolling.

"Twenty years ago. Wow," Joe suddenly muses aloud. It is our first mention of the date, though I can somehow tell that it's been on his mind as much as mine.

"What was twenty years ago?" Sylvie asks without looking up from her phone.

"Your father's emergency landing," I say—because I don't like saying *crash*. I shiver, remembering the cold.

"Oh. That. Yeah," she says.

I wait for Joe to say something more—something profound—which he's become so much more capable of over the years. Instead, he smiles, those gorgeous, crinkly lines appearing around his eyes.

"That's what you get for trying to dump me," he says, giving me a wink.

I laugh and say, "Well, that's a fresh take on things."

"You tried to break up with Dad?" Sylvie asks, giving me a horrified, accusatory look.

"Tried? Your mother *did* break up with me. She called off our engagement."

"Wait. You weren't married when you crashed?"

"We didn't crash," Joe says, hating the word, too. "I successfully and skillfully *ditched* the aircraft."

"Yeah, dummy," Finn says, returning to the table and taking his seat next to me. "Dad ditched . . . and they were flying to Uncle Peter's wedding. Mom and Dad got married three months later."

Sylvie rolls her eyes and says, "Like I'm supposed to memorize our whole family time line."

"It's kind of a big thing," Finn says. "The night your parents almost died and all."

"But they *didn't* die," Sylvie says.

"No *duh,* Captain Obvious," Finn shoots back at her.

"All right. Enough," I say, doing my best to nip their bickering in the bud before it escalates into an argument.

"So, Mom," Sylvie says. "What gives? Why did you try to dump Dad?"

"It's a long story," I say.

"Oh my God. Did someone cheat?" Sylvie asks, her eyes lighting up. To her, any drama is good drama.

"No, Sylvie. Nobody cheated," Joe says.

"It was just a complicated time," I add.

"Complicated, how?" Finn presses.

"Well, Grandpa had just gotten out of prison. Which was very stressful."

"And that was Dad's fault . . . *how*?" Sylvie says.

"I didn't say it was Dad's fault. I said it was complicated. I was upset and embarrassed and in shock . . . about Grandpa . . . and I was worried maybe your father and I didn't belong together. That we were too different."

"Dad. Is that true?" Sylvie asks, clearly intrigued by this twist on our family lore.

"It's true that your mother felt that way," Joe confirms. "But obviously, it wasn't the *truth*. We were clearly meant to be." He leans over and kisses me on the cheek. "And as you can see, I won her back over."

"Yes," I say, smiling. "And besides, our fight isn't really the point here."

"What is the point?" Finn asks, always wanting the bottom line.

"The point is gratitude," I say.

"Yes," Joe says. "We have so much to be grateful for . . . which is why we have a responsibility to give back to others."

"We know, Dad," Sylvie says. "To whom much is given—"

"Much is expected," Finn says, nodding.

"Yes. Exactly," Joe says.

He glances at me, and we lock eyes for a few seconds before he turns back to the kids. "And so . . . on *that* note . . . there's something we want to talk to you about."

"Hold on," Sylvie says. "Are we in trouble?"

"No," Joe says with a laugh. "I mean—yes—but not in the way you might think. . . . We want to talk to you about the state of the world."

"Ugh. Politics again?" Sylvie says.

"If by politics you mean morality and fighting for what is right, then yes," Joe says. "There is so much more work to do."

"Are you gonna run for president, Dad?" Finn says, his eyes lit up with excitement.

Joe looks at me.

"Only with both of your blessings," I answer.

We've gone back and forth for such a long time, and this is what Joe and I finally decided. He should run, but only if the kids are okay with it. It has to be a family decision.

"Would I have to give up social media?" Sylvie asks in classic Sylvie fashion.

"Yes," I say. "You probably would."

She groans and says, "Well, then I say no."

"*Gah,* Syl. That's so selfish," Finn says, relishing his sister's misstep.

Sylvie tries to backtrack, saying that she was only joking, but I don't believe her.

"I understand that would be hard," I tell her. "Maybe you can keep Instagram. Just stay private and post more judiciously."

"Okay!" Sylvie says. "I'm in! I hear there's a bowling alley in the White House!"

Joe laughs and says, "Easy sell!"

"You mean sell*out,* Dad," Finn says, making a face at Sylvie.

"Shut it, Finn," she says.

"So, you think you can win, Dad?" Finn asks, his blue eyes as big as quarters.

"I don't know, Finn," Joe says. "But I think we have a good shot—"

"A *really* good shot," I say.

Joe looks at me and smiles.

"What if you lose, Dad?" Sylvie says. "Will you be really sad?"

"Probably so," Joe says. "But that's not a reason not to try, is it?"

Sylvie shakes her head, looking solemn. "No. It's not."

"And even if you lose, you'll still be a senator, right?" Finn asks.

"If the good people of New York allow me to keep my job," Joe says.

"They will," the kids say in unison.

"The more important question: will your mother keep me, too?" Joe says, coming over to my chair, then pulling me up and into his arms.

I laugh and say, "Yes . . . I can't get rid of you. I tried that once. . . ."

"Yes, you *did*," he says, nuzzling his face against mine. "And you see how that turned out."

"Okay, you guys are getting gross," Finn says, getting up from the table.

"Your face is gross," Sylvie says, cracking herself up and following her brother into the family room, where we plan on watching *Casablanca*, in memory of Joe's grandmother. She passed away before the kids were born, but they've heard so much about her, along with the legacy of their grandfather.

I start to follow them, but Joe holds on to me tighter.

"So, we're really doing this?" he whispers in my ear.

"Yes," I say, pulling back just enough to gaze into his eyes. "We are."

I get a quick flash of the White House, imagining what it would be like to live there with Joe and the kids and our two dogs. It's obviously a long, difficult road ahead, but I have faith in my husband, feeling certain that he will prevail. He *always* finds a way.

But win or lose, we will have each other, and that's all that really matters. I tell him as much, and he smiles and nods. Then we both turn and join our children by the fire.

Author's Note

Ever since I was a little girl, I have been fascinated by the Kennedy family. My mother inspired this early intrigue, sharing vivid recollections of her own childhood with the romantic backdrop of Camelot. I remember her showing me a copy of *Life* magazine that she'd saved from July 1953, when she was only eight years old. On the cover was a photo of John F. Kennedy and Jacqueline Lee Bouvier smiling on a sailboat, the headline reading "Senator Kennedy Goes-a-Courting." I loved looking at that picture, as well as so many other happy images of Jack and Jackie over the years with their two adorable children, Caroline and John, Jr.

Of course, I knew how their story ended, my mother also telling me how CBS News interrupted her soap opera, *As the World Turns*, with a news bulletin as Walter Cronkite informed a shocked nation that President Kennedy had died from gunshot wounds.

From all these stories and photos, both the beautiful and tragic ones, I understood that the Kennedys had captured the imagination of a nation and had taken on a cultural and emotional significance beyond politics. We cared about these people not because they had money or power or fame—but because we had shared some of their most intimate moments, from their wedding day to the birth of their children to the funeral of a father and husband, son and brother. How could we *not* feel like we knew them?

As I grew older, so did my interest in the Kennedys and politics. I majored in history in college, then went on to law school at the University of Virginia (Robert and Ted Kennedy's alma mater) where I studied the Constitution and civil rights and so many of the things the Kennedy family fought for. I admired their spirit of service and sense of idealism, but I also knew of the scandals and tragedies that plagued them. I came to understand the layers of hypocrisy and self-destruction that so often seem to accompany unchecked privilege and ambition. Ultimately, I hoped that John, Jr., would rise above these things, escape the so-called Kennedy curse, and fulfill his father's legacy. I think many Americans shared this wish.

After I graduated from law school in 1997, I moved to New York, took the bar exam, and went to work at a large firm. It was an exciting time for me, both personally and professionally. I had never lived in a big city before, and it was crazy to think that I might at any moment run into JFK, Jr., or his wife, Carolyn Bessette-Kennedy, whether on the subway, in Central Park, or at their usual Tribeca haunts, from El Teddy's to Bubby's to The Odeon. I respected their privacy—and had always been wary of the tabloids—but I remember sheepishly picking up magazines with John and Carolyn on the cover, captivated by his charisma and her amazing sense of style. There was no getting around the fact that they were icons—no matter how much they both may have wanted to lead normal lives.

Fast forward two years to July 16, 1999. It was a Friday, and I left my law office that evening, taking the escalator down into Grand Central Station. I passed through the terminal several times a day, to and from work in the Met Life building, which adjoined the station. Often I was in too much of a hurry to notice its beauty. That night, though, I felt oddly contemplative and melancholy, thinking of John's mother, Jackie, who had fought to preserve and restore the historic landmark decades earlier. It was long before we had smartphones, but for some reason I had an actual camera with me, and I stopped to take two photographs—one of the celestial blue ceiling, the other of the Tiffany glass clock in the middle of the station. I then went on my way, headed to the Jitney stop, where I boarded a bus to the Hamptons. Like many twenty-somethings, my friends and I had a summer share, all of us cramming into a small house on the weekends so we could escape our jobs and the heat of the city.

The following morning, I woke up in the basement of our rental, where about a dozen of us had crashed on pull-out sofa beds and sleeping bags. A small television was on, and reporters were talking about a plane crash. I was still half asleep, not paying too much attention, until I realized that it was John's plane that had gone down off the coast of Martha's Vineyard, en route to his cousin Rory's wedding. Carolyn and her sister Lauren were both on board. I watched the coverage all day in a state of shock and disbelief, refusing to believe that they were gone, holding out dumb hope that John would suddenly appear with his trademark goofy grin and another one of his crazy stories. Of course, that never happened, and the loss of those three young people has haunted me ever since.

Though I was still practicing law at the time, I was already writing my first novel with the hope of one day being published, and the storyteller in me began to obsess over the personal component of their very public lives and deaths. I wondered what it must have been like to be John—the pressure he must have felt to carry his father's torch. I thought a lot about Carolyn, too—how difficult it must have been to marry into that famed family.

As a writer, I often ask myself *what if*. And it is this question that I always return to when I think of John and Carolyn. What if John hadn't flown his plane that night? What if the weather had been different? What if he had been able to safely land his plane? What would the two have done with their lives? Would they have had their own children? Would they have survived the flashbulbs that followed them everywhere? Would they have found the happily-ever-after that eluded his parents?

Meant to Be is my eleventh novel (twelfth if you count the one that I was writing during my lawyering days, which was never published), but I first thought about writing this book years ago as I wondered about those *what if* questions. When I finally decided it was time to tell the story, I imagined and created Joe Kingsley and Cate Cooper. Like Joe, John felt the crushing weight of expectations and history. And like Carolyn, Cate found herself in the shadow of an iconic man and family. But beyond that framework, Joe and Cate are purely fictional characters with unique interior lives and backstories, hopes and dreams.

In this sense, it is important to remember that we won't ever know the full truth about John and Carolyn's relationship and their final moments together, just as we will never know what their lives would have looked like had tragedy not intervened. I do believe that this is part of the magic and beauty of fiction—we can take a sad story and transform it into something completely different.

So much has happened since July 1999. The world has changed many times over. We entered a new millennium; we suffered through 9/11; and we all went online. But some things have endured, including the mythology of the Kennedy family. In the words of the popular Broadway musical Jackie Kennedy so loved: "Don't let it be forgot, that once there was a spot, for one brief shining moment, that was known as Camelot." It is my hope that *Meant to Be* captures that fleeting bright light while examining the darker side of the story. Most of all, I hope it inspires my readers to imagine *what if. . . .*

Acknowledgments

First and foremost, I would like to thank my editor, Jennifer Hershey. I've wanted to tell this story for a long time, and I'm so grateful to her for giving me the encouragement to finally do so, as well as all her insight along the way.

Thank you to Sarah Giffin, always my biggest cheerleader, who helped me to the finish line of a first draft during my writing retreat in Wisconsin. There isn't a better sister in the world.

To my mother, Mary Ann Elgin, who instilled in me a love of books and fairy tales—including Camelot.

To my bestie, Nancy LeCroy Mohler, who scrutinized and discussed every sentence of this novel with me (and also wrote Cate's line in French!).

To my assistant, Kate Hardie Patterson, a real-life Mary Poppins, who is "practically perfect in every way." I'm so lucky to have her, both personally and professionally, along with my loyal publicist, Stephen Lee, and my wonderful new agent, Brettne Bloom.

To Gina Centrello, Kara Welsh, Susan Corcoran, Jennifer Garza, Debbie Aroff, Kim Hovey, Allyson Lord, Corina Diez, Paolo Pepe, Loren Noveck, Erin Kane, and my entire talented team at Penguin Random House, as well as Elena Giavaldi, who brought my vision for this cover to life.

To all my friends and family who provided input or otherwise supported me while I wrote this book, especially Allyson Jacoutot, Jennifer New, John Tully, Jeff MacFarland, Laryn Gardner, Julie Portera, Michelle Fuller, Sloane Alford, Steve Fallon, Martha Arias, Ralph Sampson, Harlan Coben, Charles and Andrew Vance-Broussard, Lea Journo, Jim Konrad, Katie Moss, and Troy Baker.

Above all, my heartfelt gratitude to my innermost circle: Buddy, Edward, George, and Harriet. I love you endlessly.

ABOUT THE AUTHOR

EMILY GIFFIN is the author of ten internationally bestselling novels: *Something Borrowed, Something Blue, Baby Proof, Love the One You're With, Heart of the Matter, Where We Belong, The One & Only, First Comes Love, All We Ever Wanted,* and *The Lies That Bind.* She lives in Atlanta with her husband and three children.

emilygiffin.com
Facebook.com/EmilyGiffinFans
Instagram: @emilygiffinauthor

ABOUT THE TYPE

This book was set in Sabon, a typeface designed by the well-known German typographer Jan Tschichold (1902–74). Sabon's design is based upon the original letter forms of sixteenth-century French type designer Claude Garamond and was created specifically to be used for three sources: foundry type for hand composition, Linotype, and Monotype. Tschichold named his typeface for the famous Frankfurt typefounder Jacques Sabon (c. 1520–80).